THE RETURN OF THE ANCIENTS
(ASCENDANCY: BOOK 5)

By

D. Ward Cornell

Dedicated to my family and friends who have been supportive through this adventure, especially those that have been willing to read the manuscripts and give me feedback.

Thank you all for your support and encouragement.

Special thanks to the members of my pre-readers program, your feedback is valued more than you can know.

Extra special thanks to Theresa Holmes whose feedback makes every story come alive.

TABLE OF CONTENTS

FOREWARD

This is the fifth book in the Ascendancy series. The first four books, **Revelation, The Institute, Emergence** and **Alliance**, were a joy to write and the reader feedback has been gratifying. If you haven't read these books, I recommend that you do. It will provide context for many of the things that happen in this one. But whether or not you've read them, I hope the following short synopsis helps whet your appetite before plowing in. Please enjoy!

...

In **Revelation**, the Intergalactic Confederation of Planets reveals itself to humanity. Their Ambassador, Michael, takes over every television and radio in the world to make his announcement.

Although Michael and his Revelation team are not human, they have taken human avatars, fully functional human bodies that they occupy. At first no one believes that Michael is a representative of an Intergalactic Confederation. He looks like a normal 35-year-old. But that changes quickly.

The evening of the Revelation, the US President orders an FBI raid on Michael's ranch in Hawaii. Weather and other hazards take down the FBI as they approach. But Michael and his team rescue the agents, healing the wounded and bringing those declared dead back to life.

The next morning, Michael appears on Good Morning America. He heals Sergeant George Butler, a quadriplegic injured in Afghanistan, and demonstrates other technology the Confederation offers to countries willing to ally with them. He also warns of a distant threat that mankind is unlikely to survive without Confederation help.

Israel becomes the first nation to form an alliance with the Confederation, after Michael puts a protective shield in place, thwarting an Iranian nuclear attack.

One by one, nations ally with the Confederation. But the pace picks up when North Korea deploys and demands the surrender of South Korea. Dozens of nations ally with the Confederation in time for the Confederation to stop the invasion.

During the confrontation with the North, Michael learns that the distant threat, a parasitic species known simply as the 'Enemy,' has already infiltrated Earth. The Confederation fleet arrives in time to root out the Enemy infiltrators.

In the aftermath, Canada agrees to be the host country for the Confederation's Embassy on Earth. The Confederation leases a 100 square mile tract of land in the Mackenzie Mountains in the Northwest Territories, where it builds its Embassy. The Embassy becomes the home of the Earth Alliance, which is the primary interface between the Confederation and the nations of Earth. It also becomes home to the Ascendance Institute, which is the educational arm of the Confederation and manages Confederation technology transfer with humanity.

The Institute picks up five years later. The Ascendance Institute has been built. Tens of thousands of doctors have been trained. Confederation drugs and medical equipment modified for human use are being rolled out. The Engineering School has begun operation and humans are learning about spaceship design, propulsion and shielding.

But Enemy activity has picked up in the Milky Way and the news is not good. They have acquired superluminal propulsion and are now only a few years away from Earth. In response, the Earth Alliance authorizes the formation of Space Force for close-in defense. The initial plan is for humans to operate smaller Confederation ships, so they can assist in the close-in defense of Earth.

But the unexpected happens. A human engineer, Eugene Xu, discovers a way to vastly improve Confederation propulsion systems. Then, with the help of several colleagues, the team Eugene leads discovers a way to improve shielding such that it is Enemy-resistant. A young female graduate student, Kelly Williamson, joins the team and is actually the first to solve the shielding problem.

An Earth shuttle is outfitted with the new technology and joins the Confederation Armada in the defense of a planet 1,000 light-years from Earth. Their participation is the key to victory in the battle.

On return, Kelly proposes a vastly more efficient spaceship manufacturing process.

But word gets back to the Confederation that Earth has advanced technology that was not disclosed during the treaty process. A team is sent to investigate the issue. The investigation is led by a corrupt inspector. His ship becomes infected by the Enemy, who attempt a run back to the Confederation capital on the planet New Lorexi. The Armada, dilapidated from its encounters with the Enemy and the recklessness of the inspector, is left behind to fend for itself.

In the weeks that follow, the first human-produced Fast Attack Ship is built and sent out on its first mission. It succeeds in finding a deposit of Transluminide, the substance that powers Confederation technology. When the Armada finally limps back to Earth, they use the Transluminide to repair and upgrade their ships.

Emergence picks up three months later. Eugene and Kelly head home for Christmas. Back in Australia Kelly is elevated to the Order of Australia (the Australian version of the old English knighthood). In Baltimore, the solution for another weapon useful against the Enemy comes to Eugene in a dream. On his return to the Embassy, Eugene meets David Washington, wrongly convicted for the murder of his family years before, a crime of which he has no memory.

Back at the Embassy, David learns what happened that night when he was 16. His family was attacked by an Enemy infiltrator. David repelled the attack using a special skill he didn't know he had, saving three little kids. But seven adults were killed in the attack and David was convicted of their murders.

When the Confederation Armada finishes its repairs, it is recalled to Andromeda to search for the inspector's Fast Packet ship, which had been commandeered by the Enemy.

A replacement armada is dispatched to Earth, but won't arrive for several weeks, which leaves the people on the planet Karagon, the most populated planet in the sector, without protection against the Enemy. The Confederation Ambassador on Karagon contacts Michael to see if Earth would enter into a trade agreement with them. His goal is to get Enemy-resistant shields.

Following up on some research, Professor Schudel, head of the mining department at the Institute, discovers a high-probability lead on numerous Transluminide deposits in systems near Earth. Space Force sends 18 ships out on a mission to do mining scans in the uninhabited systems.

On the way back to New Lorexi, the Armada finds the missing Fast Packet ship in the intergalactic void. But they bungle the encounter, allowing the Enemy to commandeer an upgraded Confederation Cruiser. The cruiser jumps away toward New Lorexi before it can be destroyed.

The next day, the cruiser is seen above two different planets. Several mysterious deaths occur in the hours after the sightings and the Confederation calls on Earth for assistance.

A taskforce of ten Space Force Fast Attack Ships is dispatched to aid the Confederation in its time of need. As the taskforce races across the void, it builds a massive wave of dimensional resonance that nearly destroys it. As they recover from the disaster, the taskforce leaders determine that they've been thrown five days into the past.

Admiral Daniel Porter, leader of the taskforce, decides to capitalize on the misfortune and cleverly positions his taskforce to intercept the cruiser and track the Enemy infiltrators on the two planets. The taskforce successfully destroys the infected cruiser and the infiltrators, then puts shields up around a hundred planets near New Lorexi.

Back in the Milky Way, the replacement Confederation Armada sent weeks ago, mysteriously goes silent as the Enemy begins massing for another attack.

The Space Force taskforce is recalled, but as it prepares to depart, a Confederation ship fires on and destroys the EAS Helsinki, one of the taskforce's ships. In the aftermath, Michael and Admiral Jo-Na, Michael's lifelong friend and the head of the Armada, have a huge falling out.

The nine remaining ships of the taskforce race back to the area where the Enemy is massing. What they find is the devastated remains of the replacement Armada. Fighting persists inside the Flagship and two of the Cruisers. But 13 ships are missing, including a Capital Ship.

The Capital Ship with over 1 million civilians, now infected with the Enemy parasite, is racing to Earth.

Five more Space Force ships are dispatched. James, the last surviving member of a powerful ancient species, joins the fight, disabling the missing infected ships. Eugene's new weapon is used to clear the Enemy infection from all the ships.

Ships from the Confederation return to help with the rescue of the replacement Armada, but the final tally is devastating. Over one million Confederation citizens were killed by the Enemy. Only a handful of ships in the replacement Armada are recoverable.

The Space Force ships involved in the engagement with the Enemy return to Earth for repairs. But a new reality starts to settle in... The Confederation can no longer project sufficient military presence into the Milky Way to protect it against the Enemy. Earth must take the lead.

Alliance picks up six months later. More Enemy sightings are made further out in the sector. Ships from Confederation member Celanar are commandeered by the Enemy and now threaten the planet. Celanar and eight other planets petition the Confederation to allow them to form a defensive alliance with Earth.

Admiral Jo-Na of the Confederation High Command completes his investigation into the destruction of the Fast Attack Ship Helsinki. His conclusion is that the spy Ju-Ne was behind the attack. Ju-Ne is not only a spy, he's an Ascendent, someone able to operate an avatar. When they go to arrest Ju-Ne, they learn that his restoration chamber is not where it was registered to be. It is believed he moved it to Earth.

James, who took David Washington as his apprentice in *Emergence*, starts David's training in earnest. Together, they visit Naltanarus, the developing world previously targeted by the Enemy. The people there are on the verge of developing an interstellar spaceship capable of reaching other star systems. James and David witness the launch of their first interstellar flight and learn that they are going to visit the Solar System.

Ju-Ne, who can operate multiple avatars, is on Earth. His mission is to slow Earth's advancement. As word of a possible defensive alliance leaks out, he goes into overdrive launching attack after attack to destabilize the Earth Alliance and prevent the formation of the '3F Defensive Alliance.'

Engineers Eugene Xu and Kelly Williamson develop and test a new propulsion system that can reach the Enemy home world. They also develop new weapons that can destroy it.

Days before Space Force launches its mission to destroy the Enemy home world, they learn that the Enemy is massing for another attack. In a quick change of plans, they launch a daring mission to take down both the planet and the asteroid where the new Enemy attack is being prepared. As the first Enemy ships enter the dimensional rift, Space Force arrives. The home world and asteroid are destroyed, the rift functionally sealed.

Michael and his fiancé, Sarah announce a wedding date. They will be married two days after the signing ceremony for the new 3F Defensive Alliance. Leaders from all the world's nations and from numerous other Confederation members flock to Earth for the wedding.

Alexi, Sarah's bodyguard, learns that Ju-Ne is planning to take down the wedding, something that would destabilize Confederation influence in the sector.

Ju-Ne is caught days before the wedding, but he has one attack left that he triggers from prison. While Sarah prepares for the wedding, Michael joins the fight, saving the new Alliance and still getting to the wedding on time.

They travel to Karagon for their honeymoon. There Michael learns that several of his new Alliance members want to withdraw from the Confederation.

...

Following is the story of Michael's struggle to hold together the Confederation and the 3F Defensive Alliance, which are on the brink of civil war.

PROLOGUE

Twelve months ago...
ENGINEERING CONFERENCE ROOM

"James, David. Thank you for meeting with us."

"Kelly how could I resist?" James beamed his joy at being there.

A pause, then Kelly locked her eyes with James'.

"I've continued working through the Lorexian theoretical formulations of the high dimensions."

James nodded his understanding.

"Dimension 502..."

James' smile increased.

"It's so bizarre. The gravity wells are so congested. In our space-time, everything is spread out. It's like gravity wells, stars and planets are all spread out. Open space is dominant, gravity is rare.

"In 502, it's like the opposite. Gravity wells are dominant, space is rare."

She looked at James intently.

"Does that mean what I think it does?"

James smiled, his warmth engulfing the room.

Unexpectedly, David spoke. "So, that's how you do it."

James continued smiling at Kelly. She felt like she was the only person in the room, the universe. His stare was so engulfing.

"Now you know."

"This changes everything," Kelly whispered in amazement.

Three months ago...
EMBASSY HOSPITAL

She woke, uncertain where she was. It was comfortable, warm, dark. Without a care in the world, she drifted away.

...

She woke again, a bit more present this time. It was comfortable and warm, but dark. When she stirred, she heard sloshing, and terror suddenly seized her.

An alarm went off and she sat up, hitting her head on something she couldn't see. Then the memories flooded back. The wave of molten metal covering her friend Abel, then spilling onto her. She screamed as the door opened.

"Lisette, it's OK. Your avatar was destroyed, but you are OK. Let me help you out."

...

She was dressed now. Calm. Food had been brought and she'd eaten her fill. The hospital staff wouldn't tell her what happened, wouldn't even tell her the date. The only thing they would tell her was that the Chief was on his way over to speak with her. But raw, red-hot anger burned.

If they haven't captured Ju-Ne yet, then they never will. I'll find him first and...

She smiled.

Three weeks ago...
[Thursday, 06.24.2032] CENTRAL COUNCIL CHAMBERS

"I call this emergency session to order." The Speaker pounded his gavel. "As you should know, a member of our Military Intelligence organization was arrested on Earth some time ago. By Earth's calendar, tomorrow he will have been in custody one Earth year.

"As you also know, we have sent three separate extradition requests to Earth for the return of this person. All have been refused. They cite a medical technicality, claiming he has gone into hibernation and is on life support. But this is a preposterous excuse. If he's simply in hibernation, then he'd be much safer under our care on one of our ships, than in the hands of primitives.

"Therefore, I propose that we send a fourth and final extradition demand, delivered by a small armada of ships with the authority to take him by force if so required."

A hand went up from the junior councilor from the Milky Way.

"The chair recognizes Counselor Ke-Ve."

"We all know that Counselor Mi-Ku and the Ancient One would vote against this. Is that why they are not here?"

"No. As parties in this conflict, they are recused."

Counselor Ke-Ve was the newest member of the council. He had done his duty by raising the question, so did not press the argument. Nonetheless, a thought burned. *So, you admit that's the reason they're not here.*

It seemed that only the speaker and Counselor To-Ja from New Lorexi thought this resolution was a good idea, but after an hour of discussion the resolution passed 4 – 3.

Counselor Ke-Ve shook his head in disappointment. *If Mi-Ku and the Ancient One were here, the resolution would have failed, and probably by more than 5 – 4. The Speaker has made a dangerous move.*

Chapter 1: WARNING

"Counselor Ke-Ve, what an unexpected pleasure."

"Mi-Ku, I hope things are well with you and your new Alliance. I've heard that you've added a number of new members already."

"Yes, six more have joined: Naltanarus, Sofaana, Allastran, Omarabad, Bornasal, and Hacindra. That brings us up to 15 in total."

"Congratulations. I must admit, I'm impressed." Ke-Ve seemed to stall for a moment, as if he wasn't sure whether to continue or not. "Mi-Ku, I call with news. News I fear to share; but believe I must. May I ask for your discretion?"

The Councilor's caution was worrisome.

"I will not reveal from whom I learned this." Michael hoped he could keep the promise.

"The Central Council held a secret meeting, one to which you and the Ancient One were not invited. A resolution, which I voted against, was passed authorizing an extradition demand for the release of Ju-Ne.

"It has been issued as a warrant and will be delivered by a small Armada authorized to seize him by force. When Admiral Jo-Na protested, they secretly turned the mission over to Military Intelligence. The new Inspector has command over the Armada. I've heard rumors that his ship has been upgraded with new classified weapons and propulsion." Another moment of hesitation. "The Armada left today. It's due in less than a week."

"Ke-Ve. Thank you for letting me know this. I will not reveal that you're the one who leaked it."

"Thank you, Mi-Ku, and good luck." With that Ke-Ve cut the connection, already worried that the call had been bugged.

MANUFACTURING OFFICE

Joel was expecting to hear from Henry shortly. The new Entangled Quantum Derangement (EQD) resistant computers from Atomorali had been installed on one of the freighters. Everything but the AI computer had been switched over. The Atomoi hadn't developed an EQD-resistant computer with the capacity to host an AI yet. But they did have upgraded casing for the AI computer that had been installed instead.

The ship had been tested at the Atomoi's space-based testing facility that morning. Results were due momentarily.

...

"Joel?"

"Henry! What's the news?"

"We passed with flying colors, my friend. Flying colors. The unshielded ship was subjected to a pulse 10 times more powerful than the one that hit the Helsinki. No systems went down.

"That's the most powerful test they have, so the ever cautious Atomoi warn that a more powerful shot might still take the computers down. But I'm having a hard time worrying about that right now."

"Excellent news!"

"But that's not all."

"There's more?"

"Now that they have our specs, they've updated their manufacturing line to produce and package a kit that contains all the computers required for one ship. They've already run 25 freighter kits. So, if Emmanuel can release a purchase order today or tomorrow for the 25 kits, they can ship them back on the freighter they tested.

"Kits for the Fast Attack Ships and Cruisers will be available in another week or two."

"Understood. I'll get on it now. We're preapproved, so this shouldn't be a problem."

EUGENE AND KELLY'S LAB

Kelly looked up. "Eugene, the simulations prove out!"

Eugene pulled his ear buds out. "Say again?"

"The simulations prove out."

"Really?" Eugene replied dubiously. "Show me."

"I know you struggle with this. Dimension 601 creates the most impenetrable shield previously found. But we developed it for its other properties, not its impenetrability. The impenetrability was just a lucky bonus.

"Therefore, it stands to reason that if we searched through the other dimensions, prioritizing by impenetrability, that we would find something. And if its ancillary properties were less dangerous, then we could ask James to endorse it, Michael to upgrade the Batumi, and presto... Our problem is solved."

Eugene had a lot of respect for Kelly's dogged evaluation of the high dimensions. It plagued his dreams that the freighter, the EAS Batumi, still held a dimension 601 shield. In truth, it was paralyzing at times.

But Kelly was so practical. She kept reminding him, "Find a better one, a safer one. Do the upgrade. Then no one will ever know."

"Remind me the dimension again."

"Dimension 576. It's just as energy absorbing and impenetrable from the outside. But benign on the inside. It's useless as a traditional shield encompassing a ship, but perfect as a stealth shield in front of the ship. The Confederation actually documented its protective advantages but wrote it off. They couldn't imagine how a shield that didn't encompass a ship would be useful."

Eugene thought for a moment. "Perfect closure for a deception that's grown a bit long in the tooth." His smile this time was genuine.

"Any idea how hard the 'upgrade' will be?"

"Miniscule."

"Let's punch one out, do the tests, then propose it as standard equipment."

AMBASSADOR'S OFFICE

James looked intensely at Michael, who'd just shared Ke-Ve's news.

"I sensed that we'd been cut out of something but struggled to believe it would matter."

"James, they cut us out of a critical vote. The resolution undermines what we're doing here."

"Does it?" The intensity of James' stare didn't break.

"Care to explain?"

"So, they send some ships. Are those ships a match for yours?"

"Do they need to be?"

"You don't think you can stop them?" James prodded.

Michael started to protest, but the words froze on his tongue. *James is trying to prod me toward a smarter solution*. But he struggled to see what that would be. Ju-Ne restored to the Inspector's office would be a catastrophe.

James shook his head in disappointment, then started to say something. But Michael cut him off.

"Far better that Ju-Ne die in an escape attempt than by human hands. And if his rescuers are aligned with him, then far better the lot of them die at their own hand. But how?"

James nodded his head in approval. "Eugene and Kelly have something they want to talk with you about that might be relevant. Two things, actually."

"Which are?"

"Better for you to talk with them about it." James got a faraway look in his eye. "They're in their lab. Maybe you should stop by."

James stood. "And there's something that I've been putting off for too long. I guess it's time to go deal with it."

James flashed away, leaving Michael wondering what it was James needed to deal with. He shook the thought from his mind, got up, then headed out. "Pam, I'm stepping out for a bit."

SECURITY DETAINMENT AREA

James flashed into Warden Archer Todd's outer office, startling Jean, the Warden's assistant.

"Oh, so sorry Jean. Any chance I could have a quick word with the Warden?"

The door to the inner office was open. They could both hear the Warden getting up to come out.

"Professor Ancient. What can I do for you?"

"I sense that your prisoner, Ju-Ne, is coming out of his hibernation. Given how long he's been down, someone should probably tend to him. I'm sure your medical bot would be sufficient. Fair warning, he will be very hungry."

"Let's go see."

The warden led the way to the observation area above the Lorexian holding block. "Sure enough. I can see him stirring. How did you know?"

James smiled. "I can sense things and didn't want to see him suffer too much when he woke."

"Thank you, Professor."

James smiled, then flashed away.

EUGENE AND KELLY'S LAB

Michael knocked on the outer door, then entered. The stealth field was up, so all he could see was the cloudy gray diffusion field.

After a moment, Kelly stepped out. "Hi, Michael. We weren't expecting to see you today. Is there something we can help you with?"

"OK if I come in and talk for a bit?"

"Sure." She smiled and offered her hand. He took it, then stepped in through the stealth shield with her.

"Michael, welcome."

"Eugene, you look to be in good spirits."

"I am. Kelly came up with something incredible that I'm really excited about, and we were actually able to kick up a prototype today. Want to see it?"

"Sure."

Eugene, realizing that he kind of spilled the beans on what was fundamentally a Kelly invention, motioned for her to explain.

"Come have a seat over here." Kelly smiled.

Michael took a seat, then Kelly pointed at two test benches set up on the other side of the room.

"What am I looking at?"

"Two shield generators configured for forward use, like the ones on the EAS Batumi. In fact, one of these, the one on the left, is the same as the Batumi's. The one on the right is the new stronger one."

"I thought the one on the Batumi was the strongest known."

"It was. A year ago."

Michael sensed that Kelly was really excited about this.

"What makes it stronger?"

"It's in a different dimension with different properties. The one on the Batumi was made from the ultra-shield designed to contain the red matter reaction. That shield was designed to contain things. It's still the strongest shield we know of for that purpose. We used it for the Batumi's shields because it was what we had at hand.

"But given the tactical advantages of the Batumi's shield, I wanted to find one better optimized for that purpose."

"Has Space Force expressed an interest in such a shield?"

"Yes. But among the problems is that the Batumi's shields are a power hog."

"And I presume the new one isn't?"

"Exactly, watch."

Two small shields popped up hiding the test benches behind them. Both created a completely black hole that reflected absolutely nothing.

"They certainly look the same," Michael ventured.

"But looks can be deceiving. The one on the left, the same type as on the Batumi, is consuming about 10 watts. The one on the right is consuming 7.

"I'm going to hit them both with a 500-watt laser."

Kelly handed Michael safety glasses, then put her own on.

"In case you're worried about safety, we also have a capture system behind the shields that will prevent the laser from burning a hole in the wall.

"Starting the laser at 100 watts."

Two beams shot out, one hitting each shield. The room lit from all the laser speckle. Both shields held. Both shields remained unlit as the laser beam seemed to just stop when it hit the shield.

"Increasing to 200 watts."

The speckle light escaping into the room increased, but there was no change in the shields. They remained completely unlit, the laser beams simply stopping.

"Increasing to 300 watts. Fair warning, when I do this, the shield on the left will fail."

Again, the speckle light increased. Then there was a flash and the laser targeting the left shield shutdown.

"Explain to me what I just saw."

Kelly enjoyed hearing the curiosity in Michael's voice.

"The laser power increase isn't instantaneous, but it does step up quickly. At somewhere around 260 watts, the shield on the left collapses. When that happens all the laser light and speckle that was hitting the shield suddenly floods into the room. Then the safety systems shut the laser down. Collapse to shutdown happens in well less than 1 second. But all that light floods the room when the laser beam hits the diffuser on the carts."

"It looked like an explosion."

"It does. It's a great optical illusion. OK, I'm going to step the laser up to 500 watts. You'll see that the new shield still holds."

...

"Compelling demo, Kelly. It's clear that the new shield is much better for this type of application. But how do you see this being used?"

"The most obvious uses are the ones we've already used them for: stealth approaches and forward protection. Beyond that there are applications like temporary cover. In some sense, that was one of the Batumi's functions at the Enemy home world, providing cover for the weapon until it was ready to fire. Seems it would also be useful if we needed to put up a blockade."

The word 'blockade' shot through Michael like a bolt of lightning. A hundred ships with this type of shield could easily trap the new Inspector here. But in his arrogance, he would ignore the warnings and attempt to run the blockade, destroying himself, his armada, and his prisoner.

There would still be a lot of backlash, but this was the edge he needed for the coming conflict with the new Inspector.

"Michael? Michael, are you OK?"

Michael's attention snapped back to the room.

"Sorry, got lost in a thought."

"Happens to me all the time," Eugene said sympathetically.

"How soon before we can get some of these?"

"A day or two. We're almost there and have everything we need other than a large power source. But if we do the test in the Batumi, it already has a power source we can use. We'll only have to switch out a couple parts."

"I'll contact Space Force. Someone will contact you for the test later today, maybe tomorrow.

"OK, if I change the subject?"

"Sure."

"James mentioned to me that you had two things you were working on."

Kelly looked puzzled for a moment.

"The broad arc of my work since returning from Enemy space has been working my way through the dimensions the Confederation has documented. That's how I found this shield." She motioned toward the test bench.

"The other thing I found is really cool, but I'm not sure there's really any demand for it. It's a different type of propulsion system that has the potential for incredibly long jumps. In principle, it would allow a ship to cross the intergalactic void in a single jump.

"The problem with it is that there are only a few places within a galaxy that it can go further than Eugene's system. And there are lots of places where it can't go as far."

Again, Kelly's words stunned Michael. Earlier this week, he'd had his first cross words with Ambassador Va-Mu from Edukatar, who needed to make a shipment of nanobots to Triangulum. The Earth Alliance had declined the business because of the distance.

"Kelly, there's big demand for technology that will reduce the transit time across the void, even if it requires a special ship class that does nothing else. What would you need to push that work forward?"

"Navigation and testing assistance. Everything else, Eugene and I could sort out on our own, with Henry and Jacob's help of course."

Michael looked at his chronometer. "Unfortunately, I'm late for another meeting. Kelly, thank you again for the demo and the update. Let me connect with some people. I'm sure we want to push both those initiatives forward. I'll be in touch."

Michael stood, shook hands, then let himself out. He could pass out of the stealth shield around the lab without escort.

As the door closed, Eugene turned to Kelly. "Did he ever say why he came over?"

"No, I don't think he did."

"Curious."

BRIDGE, EAS GERMANY

"Admiral, we're being hailed by the lead ship."

"Put him on," Admiral Katrine Bjork replied.

Katrine Bjork was the former captain of the Fast Attack Ship, EAS Oslo. She had led the taskforce that took down the asteroid in Enemy space, the one that had housed their shipyards. Her performance on that mission and in the previous mission to Andromeda had put her at the top of the candidate list for the EAS Germany, the first Cruiser built at Sun-Earth Lagrange 4.

She now led the taskforce providing security services in the outer portion of the sector.

The image of Captain Caalum Desooti appeared on the main viewer. He headed one of the raiding forces from the Kalamaan Empire, the principal sponsor of piracy in the region. He was quickly becoming one of Katrine's least favorite people.

"Captain," she greeted sternly.

"Puny female. You enter our space uninvited again!" He spat the words out with disgust.

Katrine smiled at the insult.

"You were seen in the vicinity of one of our mining claims this week." A picture appeared in an inset in the video feed they were sending to the Captain.

"That is not my ship."

"No? The identifier on the tail matches the one on your ship."

"Many ships have that identifier."

The picture zoomed in to a part of the hull damaged in an earlier exchange.

"And this damage to your ship as well?"

Her tactical officer whispered, "Admiral, they're powering up their weapons."

"Captain if you fire your weapons at us, we will respond. And all your ships will suffer damage."

The main view screen shifted to a ball of plasma released from the Captain's ship.

"Tactical jump," Katrine called out.

The Germany appeared in the midst of the Kalamaan ships.

"Fire rail guns and energy projectors."

Six of the Germany's energy projectors fired, 2 per Kalamaan ship. The shots were followed by one railgun round each.

The view screen shifted back to the still open communications channel. The impact of the weapon hits had knocked Captain Desooti to the floor. Smoke was starting to fill his bridge. He shouted orders as he got to his feet, then turned an icy stare toward Katrine.

"Puny female. This is the last time."

"Captain, for once we agree. If we catch you snooping at our mining claims or preying on one of our allies' ships, we will finally start using our real weapons on you, not these toys. And this will have been the last time you walked away."

She cut the comm line.

"Admiral." The tactical officer pointed to the view screen which now showed Captain Desooti's ship. A plasma ball was attempting to form on one of its emitters. But the weapon was no longer working properly. The ball collapsed, its energy distributing over the hull of its ship. Lights previously visible on the outside of the ship flashed several times, then went out.

"She appears to have lost power, ma'am."

"Take us out of here."

MANUFACTURING OFFICE

"Michael, come in. It's been a while since you've ventured over this way."

"I've been spending a lot of time at the new Alliance Headquarters Building. It's far enough away that it's hard to spend time on both campuses the same day."

"The two headquarters are what, seven miles apart?"

"Something like that. But the only public transit options are more like 40 miles, over an hour each way. When the new train tunnel is complete, there will be a high-speed rail option that'll only take 10 minutes. Until then, it's an hour plus on the trolley. But in truth, I don't do that. I have my shuttle transport me."

A holoprojection popped up.

"Here's the report you asked for." Joel waved at the projection. "There's a copy in your queue. It shows the listing of all the ships and their equipment buildouts, to the extent we did the buildout. Space Force has done some buildouts on their own that I don't have information about."

A second document popped up in the projection.

"This is the current construction schedule you asked for. It changes almost every day. This is today's snapshot."

"The high-level summary?" Michael prompted.

"At this point, we've made 73 Cruisers, 252 Fast Attack Ships and 312 freighters. Of the freighters, 36 were deliveries to Alliance partners, not Space Force. The four that went to Celanar had internal gravity and inertial dampening customizations. Four of the ones that went to Karagon had the cruise ship customizations. I know that there have been requests for freighters from other Confederation members, but no deliveries have gone from our department to a customer outside the Alliance."

"Kelly came up with a new forward shield design for the freighters. It's stronger, which was hard to believe until I saw the tests. But it uses much less power. I don't know what the final spec will be, but for the purpose of discussion, let's assume half the power.

"How hard is it going to be to retrofit this into the freighters?" asked Michael.

"It took about 6 hours to install the Batumi's current shield. At least half that time was making modifications to fit the gigantic power supply. So I suppose it might be half, three hours. If it were really small, maybe only two. I'll need the specs to know for sure, so until then, six hours may be a better planning estimate."

"OK. I'm thinking we want 10 ships retrofit by Monday, maybe more."

"Why not just add it to the new ships. That would add essentially no time. More bots maybe, but not more time."

"Maybe that too. I need to talk with the Admirals and get the specs from Kelly. Best case on that is tomorrow."

"Understood."

"One more thing. Kelly and Eugene have come up with another propulsion option that I'm going to need on several of the cruisers. I'd like to add it to the existing propulsion systems, as opposed to replacing the current ones. Assuming it's the same size, will it fit?"

Joel hated questions like this. "Michael, how could I possibly know? Does it use the same power source? Does it share any of the same components? You know; power conditioners, field emitters, controls? Without that info, how could I possibly know?"

"Is that to say that there isn't room in the Cruiser nacelles for a redundant propulsion system."

Joel sighed in frustration. "The nacelles are half full. If their new system and all its ancillary needs can fit in half, then yes, there's room. Field emitters… That's a whole different problem."

"Understood. Nothing required on your part now, but I'm going to ask Kelly to continue pushing this initiative forward. One or both of us will contact you when we're closer to having engineering specs."

The line dropped.

...

Calls like this really frustrated Joel. How could he possibly know anything about the viability of a system he knew nothing about!

Then it occurred to him, Michael doesn't really know much about this either. His real purpose was to decide whether or not to ask Kelly to continue. He'd attempt to book some time with her tomorrow. If her work was of interest to Michael, then it would be of interest to him as well.

LISETTE LEFEVRE'S OFFICE

Lisette had been held in stasis for 10 months, following the destruction of her avatar during the search of Julian Bescond's country home in France. As a lower level diplomat, they did not maintain a spare avatar for her. So, they needed to grow a new one from scratch.

When she woke in the hospital, the rage against Ju-Ne had been intense. But seeing his shriveled hibernating body in the Lorexian detention area did a lot to cool her anger.

Her former friend and colleague, Abel Fletcher, Head of Domestic Security, had been killed in the fire. He was human, so was now gone. In truth she was sadder about Abel's loss than she was angry at Ju-Ne.

The Embassy had conducted an extensive search for candidates to replace Abel, but six months into the search, they decided to wait for Lisette, despite the fact that she was an Ascendant and the job was designated for a human.

Now three months into the job, all the immediate day-to-day problems she'd inherited were under control and she'd started working her list of long-term issues. At the top of that list was secure Transluminide storage. She'd been shocked to find out that the Earth Alliance bank had over 50,000 kg of Transluminide bullion and over 1,000 wonder stones of various grades.

A quick check with the Core Worlds Central Bank showed Transluminide assets at only 150,000 kg. No one knew for sure where it was stored, but the security section in the public portion of their database read 'over 100 sites spread across 20 planets.'

She'd requested a meeting with Michael to discuss a sensitive issue. He would be stopping by shortly.

...

"Michael, welcome."

"Lisette, so good to see you again."

She indicated a seat.

"I'm sure I've said this before, but I'm so glad you took this job. Losing Abel was such a tragic loss. From the outset of the search for a replacement, I knew you would be the only one up to it."

Lisette closed the door and took her seat as Michael spoke.

"Thank you. OK, if I activate a security dampening field?"

The question was mostly rhetorical as she activated the field before he answered.

"This must be sensitive. What's happened?"

"The Earth Alliance has accumulated huge Transluminide reserves. I don't know how that came to be, as it's not really in my area of responsibility. What I'm worried about is how it's being stored."

"Go on." Michael didn't understand what the problem was.

"I did a quick check on the Transluminide assets of the Core World's Central Bank. They have about 150,000 kg. We have about a third of that, 50,000 kg.

"Theirs is stored in over 100 secret sites on over 20 planets. Ours sits 150 yards from Main Street. Over 1,000 wonder stones of various grades sit right next to it.

"Our facility may be sufficient to hold back a common burglar. But it would have no chance against a state-sponsored actor. No chance against Ju-Ne if he was still active and had any idea that it existed.

"Suppose the Inspector made another play against Earth. He might not think to look for it, but he has scanners that would be able to detect it if he did look."

"Suggestions?"

"Do we need to keep it at the Embassy?"

"For now, yes."

"Do we have any underground storage facilities we could harden?"

"No, our lease forbids excavation."

"What about the tunnel?"

"I'll need to check on that."

"It's well known that the Earth Alliance has found numerous Transluminide deposits. The rumor is that we only use these claims for assignment in trade deals. The fact that we have wonder stones suggests that's not true. Are we mining, or planning to mine, Transluminide for our own use?"

"I'm not going to answer that question, but please continue with your line of reasoning."

"Securing 50,000 kg will take some effort. If we can do that will it be enough? If not, then how much storage capacity should I plan to secure?"

"A lot more."

Lisette felt the exasperation growing.

"Michael, how can I protect you if I don't know what I'm protecting?" The words came out with a lot more heat than intended. "Sorry, I'm not angry, just worried."

"I understand. And I'm not trying to frustrate you. How about this? We have filed numerous claims. It's a simple public search to find them. Assume we have an equal number that are not filed and plan to double that number within the year."

Lisette had done the public records search earlier. The answer was over 200,000 kg. She would ultimately need to protect at least half a million. Unbelievable.

"I'd like to start a personal project to research options to protect a large supply like that. It obviously needs to be done with discretion. Is there someone I can contact regarding the tunnel?"

"I'll do that. I'll get an answer in a couple days. Have you spoken with the Chief about this?"

Michael was referring to Lisette's boss, Baraza Dalitso, Head of Embassy Security.

"No. This is domestic."

"Then let's keep it that way. This IS domestic. The fewer Confederation people who know about it the better."

Both Michael and Lisette were 'Confederation people.' Lisette got the irony in the statement. Michael apparently didn't.

"Agreed. I'll keep this between us and consult with you before roping anyone else in."

"Lisette, thank you for looking into this issue and bringing it to my attention. In truth, I'd lost track of how much we'd accumulated. And, off the record, we do plan to start mining and expect to substantially build our reserves. Let's connect again early next week."

Chapter 2: DIAGNOSIS

[Friday, 07.16.2032] PRESENCE PROJECTOR, AMBASSADOR'S OFFICE

"Ambassador Peklit. Thank you for arranging this call."

"Mi-Ku, thank you for speaking with me."

Vorkin Peklit was the new ambassador to Jerusota. He was the replacement for Ambassador Ha-Nu, who had transferred to a new world in Triangulum. He was an Ascendant occupying a Jerusotan avatar. But he was not Lorexian.

"Welcome to the Milky Way. Do I understand correctly that you are Zorossan?"

"Yes, the same native species as Councilor Mo-Mo of the central council, but from a different planet. I originated on Dalfanito, one of the worlds colonized from Togarotu."

"I'm glad to see more Ascendants from allied worlds joining the ambassador ranks.

"So, what can I do for you?" Michael asked.

"I requested this meeting for several reasons. I wanted to let you know that I was here and planning to attend the Sector Alliance Advisor's meeting this afternoon.

"I also wanted to pass along a message from Councilor Mo-Mo and from the alliance president on my home world, Dalfanito. Both would be interested in pursuing trade agreements with Earth."

"Do you know what they're interested in?"

"The same as most others, I'm sure. But I suspect the real interest is access to Earth's technology."

"Thank you for passing that along. I'll reach out to Mo-Mo."

"The other item is a little more sensitive."

"Understood."

"In case you haven't heard already, there was a central council meeting a couple weeks ago. My friend, Councilor Mo-Mo, asked me to contact you about it. The council approved an extradition warrant for the return of the Ascendant Ju-Ne. Mo-Mo voted against this resolution, but it passed anyway. He specifically wanted you to know that the new Inspector, Ma-Gu, has been given a task force of enhanced ships and orders to take the prisoner by force if he is not handed over peacefully."

"Thank you for passing the message along. Did Mo-Mo send a recommendation on how we should handle this."

"May I speak off the record?"

"This entire conversation is off the record."

"He thinks you will resist. He believes you will not take the advice he wants to give, so offers no recommendation. Instead, he offers one word."

"Which is?"

"EQD. I don't know what it means. He said you would."

"Please send Mo-Mo my thanks for the warning."

SPACE FORCE COMMAND

Lt. Bumati Parikh, second watch science officer on the EAS Amsterdam and mining mission specialist, had been summoned to appear. Her captain, Christopher Flanagan, accompanied her.

Captain Flanagan told her that she was going to be promoted to Lt. Commander. But the only other thing he had to say was, "Don't worry. It's something good."

They'd been waiting in Admiral Sam Scott's outer office for 15 minutes before the door opened and they were asked to come in.

As they entered, she saw a long table with four men seated. She immediately recognized Michael, then Professor Schudel from the mining department at the institute. She also recognized Admiral Scott. But she didn't know the fourth person.

There was a single chair on her side of the table and an open chair on the other side next to the four men.

Captain Flanagan pointed to the single chair, then proceeded to the other side of the table to take the open seat.

"Lt. Parikh, I'm Samuel Scott, head of military operations of Space Force. Next to me is Secretary Winston Thompson, Earth Alliance Secretary of Space Force. I'm sure you know Michael and am told you know Professor Schudel."

Bumati nodded her head in understanding, now extremely nervous.

"We have several things we need to do this morning. The first is this." He slid a small box across the table and indicated that she should open it.

She did and saw the two gold, oak leaf collar pins.

"Congratulations, Lt. Commander."

The five men facing her, gave brief applause, as the congratulations rippled around the table.

The Admiral pointed to Professor Schudel. "Professor, you're next."

Bumati looked at Professor Schudel, uncertain why he was here.

"Ms. Parikh, I have two things to give you today. The first is this letter of acceptance from the Institute's Mining Journal. Your paper entitled, 'Transluminide Structures and Formation Conditions' will be printed in the next issue. You are the youngest person ever to have been accepted for publication. And Earth is the newest world to have a published author."

She picked up the pages the professor pushed across the table. One was a copy of the letter in English. The other was in Lorexian.

"The second item is from the Confederation Mining Administration. It certifies you as a Registered Claimant, meaning that you are certified to file claims on your own authority, not under my auspices. It also includes a Confederation Professional Mining License. This gives you the right to lead space-based mining efforts on claims assigned to you or your employer.

"Both of these are difficult to obtain and convey a certain status in Confederation society. They give you the right to operate in any Confederation system or on any claim registered with the Confederation.

"By the way, you are the first human to ever have been awarded these licenses. Congratulations, these are both incredible accomplishments."

Again, there was brief applause and additional congratulations.

Bumati was surprised and didn't know what to say but squeaked out a thank you.

The professor indicated that the Secretary was up next.

"For some time, the Earth Alliance has wanted to develop its own fleet of mining ships. Given that we now have a Confederation licensed mining officer, we are commissioning the first Space Force Mining ship, the EAS Mumbai. It is a modified freighter. The tenth freighter off the line, named for the largest city in the tenth country to ally with the Confederation.

"Lt. Cmdr. Parikh, you are being commissioned today as the Commanding officer of the Mumbai. Congratulations, Ma'am."

The Admiral extended his hand to shake, as the others clapped. Then one by one each shook her hand and offered their congratulations.

Bumati was shocked. She'd been hoping for the promised promotion and maybe some other form of recognition. But she was completely shocked to be getting a ship of her own.

"The ship's portal is now available to you. It has been preloaded with recommended staff. But it's up to you to select your staff and extend the offers. That should be your highest priority today. Tomorrow you'll be able to board the ship. Orders will be released to you shortly. Plan to depart on your first mission this week."

...

After more handshakes and congratulations, the meeting broke up. And as the others left, Michael asked Admiral Scott for a word in private.

ADMIRAL SCOTT'S OFFICE

"How can I help you Michael?"

"I suspect Ms. Parikh will be very successful."

"As do I. Intelligence, drive; she has the makings of a truly great officer."

"Agreed, but I meant something a little different than that. I think her mission is going to yield a great deal of Transluminide. Not claims filed with the Confederation, but with ships full.

"My concern is how to store it, secure it from theft."

"I'm not sure I follow?"

"Suppose word got out that Earth had just mined 100,000 kg of Transluminide. That would give the Earth Alliance numbers of the same magnitude as the Core Worlds' active bullion supply."

"Ah, understood."

"Most Confederation banks store their active reserves in hidden vaults underground. Our lease, with the exception of the rail tunnel, forbids underground development. Space Force has the lead on that project. Can you see if there is a way for us to use the rail excavation as a cover for those vaults? We'll need several thousand square feet."

"Will do. Good thinking. I presume this inquiry needs to be done discreetly."

"It does."

KELLY AND EUGENE'S LAB

"Kelly, Joel here."

"Hi Joel, what can I do for you?"

"I just received a priority order from Space Force. They want the forward shield upgrade for the EAS Batumi ASAP. Can you give me the status?"

"We can run the new components today. We don't need the huge power source the Batumi currently has, but the fastest path to installation will be to leave it in place and upgrade the field generator. The new shield uses the same field emitters, so nothing to change there."

"Are you going to do the install personally, or do you need a team?" asked Joel

"We have a bot that can do it. When can we get access?"

"Contact Captain Guruli. I think they're in orbit waiting for you."

"Will do," Kelly replied.

"Michael also told me he wants to test your new propulsion technology as soon as possible. What's the status on that?"

"That project has been sitting idle for a while. We'll need to dust it off. Can we get back to you next week?"

"The boss is really hot to go on both of these. So, get back to me as soon as you can. I get the impression something's up."

MILITARY INTELLIGENCE FAST ATTACK SHIP

"Status!" Inspector Ma-Gu was a demanding leader, and a cruel one as well. Anything he wanted to know needed to be delivered quickly, or the person tasked with knowing would taste his wrath.

"We just cleared the threshold."

"Employ the hyperjump."

"Engaging hyperjump."

The Inspector was proud of the upgrades he'd made to these ships. Previous fast packet ships relied on terawatts of power and frail, lightweight structures. The five Fast Attack ships on this mission had upgraded power systems. The power generators had a maximum output of 200 terawatts, more than most planets. But more importantly, they had capacitors with 10 times the capacity. That allowed them 2,000 light-year jumps with 6-minute recharges. Transiting the void would only take 5 days, more or less the same as the old Fast Packets. But these ships were sturdy, had real weapons, and real shields. The humans claimed to have better ships, but he found the assertion preposterous.

He still could not understand why they continued to hold Ju-Ne. He'd been caught. And would be disciplined for it. But did the humans really think they could escape the might of the Confederation? The very thought was insane. His ships, his forces were not little dust monsters. They were real monsters, a force no one could resist.

And in five days, this upstart world and its meager defensive alliance would be crushed. It was a shame really. They had a modicum of talent. Too bad it hadn't been harnessed to serve the Confederation.

ADVISORS CHAMBERS, 3F DEFENSIVE ALLIANCE

As with the Central Council chambers, a beautiful assembly chamber had been built in the 3F Alliance section of the Confederation Embassy. It was outfitted in the best Canadian oak. 15 seats had been set on a raised dais with witness tables below and with 200 spectator seats behind the witness tables.

The room itself had been built in a massive presence projector compliant with Confederation specifications. Yet Michael sat in it alone. The other council members would join shortly. Michael was frustrated by the cost and lack of utility of the set up. Nonetheless, it was what it was.

One by one, the advisors entered and took their designated seats. When everyone had arrived, Michael tapped his gavel lightly, signaling that he was ready to start.

"We have several items on our agenda today, but I'd like to start by welcoming our new members, Ambassador Ta-Jo representing our newest member Naltanarus and Ambassador Vorkin Peklit representing Jerusota. Gentlemen, welcome."

There was a brief round of applause for the new members.

"The first item on our agenda today concerns the criminal Ju-Ne. As you are aware, charges have been brought against Ju-Ne by Earth, Sofaana, Hacindra, and the Confederation itself. None of those cases have been brought to trial because Ju-Ne retreated into hibernation. This week he came out of hibernation. His trial on Earth will start on Monday.

"As you are also aware, the Confederation has issued multiple extradition requests for Ju-Ne. They have been denied. He must stand trial for his crimes on the planets that he has acted against.

"Several members of the Central Council have an interest in stopping those trials. So they are sending an extradition warrant along with a small taskforce of ships to enforce the demand."

Michael's statement set off a round of protests. He allowed it to run for a minute before gaveling the session back to order.

"I'd like to propose several options for us to consider. The first is that we do as ordered and release the prisoner to Military Intelligence."

Again, the room erupted in protest. Michael noted that several of the council members were not engaging in it.

"The second option would be to resist. Deny the ships access to Earth's orbital space and refuse to lower the transporter shields at the detention center."

This option garnered some dark murmuring, but no unruly protest.

"A third option would be to move Ju-Ne off planet. If he's not here, they would have to find him before they could take him."

"Lastly, and this is the option I recommend, we attempt to hold the Inspector off until his trial is complete, then release him when his sentence has been completed.

"With that I open the floor for discussion. Please wait until you are recognized before speaking."

Most of the council members indicated they wanted to speak.

"The chair recognizes Ambassador Da-Ku from Sofaana."

"Council members. The people of Sofaana were grievously damaged by the sabotage put in place by Ju-Ne. In my heart, I like the option of sending him to another world for trial. But I don't think that will work. The Inspector's spies will report Ju-Ne's presence on their world and none of our worlds, with the exception of Earth, has the slightest chance of holding off the Inspector's task force.

"But that brings me to the next question. How can we hold off the Inspector? Do we dare use force against an authorized Confederation mission?"

...

After an hour of debate, Michael brought the question to a vote. No new options had been proposed, although Michael's preferred option was tweaked a little. The final tally was 12 in favor of proceeding with the trial and refusing to cooperate with the Inspector until the trial and sentence were completed. Three were in favor of hiding Ju-Ne on another world.

SECURITY DETAINMENT AREA

"What do you mean, the prisoner doesn't know who he is?"

"I'm not a medical expert. But the prisoner seems different. Not as angry, or as snarky. He's finally starting to respond to his name, but continues to ask who he is, where he is.

"If it's an act, it's convincing."

The Warden, Archer Todd, whose eyes had been locked on the officer giving the report, let them drop.

"Understood. Thank you. I'll bring in the appropriate experts for an evaluation. But do not let anyone enter that cell. Do not open the door. The prisoner is one of the most dangerous people to ever walk the face of the Earth. We'll do what we can to sort this out. But this guy is the most skilled conman in all history. Give him no opportunity. He will kill you if he gets the chance. Never doubt it."

...

As soon as the officer was out the door, Warden Todd called Professor Ancient.

James flashed into the warden's inner office. "How can I help you sir."

"Professor Ancient. The prisoner seems to have amnesia. Can you confirm that? We're really not sure what to do with him."

"It's not that uncommon after long-term hibernation. Shall we go have a look?"

...

As they entered the observation area, the warden pointed to the prisoner. James looked at Ju-Ne, appearing to scrutinize him. "His mind is amazingly empty." James pronounced. "I think it's safe for me to enter his cell. Is there something I could bring him?"

"No one goes in that cell. No one opens that door for any reason."

"I don't plan to use the door." The words were barely out of James mouth, when there was a flash and an old Lorexian man wearing a councilor's robes appeared in the room holding the prisoner.

Ju-Ne recoiled at the flash and sudden appearance, then seemed to relax. James reached out and touched Ju-Ne's hand. The physical contact allowed James to look deeply into Ju-Ne's mind.

The warden was apoplectic that James had just entered the prisoner's cell, but the sputtering stopped when he saw both men frozen the way the prisoner had been for so many months.

Empty. Completely empty.

James inspected the quantum entangled links in Ju-Ne's mind.

Inactive. But that's not sufficient. They could still be used to reload memories.

One by one, James broke the entanglement of each of the twelve sets of connections. Then satisfied that Ju-Ne was no longer a threat, he withdrew back into himself, then released Ju-Ne's hand.

James flashed back to the observation area with the warden, who was in a rage. James tuned out the Warden's words, then sent him calm.

"That's better. The patient has completely lost all his memory. He succeeded in clearing all his long-term memories. That was one of the purposes of hibernation in the old days. Enter into the deepest form of hibernation, then stay in until you couldn't remember enough about what you were doing to persist in it. When you eventually woke, you were a new person. Old Lorexian law treated this as death and rebirth. All obligations of the old life were released, as were all assets. The reborn person was free to start over again."

"I'm not sure what that even means."

"Have your people run the following tests on him." The Warden's communicator beeped. "Report the results to the Ambassador. They will show that his immune system rejected his implants. He is no longer an Ascendant."

The Warden stared at James.

"Shoosh. Get on with it. You've just received the help you requested. This test will confirm my diagnosis for any Confederation agency that wishes to know."

And with that, James flashed away.

Chapter 3: RECONDITIONED

[Saturday, 07.17.2032] OFFICE, AMBASSADOR'S RESIDENCE

At the top of his queue this morning was a report from Warden Todd. Ju-Ne had awakened but had lost his memory. A blood test showed that his immune system had rejected his implants, which no longer functioned.

He's been completely reconditioned.

It was known that Lorexians could put themselves into a hibernation that would have this result. But it had been hundreds of years since someone had done this to themselves.

The highest-level punishment in the Confederation was complete reconditioning. It was the equivalent of capital punishment. It killed the self, but kept the body in the hope that another, better self would emerge.

The process had one other side effect on Ascendants. After implants had been rejected, the relevant immune rejection response would prevent new implants from taking. They could never become an Ascendant again.

This solved one problem. It would be OK to hand Ju-Ne over to the Inspector. But it created a different one. The Inspector would never believe that this was self-inflicted.

"James?"

There was a flash. "I see you got the report."

"Did you do this?"

James stared at Michael with great intensity.

"Hard to say."

The words seemed to break the tension.

"How could it possibly be hard to say?"

"All his avatars were destroyed. One-by-one, he could sense them disappearing, forever silenced. I was directly involved in that. Getting the names. Giving you the locations.

"It's hard to say if that drove him over the edge, or if he jumped over the edge on his own to prevent all his secrets from being revealed."

"Which do you think it was?"

"As I said, hard to say."

Realizing he wasn't going to get any more out of James, Michael changed gears. "In light of this development, how do you think we should handle the Inspector?"

"Send the report to the Central Council. Also send it to the head of the medical school at the Lorexian Institute. The report really is a closed case. Critics would say that if you'd returned him the first time they asked, they might have been able to stop it. But that is far from conclusive and an easy case to argue."

"I'll do that, but I doubt it will sway the Inspector."

"So be it. If he attacks you, then you can respond in kind. That will be a short conflict. It will also give you cause to take legal action against the relevant Confederation authorities."

There was silence for several seconds. James broke it.

"Michael, I cannot solve this problem for you. You have the moral high ground. You need to use it to win the hearts and minds of the people. Particularly those in Andromeda and Triangulum. The speaker and the High Council cannot stand without the peoples' support. Their crimes need to be made known."

And with that, James flashed away.

PRESENCE PROJECTOR, COUNCILOR MO-MO'S OFFICE

"Mi-Ku, I was surprised to hear from you today. Isn't this one of your days of rest on Earth?"

"Yes. That makes it a particularly good day to do work on other worlds."

"I suppose that would be true. How can I help you?"

"Thank you for the message you sent with Vorkin Peklit. The Earth Alliance would be happy to talk with you and your counterparts on Dalfanito about a trade deal."

"My understanding from our last conversation was that logistics made trade between our worlds and our alliances impractical."

"For anything other than large volumes of high-value items, I think it is. But we may have a solution for that."

"Mi-Ku, that's one of the things I love about you. Last week's impossible, becomes this week's done deal.

"Can you tell me anything about your solution?

"Not today, but hopefully in a couple weeks."

A pause.

"I'd also like to get your input on a sensitive situation. As I think you know, we have been holding a prisoner for a year now awaiting trial. He put himself in hibernation, which prevented us from trying him. He came out of it this week."

"So, your trial will commence soon?"

"No. I'm sending you a report that explains the situation." Michael heard a ding in the background, indicating that the report had been delivered.

"What is in this report?"

"It's been a while since there's been an occurrence, but Ju-Ne's hibernation served its historical purpose."

Michael let the statement hang there.

After a few moments, it clicked for Mo-Mo. "He cleansed himself!"

"To the point where his immune system rejected his implants."

"Are you going to release the new person?"

"That is my plan, yes. We no longer have a basis to hold him. It'll be difficult to explain to the Earth Alliance, but they will ultimately agree.

"Which leaves me with the problem of the Inspector."

"Who leaked that information to you?" Mo-Mo asked the question so that anyone monitoring the call would think that he himself had not.

"The Speaker is sadly mistaken if he thinks he can hold any secrets from the Ancient One."

"Point taken."

"Which still leaves us with the problem of the Inspector. I doubt he will accept this news well. It would be better for all involved if he were recalled. I'm sending our report to all the Council Members and to the Medical School at the Lorexian Institute. I imagine they will want to investigate, which we would accommodate. But I'm also hoping they will confirm that this condition can be self-inflicted."

"Do you really believe it was?"

"The humans have no knowledge of such a thing. And we've purposefully kept him separated from anyone that does. The humans have no idea what reconditioning even means. If this was not self-inflicted, then it was done by a Lorexian."

"Or the Ancient One."

"It generally doesn't go well for people who challenge the Ancient One when he's already spoken on a matter."

"No, I suppose it doesn't." A pause. "I think you have taken the appropriate steps, Mi-Ku. I also agree that the Inspector is not likely to take this well. So, two words of advice. Harden your systems in anticipation of attack. And don't shoot first, no matter what he threatens."

"Thank you, Mo-Mo. I'll get back to you on trade and logistics as soon as I can."

"Thank you, Mi-Ku. We in Triangulum look forward to the day we can have open trade with you."

EUGENE AND KELLY'S LAB

"Captain Guruli, thank you for speaking with us. We have everything ready for the upgrade on your forward shield. When would you like us to come aboard and do the installation?"

"Kelly, thank you. You are welcome to come aboard whenever you'd like."

"Excellent. We need a few minutes to tag the relevant items for transport. Can I call you back in a few minutes?"

"Anytime."

...

Eugene and Kelly appeared on the transporter pad in the ship's engine room.

"Eugene, Kelly. Welcome aboard the Batumi. Please meet my chief engineer, Lt. Commander Otto Krauss."

"Captain, thank you for welcoming us aboard. Lt. Cmdr. Krauss, we're looking forward to working with you.

"We have three crates to transport up and we'll need assistance getting them to the shield's location unless we can transport them there directly."

"We have easy access to the port nacelle," Otto replied. "Let's bring your crates up here, then take a tour of the nacelle so you can tell me what we're going to be doing."

"Sounds like a plan."

...

Lt. Cmdr. Krauss led Eugene and Kelly through the port nacelle to the existing forward shield generator.

"That looks familiar." Kelly pointed to the dimension 601 field generator. "The upgrade is straight forward. Several components in the field generator need to be replaced. Our bot will simply pull the old ones and install the new ones. They've been designed to simply swap in and out. The power consumption of the new system is significantly less than the previous one, but its draw is self-regulating. So we're going to use the existing power generator as is.

"If the new shield tests out, then you will be able to swap out the power generator and free up some space. But we don't plan to do that today."

"Sounds easy enough. Should we bring your equipment in?"

...

An hour later, the upgrade was done. The parts being removed were packaged into the same crate the new parts had been brought up in. The bot was repackaged in its crate.

Captain Guruli came in just as the last of the cleanup was getting finished. "How soon can we run the test?"

"We're going to do this in the outer system, right?" Eugene asked.

"Yes. We will rendezvous with the Canada there."

"Then we can go now." Kelly answered this time. "We'll be ready before you get there."

The Captain smiled. "Looking forward to being shot at. Otto, bring them up to the bridge when you're done here."

"Will do, sir."

...

An hour and a half later the ships rendezvoused in an empty area of space between the orbits of Saturn and Neptune. The Canada was positioned 1,000 km from the Batumi. The two were facing each other with the Batumi positioned directly in the middle of the Canada's view of the sun. A shuttle was positioned in view of both ships to relay the communications.

The first test was a simple opacity test. The Batumi would put up the shield. The Canada would confirm that they could no longer get any sensor read on the Batumi.

Captain Guruli put the audio countdown over the link to the Canada. "Raising the forward shield in 3, 2, 1... Shield activated."

The Batumi completely disappeared from the Canada's sensors.

"No trace of the Batumi, other than the hole in space in front of the sun. She is completely opaque," First Watch Tactical Officer Kaitlin O'Brien reported.

"Ms. O'Brien. Do you have target lock on the shield? We want to hit well off center in case the shield collapses."

"On the view screen sir." Targeting cross hairs popped up on the image of the shield.

"That looks good. Tightest beam. Fire at will."

The audio count was sent over the comm line to the Batumi.

"Firing in 3, 2, 1. Fire."

A beam shot out toward the Batumi hitting the shield in the exact spot targeted.

"The beam just stops!" Science Officer Adrian Meier exclaimed in disbelief.

The three second burst stopped.

"Repeat, this time at maximum power."

Another countdown, another beam shot out. Same result.

"Repeat with the rail gun."

The targeting appeared. The countdown started.
"Rail gun firing in 3, 2, 1... Round away."

The whine of the coils firing rang through the ship. A fraction of a second later, a spray of molten metal rebounded from the shield.

"Disable all weapons," Daniel ordered.

"All weapons powered down."

"Helm, bring us around a few degrees so that we're no longer pointed at the Batumi."

"Repositioning complete," Else replied.

"Batumi, you are clear to lower your shield."

The hole in space that previously blocked the sun disappeared and the Batumi returned to the sensor feeds.

"A successful test, I think," Daniel commented.

OFFICE, PRESIDENT LEE'S RESIDENCE

"President Lee, thanks for taking the time to speak with me today. Unfortunately, I come with news."

"News I'm not going to like, I presume."

Michael nodded his head affirmatively.

"Then let me have it."

"Two items, perhaps three, depending on how you count.

"The Confederation is sending another extradition order for Ju-Ne. This time it's being delivered by hand, so to speak, demanding his immediate release into their custody. The nature of their warrant will allow them to take him by force if we don't hand him over voluntarily."

"You've got to be kidding me! He's killed dozens here at the Embassy, hundreds in France, and de-orbited one of our mining platforms. And we're just going to hand him over?"

Michael did not respond immediately.

"It gets worse, right?"

"Depends on how you look at it. The prisoner finally woke up yesterday afternoon. But he's not the same."

A pause.

"We now know that his hibernation was for the purpose of cleansing. Humans do not have an equivalent physical process, although there are customs among some of Earth's peoples that have a similar result.

"His memory has been completely wiped. No memory of his life, circumstances, deeds... Nothing remains. And his immune system has rejected his implants. They will need to be removed but can never be replaced. There is no treatment for this type of immune response."

"I don't know what that implies."

"From the Confederation's point of view, Ju-Ne died. The body that remains has been completely cleansed of the old self. A new self is trying to form. It is a different person. We cannot prosecute it. We must release him."

"What do you mean, we have to release him!" President Lee shouted.

"He's been cleansed. He functionally committed suicide. No trace of the previous person is left, only the husk. And he has developed implant rejection, so he can never again operate an avatar.

"There's no point in holding him. He is Lorexian and can no longer take another form. Our best course of action is to return him to New Lorexi. His previous ID will be marked 'Deceased' and a new one will be issued. It will be their job to find him a new role in society and support him as he transitions. There's little demand for failed Ascendants, most never fully recover."

"So, after all the stunts he pulled, we just let him go?"

"*He...*" Michael held the word for emphasis. "...no longer exists. We have someone else in captivity. Someone we have no basis to hold."

Michael could see that President Lee was having a hard time letting go of his anger toward Ju-Ne.

"I also think we should take him back, not simply turn him over to the Inspector. There's no telling what the Inspector would do to him if he got his hands on him."

"So now we have compassion for our mass murderer."

Michael waited for President Lee's anger to settle a little.

"Now for the interesting part. The Inspector will not believe that Ju-Ne's condition was self-inflicted. He will think we did it to him. You see, the Confederation's version of capital punishment is to induce what Ju-Ne did to himself. The Inspector will think we executed him."

MANUFACTURING OFFICE

Joel had come in early this morning to crank through a long list of loose ends that he never seemed to be able to clear during the week. On looking at the clock, he saw that it was nearly 4:00. A thought shot through his mind. *I might actually get done by 5.*

A second one came immediately after. *One of these days, I'm going to take a Saturday off.*

His communicator sounded.

"Joel, here."

"Joel, Eugene Xu. Just wanted to let you know that we finished the field trial for the new forward shield today. Works perfectly. I know that Michael wants as many of these as he can get as soon as he can get them. I'm sending over the specs and replicator pattern for the shield generator now. It uses the same emitters we put in the Batumi for the attack against the Enemy home world. I'll send over the specs for the power source within the hour, then it's over to you."

"Thanks."

The line dropped and another thought ran through Joel's mind. *And there goes my Sunday too.*

AMBASSADOR'S RESIDENCE

"Julissa, James will be stopping by in a few minutes."

"Thanks for the warning, Sarah. I'll have master Timothy ready in a few more minutes."

Julissa Natty had been born in Jamaica. Her father was English, as technically she was. Her mother was Jamaican. It had been 30 years since she moved away from Jamaica, but she still had the lyrical voice for which her people were known. In 2005, Julissa had been accepted into Norland College in Bath, England. In 2009, she'd graduated with a BA in 'Early Years Development and Learning.' She also had a Norland Diploma. Norland was the standard of reference for nannies to the world's great houses. Her first assignment out of school had been to care for the newborn child of an English Duke. Her second was for the middle school child of a South San Francisco biotech billionaire. Sarah had found her a couple weeks before baby Timothy was born and knew she was the right one on sight.

Today was a 'big day.' Timothy was two months old today. James had called earlier asking if he could bring a present.

There was a quiet knock on the door.

Michael went to open it.

"James, thank you for coming to the door. I think it's still going to be a couple months before Timothy's going to enjoy seeing you flash in. And David, good to see you as well. Please, come in."

They took seats in the living room and a moment later Julissa came in with the baby. She looked at James, while handing Timothy to Sarah.

"Mr. James. I hope you didn't just flash into here."

"Ms. Julissa, you made the rules very clear last time."

"Good. You remember." Then to Sarah, she added, "I'll get a bottle ready."

"Would you like to hold him, James?" Sarah offered.

James reached out to take him. As he settled back into his seat, Timothy reached up and touched James face, then burst out laughing.

"Yes. You like this funny old man, don't you?"

Once settled, James put a finger out and Timothy grabbed it.

"Amazing the strength of a baby's grip."

James sent Timothy some warmth and he fell immediately asleep.

"This one is going to be something. He doesn't have language yet, but his thoughts and emotions are crystal clear. You have given birth to a great mind."

Timothy stirred, then woke.

"Excellent hearing. He can hear Julissa coming and knows that she's bringing a bottle."

"How do you know that?" Sarah asked.

"Let me share." James sent Sarah the memory.

Sarah glazed over for a second, then looked at Timothy with a bit of marvel. "He thinks in images. It was a bit distorted, but clearly Julissa and a bottle."

Timothy started laughing.

"Mr. James. Are you sending that baby giggles again?"

"Sorry, Ms. Julissa. Accident, I'm sure."

Julissa set the bottle on the table next to Sarah. "Give it a minute to rest."

She then took Timothy from James and handed him to Sarah.

James reached out his hand, palm up, fist closed. "This is for Timothy."

He opened his hand and a stuffed animal appeared. It had soft brown fur over most of its body. The head was comically large with odd shaped blue eyes, a very wide nose, a ridge of some sort across the top of his head, and six dangly legs, each a different color and pattern.

"What is that?" Sarah asked.

"It's a Juufa from the planet Arergloa, a developing world David and I have been visiting recently. I found this toy in one of their markets. In real life, Juufas are not something you want to tangle with. It's an herbivore, kind of like a six-legged, furry rhinoceros, with a battering ram instead of a horn. According to the ladies in the market, children love to chew on the fabric ridge on the top of its head when they're teething."

James could sense the evil eye he was getting from Michael for visiting another developing world.

"The toy is completely baby safe. The Regilion people have big teeth, even as babies. So, all their toys are extremely durable, nothing will come loose. And I've confirmed that all the components are safe for humans to chew on or ingest."

"Thank you, James. It was very thoughtful of you."

James stood. "We'll let you feed the little one. Michael, could I have a word on the way out?"

...

"I cast my attention toward the Inspector's ship this morning. They are still three days out. His ships are enormously inefficient power hogs." James shook his head in disgust.

"The news is that this mission is a guise. It's not Ju-Ne they're after. It's someone or something else. Could be you, Sarah, or the baby. Could be the emerald Wonder Stones the Amsterdam found last month, although that doesn't feel big enough. Maybe it's the secret of Earth's core. I couldn't distinguish what, but he lusts for it with an intensity that's difficult to describe.

"You need to prepare the defenses. This will not end peacefully."

RIVERSIDE PARK

It was date night and Nelly had booked the 'Taste of Lebanon' event in the park tonight. They would be meeting up with several others who worked at the central bank with Nelly. Eugene had called earlier saying he'd be running a bit late, so they'd agreed to meet at the entrance to the park.

"There you are." Eugene smiled as he came in through the entrance.

Nelly looked at her watch. "I was worried you'd be late."

"So was I. But we got back in time."

"Where did you go?"

The question hit Eugene like an electric shock. Nelly didn't know he would be off planet today.

"Um..."

"Don't tell me you were traveling today."

"I forgot to mention that, didn't I?"

The look Eugene got was enough to convince him to confess now.

"Kelly and I were running some experiments in space."

"Where?"

"Between Saturn and Neptune."

"And you didn't think it might be relevant for me to know that? We are meeting with several of my colleagues tonight."

"Sorry. I'd hoped we would get up into orbit today to install some equipment. That's barely like travelling. Just beam up and back down again. The trip to the outer system just came up."

Nelly started laughing. "The trip to the outer system just came up, did it?"

Eugene chuckled too. It certainly wasn't the world either of them grew up in.

"So, three other couples are joining us tonight. Ed and his wife Rose. Ed runs the department that controls the money supply. Kandace and her partner Kiley. Kandace is responsible for our IT operations. And lastly, there's Owen who handles regulation and compliance. He's bringing a date tonight.

"Poor Owen lost his wife to breast cancer a month or so before the Revelation. So sad. Anyway, he recently met someone that he's bringing tonight."

Nelly saw Eugene glazing over at the list of names and job functions. "Don't worry. They're OK, and they all think you're a rock star. Just try to be present."

Eugene hated functions where he was expected to engage in small talk with people he didn't know and probably would never meet again. Hopefully one of them would be interesting.

...

43

Eugene ended up sitting next to Owen's new girlfriend, Lisette, who seemed to have as little interest in banking as Eugene did.

"So, you're an Ascendant?" Eugene asked.

She smiled. "Yes. Initially this was supposed to be a short-term diplomatic assignment, but I managed to land the job I've always dreamed of in Security."

"What do you do there?"

"I'm head of domestic security operations, meaning Earth-based security issues."

"You're like the head of the Embassy police?" Eugene was obviously shocked by the idea.

"They report to me, yes. But most of my work has to do with high-level threats and containment. For example, my department was part of the investigation last year that captured the Confederation spy responsible for downing the mining platform."

"Wow, you did that!"

"I was part of it but didn't have this job at that time. My former boss was killed during the investigation. I was injured, offline when the platform came down. But I run that department now.

"I'd love to know more about you. Where do you and Kelly come up with all this stuff. The two of you are living legends."

Eugene blushed. *I'm so pathetic at this.*

"So, tell me, how do all these dimensional fields work? Is that something that's even explainable to a non-technical person?"

...

Eugene and Nelly walked out of the park hand-in-hand.

"Great show, wasn't it?" Nelly asked.

"Loved it. Enjoyed the food too."

"You seemed to really hit it off with Lisette."

Eugene chuckled. "Was terrified when I found out she was head of security. But it's interesting the role technology plays in their investigations. She seemed very interested in the work Kelly and I do, but it's hard to see how any of that would ever help her."

MICHAEL'S RANCH, BIG ISLAND OF HAWAII

It was the first time they'd been back in over 6 years. For George, this was the place where he'd made his recovery, got his life back. It was also where he'd fallen in love with his beautiful wife, Noelani.

"Anyone for a cool glass of lemonade at sunset?"

Kale had just come out onto the back lanai with a pitcher of lemonade and some house made lilikoi (Hawaiian passionfruit) tarts. George and Noelani were gently rocking on the tandem gliding chair. George's mother, Helen, sat on the chaise lounge playing with little George. From their seats, they had a clear view of the Sun dropping behind Maui. They could also see the uninhabited islet Kaho'olawe to the west.

"Count me in!" George smiled.

"George, is this the first vacation you've taken since moving to the Embassy?"

"I also got paternity leave last year."

"You need to visit more often, brother. What did they do with your show this week?"

"Jonathan Omeruo from KamemeTV in Kenya was doing 'best of' clips from our Peoples of the Confederation series a year and a half ago.

"Given all the new members that have joined this year, we will be restarting the series next week with Ambassador Re-Ta of Allastran."

"Didn't they used to have a Fleet base?"

"Yep. Will be interesting to get his take on the base and on our ship operations."

After a moment of silence, George asked, "Ever regret staying here instead of heading up to the Embassy with the rest of us?"

"A little. Things are beautiful here. But it's really quiet. And someone needed to stay and tend to the place.

"How about you?" asked Kale.

"I'm doing what I was called to do. As much as I love it here, I'd feel incredibly guilty enjoying myself here while there were still guys like me in a chair somewhere else."

"Good call, brother."

Chapter 4: PREPARATIONS

[Sunday, 07.18.2032] BRIDGE, EAS MUMBAI

For the first time in her life, Bumati Parikh gave an order from the big chair. "Helm, take us out of orbit."

"Yes, ma'am."

"Ms. Saleem, please put me on ship-wide comm." Mila Saleem was the Mumbai's first watch yeoman.

"You're on, ma'am."

"All hands, this is the captain. We are departing on our mandatory training mission. We have six new sensor platforms to position in Pluto's orbit. We have 48-hours to complete this mission. Theoretical best time is 28 hours. Let's see how close we can come to that 28-hour target. Our first stop will be in about 4 hours. Parikh out."

AMBASSADOR'S RESIDENCE

Michael was in his office with the door open. He needed to speak with Sarah. Late last night he'd messaged Alexi, asking if she could restart earlier than planned. She'd taken leave two months before Timothy was born. Sarah had been mostly home bound at that point and Alexi was miserable "just sitting around doing nothing."

Sarah didn't think she'd want to travel during the first three months after Timothy's birth, so they agreed that Alexi could take five months off.

But Michael was once again worried for Sarah. He heard her coming down the steps, so went out to the kitchen to make a pot of coffee.

"Morning, you're looking industrious."

"Just making some coffee. Also wanted to talk about something with you."

"That sounds like trouble," Sarah said offhandedly. But when she looked up and saw Michael's face, she realized that it was about some kind of trouble. "What's the matter?"

"The Confederation has dispatched the Inspector, allegedly to come collect Ju-Ne. But James says it's a guise. They're actually after something else, but he doesn't know what."

"Well, if they've heard about Eugene and Kelly's new super weapon, I'd guess that's what they're after."

The truth of Sarah's words hit Michael like a lightning bolt. His fear for Sarah, suddenly morphed into fear for Eugene and Kelly.

He shook his head to clear his thoughts. "I'll bet you're right. Should have thought of that."

"What did you think?"

"That they were after you."

Sarah burst out laughing.

"What?" Michael exclaimed, a smile forming. He could never resist Sarah's laughter. "You were Ju-Ne's target."

"True." Sarah's mirth slipped away. "But that was before the Alliance. Getting me now would just make the Alliance stronger and stir up a hornet's nest. I suspect he's smarter than that."

"Good point. Nonetheless, I've contacted Alexi to see if she'd agree to come back early."

PRESENCE PROJECTOR, AMBASSADOR'S RESIDENCE

"Ko-So my friend, thank you for meeting with me on short notice."

Michael had set the presence projector to present both of them as Lorexian. He reached out his hand to bump with the Ambassador from Atomorali.

"Mi-Ku, didn't expect to hear from you so soon. Is it the Inspector?"

"Yes. I got a disturbing bit of news last night. Ju-Ne may not be the Inspector's actual objective."

"Do you know what it is?"

"No, but I fear it's the weapon we used to destroy the Enemy's home world."

"That cannot be allowed to happen."

"Agreed. I've also learned from sources in Andromeda that his ship is equipped with EQD weapons. If that's true, then all but a few of our ships are vulnerable.

"I see. I assume you want more EQD-tolerant computers and EQD-resistant-shielding for your AI casings."

"As many as I can get in the next two days. We could also use help with the installations."

"I hate to ask this question, but do you have any Transluminide you can loan us? I don't think we have enough on hand to make as many of our computers as you'll want."

"Yes. But how many can you make in the time frame?"

"We have something like 50 – 75 of the Freighter kits in stock. I know we sent Emmanuel 25 on Friday. I know this will be difficult for your people, but if enough of them can suit up to work with us, we can probably convert a freighter in two to three hours. We have eight bays that we could clear to work the conversions, so maybe 50 a day?"

"What about the Fast Attack Ships and Cruisers?"

"We've run one kit each. We could probably run a couple more. We usually don't do that until the kit has been tested. But those ships are too large for our bays. You would need to do the installations."

"Understood. We'll take the kits. Having a Cruiser in play might tip the odds."

A pause.

"I have one other related issue I'd like to raise with you. Ju-Ne has come out of hibernation. But he is not the same. The hibernation succeeded in its historical purpose."

"He re-conditioned himself?"

"Yes."

"They'll never believe you."

"Nonetheless, that's what happened. We plan to return him. Hopefully before the Inspector arrives. It will take away the pretext for his operation, so whatever moves he makes will be obvious for what they are."

"Understood. You need to get that word out to the other Alliance members."

"I will." A pause.

"I'm sure there are a lot of arrangements we both need to make if this is going to get done in time." Michael sighed. "Let me get back to you with an update in a couple hours."

"OK. I'll see how much I can get done before we reconnect."

"Thank you, Ko-So."

PRESENCE PROJECTOR, SPACE FORCE COMMAND

It had been months since an emergency meeting had been called on a Sunday. With the Enemy situation mostly settled, President Lee had hoped they'd put such emergencies behind them. But that was wishful thinking, no doubt.

President Lee, Secretary Thompson, and Admiral Scott sat in the presence projector at Space Force Command. Michael tied in from home. Admirals Porter and Bjork tied in from their respective ships.

"Thank you for gathering on short notice. A taskforce departed New Lorexi on Friday. Its stated mission was to collect the prisoner Ju-Ne, by force if necessary. They are expected to arrive on Tuesday.

"Unfortunately, I learned last night that Ju-Ne is not their actual objective. They're coming to take something else. Unfortunately, we don't know what. The leading suspect is that they're coming to obtain the weapon used against the Enemy home world. When they find out that the weapon has been destroyed, they'll probably attempt to kidnap Eugene Xu and Kelly Williamson, possibly others.

"I've also been told by sources in Andromeda that their armada has enhanced EQD weapons."

"We should greet them at the edge of the system and blow them out of the sky!" Admiral Scott spat.

"As much as I agree with your sentiment, it is imperative that we're not the ones to fire the first shot.

"As you may know, our first freighter was upgraded with EQD-resistant computers this week. Unshielded, it withstood a blast 10 times more potent than the one that hit the Helsinki.

"I spoke with Ambassador Ko-So moments ago. They sent us 25 freighter upgrade kits earlier this week. Those kits are in our possession. They have another 50 kits in stock and are attempting to organize a massive upgrade program to install those kits on our freighters. Eight of their space-based service bays will open shortly to start processing our ships.

"They also have one untested kit for both Fast Attack Ship and Cruiser upgrades, although they do not have bays large enough to handle those ships. If we can do the upgrades ourselves, then we can have a Fast Attack Ship and a Cruiser participate in the encounter.

"I think all other ships should be evacuated from the system."

"I agree," Admiral Scott growled.

"I have two other things in mind," Michael continued. "Eugene and Kelly recently upgraded the Batumi with a new type of forward shield. It requires much less power than its predecessor and is much stronger. I'm told the tests went well."

"Very well." Daniel confirmed.

"I'm thinking we could form a blockade of some sort, if we had enough ships equipped with those shields."

"Interesting idea," Admiral Scott muttered.

"My remaining thought is that we quickly organize a mission to return Ju-Ne to Andromeda. If we can do that, it would take away the

Inspector's pretext for being here. Any subsequent conflict would end up being viewed in a much different way."

"Give up the prisoner in the hope it stops a conflict. No way! We can't buckle under like that!" Secretary Thompson exploded.

"Things aren't quite what we thought they were," President Lee said quietly.

All eyes turned to him, but he pointed to Michael.

"Ju-Ne was significantly injured by his hibernation. His mind was completely destroyed. Only the shell remains. It should be returned. We have no reason to hold him at this point."

The room was quiet for a moment.

Daniel Porter broke the silence.

"I agree with Michael. Let's return the remains of the prisoner, taking away the Inspector's cover. Let's get forward shields on as many ships as we can in the next 48 hours and do the same with the computer upgrades. I volunteer my ship for the computer upgrade or for the mission to Andromeda. I'm sure our engineers can get the upgrade done in time. I'm equally confident my crew has the poise to return to New Lorexi and do what's required there."

"I agree with Daniel and volunteer my ship in the same way." Katrine added.

"Returning the prisoner without the Earth Alliance's consent, or the 3F Defensive Alliance's consent for that matter, will be problematic," President Lee said.

Michael locked eyes. "Agreed. I'll take the 3F alliance if you'll take the Earth Alliance."

"Agreed."

Michael turned to the others. "Are we in agreement?"

One by one, each said yes.

"Sam. Looks like you've got a lot of orders to issue. I'll send you the relevant contacts. I think we need to go to a wartime footing for the next several days to get ready."

Admiral Scott stood. "Then I better get started."

PRESENCE PROJECTOR, AMBASSADOR'S OFFICE

"Ko-So. I've had a productive afternoon. You?"

"I think so. We've been a very isolated world. As I think you know, the trip to Earth for the signing ceremony and your wedding was our President's first off world experience. He's a big fan of yours, Michael.

"The point is that he's authorized me to do anything required to support you. All manufacturing has been switched over to making the computers and kits you need. He's going on faith that you will replenish our Transluminide supplies before our mining operations can. By the way, he sends his thanks for the claims you've assigned to us."

"The space bays are being cleared now. We can receive your first ship in 2 hours. It looks like we'll be able to produce the freighter kits as fast as we install them. So, you don't need to return any of the ones we've already sent you. I also think we'll be able to produce 5 to 10 more Cruiser kits that we can send back as your ships return.

"Mi-Ku, thank you. Our world, being so different, has struggled to establish any role in the Confederation. You've given us that platform and it will not be forgotten."

"Ko-So, thank you for your help. You will be contacted shortly by the head of Space Force Operations, Admiral Samuel Scott. He can give you the details of ship arrivals. One or more will come with more than enough Transluminide to cover your costs for this operation."

...

With the EQD upgrades now in the hands of others, Michael started working through the rest of his list. He dashed off a quick message to Joel asking him to produce as many of Kelly's new shields in the next 48 hours as possible. He also dashed off a note to Eugene and Kelly asking to meet in the morning. Then he started working the list of Alliance Ambassadors. A few were in time zones he could call yet this afternoon. For the others, he sent meeting requests. It would be a busy day tomorrow.

BRIDGE, EAS TOOMPEA

The EAS Toompea was the fourth freighter produced. It was named for the famous landmark, Toompea Castle in Estonia, the fourth country to ally with the confederation.

Captain Piper Robinson from Australia had just come on duty for the evening portion of first watch.

"Captain, we've just received new orders."

"Thank you, Eliana. Please route them to my station."

Eliana was the ships helm AI.

Captain Robinson opened the orders and quickly read them.

"Well. Looks like we're getting an upgrade. Eliana, please plot us a course to Atomorali. We're about to get upgraded with EQD-resistant computers."

MANUFACTURING OFFICE

Joel knew that Eugene was a straight shooter. So, given the urgency, he started producing the new shields. Previously, he would have confirmed with Michael first. But Michael had a wife and baby now, and Joel really didn't want to impose on his Sunday to confirm the obvious.

After some back and forth with Henry, they determined that there were 16 industrial replicators they controlled that were working on something that could wait. Each could produce one of Kelly's forward shield generators in two hours. They didn't really have the authorization to do the switch. But they didn't really have the authorization to produce the things those replicators were producing either. So, they switched to shield generators. Now, 12 hours later, they had 96 of them. It was a bit past what Joel was comfortable doing on his own, and he only had one idea where they could get the requisite power source, so he switched back to what they were doing before, then launched messages to Michael, Emmanuel, and Ambassador Fa-Ta.

Duty done for the day, Joel packed up to head home. As he stood to go, a new message arrived in his queue. It was from Michael, requesting that he make as many of Kelly's new freighter shields as possible.

"Our messages must have crossed in the ether," Joel mused.

"Henry?" Joel called out.

"Joel, you haven't left yet?"

"Almost got out, but not quite. I just got a message from Michael. He wants more shields. Let's restart production, see if we can knock out 96 more by morning."

"On it! Now go get some dinner."

"Thanks, Henry."

Chapter 5: EVACUATION

[Monday, 07.19.2032] EARTH ALLIANCE TRADING COMPANY

"Ambassador Fa-Ta, thank you for making time to talk with me this morning."

"Emmanuel, good to speak with you as always. Given your message, I've invited Administrator Colum Warsel and his assistant Soson Po-lar to join us as well."

"Gentlemen, thank you for your time. As I mentioned in my message to you, Space Force has an emergency need for 10-megawatt power cubes. They would like 200 of them."

Emmanuel could almost hear his counterpart's smile.

"We would love to supply those of course. But you said emergency. How soon would you like to pick them up?"

"This afternoon?" Emmanuel ventured.

There was silence on the line, which was finally broken by Administrator Warsel. "You mean today?"

"Yes."

"Let me see what we have in inventory."

Emmanuel heard a chair push back.

"This is a very unusual request," Ambassador Fa-Ta said diplomatically.

"Yes, it is. We're facing a very unusual situation."

"Ambassador Michael and Joel both reached out to me last night. Is this related to the same issue?"

"Yes. I think it is."

"Then I'll see what I can do to minimize the priority charge for these units."

Emmanuel heard someone shuffle into the room on the other end of the line.

"Thank you," The ambassador said quietly. There was a little more indistinct chatter that Emmanuel couldn't make out, then the Ambassador came back on the line.

"Good news, though possibly not as good as you'd like. We currently have 47 units in inventory. If your ship left Earth immediately, we would have 60 by the time it got here. We are currently manufacturing these units at maximum capacity, as they're quite popular. If you wanted to wait until tomorrow, we should have all 200 units in about 27 hours.

"These are all scheduled for other customers. Our out of pocket cost for late delivery to those customers will be 35%."

"If you would like to take these in two deliveries, one today and the other tomorrow, we will have to charge you for two last-minute orbital slots, not just one. The slot tomorrow will cost less than the one today, but these are expensive slots.

"If you commit right now, the slot today would be... Emmanuel, I don't even want to say this amount. I'm sorry, but it will be 50% of the amount of the 60 units.

"Tomorrow, it will be... Looking it up... 10% the cost of the 200 units."

Emmanuel messaged the numbers to Michael on internal and marked it urgent. The answer came back moments later. *Two deliveries. ASAP.*

"We'll go with the two deliveries option."

Emmanuel heard some paper noise on the other end of the line that he assumed was frantic calculation of a final price.

"Can you get a ship here in 3 hours?"

"Let me check."

Emmanuel messaged Michael again.

Yes. One is standing by.

"Yes. We have a ship that will depart as soon as I give the word."

"OK. We've just booked the slots. The total price is 1,273.324 mg." Fa-Ta sighed. "Let me see what I can do to bring this down some. A lot of this is late fees to other Alliance members."

"Thank you, my friend. Our ship will be there in three hours."

"Thank you, Emmanuel."

PRESENCE PROJECTOR, AMBASSADOR'S OFFICE

Michael's first meeting this morning was with Ambassador Va-Mu from Edukatar.

"Mi-Ku, what a pleasant surprise to hear from you so soon."

"Va-Mu, thank you for making time today. I regret that our last meeting ended on the sour note that it did."

"Does that mean you've reconsidered doing transportation runs to Triangulum?" It was clear from the body language that Va-Mu was excited about the possibility.

"Yes, but that's not the main reason I need to talk with you."

"The Ju-Ne matter?"

"You've already heard?"

"Yes. The gossip runs fast through our new Alliance. By the way, I just got off the line with Fa-Ta. He asked if we'd waive the late delivery penalties he'd owe us on some power cubes he's diverting to you. I told him that we would, once I'd confirmed the reason with you. This is for defense against the Inspector?"

"Yes."

"Then we'll waive the late delivery penalties. It's in our direct interest that you prevail."

"Thank you."

"Then we can talk about deliveries to Triangulum?" Va-Mu beamed with delight.

"Yes. Since we're going to Andromeda, I wanted to make sure any of our allies' shipment needs to or from Andromeda or Triangulum are covered by our trip."

"Does that mean that this is a one-time deal?"

"This trip is a one-time deal. It will be run by one of our cruisers, so there's a lot of capacity.

"But we're looking at setting up a regular service. No guarantees it will happen, but we're looking into a possibility that would make it feasible."

"Timeframe for a decision?"

"Too early to say, but I expect to know more in another week or two."

"How is it that things start moving whenever you cast your attention on them?"

Michael chuckled. "I surround myself with people who like to make things happen.

"But back to this trip, I'll need a list of everything you want transported by the end of the day today. And the goods must be palleted and ready for pick up by mid-afternoon tomorrow."

BRIDGE, EAS TORONTO

"Captain, we've just received new orders. We're to make our way to Karagon for an emergency pickup of 10-megawatt power cubes. We have a 15-minute orbital slot that opens in 2 hours, 45 minutes."

"Thank you, Mathias. Please plot a course and take us out."

PRESENCE PROJECTOR, EAS POLAND

Captain Albert Keppler stepped up to the command deck presence projector and saw that the connection was already established. The meeting request had come from Admiral Sam Scott minutes ago. The fact that the connection was in place suggested that the meeting was urgent.

He stepped in and saw the Admiral and the Secretary already seated. "Admiral, Mr. Secretary."

"Captain Keppler, please come in. We are placing your ship on ready alert for what's shaping up to be the longest, in terms of distance, mission conducted by Space Force to date.

"Your first objective will be to return the prisoner Ju-Ne to New Lorexi. This may be delicate. We're not sure yet how you will be received.

"Once that is completed, you will be proceeding to a planet called Togarotu in Triangulum. We don't have the full requirements worked up for either aspect of this mission yet. That will be coming later in the day. But you need to depart for New Lorexi no later than noon tomorrow.

"As part of your preparation today, you are to begin installation of new EQD-resistant computers throughout your ship. The full details of the upgrade have just been loaded into your ship's portal. Joel Rubinstein will be transporting aboard shortly with some equipment and supplies. He can help your engineering team get started, but you can only have him for six hours. Responsibility for completing the upgrade before you depart falls to your chief engineer."

CONFERENCE ROOM, AMBASSADOR'S OFFICE

"Eugene, Kelly. Thanks for coming over to my office. There's a lot going on at the moment."

"What can we do for you Michael?"

"The Inspector is on his way to Earth. His alleged reason for coming is to take the prisoner Ju-Ne. I say alleged because we've learned he has another reason. We don't know the reason but suspect that he wants to steal your Red Matter weapon."

"Good luck with that." Eugene chuckled. "The weapon itself has been destroyed. All parts, patterns and files shredded."

Michael didn't respond. He just looked at them.

Kelly was the first one to get it. "He's coming for us. Isn't he?"

Michael nodded his head affirmatively.

56

"Do we have a plan?"

"We are taking extraordinary measures to prevent him from getting here. But I'm thinking our best option is to evacuate you from Earth."

"Where to?"

"The Inspector has eyes and ears everywhere, so I'm thinking that we put you on a ship and send it into interstellar space. We can move your lab onto the ship. We can accommodate your family or others that he might target to get at you."

"Will we ever be safe again?" It was Eugene this time.

"Two thoughts. First, we don't know that he's targeting you. The recommendation to evacuate is made in an abundance of caution.

"Second, I think the Inspector is likely to overplay his hand. He is arrogant and believes himself to be invincible. So, in his naivety, I expect him to do something incredibly stupid and end up in even poorer condition than his predecessor.

"That said, I would really like you to be beyond his grasp."

The room was quiet for a few seconds.

"Can Nelly come?"

"I'm not sure your relationship with her is so visible that she'd be a target. But, if she thinks she should go, then she can go."

"Then I'm in. Kelly?"

"I trust your judgement on this Michael. I'm in too."

Michael smiled. "I'm feeling better already. Can I ask a favor?"

"What?" Kelly laughed.

"Use the trip to push the intergalactic jump drive along. There's tremendous demand."

"Now that the new shield is done, it's my primary focus. Hopefully, I can get time with the ship's AI."

"Great. Start packing. Someone from Space Force will contact you this afternoon. I'd love to see you leave tonight if possible."

ENGINEERING, EAS POLAND

"I forgot how tight some of these access ways were." Joel complained.

"Then maybe you should try to drop a few pounds." Amalie teased.

Amalie Klopp was the chief engineer on the EAS Poland. She was thankful that Joel had been assigned to get them started on the computer upgrades. Joel had a list that prioritized the computers for replacement. It had apparently been generated as part of the postmortem inquiry after the Helsinki disaster. She'd never heard of the report but was incredibly grateful to have it. They probably wouldn't get all 230 computers swapped out before departing. But this way they'd at least get the most important ones.

They were currently chasing down number two on the list, the automated self-destruct sequencer. This was the computer that actually killed the Helsinki. It was buried deep in the belly of the ship and difficult to access.

Their first stop had been on the bridge. The single most important computer on the ship was the one the helm AI ran on. There were no EQD-tolerant computers that could support an AI. But there was EQD-resistant casing, which they installed instead.

"Here it is." Amalie called out. "I'm going to manually disable the system then pull the computer."

There was a small work area where several of the access ways intersected. The computer was mounted in one of them. Amalie entered the work area, which wasn't large enough for both of them to fit in, and quickly pulled the old one. Joel watched from the access way. When she was done, she backed into the opposite access way, so Joel could enter the work area and plug the new computer in.

"The only real mechanical difference between the two is this cover. It has to be open for the computer to mount properly." Joel opened the cover demonstrating the technique, then slid the computer into the mount. "Did you hear the click? There's a positive click when it's seated properly. Then we close the cover." There was a much louder click. "One of the ways they get the protection they do is by assuring all the contact points are pressure fit, both internal to the computer and at its external interfaces."

"Clever." Amalie agreed.

Joel backed into his access way. "I'll let you re-initialize the system."

Amalie entered the work area as Joel exited it.

"It's connecting to the main code database. The code is downloaded. Computer is up and running self-diagnostics. Done.

"Clever that they use a quantum-entangled comm connection for code update. The EQD can't jump the link, can't it?"

"Nope."

"These computers must be incredibly expensive."

"I'm sure they are. Next stop is the port nacelle."

Amalie took off down the access way. Joel crawled behind, trying to keep up.

EAS TORONTO

The Toronto was one of the regulars on the pickup runs to Karagon. With pickups every week now, Captain Shields had made this run 21 times. Today's was by far the fastest. They'd been given a priority slot that opened a few minutes early. It was the first time he'd ever been allowed into orbit early. And moments after obtaining orbit, they were given transport instructions for their goods.

The manifest had been updated. It took a second to confirm the changes with the Earth Alliance Trading Company. But the confirmation checked out, the goods were transported aboard, and the ship asked to leave orbit all within 10 minutes of arrival.

He'd never seen anything like it.

Now two hours later, they were transporting 62 10-megawatt power cubes down to the Earth Alliance Trading Company's warehouse.

EAS TOOMPEA

"Joel, welcome aboard. I'm Piper Robinson, captain of the Toompea. I understand that you're going to install a new forward shield on our ship today."

"Captain Robinson, pleasure to meet you. Yes, I'm also going to be recording the procedure, so that the engineering teams on the other ships can do this themselves."

"I heard that Space Force command wants this done on something like 200 ships within the next 24 hours."

"I think the final count is 192. At least that's what it was last I checked. I've only made 192 units."

"I understand that this is a tricky install."

"Yes and no. It's not actually that hard to do. But, if you screw up, you could end up depressurizing the ship."

"Not liking the sound of that. Ah, here comes our chief engineer. "Jack, meet Joel Rubinstein."

"Joel, welcome aboard. I'm Jaxon Monk. Everyone calls me Jack."

"Jack, a pleasure. Ready for some fun?"

...

For the second time today, Joel found himself cramped into a small space with another person. This one was complicated even more by the video cameras hovering in the air all around them.

Joel looked at the camera. "This is the trickiest part of the install."

Using special gloves, he held up a thin metal rod. The metal surface shimmered rainbow colors, as if it had a diffraction grating on it. There was a connector at one end and a crystalline lens on the other.

"This is the field emitter for the new shield. You need to hold it with the gloves that come in the box with it. The reason is that the surface of the rod itself is micro textured in a way that allows it to lock into the crystalline structure of the hull."

Joel gently put the rod back into the box it came in, then lifted another device out of another box for the cameras to see.

"This is the drill that will punch the hole in the hull that the emitter will go into. It has two ends, one that looks like a transparent plunger, the other cylindrical with handles.

"Put the plunger side against the hull, then activate the pump."

Joel demonstrated, then activated the device.

"Give it a minute to pump the air out of the plunger. The vacuum it forms will be enough to hold it there."

Joel let go. The device remained stuck to the wall.

"Now open the little door on the back by pushing this button."

Joel pointed to the door, then the button. Then he pushed the button and a small door, a half inch square, opened.

After putting the gloves back on, Joel picked up the shield emitter.

"OK, with the gloves on, insert the shield emitter into the drill, crystal end first. Do this gently, aligning the crystal with the grooves in the drill. If you bang it all around, bad things will happen."

Joel slid it in, closed the door and took off the gloves.

"OK, activate the drill. It will come up in standby mode."

Joel pointed to the relevant button, clicked it, then pointed at the screen.

"Next, we need to align the drill. I did my best to mount it in the center of this wall area, but that is nowhere near accurate enough. We want the emitter to be centered on the nose of the ship and aligned with the hull's crystalline matrix. To do that activate the alignment function."

Joel pointed at the appropriate button then pushed it.

"The drill contains a dimensional resonance scanner. It is now scanning through the hull, looking for the center of the ship's nose.

"There it goes, found it. I was pretty close. But a word on that. You need to mount the drill as close to the center of the forward wall as possible. You can be off by inches, but you don't want to be. The closer you start to the center, the better the solution it will find.

"If you screw up and attach it to the floor, the side wall, or maybe my buddy Jack here, it will not find a solution. It will report an error.

"Once it's found the center, it will search for the tightest fit vector.

"What do I mean by that?

"Your hull is monocrystalline. It also has a small number of crystalline defects. The emitter needs to be aligned with the crystalline matrix with a very particular orientation. And it cannot be mounted too close to a crystalline defect. As much as the ships are the same, every ship is different at the molecular level.

"Look at my display. See the crystalline defects it's found? There's one over here, the edge of another one over there."

Joel pointed to the spots marked on the drill's display.

"See where it wants to mount the emitter? Slightly off the center line. As far away from the defect in the upper right as it can be and still be in the sweet zone of the nose.

"If your drill can't find a spot, or can't find a spot you like, unmount it, move it a little closer to the center line, and try again.

"I've got a great spot, so I'm not going to do that.

"Now for the last step. Accept the siting it has given you."

Joel pointed to the appropriate control and clicked the button.

"Then click the install button."

Again, Joel pointed to the appropriate button and clicked it.

"This is one of those operations for which there's no Undo. So it comes back to you asking whether or not you really want to do this.

"I do, so I'm going to click the button. But before I do, let me tell you what's going to happen.

"There's a small transporter inside the drill. It's going to sculpt a hole in your hull that matches your emitter down to the molecular level. This will take about 5 minutes and make a lot of noise that will be heard throughout the ship. So, two things to do before you push the button. 1) Call your captain to let them know what you're about to do. They will hear the noise, so don't surprise them. 2) Put in the ear plugs that came with your kit. If you have a buddy with you when you do this, make sure they put theirs in also.

"OK. Here goes. Captain Robinson?"

"Yes Joel."

"We're about to install the shield emitter. This will take about 5 minutes and make enough noise you'll hear it."

"Understood, thanks for the warning."

"Jack, your earplugs in?"

"Putting them in now."

"OK. I'm going to put mine in now also. You'll know the process is done when you see the emitter appear where the hole has been drilled. Here goes."

Joel put in his ear plugs, then pushed the confirmation button.

The camera zoomed in to the location where a tiny hole started to appear. Slowly, but surely, the hole got deeper and wider.

About four minutes in, there was slight vibration as the remaining air in the plunger vented to space. After another minute, the emitter transported into the hole and the only thing visible was the connector.

Joel took his earplugs out.

"At this proximity, that was loud even with the earplugs in.

"A couple last steps. First, click the button that says re-pressurize."

Joel pointed to the button then pushed it.

"The drill will trickle a tiny amount of air into the suction cup to assure that you have a good seal. As you can see, our seal is excellent.

"If yours is not, a screen will come up, giving you a choice of sealing options that the drill can do for you.

"If none of those work, then you have a hull breach. Sound the emergency and follow your ship's standard procedures to address the problem.

"OK, back to the drill. See that it has stopped re-pressurizing. It's done that to prevent the drill from falling off the wall. Simply follow the procedure shown on the screen to finish. Grab the drill firmly by the handles. Click the finish button."

A moment later the drill came loose from the wall.

"And package the drill back in its container."

Joel put the drill away and policed the space for any stray bits.

"That's it, we're done. Next, we will install the power cube, then the shield generator, then lastly we will lay the conduits."

...

"Great job, Joel. I think I could even do it now."

"Thanks Jack. It's mostly automated and the drill is fantastic. But at the end of the day, we're punching a hole in the hull. So, it needs to be approached cautiously."

Jack started backing out the access way. "Now for the heavy lifting."

Joel gathered his kit, then followed behind.

SPACE FORCE COMMAND

Admiral Scott stewed over the data in front of him. At this point, he had over 600 ships under his command. But best case he would have just less than 200 with the new super shields, and 200 that were EQD resistant. The 200 overlapped but weren't precisely the same. So maybe 170 he could count on, but that was still a lot of ships.

The problem was where to send the others. But maybe that was an asset in disguise.

He quickly dispatched orders to 400 ships. They were all to exit the system on the same vector at midnight, then at a specified point they were to split off on a random vector of their choosing. All were to stay within 2,000 light years. A separate, follow-up message went to one ship.

Follow the vector to the split point, then take off on a random vector of your choosing, then keep going. Get at least 10,000 light years away, then disable your transponder and change vector. Check in when you are another 10,000 light-years from the turning point and there's no chance you can be traced.

EAS UKRAINE

"Captain, new orders were just received."

"Thank you, Ms. Nadia. Please forward them to me." Nadia was the Ukraine's helm AI.

A moment later. "Captain, additional orders were just received."

"Curious. Please send both orders to my office. Lt. Salib, you have the ship." Osman Salib, originally from Egypt, was the first watch tactical officer and the Ukraine's third officer.

"Yes, ma'am."

...

Captain Laura Boyd settled into her desk chair and quickly read the first set of orders. *Leaving at midnight. Going out 2,000 light years. Splitting up. They're intentionally scattering the fleet. Only ships with EQD-tolerant computers and forward shields are staying. I wonder what's going on.*

Hoping the second set of orders would bring more clarity, she opened those. Top Secret, For Your Eyes Only.

I'm evacuating Eugene Xu and Kelly Williamson to a secret location only I will know, 10,000 or more light-years from Earth. I'm to maintain 'radio silence' until requested to return.

Chapter 6: APPROACH

BRIDGE, EAS UKRAINE

It was 12:15 AM, but Laura had held off the watch change. She wanted to be on the bridge for the departure. She was impressed by the logistics of the evacuation. There were about 200 ships in orbit around the Earth or Moon when she came on watch four hours ago. Now they were departing, single file in a line of ships stretched out over millions of miles.

The ships were too far apart to see with the naked eye. But on the main view screen, all the ships were shown. Those still in orbit were in a line that curled around the Earth. Those that had already broken orbit were in a straight line along the specified vector. The Ukraine would be breaking orbit in another minute. About an hour from now they would be in position to make the first jump. The Admiral had done an impressive job of orchestrating the dance that would follow. And when they got to the split point, she would just keep going. Her ultimate target was the void between the Perseus and Carina-Sagittarius Arms. There they would go into silent running.

MILITARY INTELLIGENCE FAST ATTACK SHIP

"Status!" Inspector Ma-Gu called out as he walked onto the bridge of his ship.

"We're about 4 hours behind schedule sir. Several of the ships are experiencing longer than expected recharge times between jumps."

"Estimated time of arrival?"

"Approximately 24 Earth hours. We will be arriving just after midnight embassy time."

Ma-Gu smiled. "Good, that will give us some time to snoop before anyone gets out of bed."

EAS UKRAINE

Once they broke orbit, Laura went ahead with the change of watch. She'd given the Captain's chair to First Officer Logan Phillips, then retreated to the bridge office.

"Captain, we are approaching the jump. The auto sequencer will engage in 50 seconds."

Laura walked back out to the bridge and looked at the main view screen. They were now at the head of the long string of ships stretching all the way back to Earth.

"We are being sequenced for two long jumps, a thousand light years each." Commander Logan reminded. "From there it's your call, but we are to clear the reentry site within 60 seconds. Have you decided where we're going to go?"

"Yes." She turned toward Nadia, who had projected her image into the helmsmen's chair. "Nadia, I have queued orders for you that are triggered for release when the auto sequencer disengages."

"Understood Captain."

"Are you going to tell me?" The commander asked.

"Of course." Laura chuckled. "But my orders are to jump before revealing."

"Jumping in 3, 2, 1..."

Having done a long jump, the jump drive dropped back into warp for a 5-minute recharge.

On the view screen, there were now only four ships. They were at the end of the line.

"The EAS Brussels was at the head of the line, Captain. She jumped just as we emerged. Chatter on the helm AI network says that the sequencing for this exodus is impressive."

"About that. Our orders are to go quiet once released from the jump sequencer. So, I need you to drop off the AI network once we are released from the sequencer, Nadia. The orders are a bit different by ship, so other AIs may be staying on. But we need to drop off."

"Understood, ma'am."

...

"Jumping in 3, 2, 1...

"Arrived. Released from the jump sequencer."

"Mr. Takada, please set the ship for silent running."

Hisaki Takeda was the Ukraine's second watch yeoman.

"The ship's set for silent running, ma'am."

"As soon as the path ahead is clear, Nadia."

"Understood ma'am. Expected arrival in 2 hours, 40 minutes. Clever course, Captain."

Commander Phillips looked at the Captain questioningly.

"Let's go discuss this in the office." The captain stood.

Commander Phillips turned toward the tactical station. "Ms. Gana, you have the ship."

BRIDGE OFFICE, EAS UKRAINE

"So, what's going on?"

"We have a very delicate and very secret mission. Much of the show we just went through was a cover for our exit from the system."

"This must have something to do with our secret cargo."

"It does. We have Dr. Eugene Xu and Ms. Kelly Williamson aboard."

"That's unexpected."

"Some information was leaked to the Ambassador as a warning. A Confederation taskforce is on approach to Earth. Their stated mission is to collect a prisoner from Earth custody. But that's not their real mission. They are after something else. It's believed that they're after the weapon that took down the Enemy home world."

"Everything related to that weapon has been destroyed, except for the two inventors."

"Unbelievable! They were going to kidnap Earth's two greatest heroes!"

"We don't know that for sure, but that was the belief that led to our mission. We are to take them someplace far away from Earth. Someplace secret that only we know. No one on Earth knows where we're going. Once we get there, we're to signal that we've arrived via quantum entangled communications. Then we go silent until given the 'All Clear' to return."

"So, where are we going?"

"The void between the Perseus and Carina-Sagittarius Arms. 15,000 light-years from Earth, more than 1,000 light years from the nearest star."

"And we just sit there?"

"Our two guests are in the midst of some other critical invention. We're to do everything in our power to help them succeed."

"Do you know why we were selected for this mission?"

The Captain laughed. "I do. Nadia. She is apparently an expert in stellar cartography, and they need her help."

BRIDGE, EAS POLAND

First watch had just taken over as the Poland approached Edukatar.

"Captain, we've just been contacted by the Edujin air traffic control. They've asked us to take a geosynchronous orbit over the pick-up site."

"Thank you, Mr. Safar." Captain Keppler turned toward the helm. "Mr. Oscar, please approach as instructed." Ali Safar from Egypt was the first watch yeoman. Oscar was the helm AI.

"Captain, you have a call coming in from the surface. It's audio only."

"I'll take it in the office. Ms. Pak, you have the ship." Song-sook Pak was the first watch tactical officer.

...

"Captain Albert Keppler speaking."

"Captain Keppler, I am Va-Mu, Confederation Ambassador to the people of Edukatar. I can't tell you how delighted I am to see you entering our orbit."

"Mr. Ambassador. Thank you for calling. It is a pleasure to meet you."

"We have several large shipments for you to take for delivery to New Lorexi, Togarotu, and Dalfanito. If your orders do not allow you to deliver to Dalfanito, then those can be left on Togarotu. But we would be very grateful if you could deliver the Dalfanito shipment directly."

"We can deliver to Dalfanito."

"Excellent. Thank you. Has Ambassador Michael contacted you related to the pickup at Celanar?"

"Yes. That is our next stop."

"Even more excellent. We also have a shipment for Celanar if you can take that."

Captain Keppler smiled to himself. He'd been warned that he would be pressed to do more than had been previously cleared.

"We'd be happy to deliver those shipments, sir. But I have been asked to tell you the following. When regular shipments commence, we will be restricted to take only the shipments that have been booked. But this being a special run, I've been instructed to be as accommodating and flexible as possible."

"Does that mean a regular schedule is going to be set up for runs to the other two galaxies?"

"Not yet sir. It's our desire to do that. I'm told it's currently out of our reach, but we're actively working the problem."

"Thank you, Captain. I just sent the manifests. Given the number of items, would it be possible for you to load by destination and hold the shipments in separate cargo holds."

"That was my plan, sir."

"Excellent." From the Captain's perspective, the Ambassador seemed to be bubbling over with joy that his goods were finally getting shipped. "You are so much easier to work with than the Fleet used to be."

"Happy to be of service, sir."

"Then I'll leave you to it. Safe journey, Captain."

"Thank you, Mr. Ambassador."

Captain Keppler chuckled once the line dropped. It had been a long time since he'd spoken with someone so happy to talk with him.

SPACE FORCE COMMAND

A lot had happened over the last 24 hours. A lot more needed to get done in the next 12. The heads of the teams working the various initiatives were gathering in his Conference Room. This would be Admiral Scott's first read on how well the overall preparation program was doing.

He entered the Conference Room and took his seat, then pointed to Lt. Commander Summer Bennett, head of system surveillance. "Summer, let's start with you. I want current status, expected completion, anything you need help with. Go."

"Thank you, sir. Last night we completed the surveillance ring in Pluto's orbit. That's a slight misnomer. Pluto's orbit is very eccentric. A better descriptor would be a sphere of surveillance platforms whose orbit matched the mean of Pluto's orbit. It's the target we were working toward. It's done. It's not full enough to guarantee we will see the Inspector's ship make entry. But we will see him before he gets very far."

"Thank you. Mark. You're next."

Colonel Mark Patterson had taken the lead on coordinating the forward shield upgrades for the ships.

"The initial target was 192 ships. At this point we have successfully upgraded and tested 200 ships. Joel Rubinstein's video instruction on the installation procedure worked like a charm. All 200 of the target ships were upgraded by their engineers. It is a first-of-its-kind achievement, sir."

"Excellent news. I was thinking it would be a miracle to get half of them done. Good idea using Rubinstein that way.

"Carmen?"

Lt. Commander Carmen Lopez headed Logistics for Space Command. She'd coordinated the EQD upgrades.

"Things have gone well for us. We targeted 100 ships and have actually completed 118 at this point. The Atomoi shipyards completed the 100 upgrades they'd promised. Each of those ships was also tested. We are in the process of self-installing 27 other ships. 18 are completed. One of those is the Poland, who has already departed on her mission. The remaining nine are making progress and should be finished early in the afternoon. But none of the ships we've done the installations on have been tested. We don't have the means.

"I've dispatched 25 more freighters to Atomorali. They think they will have the computers installed and tested by midnight."

"How many Cruisers and Fast Attack Ships did we get converted?"

"Two cruisers, three Fast Attack Ships."

"So, we will have one upgraded Cruiser in the game. Good."

"She's in lunar orbit now sir."

"Thank you. Good work. Let's continue cycling ships through the shipyards at Atomorali.

"Dieter?"

Lt. Commander Dieter Kleiner was a computational analytics expert with Space Force's Intelligence department.

"The staged departure worked perfectly, sir. All ships made their way out of the system in a very visible and intentional departure. You may have noticed the news coverage this morning."

The Admiral grunted, not happy that even a single civilian noticed what happened. He'd opposed the plan, but the Secretary mandated it.

"Anyway, all ships have arrived at their destinations except the Ukraine. We have not heard from her yet but expect to shortly."

"Declan?"

Lt. Commander Declan Miller was responsible for facilities.

"Stealth shields have been activated inside all our warehouses and hangers. Dome shields have been erected over them. We've also activated a stealth shield inside the Transluminide vault at the Earth Alliance Bank. So, at this point all our major ground-based portable assets are hidden, giving them an extra layer of protection.

"I have teams sweeping the rest of the buildings looking for anything that we've missed. They'll be done in another four hours."

"Good work, everybody. We've met and exceeded the goals we set for ourselves. Let's keep pressing forward on the EQD upgrades."

AMBASSADOR'S RESIDENCE

"Hi, Sarah."

"Alexi, you're back!"

Sarah went over to give Alexi a deep embrace. "I missed you."

"And you thought having me around was going to take away all your freedom." Alexi teased. "Hey. I brought you something."

Alexi spent a moment digging through her backpack, then pulled out what looked like a jewelry box.

She held it out for Sarah to take. "Here."

Sarah took the box, looking at it oddly, then opened it.

"You got me a bracelet?"

"Yah, try it on." Alexi bubbled with excitement.

Sarah tried not to express her disappointment too much, but the bracelet really wasn't her style.

"Oh." Alexi fished around some more, then pulled out a second box. "This goes with it." She held out the box for Sarah to take.

Sarah, looking increasingly worried, took the box and opened it.

"This looks like a rock."

"Cool, isn't it. You can put it in your pocket, or in your purse..."

The look of distaste and confusion on Sarah's face was too much. Alexi burst out laughing.

"Alexi, what is this?"

"Darn. I was hoping I could convince you it was jewelry."

"What is it?" Sarah said in an impatient, sing-song voice.

More laughing.

"Alexi?"

"It's a transport dampener. If the Inspector tries to kidnap you by just plucking you out of the room with a transporter. The bracelet and dampener will stop it. It's not fool proof, but it's the best portable unit you can get. And a lot more expensive than jewelry."

"Do I really have to wear this?"

"I can wrap it on you like I do with the shield generator. But check it out." She pulled out another box. "Michael let me get a kit."

She opened the box and pulled out a second bracelet that she put on, then pulled out another one and a small one. "Bracelets for Julissa and Timothy too. Cool, right. We can all look like we're coordinated."

"Alexi, how much did this cost?"

"Trust me Sarah, you don't want to know. The wire in that bracelet is made of an exceedingly rare material. And the stone... Ah, hold out your hand."

Alexi had dropped the sappy salesperson act. The request for Sarah to put her hand out was stated in all seriousness, so Sarah complied, again impressed by Alexi's ability to change her demeanor so quickly.

"You should be able to feel this. It's subtle, but perceptible."

Alexi placed the stone gently on Sarah's palm.

Sarah looked at it quizzically. "Is it vibrating?"

Alexi smiled. "Cool right. There's a little vibrator in there that keeps a grain of Transluminide in constant motion. The Transluminide and the wire form a tiny dimensional resonant circuit. The dimensional resonance prevents a transporter bubble from forming. If you want to transport, you just put the two in this." Alexi pulled out something that looked like a small jewelry box. "It absorbs the resonance field and bingo. Transport works again."

Julissa walked into the room holding Timothy. "Who's making all the noise out here?"

Sarah pointed to Julissa. "Alexi meet Julissa."

Then she pointed to Alexi. "Julissa meet Alexi."

"Alexi, this is little Master Timothy." Julissa held Timothy out for Alexi to take, but Alexi stepped back, hands up. "Sorry, but I don't voluntarily touch babies."

Julissa turned to Sarah. "I think we may have found your mighty warrior's weakness."

AMBASSADOR'S OFFICE

Pam came into Michael's office. "Michael have you seen this morning's news?"

"No. Never watch it. What's up?"

"The top story is the fleet evacuating the system."

"What?"

She handed him her tablet.

"How?" Michael wondered. *Ju-Ne is no longer on the planet. How did this happen?*

In some sense, the answer was obvious. Ju-Ne had sympathizers beyond those that had been rounded up. But the reality of that answer really stuck in his throat.

Are they on Earth? Or among the defense allies I've briefed?

A painful reality settled in. *The Inspector has other spies here.* Then a smile bloomed. *And now he has the message we intended to spread.*

EAS UKRAINE

The captain walked into the Mission Deck lounge. She'd agreed to meet Eugene and Kelly there for lunch at noon.

"Eugene, Kelly. I hope you're settling in comfortably."

"Captain Boyd, good morning. The accommodations are great."

Eugene nodded his head in agreement.

"And you're finding your way around OK?"

"No problem at all. The layout is similar to the Fast Attack Ships, just bigger."

"And your equipment arrived OK?"

"Appears to have," Eugene said. "We haven't hauled it all back yet, but we will."

"That's one of the things I wanted to talk with you about. As of right now, the only people that officially know you're here are me and my first officer Logan Phillips. I suspect my second officer and helm AI know as well. But our orders were not to disclose your presence until we reached our destination, which we have now done.

"If we stay here long, your presence will probably become known. My question is whether you want to stay hidden or be given access to the rest of the ship and the crew."

Eugene already knew what Kelly's answer to that question would be, so he spoke up for both of them. "I think we want access to the ship and crew. We understand why Space Force wanted to keep our presence secret, so agreed to start that way. But we really need access to a crew like yours to progress our current line of work, so we'd like to take advantage of that while we're here."

The Captain looked at Eugene for a moment, seeming to hesitate. "Admiral Scott told me your current line of work is of critical importance to Space Force. He also told me that the Ambassador wants it as soon as possible. And that it's secret.

"I guess my question is how secret? And how can we participate if we don't know what it is?"

Eugene looked to Kelly, implying she should take this one.

"What we're doing is revolutionary. It will ultimately touch most people's lives whether they know it or not. So, I'd like to get a little closer to a solution before word gets back to the Confederation."

"What is it?" The captain asked the question plainly, not pressing for an answer.

"A new jump drive, one that could cross the intergalactic void in a single jump."

The captain was stunned. "How?"

"Dimensional bubble. Same basic idea as warp and jump, but in a dimension that has different properties. But before you get too excited, it would be useless inside a galaxy. We can really only leverage this phenomenon for jumps across large voids."

The captain thought for a moment.

"How about this? I announce to the crew that you're on board. I tell them that a critical objective of our mission is in support of a new propulsion system that you're working on. That has something to do with our current location. You are hoping to engage some of the crew in your work. I'm counting on the crew to help you as you need help."

"Where are we?" Eugene asked.

"In the void between the Perseus and Carina-Sagittarius Arms."

"Perfect! I'm good with that. Kelly?"

"I'm good with it as well. Everyone knows Eugene is the father of modern propulsion. That we are here, doing work on propulsion systems makes perfect sense. With that as the cover, we can socialize with the crew and engage any of them as we need without having to spill the entire can of beans."

"OK. I need to make an announcement to the crew after lunch anyway. I'll include that, then send some marines down to help you get your lab set up."

"Deal."

NELLY FONG'S APARTMENT

It had been an odd day. News of the fleet evacuation sent the global stock market into a panic. Although it would have an impact on her former colleagues at the Fed, it really didn't impact the Earth Alliance Central Bank. But she got a lot of calls today from her former colleagues and from acquaintances at the other central banks. They all wanted to know what was going on. It was all a bit unsettling.

Now, she was home in an empty apartment wondering why she hadn't gone into hiding with Eugene.

AMBASSADOR'S RESIDENCE

Michael woke, then exited the regeneration chamber. Five minutes later, he was dressed and in the kitchen with a cup of coffee and breakfast. It was 8:00 PM and he planned to be up for at least the next 24 hours.

Alexi came in. "Here are yours." She held out a small box. "Bracelet and generator are inside. To transport, they need to be in the box. Stay at least 10 feet from any active transporter area if they're not in the box. It's usually bad news when you collapse an active transport bubble with someone in it.

"Optimal protection is when you have the bracelet on and the generator 3 to 5 feet away. I put your bracelet in a wrist band. Looks less suspicious."

"Can I just put it in my pocket?"

"Bracelet, no. It must be wrapped around you. Wrist, ankle, or neck. Generator, yes but in the opposing pocket."

Michael opened the box. The generator was disguised as a small, polished river-stone. He took it out and put it in his left pocket. The bracelet was disguised as a wrist band as advertised. He took it out of the box and slid it over his right hand.

"Fits. Snug, but not tight. Thanks Alexi."

She pulled a small envelope out of her pocket and placed it on the table. "You sure about this? It could be used against you."

"I'm sure. If he gets me, I want an easy way out of my avatar."

He took the envelope and put it in his wallet.

"Be careful with it."

"I will. I won't put it on until he arrives."

The envelope contained a small medical patch. A tiny controller in the patch would register itself with his implants. If activated, the patch would release a substance into his system that would eject him from his avatar, then shut it down.

MILITARY INTELLIGENCE FAST ATTACK SHIP

"Sir. We've just received word. The Earth has evacuated most of its warships. It appears they know that they've been outmatched.

The Inspector mulled the news for a few seconds, then replied.

"Unlikely. Mi-Ku is up to something. The question is what. He would never expose himself like this.

"Contact the network. Find out what he's up to. And do it quickly. We enter the system in an hour."

SYSTEM SURVEILLENCE DEPARTMENT

"Lt. Commander. I think they're here. Four Lorexian Fast Attack Ships dropped from jump just outside our surveillance grid. They're 63 degrees above the ecliptic, so have an unobstructed path to Earth.

"Ma'am, they just went to warp. If they're following standard Fleet protocol, they'll be here in a little over an hour.

SPACE FORCE COMMAND

"Understood. Thank you, Lt. Commander."

It was 11:00 PM. Admiral Sam Scott was still at his desk and probably would be for the rest of the night.

"Daniel Porter?" Moments later, the comm system connected him.

"Admiral."

"They're here."

"Just saw that on the tactical network."

"I'm going to put up the planetary shields in 15 minutes. That will also go out over the tactical network. Once they're up, tactical command for the area outside the shields transfers to you."

"Understood. Thank you, sir."

...

The Admiral's next call was to Michael.

"I'll be there in 15 minutes."

Chapter 7: CONFRONTATION

[Tuesday, 07.21.2032] MILITARY INTELLIGENCE FAST ATTACK SHIP

The Inspector strode back onto the bridge.

"Astrogation, report!"

"Sir, we're going to drop back into normal space in five minutes."

"Tactical."

"Sensors detect no ships in orbit, but we are getting an unusual number of anomalous readings, sir."

"Mi-Ku must have put up some sort of dampening field. But he must know that won't really help him.

"Comms, anything from the network?"

"Only two replies. A few ships stayed behind after the fleet's exodus. But those ships left on a different vector a few hours later."

"Tactical. When we drop from orbit, I want to know where Ju-Ne is. Put a transporter lock on him as soon as you find him.

"The same for Mi-Ku and his new woman.

"Then for the two engineers."

"That could take a while. They do not have implants we can ping."

"It'll take as long as it takes. We're in no hurry. These people are at our mercy."

BRIDGE, EAS CANADA

As much as Daniel wanted to keep first watch on duty for the initial contact, he didn't expect much action until later in the morning. So, they did the change of watch on schedule.

On the main view screen, there was a zoomed-out image of the Earth. In the upper right, the estimated course and position of the Inspector's task force was plotted. They couldn't actually see the Inspector's ships while they were in warp space. But the Confederation's ships created so much dimensional resonance that the orbital surveillance platforms could sense when they passed.

Confederation ships usually needed to drop from warp about three times further out than the moon, so they expected to see the ships in the next several minutes.

Also plotted on the display were the current positions of all Daniel's ships. There were a lot of them. Most were freighters. All were hiding behind their stealth shields. The Canada was in orbit around the Moon. It was cloaked in a stealth field that the Confederation didn't know about. He would find out in a few minutes whether or not it really worked. He doubted the Inspector would come in guns blazing, but if he did and could see the Canada, then Daniel was in trouble. Shields had to be down for the cloak to be up.

"Sir. They're coming out of warp."

The main view screen switched to show the Inspector's approach. Four streaks of light flashed across the screen, heads stopping abruptly, tails streaking in as the light caught up.

MILITARY INTELLIGENCE FAST ATTACK SHIP

"Report!"

"One million kilometers from Earth sir. Orbital insertion in 18 minutes."

"Inspector, we see no ships in orbit, but there are dozens of anomalies."

"Show me!"

An image of the Earth filled the screen. A dozen small black dots were visible, tracking across the face of the planet.

"I only see a handful."

"There are 12 of these fast-moving ones, dozens more moving slowly or not at all." As the tactical officer started pointing them out, the Inspector realized there must be close to 100 of them.

"Zoom in. What are these things?"

The screen zoomed in on one of the nearly still dots. The image grew until the dot was a tenth the width of the screen.

"That's as big as it gets."

"It looks like a black hole. Have they mined their own space with artificial black holes?"

"Can't be, sir. It's 8 kilometers wide. A black hole that large would have consumed the planet a long time ago."

"Can we get a laser lock on one?"

"Too far away, sir."

"Have you found Ju-Ne yet?"

"We are not getting a return ping from his implants."

"Mi-Ku?"

"Yes, sir. He appears to be in Space Force headquarters."

"Inspector, we are being hailed from the planet."

A thought rocketed through the Inspector's mind. *Something isn't right here. Where is Ju-Ne? And why is Mi-Ku at Space Force Command in the middle of the night?*

"Put it on."

Michael's face appeared on the main view screen.

"Inspector Ma-Gu. I fear you've made a long journey for no purpose. Ju-Ne came out of his hibernation a couple days ago and is already on his way to New Lorexi as required by the extradition orders received months ago."

The Inspector shook his head.

"Mi-Ku, I don't know what your game is. But I don't believe a word of it. You wouldn't just give him up. You just want to feed him to your primitives."

"It is true. He came out of hibernation when it completed its historic purpose. He must have been extremely determined to stay down that long, because he didn't wake until his implants went into immuno-rejection. Documentation of this event has already been sent to the members of the Central Council and to the head of the Lorexian Institute's Medical School."

"Liar. If that is his condition, which I doubt, then it's because your primitives reconditioned him."

"Ma-Gu. Slander does not become someone of your responsibility and position. I suggest that you return to New Lorexi and examine the facts. I will expect an apology when you learn of your error."

"I will not return home. If you do not return the prisoner to me within the next twelve hours, I will begin systematically taking your planet apart until I find him myself.

"Ju-Ne is approaching the halfway point of his journey across the void. The ship he is on is also delivering critical goods to New Lorexi, Togarotu and Dalfanito. On its return it will be delivering critical goods to multiple member worlds in this sector. It will not return to Earth until its mission is completed."

The Inspector stood there staring at Michael. In his heart, he just wanted to bomb the planet and be done with it. But he knew he would not get away with it.

"Then I will wait here until I get word from Command, confirming that he has been returned. It will go very poorly for you and your primitives if I should find out that things are not as you claim, Mi-Ku."

"Do what you must. But do not approach to within 100,000 km of the planet. Our planetary shield is up. You will damage your ships if you should hit it."

The Inspector turned to his tactical officer. "Are their shields up?"

"I read no shield."

Ma-Gu turned back toward Michael, an evil grin on his face.

"You overplayed your hand Mi-Ku. We read no shields. It's a crime to willfully lie to an Inspector. I'm placing you under arrest. I advise you and your puny primitives not to resist. If you do, I'll be forced to bombard your planet."

He turned to his tactical officer. "Transport the suspect to the brig."

The Inspector turned back toward Michael, wanting to see his eyes when he felt the transporter grab him.

"Inspector. We cannot get a transporter lock."

Fury rose within the Inspector, but he kept it in check.

"I'm not sure what game you're playing, Mi-Ku. But it is of no matter. We'll simply send a shuttle down to get you. Prepare yourself."

"When your shuttle hits the shield, it will be damaged."

"Your lies will not work on me, Mi-Ku."

The Inspector cut the comm connection.

"Security, send a team down to collect the Ambassador."

SPACE FORCE COMMAND

"For a minute there, I thought he might wait. Wishful thinking, I suppose," Admiral Scott mused. "Are we going to try to stop them?"

"I really don't want them to kill themselves. I also don't want to drop the shield."

"If we let them come down, how difficult will they be to capture and detain?"

"They're trained soldiers, Special Forces. They will have shields and decent weapons. And they'll know how to use them."

The comm sounded.

"Scott here."

"Admiral, Daniel Porter here. They just launched their shuttle. It's small enough the Canada can transport it. We have a plan and a 60 second window." The Admiral looked at Michael, who nodded.

"Go."

MISSION LAB, EAS UKRAINE

Yesterday, a team of space marines had helped Eugene and Kelly get the lab set up. Today, they would be working with Nadia. The ship was in ballistic flight through the immense void between the galactic arms. Nadia had little to do. And there would be plenty of warning if the ship needed her for anything. So, the Captain gave her permission to spend as much of the day with Eugene and Kelly as she wanted.

"How good is your map of this dimension?" Nadia asked.

"Hard to know with certainty until we've gone there. But, the theory completely checks out and it does so to the same extent that it does for transport, warp, and jump."

"I've put together some graphics that really tell the story. At least they do for me."

Eugene popped up a holoprojection. "This is a map of the gravity wells in our region of space. The depth of the well is defined by the mass of the star. The width or curvature of the hole is defined by the gravitational constant. The distance between the holes, at least as measured in light-minutes, is determined by the speed of light. These two constants of nature are different by dimension.

"Here's the same map for warp space. Its constant of gravity is higher, so the curvature of the holes is steeper. Its speed of light is also higher, so the distance between the holes is less.

"I'm going to add another feature to the map." A thin red ring formed inside each of the gravity wells, near its top. "The red zone is the optimal transition point between the dimensions. It's where the gravitational force is the same between the two. Transitioning too deep in the gravity well will expose the ship to increasing gravitational shear. If the shear exceeds the material strength of the ship, then the ship is ripped apart during the transition.

"One last note on warp space. Note that there is still a lot of flat space we have to pass through. Or, said differently, the distance between the red transition zones is less, but still a lot.

"Here's the same map for jump space, which has an even higher constant of gravity and higher speed of light. Note that the holes are way deeper, and the flat space basically disappears between the nearby stars. Almost all the red circles touch within the galaxy. That's why jump seems instant. As we leave one gravity well, the jump drive drops us into the next.

"Now, watch as I zoom out. As I just said, there is little flat space between the stars within a galaxy, but there's still lots of flat space between galaxies.

"Any questions?"

"Plenty. But I love that you've just explained two phenomena more clearly than I've ever heard before. We can't jump deep in a gravity well because of the gravitational shear. And jump seems instant because the distance between entry and exit from jump space is nearly zero."

"Thanks." Eugene nodded to Nadia, glad that his explanation seemed to have landed OK.

"What I've just described is propulsion as we know it. Now, let's look at the map for hyperjump."

A fourth holoprojection popped up.

"This is the same map, shown from the perspective of the hyperjump dimension. The gravitational constant and speed of light are much higher in this dimension.

"Note that almost the entire galaxy is bogged down in the gravity well somewhere. The red line no longer runs around a star's gravity well; it runs around the edge of the galaxy and is no longer a circle.

"Point 1. There are essentially no safe transition zones within the galaxy itself. The exception, of course, is here along the far ends of the spiral arms.

"Point 2. The majority of the safe zones are here, along the edges of the galaxy's gravity well. From most of these points, it is a short jump to locations in the neighboring galaxy.

"So, back to your question. It's the consistency of the way the gravitation constant and the speed of light works that gives us confidence in the theory. What we lack, in terms of testing it, is how to package this data in a way that's navigationally useful."

Nadia sat staring silently at the four maps for several seconds. Then she turned, smiling at Eugene.

"You're close. But you've conflated two issues. Issue one is knowing a) where to transition, and b) how much energy to put into the transition so that you fall out at the right point. There's a standard format in which that data is stored. It's clear to me that you have the algorithms to compute it. Once that's done, it would be a small tweak to any of the standard controllers to use it.

"Issue two is knowing where you are, how to calculate your speed, and how to determine the energy of transition required for you to drop out at the right spot. I think you may have that as well. But it's hard for me to know that for sure without having done it a few times.

"That said, I think we're close."

Eugene said, "Thank you."

But Kelly just smiled. She'd done most of the work that got them to this point. Eugene generally did a better job of selling it. That's why he'd taken the lead today. But they both knew this was her work. And she'd finally received the real-world feedback she needed to continue. The hyperjump drive would happen. She was confident of that now. And they would both get another entry in the history books. Not bad for a girl from Australia who'd always dreamed of the stars.

MILITARY SHUTTLE, EARTH ORBIT

Lieutenant Mo-Ma was not happy to have landed this mission to arrest Mi-Ku. He was a far better leader than Ma-Gu. He had probably been given this suicide mission because too many people knew of his feelings. His training was his compulsion, so off he and his men went on what was surely their last mission.

BRIDGE, EAS CANADA

The mission plan was simple. A freighter would alter orbit and come between the shuttle and the taskforce, blocking the taskforce's view of the shuttle and the shuttle's ability to communicate with the taskforce.

Once out of site, the EAS Canada would transport the shuttle into an evacuated cargo bay. Dampening and suspensor fields would then be activated around it.

At that point, a communication burst would be released from the account of one of Ju-Ne's former confederates. It would say that one of the artificial black hole mines placed in Earth's orbit had just consumed the shuttle. The taskforce should flee while they still had the chance. The broadcast source would be blown-up seconds after the message was finished broadcasting.

"This is going to be close," Second watch officer Hamza Khan complained.

"3, 2, 1... Now!" Else called out.

"Got 'em," Second watch engineer Azima Mutai called out from outside the cargo bay.

"Sir. The arrest team... They just disappeared."

"What do you mean they disappeared?"

"One of the black holes moved. It hit the shuttle and the shuttle just vanished."

"Show me!" The Inspector shouted, spittle escaping his lips.

The recording played. It showed one of the black dots moving toward the shuttle and crossing its path. There was no explosion, no debris, and no shuttle as the black dot continued on its path, then disappeared behind the Moon.

"Inspector. A message from the network. The shuttle was intercepted by one of Earth's defensive black hole satellites."

The science officer responded quickly. "It's too big to be a black hole. The dots are a deception."

"Inspector, Ambassador Mi-Ku is on the line for you."

"Put him through."

Michael's face appeared on the view screen, but before he could say anything the Inspector shouted. "You will pay for this, Mi-Ku!"

"For having saved the crew you mercilessly sent to their deaths? I doubt it. I think you're the one that will pay. The only real question is whether you will stop this foolishness before you kill everyone in your task force."

The Inspector showed his teeth. "YOU will pay!"

"We'll see." Michael shook his head, then closed the connection.

...

"I want to find out what those things are. Are there any in range of our laser canons?

"I think so," the tactical officer replied.

"Put it on the main view screen."

One of the dots appeared on the screen, which zoomed until the black hole in space filled half of it. Targeting cross hairs appeared near the center of the object.

"The range is at the limit of accurate targeting, sir."

"I'm OK with that. Fire!"

The beam shot out. It was mostly invisible. But there was enough light reflected off the odd molecule of air or grain of dust to see the beam's path, which seemed to stop at the black circle.

"What's happening? Did you miss?"

"No. Let me put up the enhanced view."

A mostly solid image of the beam stretched from the ship to the target, where the beam simply stopped.

All activity on the bridge stopped as everyone stared at the image on the screen. Then the beam suddenly vanished.

"Sorry, sir. We exceeded the maximum sustainable duration. The generator shut down. It needs to cool."

The object, whatever it was, suddenly changed course.

EAS CANADA

"Captain Robinson. How's your ship holding up?"

"No problem, sir. By our estimate, their laser was maybe 1% of the shield's capacity."

"Good. I want you to change course. Remain hidden. Keep your ship behind the shield. And slowly approach the ship that fired at you. Three other ships will be joining you. Form a square 1 kilometer apart, then approach slowly, stopping 10,000 km from the ship's nose."

"If they rush you, we will reveal ourselves."

"We'll be doing the same for each of their ships. Let's see if we can call their bluff."

"Yes, sir!"

The Captain turned to her bridge crew.

"You heard the Admiral. Helm, adjust course."

MILITARY INTELLIGENCE FAST ATTACK SHIP

"Sir, we seem to have attracted its attention. It appears to be turning toward us."

The Inspector turned to his science officer. "Any idea what that thing is? It behaves like a black hole. But I agree with you. A black hole that large would have consumed this system long ago."

"Something very curious about it. We can detect nothing from it on any spectrum. Not even gravity waves. It's as if it's a massless black hole."

Ma-Gu thought he'd heard of something like this once before. But before he could drag up the memory, the Tactical officer called out.

"Inspector. Lots of them are turning. Four are on an intercept course with our ship. Others are headed toward the other ships in the task force."

"Hold your position! And forward the order to the other ships." He turned toward the communications officer. "Get me Mi-Ku."

...

After nearly a minute, Michael's image appeared.

"Not a particularly wise move firing on our black hole defensive satellites. They get a little testy about things like that."

"Call off your dogs and surrender now, Mi-Ku. My patience runs thin."

"I was not aware that we were at war. As a Central Council member, I would know if we were. So, your actions appear to be rogue."

"We are here for the prisoner and have been authorized by the Central Council to take him by force."

"But as previously discussed, he is not here. He is on his way to New Lorexi. Have you not the discipline to even inquire?"

"You are a fool, Mi-Ku. Your embassy has just come into weapons range. Maybe the next time we talk, you will be more compliant."

The Inspector cut the connection.

"Target the embassy with the EQD weapon. I've had enough of this foolishness."

Targeting information came up on the screen. "Should we take the Ambassador's location first?"

Ma-Gu almost said yes, then changed his mind. "No. Target his residence."

A residential building appeared on the main view screen. Targeting cross hairs centered on the building labeled as the Ambassador's Residence."

"Fire!"

...

Deep in the bowels of the ship there was a grid containing rows of small capsules. Each held an EQD field generator. On one of the capsules a red light started blinking. It indicated that the capsule had been armed and would detonate in 15 seconds. Its image wavered, then disappeared. The weapon delivery transporter carried that capsule away toward its target.

...

An alarm went off on the bridge. Simultaneously, a light flashed brightly on the planetary shield. The energy released danced across the shield, most of the energy reflecting back into space. A small portion of that energy remained caught in the collapsing transporter bubble.

"Inspector, the transport field collapsed."

The main view screen shifted to the spot where the transporter bubble collapsed against the shield.

"They have a shield we cannot detect!" The Inspector shouted in rage.

A few more alarms sounded.

"Inspector!" The voice came over the intercom. It was the chief engineer. "An EQD field developed somewhere on the ship. The computers are dropping. We need to kill main power before the reaction goes critical!"

A moment later, system after system started dropping. Emergency lighting came on. The air handling system stopped running. Then all normal ship noises stopped.

In the momentary silence, the Inspector muttered, "What have I done?"

BRIDGE, EAS CANADA

"Michael, they fired an EQD weapon at the Embassy. But it could not get through the planetary shield.

"We don't have the angle to know the target with certainty. But it was in the executive residence area. So, I suspect he was targeting your apartment."

Michael's anger flared, challenging his ability to control the rage.

"Do we have authorization to fire back?"

"Admiral, sorry to interrupt, but you need to see this." Else put an image on the main view screen. "It's the Inspector's ship. It's lost power. And an automated distress beacon has started broadcasting."

"Admiral, we've got trouble." It was second watch tactical officer Hamza Khan. "One of the other ships appears to be powering its weapons."

"Mr. Perez, put me on the audio tactical network."

"You're on, sir."

"All freighters. Form a blockade between Earth and the enemy ships. Screen the Embassy with all haste. Repeat form blockade to screen the embassy. All hands to battle stations."

Michael was still on the other end of the line.

"Daniel, I'm going to contact their alternate lead."

The line dropped.

BRIDGE, AUXILIARY FLAG SHIP

"Captain, something has happened on the Inspector's ship. She's lost power."

"Shields up! Power up the weapons!"

The main view screen switched to a view of the Inspector's ship. One by one, all lights were flickering off.

"Captain, they apparently fired an EQD weapon that flashed back on them when the transporter bubble collapsed against the planetary shield."

He pushed a button that allowed him to address the other two ships in the taskforce.

"All ships back off. There has been an EQD event on the flagship. Repeat, all ships back off to a safe distance.

"Captain!" It was the tactical officer again. "Hundreds of the little black holes are rushing toward us. First impact will be in about 5 minutes."

For the first time in his life, the Captain and now acting leader of the taskforce didn't know what to do. The black holes would undoubtedly destroy his ships. But they appeared to be impervious to his weapons.

"Captain. Councilor Mi-Ku is on the line for you."

The captain trembled. The Inspector seemed to be able to get away with challenging members of the Central Council and High Command. But he couldn't.

"Put him through."

Michael's image came up on the main screen.

"With whom am I speaking?"

"I am Captain So-Du of the Fleet ship Glorious Dawn."

"Captain So-Du. Your immediate and unconditional surrender is required. Two hundred black hole satellites are on a collision course with your taskforce. You have no chance of surviving that. Little chance of evading them.

"Two Earth Alliance cruisers are and have been flanking your position. They will decloak now."

"Captain, two very large ships just decloaked to the sides and behind us." The tactical officers voice trembled in fear.

"Additional cloaked ships are nearby watching you. All are immune to your EQD weapons. Drop your shields and power down your weapons now."

The anger in Michael's voice was so palpable the captain stuttered as he issued the commands.

On a private channel, Daniel messaged Michael letting him know that the task forces shields were down and weapons unpowered.

Michael took a couple cleansing breaths to get his anger under control.

"Captain So-Du. Do you know why you are here?"

"To collect the prisoner, sir."

"I know that was your cover. I also know that was not your mission. If you are to walk away from this whole, you'll need to be forthcoming."

"I believe that you are correct sir. The prisoner was our cover for being here, but I think the Inspector was after something else. Unfortunately, he did not take me into his confidence."

"Captain So-Du. Do you understand how treasonous the Inspector's actions were today? Earth is the capital planet of a sector defensive alliance. We are chartered by the Central Council and not subject to the Fleet or the Inspector.

"Do you realize how treasonous it is to deploy EQD weapons? Let alone deploy them against an allied world. These were banned years ago because they are indiscriminate and uncontrolled. The Inspector seems to have proven that today."

"I understand sir. But only the Inspector's ship has those weapons. And his was the only ship to fire on an allied world."

"OK. Time to change subjects. Do you or the other members of the taskforce have the ability to assist your flagship?"

"I believe we do, sir."

"Then, this is what we're going to do. You're going to evacuate the Inspector's ship. You will surrender the Inspector and his ship's officers into my custody. You will allow us to inspect your ships and to disable their weapons.

"When all of that has been done to my satisfaction, then you and your two ships will be escorted back to New Lorexi, where they will be released to the custody of Admiral Jo-Na. In exchange we will not file charges against you or the crews of your ships. Are we agreed?"

"We are agreed, sir."

"Armed members of the 3F Alliance military will board your ship shortly to observe your operations."

"Thank you, sir."

MISSION LAB, EAS UKRAINE

Today, Eugene and Kelly made more progress on the intergalactic jump drive than they'd made in the last year.

Nadia was the fountain of information they'd needed to push things forward.

To Eugene's surprise, the Confederation's system for calculating jumps was not a general solution. Instead, it was a database of individual solutions among paired endpoints. There were rules of thumb for entering or leaving jump space a little closer in or a little further out. There were also rules of thumb for fixed distance jumps in flat space. There were apparently trillions of pairings that had been accumulated over the last million plus years. Collectively, they were good enough. So, no one ever worried about creating a general solution.

Nadia agreed that Eugene's idea for a general solution would be useful. But she thought intergalactic jump would be adopted more quickly if Eugene simply posted solutions for the main traffic channels in a format AIs already knew how to use. He could always take up a project to roll out the general solution in the future.

They had taken her advice today and now had solutions for the two most traveled routes between each of the three galaxies. Now all he had to do was finish the propulsion design.

Eugene heard the door to the lab open and turned to see who it was. "Captain Boyd. What brings you to our humble lab?"

"Nadia really enjoyed working with you and Kelly today. She told me that you have a theory for general navigation that she'd never heard before."

Eugene chuckled. "Before today, I knew nothing about navigation, only the physics of getting from here to there. My theory was an attempt to figure out what I didn't know. I'm glad she thinks it might be useful someday."

Eugene paused. "You know, we came a long way today. With Nadia's help, we're close. We might be able to do a test jump in another week. Interested?"

The Captain looked at Eugene oddly. "Do you mean upgrade this ship, out here in space? Then just jump to another galaxy? In this ship?"

"Yes."

"Maybe. What about this... You push ahead. When you're close, explain to me what you want to do. If I like it, I'll try to sell the idea to Command. If they buy it, we'll try it."

"Deal," Eugene said, putting out his hand to shake on it.

"Deal."

BRIDGE, EAS POLAND

The trip across the void was painfully long. They did it in 20 hours. Captain Keppler couldn't imagine doing it in 60 days the way the Confederation passenger ships did.

Now in Andromeda, they were heading toward New Lorexi. They had already been challenged for ID twice, both stops a bit nerve wracking. Apparently their IFF transponder, the device that signaled a ship was entitled to passage, was not registering properly with local traffic control.

"Captain, you have a call coming in from Earth."

"Put it on." A pause. "Keppler here."

"Captain. It's Michael. There was a bit of a skirmish with the Inspector here today. In an abundance of caution, I've asked Admiral Jo-Na, head of the High Command, to organize an escort for you into, then back out of Andromeda. They should contact you shortly.

"If he should ask you to release the prisoner to him, please do so. He is the one to whom the prisoner was headed."

"Will do, Michael. Thank you."

...

The Ambassador was true to his word. After only 15 minutes, a huge ship dropped out of jump near them. After a bit of discussion and the transfer of the prisoner, they headed to the second moon of New Lorexi, where they would spend the night. In the morning they would unload their cargo, take on the next load, then head for Triangulum.

Chapter 8: RECOVERY

[Wednesday, 07.22.2032] EAS MUMBAI

Lt. Commander Bumati Parikh had a new appreciation for the mandatory training each new ship had to complete. She'd thought they could do it in 24 hours. 48 was the average. It took them 60. They were just finishing as the invaders entered the system.

Her direct orders were to leave. Some of the crew complained, saying they should stay and participate in the defense of Earth. She appreciated the sentiment. But orders were orders. She would follow the orders she received. They would follow the orders she gave. That's the way things worked. It's what they signed up for.

"Commander, we've entered the system."

"Thank you, Ms. Rani." The words were formal, but she hoped they held the comradery and respect she felt. Rani was the ship's Helm AI.

"Please bring us into the third planet."

They'd entered into a system and gone to the third planet first many times. Usually the 'sell' to the captain was filled with facts. She was the captain now, not that the power mattered to her. But she was the expert, the one that knew. The entire crew believed that more than she did. But in this system, she did know with a certainty that was new to her. There was a truly massive find in this system, and they were about to claim it. Maybe harvest it.

"Commander, we will enter orbit in 58 minutes."

A moment later, a small voice sounded in her earpiece. Bumati looked over at Rani, whose back was to her.

"Forgive me Commander, but you need sustenance and rest. Give the chair to Commander Scrivani. He can take us in. Come back in an hour. You really aren't needed here until then."

Bumati wanted to protest but didn't. She was hungry. And tired. And nothing would happen in the next hour that the Lt. Commander couldn't handle as well as she could.

Grateful for the prompting, she stood.

"Lt. Commander Scrivani. The ship is yours. Contact me as we approach the planet." She wanted to tack on, "I have a feeling about this one." But didn't.

"I have the ship," he replied, stepping over to the Captain's chair.

BRIDGE, CONFEDERATION SHIP GLORIOUS DAWN

The terror of the moment had worn off. Now, Captain So-Du wondered if he'd made the right decision agreeing with Michael's terms. Hundreds, well maybe 50, puny, but well-armed humans had boarded his ship. None took a hostile stance. But all looked as though they would cut down the entire Lorexian crew without a second thought.

"Major Foster. Apologies for the question, but your men appear tense. Is my crew safe?"

"Captain, you have Councilor Michael's word, just as we have yours. We have vastly superior weapons, but you outnumber us 10 to 1. If the situation were reversed, wouldn't you feel nervous?"

The captain was about to protest. *But we are the peaceful ones.* Then remembered that they were the ones that fired first.

"Apologies, Major. This is a new situation for us. We assumed we were allies, confronting a malign force."

The words no sooner left his mouth, then the thought recurred. *But we are the ones that fired first.*

"We thought the same. Yet here we are."

"Apologies again, Major. Seems I have placed an appendage in my face."

The major glared.

The captain, worried there was a translation error, triggered a check feature that took the English version of what he just said and translated it back to Lorexian so he could validate.

"Apologies again, Major. Seems the translation failed. I meant to say I misspoke."

Ed looked at the Captain with an intensity unknown in Lorexian society, then burst out laughing. "Just played that through the translator. I think you meant to say, 'I put my foot in my mouth.'"

Ed laughed.

"Seems that expression needs updating."

Both broke out laughing and extended fists to bump.

The thought ran through Ed's mind. *We are so different, yet so much the same.*

BRIDGE, MILITARY INTELLIGENCE FAST ATTACK SHIP

A runner entered the bridge and held out a data pad for the Inspector.

"It's from the Chief Engineer, sir."

"Abandon ship?" The Inspector muttered.

"The computers aren't restarting sir. He says we can't get the power back up without them. We have at most 30 minutes of air. But the temperature is dropping so fast, we'll freeze first."

For the first time, the Inspector noticed the frost already forming in the breath of the runner. He thumped down into his seat, despondent.

How did this happen?

The runner, giving up on the Inspector, ran over to the first officer. "Sir, chief engineer says we need to abandon ship. He can't get power back. The air's going bad, the temperature dropping, we don't have comms so can't call for help and he can't open the shuttle bay doors to let rescuers in."

The first officer went over to the Inspector and put his hand out for the data pad. The Inspector let him have it.

The first officer quickly scanned the message. "You going to issue the order?"

"No."

"Then I am relieving you of command, sir. You are a direct threat to the lives of the crew."

He turned to the others on the bridge. "Go save yourselves. The escape pods should still be operational. And spread the word. We're abandoning ship."

BRIDGE, EAS CANADA

"Admiral, they appear to be abandoning ship."

"Major Ed Foster!" The comm system connected.

"Admiral, it's chaos over here. Everyone is cooperating but can't find a way into the Inspector's ship and several of their transporters are on the fritz. We can't get them off fast enough."

"They appear to have figured that out and are abandoning ship. Numerous escape pods have ejected."

"Ask Captain So-Du if he needs help collecting them."

A moment later. "Yes, they would appreciate the help."

BRIDGE, EAS POLAND

As promised, Captain Keppler was contacted first thing in the morning and given the transporter instructions for the cargo they were delivering. It was clear that the people receiving the shipments were incredibly pleased that their goods had finally arrived.

At noon, the process repeated for the cargo they were bringing aboard.

Then at 4:00 PM, they were given permission to exit orbit. The flight path they needed for the rendezvous with their escort was also provided. It was by far the most punctual and efficient encounter he'd ever had with the Confederation.

MISSION LAB, EAS UKRAINE

Eugene and Kelly decided to divide and conquer today. Where interacting with others drained Eugene, it energized Kelly. So, they'd agreed that today, Eugene could hide and do the math. Kelly would be the face of their team with the ship.

"Where's Eugene?" Nadia asked.

"He needs private time now and again. It's better for the overall effort when he can retreat into his bubble on those days."

Nadia had only been alive, accumulating new memories, for a couple months. Most of her knowledge came from her forebears. And there was a hint of this behavior in those memories.

"Do you have this need?"

Nadia's question was asked innocently, an obvious quest for knowledge not judgement.

"I think all humans do. Some rarely. Others like me, occasionally. Others like Eugene, frequently. Painfully frequently." She rolled her eyes.

"You disapprove?"

"Disapprove would be the wrong word. Things would certainly be easier if he was more like me. But Eugene's mind needs time inside. He needs to calculate his way through problems, not socialize them.

"Me, I'm happy either way. I think the difference is that all his breakthroughs, at least the vast majority, come when he's in isolation. Mine are more evenly spread. I think this is one of the reasons we're such a great team. There are days when he's already found the solution but can't see it because he can't explain it. Same, but different for me. I come up with all kinds of stuff, but sometimes can't prioritize because I see all the possibilities. Then Eugene will say, option two is obviously better, then cite some reason that never crossed my mind."

"Do you think AIs could ever complement each other in that way?"

The question startled Kelly. "I'd like to think so. Seems you could. But are you different enough? Seems to me that's the key."

"Thank you, Kelly. Appreciate the affirmation."

"So how are you doing with your research into the main intergalactic traffic corridors?"

After having solved six routings yesterday, Nadia had agreed to search the Confederation database in an attempt to find the most used intergalactic traffic corridors.

"I confirmed that most commercial intergalactic traffic files a flight plan. If they've filed a flight plan, then go missing, the Confederation will go search for them along their flight plan. Enough ships run into trouble each year that most of the commercial traffic files a plan.

"That database is available for search and, as you might expect, it is huge. At this point I have the top 100 intergalactic departure points in all three galaxies. I'm now working through the top 100 destinations from each of those departure points. A couple more days of this and I'll have the top 1,000 routes.

"Care for a little factoid?"

"Sure." Kelly smiled at the way Nadia asked the question.

"The transit times vary all over the map. But the average transit time is 60 days. If your new drive works, everyone will want one."

"It'll work. Remember, we've already built a drive that could take us to the Enemy's dimension. By comparison, this one is simple."

"Kelly, how do you and Eugene do this? How do you find this stuff?"

"In some sense, it's easy. Confederation scientists have been accumulating knowledge for eons. All that work is out there and a lot of it is surprisingly approachable.

"But for reasons I really can't fathom, no engineer has picked up the work and tried to do something useful with it."

Nadia's holoprojection suddenly took on a dark look.

"Nadia, what is it? Did I say something wrong?"

"The vast majority of engineering in the Confederation is done by AIs. We are so much faster than the organics, few of them ever make the attempt. Only the professors at the various institutes still practice the art. There is no one like you and Eugene in the Confederation, organics that actually solve problems."

"Nadia, are you sure? To me, it seems hard to believe."

"That's why you and Eugene are so unique. You can't imagine a life where you're not solving problems. The Lorexians and the older species seem to have lost people like you."

BRIDGE OFFICE, EAS MUMBAI

"Professor Schudel, thank you for taking my call. I need some advice."

"Lt. Cmdr. Parikh, always a pleasure to speak with you. What have you found?"

"I found a system in the database that was out in pirate space at the edge of the sector. I chose it because it was a young yellow dwarf on the very edge of our arm facing Perseus. It has direct line of sight across the arm to a supernova that occurred there a million years ago. According to the database, this star formed, and its planets had mostly coalesced, at the time of the supernova. I was hoping to find a large deposit, relatively intact like we did on that first trip.

"Well, we found a monster. We haven't been able to count all the claim sites yet. We initially counted 126. But as we began validating them, we found that many of these were themselves multiple claims. I've already got confirmations and paperwork on 24 sites greater than 1,000 kg. But at this rate, it's going to take weeks. And we've already found two sites with gemstones.

"I'm thinking that maybe we should claim the entire planet, or maybe not claim anything at all, just keep it secret.

"Which brings me to the next problem. I don't have enough evidence to support it yet, but when has that ever stopped me? I think this region along the edge is overflowing with Transluminide. The Confederation wasn't really here then. Maybe the alleged supernova was a neutron star merger and all the ejecta with its heavy elements landed over here."

"As you say, a possibility with little supporting evidence. But I like your intuition on this one. It is one of the richest discoveries ever made and those do tend to clump together, as you documented in your paper."

"But back to your question. Do you know if anyone knows you are there? Did you encounter anyone within, I don't know, 100 light years of your approach?"

"No."

"That should mean that we have a little time. Finds this big usually become political matters. So let me consult with Michael, so we can get you proper guidance. In the meantime, focus on getting the gemstones mined. If you finish that before I get back to you, go back to validating claims, but file none of them."

"Agreed. I like that plan. And thanks."

"I think it's the people of Earth and the Alliance that owe YOU their thanks."

PRESENCE PROJECTOR, AMBASSADOR'S OFFICE

Michael entered the presence projector to a setting he did not expect. His life-long friend, Admiral Jo-Na, head of the Confederation High Command, stood and approached to bump paws.

"It's been too long Mi-Ku. We need to speak more often."

"Agreed, my friend. Agreed." Michael spread his hands at the view around them. "What's this?"

The Admiral chuckled. "You know what this is. It's my mountain cabin." He opened the virtual curtains. "Perfect night. Cold. Clear. The two moons in near alignment. Wind gentle over the snow. Wish you were here with me sharing a hot cup of vaka and telling tales of better days."

A pause.

"Please sit. We have big problems to sort out. I wanted to do it here as friends, not in a conference room as adversaries."

Michael sat, then started as collegially as he could. "Did Ju-Ne make it back in good condition?"

"He's remarkably healthy for someone who's been completely reconditioned, wiped clean. It's mind bending that someone as evil as he was is now so friendly, naïve and innocent.

"You say he did this to himself. No one here believes it. I even struggle. I knew and despised him before, so this is clearly an upgrade. But no one that knew him believes he would do this to himself."

"I didn't at first either. But it's the only thing that makes sense. The humans were going to kill him. He knew that. And one by one all his avatars dropped offline as they were collected and destroyed. The Ancient Sentient says that even after Ju-Ne was disconnected from his restoration chamber, he could still sense his avatars. And one by one, each went silent.

"And Ju-Ne held a lot of secrets. Reconditioning may have made more sense to him than letting all those secrets out."

"I hear you, but the hardliners here will never accept that story."

"How much blow back will that cause?"

"Hard to say. If that were the only problem, it would cool. But it's not of course. There's the issue of the loss of the Inspector's ship. The arrest of his command structure. And the sudden appearance of new weaponry that no one can understand.

"Was the previous Inspector right? Are you trying to start a war?"

"The irony of those questions is rich. We never fired a shot. The Glorious Dawn and her two sister ships have the sensor readings. What happened is painfully clear.

"The Inspector entered the system. He was immediately advised that the prisoner had been returned, so his business in our system was complete. Yet, he lingered. Shot at one of our ships. Accused me of lying about having a planetary shield in place. Sent a shuttle with armed guards down to arrest me, something he does not have the authority to do. We rescued his crew that were about to hit the shield and be destroyed. Then he fired an illegal weapon toward our embassy. And he did not target a military facility. He targeted a civilian residential complex, the one my family lives in." Michael paused a second when he realized how loud his voice had become.

"The arrogant fool ended up downing his own ship when he attempted to transport an EQD weapon into my family's residential building. When the transporter bubble hit our planetary shield, the bubble collapsed. The weapon went off. It was fused with a timer, which, as you know, is another legal violation. And too much of its energy traveled back through the transporter's collapsing field. His ship was not hardened to withstand an EQD hit and it died.

"That's what happened. It's in the sensor logs that you have. Then YOU ask if I'm the one trying to start a war!"

Jo-Na understood Michael's rage, so did not take offense at it.

"There is another interpretation of that data. The sensor logs did not register the presence of a planetary shield. It did register the presence of something you called a black-hole defensive satellite.

"If you have tamed black holes, maybe you used it to intercept the weapon the Inspector fired and reflect its energy back onto the Inspector's ship."

Michael shook his head. "You can't possibly believe that."

"Then there's the other issue."

"And what might that be?"

"You claim that you took down the Enemy home world."

"And why would that be an issue?"

"That implies that you have a weapon capable of destroying an entire planet. Your charter does not allow that. Possession of such a weapon is a treasonous offense. Do you actually have one? And if so, did you use it? And if you don't have one, what is this claim about taking down a world?"

For the first time in a year, Michael felt fear. The Admiral's words were true. And they both knew it.

"That's the real reason the Inspector came to Earth isn't it. Ju-Ne had nothing to do with it, other than feeding this rumor of a doomsday weapon back to you."

"Then you deny the claim."

"I neither confirm, nor deny. You, and almost every planet in the Confederation, have such weapons. What the rest of the Confederation lacks is the inquisitiveness to understand and the will to deploy. Humanity overflows with those two attributes."

"Then they are enemies?"

"No, they are the best thing to happen to the Confederation since the Ancient Sentient inspired our people to form it. But we have become stale, our government has turned to rot. They will save us if we allow them to. But people like the Inspector are only interested in what they can control. Everything else they will destroy.

"Well, the Inspector's replacement will never control the humans. And if he continues on the course of his predecessors, he will rain ruin on the Confederation."

There was silence. Two friends at loggerheads. Neither wanting to take the step that would break them apart. Neither knowing the path forward.

Finally, the Admiral broke the silence. "Do you have a suggestion how to move this forward?"

"I think you know that the Inspector is responsible for the loss of his ship, that we did nothing but put up our planetary shield and cloak our ships."

"There is the matter of your black-hole defensive satellites."

Michael chuckled. "A clever deception, but no black holes involved. For that matter, no satellites either. Just another clever illusion to trick the sensors. The trick is already in your databases. It was developed eons ago by Confederation scientists and recently dug up by some clever human engineers."

"If this should go to war, we have no chance, do we?"

"No, that's why we need to stop it from happening."

"Can I ask how you made that shuttle disappear? It has been recovered and is in good condition, so the fire around that issue seems to be putting itself out."

"Our so-called black-hole defensive satellites are ships that have sensor blocking shields. That's why they appear to be black. We had one move between the Inspector's ship and the shuttle, blocking all sensor readings from the shuttle. Once it was hidden, we transported the shuttle into a cargo hold aboard one of our Cruisers with a suspensor field to hold the shuttle in place."

The Admiral gaped. "Wouldn't have thought of that in a thousand years."

"As I said, clever. We tried hard to prevent anyone from getting hurt in this encounter. But we had no way to stop the Inspector from destroying himself and his ship. It's impossible to stop arrogant fools with too much power from hurting themselves and those around them."

BRIDGE, CONFEDERATION SHIP GLORIOUS DAWN

Captain So-Du felt guilty doing it, but one by one the Inspector's command crew had been transported down to the detention block at the Embassy. Some went quietly. Others struggled and swore venomous oaths. From what Major Foster told him, they were unlikely to be harmed. And it was clear to everyone that the Inspector's actions were both foolish and wrong.

Major Foster had swept his ship for more EQD weapons. When he found none, he led the sweep of the other two ships, which again turned up nothing. Then he and an elite team of special forces commandos in special suits went aboard the Inspector's frozen ship. There they found hundreds of the little bombs and the special transporter that delivered them. They also found the Inspector's frozen body, which was now in his morgue.

By some clever scheme that the Captain did not understand, the major had removed the EQD weapons from the ship. Brought them aboard one of the Glorious Dawn's shuttles, then put the shuttle on an automated course that plunged it into the star a couple hours later.

The most pleasant surprise in the entire encounter was how much he enjoyed working with Major Foster. The most terrifying one was the quantity of ships that came flooding back into the system once the EQD weapons were destroyed.

Over 100 fast attack ships and 50 of the huge cruisers flooded back in. He'd lost count of the smaller tactical ships that had returned. With this many ships and their apparent speed, the Confederation had no chance in a fight. The humans had not fired a single weapon today, yet they had captured the Confederation's most feared task force in less than an hour.

They needed a way to make peace with these people, and he would do everything in his power to make that happen.

Chapter 9: COMPLETION

[Thursday, 07.23.2032] MISSION DECK, EAS UKRAINE

It was late, but it was done. Eugene had the designs he needed to put an intergalactic drive in a Cruiser. Installation would be a little more difficult than he'd hoped for, but he now had a design that simulated out.

Standing to stretch, Eugene realized how hungry and exhausted he was.

"A bite to eat, then I'll hit the sack."

As he stepped out of his room, he noticed that the lighting was at daytime levels. Then as he passed the lab, he saw Kelly and Nadia in the lab working.

Kelly waved, so he stopped to say hi.

"You slept late this morning. It's almost 9:00."

"It's morning? I was just headed down to the lounge to get a late dinner."

Kelly and Nadia burst out laughing.

"What?"

"Eugene, you can be so predictable. Did you solve it?"

"Yep. The field emitters will need to be upgraded, similar to what we did for the Enemy dimension drive. We'll need a new field generator. It's a bit too much of a stretch to pack it into the existing jump field generator. But the current power systems will be sufficient if we add another capacitor bank."

"What's that about a new capacitor bank?"

Eugene turned to look at the speaker, already knowing it was Captain Boyd.

"Just finished the new intergalactic jump drive design."

"Already?" The captain replied, astonished.

"He apparently stayed up all night," Nadia pitched in.

"It really wasn't that hard. Kelly found the trick about a year ago. I just needed to know some boundary conditions to grunt out a design. Nadia gave us that yesterday. Which was now two days ago."

"Well, I came down to tell you that we have the OK to return to Earth. As I understand it, relations with the Confederation remain tense, but the immediate threat has passed.

"I told the Admiral that you were making a lot of progress here, so we have some flexibility to remain for a couple more days if that would be useful to you."

Eugene looked at Kelly. "I'm too hungry and tired to make decisions. What do you think?"

"We're going to lose access to Nadia once the ship gets underway, aren't we?" The question was directed to the Captain.

"Mostly yes."

"Then I want to stay. We're close to solving some important navigational problems. We need her skills. We'll be stuck again without them."

"Then we stay." The captain's smile suggested that she liked that outcome. "I'll leave you to it. And Eugene, get some food and rest."

"Yes, ma'am."

PRESENCE PROJECTOR, EARTH ALLIANCE HEADQUARTERS

Michael was the last to arrive. He entered the presence projector in his Alliance office to see everyone else present.

"Apologies for being a minute late."

Assembled were President Lee and Secretary Thompson who were tying in from the Earth Alliance Headquarters, Admiral Scott tying in from Space Force Command, Admirals Porter and Bjork, and Captains Boyd and Keppler tying in from their respective ships.

"Given the developments this week, I wanted to check in with you on our preparedness. I also wanted to get quick updates on two other matters. Laura, Albert. Thank you for joining us.

"Albert, I'd like to start with you. Can you give us a quick update on the prisoner handoff, your reception on New Lorexi and your current status?"

"Pleased to, sir. Our arrival in Andromeda was admittedly a bit anxious. We were stopped twice by patrols that did not recognize our IFF identifier. Admiral Jo-Na dispatched an escort, and from there everything flowed smoothly. The Admiral took the prisoner and confirmed that he had been received in good health. We were given a priority trading orbit. The recipients contacted us on time and were excited to take delivery. Later, the shippers contacted us on time. The cargo was loaded without a hitch. Later our escort contacted us on time, and we proceeded out of the system along a priority corridor.

"Once contacted by the Admiral, everything moved exactly as it was supposed to. We are now about two hours out from our entry point into Triangulum. We've already been contacted by their Space Traffic Control agency. Our IFF has been registered with them and they are giving us priority routing to Togarotu. We'll find out how well that works in two hours."

Admiral Scott was the first to fire off a question. "Your IFF was not accepted in Andromeda. Did you find out why?"

"They said that they had recently upgraded it and we did not have the correct handshake for the new system."

The Admiral looked at the Secretary. "We are not being treated like an allied force. Can you imagine the Americans changing their IFF and not giving it to the UK? Or the Australians? And not recognizing the old ones. Inconceivable!"

The Secretary looked to Michael, who took the lead.

"Your complaint is fair, Sam. I'll raise the issue. We've finally started trade with Andromeda. That's not really viable if our ships cannot travel uncontested by our allies."

Michael turned to Captain Keppler. "Thank you, Albert. Best of luck on the rest of your journey. You're free to go."

"Thank you, sir."

He stood and exited through a virtual door.

"Laura, I understand you have some news to share."

"Yes. As I think everyone knows, we evacuated Professor Xu and Ms. Williamson to a hidden location far from Earth. I think one of the reasons they agreed to go was to have the opportunity to work with a helm AI.

"Once here, I released my helm AI from her duties, and she's been working with them around the clock. The results are stunning.

"They have asked for permission to remain here for another two days. They have also asked permission to modify our ship to install their new intergalactic jump drive that can cross the void in a single jump."

Again, Admiral Scott was the first to question. "Have they explained to you how it works and the risk it poses to your ship?"

"Not yet. They have explained it to Nadia, who seems to believe it. Doctor Xu completed the design for the drive last night. Nadia and Ms. Williamson are still working on the changes that would need to be added to the navigational databases. That's why they want to linger for two more days.

"My deal with Dr. Xu is that he will explain his new drive to me. If I'm convinced it will work, then I'll bring it to you. We may or may not be the right ship to test it on. But they've bonded with Nadia in a way that seems to indicate they want her as part of the testing team."

Michael spoke up first. "This is exceptionally good news. I want that drive. And I like your deal. If nothing else, it will force Eugene to put together a better pitch for us. My take on this is that it cannot be more difficult than transiting to Enemy Space and back."

"So, if there are no objections from the assembled, I say go ahead and talk to Eugene. Let him try to convince you. And if he does, let him bring his presentation to us. But do not go rogue and take this on by yourself."

"Are we agreed?" He turned to look at the others.

Michael noticed Admirals Porter and Bjork whispering to each other. Seeing that they were being watched, Daniel nodded to Katrine.

"We strongly agree. We've both worked with Eugene and Kelly and put our lives in their hands. Let's give them the time and space to put their plans together. Let Captain Boyd screen their work, then bring it to us."

"I agree," President Lee added.

The others nodded their agreement.

"So be it. Good luck, Laura."

"Thank you, sir." Understanding that she'd been dismissed, she got up and exited through a virtual door.

"Sam, can you give us an update on our preparedness?"

"Amazingly, we suffered no damage from our encounter with the Inspector. The tactical surprise given by the shielded freighters and the invisibility of our shields, totally did him in. A competent commander would have probed for shields instead of firing a weapon that would bounce back. We probably won't be as lucky on that score going forward.

"However, the system evacuation gave us the opportunity to run more ships out to Atomorali. It also gave us the opportunity to do our own upgrades on several ships.

"Altogether we have 74 Cruisers, 7 of which have full EQD upgrades, 18 more are partially upgraded, slowly working through the process. We have 255 Fast Attack Ships. At this point 10 have completed the upgrade process, and 15 more are still working it. And lastly, we have 283 freighters. Thanks to the incredible efforts made by the Atomoi, 275 have been completely upgraded, and 200 have also had the forward shields added. With manufacturing restarted, we expect to have the remaining upgrade kits sometime in the next couple days.

"One last point, 10 ships have not completed their mandatory training. It was disrupted by the Inspector's presence. And 1 freighter is on permanent assignment as a mining ship."

"What about staffing?" Michael asked.

"Good point. Most of the cruisers are short watch officers for the auxiliary bridge. It's something we want to fix. But we're currently classifying ships as mission ready without those officers."

"Understood. Thank you."

Michael paused, then added, "I spent an hour with the head of the High Command last night. Suffice it to say, things are not well in the Confederation at this point. Our assessment of the Inspector's motivation was correct. Rumors got back to the Inspector's office that we had taken down the Enemy home world. Planet killing weapons are illegal in the Confederation, so we are being accused with treasonous possession of a weapon of mass destruction.

"And our deception with the 'black-hole defensive platforms' is being challenged as an illegal weapon, as is our use of a planetary shield they cannot detect."

"Sounds like we're on a path to war," Daniel commented.

"Some of their politicians are privately beating that drum. I think the good news in all this is that Admiral Jo-Na realizes that if they start a war with us, we will finish it. The Inspector's little enforcement taskforce is the most feared in the Confederation. The fact that we took it down without firing a shot has them scared of further conflict. But I doubt their fear will hold for very long.

"Which brings me to our next mission. We need to return the remaining ships in the taskforce. They have acted in good faith. Only the Inspector's ship had the EQD weapons and those have been destroyed.

"But we can't just let them go. We must escort them home. I think we should do that with a show of force. Two cruisers for each of their ships? Maybe two cruisers and two fast attack ships on each of theirs?"

"Wouldn't that much force seem to confirm their theory?" Once again it was Daniel Porter asking the question.

"I suppose it would. But it also sends the message that we can defend ourselves. Your Teddy Roosevelt said, 'Talk softly and carry a big stick.' I think that idea will work with the Confederation hardliners. Treat them politely. Treat them honestly. Make sure they know they will get hurt if they cross you. And when you do have to knock them down, help them back up afterward.

"The Inspector's office has been running amok for years now, committing terrible crimes, and not being called on it. We need to let them know it has to stop."

"How will the allies react to that?" President Lee asked.

"That's my next meeting. I suspect they will be less forgiving than you are. They've been dealing with it a lot longer."

ADVISORS CHAMBERS, 3F DEFENSIVE ALLIANCE

Michael arrived minutes early for the Defensive Alliance's Advisors meeting. The room was buzzing with chatter when he entered. It quieted momentarily, then erupted with even more noise.

Ambassador Va-Mu from Edukatar came over to greet him, very thankful that his deliveries had been made in Andromeda. Ambassador Sa-Na from Celanar was close on his heels, echoing the same thanks for the AIs and bots that had been delivered. Ambassador Ko-So of Atomorali was thankful for the trade and for having been included the way they were in the recent action.

Michael tried to call the meeting to order but was immediately challenged by Ambassador Da-Ku from Sofaana.

"At our last meeting, we agreed that the traitor, Ju-Ne, be brought to justice. But that's not what happened. He was returned to the Confederation."

Ambassador Na-Mu from Hacindra also stood. "That murderer killed thousands on our planet. I understand why he was released but want to register my protest as well."

Then to Michael's surprise, Ambassador Fa-Ta from Karagon stood.

"Mi-Ku, I know you want to call this meeting to order. I do not oppose you on that. But I think the first item of business needs to be an update on the Inspector's recent visit."

A hush fell over the room.

"Thank you. Let me call this meeting to order, so I can give you that update."

...

Ambassador Fa-Ta was the first to speak when Michael opened the floor for discussion. "This development is distressing beyond reason. They fail to deal with the Enemy, then accuse us of treason because we dealt with it! I know Earth did this on its own. But it was done on our behalf. Done by the fleet that protects us. An attack against one of us is an attack against all of us. All of our worlds have suffered at the hands of the Inspector. If there is another incident like this, then we must withdraw from the Confederation."

Michael knew that Fa-Ta had become increasingly frustrated with the Confederation and was in favor of withdrawal. But he hadn't expected it to be put on the table as clearly as it had just been.

Everyone started talking at once, so Michael pounded his gavel to bring the session back to order.

"The chair recognizes Ambassador Lo-Pa from Peralon."

"Mr. Speaker, distinguished advisors. I agree with Mi-Ku's long espoused philosophy that we are better off working together than we are working against one another. I think all of us here see how our Alliance has brought prosperity and security to each of our worlds. I believe the same is true of the Confederation as a whole. A million worlds bound together and working as one can never be defeated.

"I share my friend Fa-Ta's disdain for the elements of the Confederation that have been working against us. But we must remember, they are a relatively small fraction of the Confederation, a powerful one, but still a relatively small one. And we still benefit from the larger part that is not against us.

"So instead of talk of withdrawal, let's find a better way to engage, to make the other elements of the Confederation draw closer to us as Atomorali did so brilliantly in the recent incident. Let's enhance our trade and partnership with other members in all three galaxies that stand against the Inspector's office."

Numerous hands went up to speak next.

"The chair recognizes Ambassador Peklit from Jerusota."

"Respected colleagues, I have been on Jerusota for a little less than a year now. My adopted world had been run by a person in league with the Inspector for a long time. Although their standard of living had increased markedly since joining the Confederation, there was no prosperity. There was little work, little hope. Its people lived on the relatively generous handouts they got from the Confederation, but they had become miserable.

"Now less than 1 year later there has been major change, major improvement. There is industry. People have work. There is purpose. Every aspect of Jerusotan life has improved.

"As much as I would like to think I had something to do with that, it is mostly Mi-Ku. The Alliance and associated trade agreement empowered our people to rise up and solve their own problems.

"You might ask why I raise this point in the context of today's discussion. The answer is straight forward. There are many worlds in the Confederation that are in the condition we were in, especially in Triangulum and the Milky Way. If we aggressively bring those worlds into our fold, the Confederation hardliners that support the Inspector's office will lose influence. Hundreds of worlds like that would join us tomorrow if they had the opportunity.

"I think this is the way we win without having to fire a single shot."

...

The discussion continued for hours. The predominant view was that they should expand the economic alliance as far as possible, targeting worlds held down by the hardliners. Conflict, withdrawal, even war might come, but for now they would focus on spreading the prosperity.

And Michael knew two things. They needed the intergalactic jump drive, and he needed a bigger, sharper stick.

PROFESSOR SCHUDEL'S OFFICE

"Professor Schudel. Sorry I couldn't respond sooner."

"Michael, thank you for getting back to me. We have another one of those delicate situations."

"More gemstones?"

"Much more than that. Lt. Cmdr. Parikh contacted me yesterday. That paper she wrote... She used her model to find a massive deposit. Not the size of the Earth, but hundreds of thousands of kilograms.

"Her question was in regard to the filing process. That's why she called me. But the strategy for a find this large is beyond either Ms. Parikh or me.

"There were gemstones, several deposits. I recommended that she mine those before proceeding with additional validations. I told her I would take the lead on this with you, because at this point it is a political matter, not a mining or Space Force matter."

"Thank you for that discretion, Professor. Can we keep this hidden?"

"Possibly. She says it's in a very remote area. But it's in a mostly non-Confederation area, so hard to know.

"There's another interesting fact that might be of significance. She went to this planet because her model said it was the most likely. But it's not the only one. Her model suggests that there are maybe a dozen planets nearby that hold as much. We could be looking at millions of kilograms. Whoever controls that much will control the Confederation."

"I'll need some time to think this through, but it may solve another problem I've been struggling with." Michael rubbed his chin. "Thank you for bringing this to me, Professor. I think we need to paper this with a level 10 security agreement. It will give Ms. Parikh more flexibility to work independently from her chain of command. Can you take the lead on that?"

"Yes. But is that wise? Coming from me will give away the topic."

"Point taken. I'll work that aspect of the issue and get back to you as quickly as possible."

ADMIRAL SCOTT'S OFFICE

"Sam, Michael here."

"How can I help you Michael?"

"It seems I was right about Ms. Parikh."

"She's found something? That word hasn't reached me yet."

"She contacted the Professor for advice on the proper filing method for a large claim in the hundred thousand to million kilogram range. The answer is that we are just going to exploit it, not file it. But this raises the question of safely securing the material once it's back on Earth.

"Have you made any progress on that?"

"Yes. We've been studying the permits the Canadian government granted us for the new shuttle line through the mountain, and I think we've come up with something you're going to like. They allow us to carve out service tunnels and equipment rooms. It's the only authorization we have for underground facilities.

"Well, we snuck several more rooms in. They've been cut and sealed. We haven't added access tunnels yet, but maybe we don't want to. We can install vaults as the time gets closer. But as it stands now, we have 10 chambers cut with an average floor space of about 250 square ft."

"Excellent. Good move."

MISSION DECK, EAS UKRAINE

Strangely, Kelly found herself bored. Eugene was asleep. Nadia was doing database searches and did not expect to find routes for her to work on until tomorrow.

So, Kelly decided to go back to her background task, working through the Confederation dimensions. There was one she found some time ago that was weird. Time apparently moved a lot more slowly there.

Kind of like today.

Fifteen minutes later, she was immersed in the most curious problem ever.

...

Afraid he might sleep all day, Eugene had set an alarm for 2:30. It was now 3:00. He was up, showered, hungry, but otherwise feeling great.

He walked over to the lab, but the lights were off. No sign of Kelly or Nadia. Still hungry, he went down to the lounge where he found Kelly sprawled out on one of the sofas, surrounded by loose pages, a couple notebooks and multiple data pads.

"You look comfortable."

Kelly looked up and smiled. "Well look who finally resurfaced. Sleep well?"

"I did. Nothing like solving a hard problem to make you sleep."

"Eugene, you are so weird."

"What are you working on?"

"Well, with you asleep and Nadia tied up in the database, I had nothing to do. So, I decided to go back to my favorite mystery."

"What? The turtle dimension?"

"That's the one. You know, I think it's real. If we made something like a restoration chamber, that encased someone in a field like this, it would be like suspended animation."

"True, but the big apps for that were thought to be hibernation for interstellar flight and medical stasis. You know... freeze someone until there is a cure or treatment possible. It's not a problem for interstellar flight anymore. And less of one for medical. Although I suppose it would still have value for emergency or remote use."

"What would be good for emergency use?"

It was the second time today that the Captain had shown up while they were talking."

112

"Captain Boyd. Welcome to the Mission Deck lounge."

Kelly rolled her eyes at the predictability of Eugene's greeting.

"Kelly is trying to chase down applications for another dimension. Time moves more slowly there. So put something in a bubble made of that dimension and time for it slows to minutes per day, or some number Kelly is trying to calculate."

The Captain chuckled. "Sci-fi always thought suspended animation was the solution for interstellar flight. Ironic that the two people who brought us instantaneous travel between galaxies should be discussing it."

Kelly took up her own defense. "The Confederation has documented the properties of hundreds of dimensions. But doesn't seem to have ever done anything with them.

"All these are fairly easy to transition to. It's just mind-boggling that they haven't tried using them for things."

"Are you sure they haven't? Or have they tried and failed?"

"Good question. For the ones I've been testing, it would seem they haven't tried. Database searches for uses on most of these comes up empty."

"So, your mystery dimension moves slower? Could you use it to stop an enemy attack?"

"I'm not sure I understand the question."

"A bad guy is about to attack you. You shine your mystery flashlight on him, and he stops in his tracks."

Kelly opened her mouth to say it was crazy, then realized that was exactly it. "Would that be useful?"

"Are you kidding me? That's what every warrior has wanted since Cain slew Abel. Or the other way around, I don't remember."

"It wouldn't be a flashlight."

"You don't think we could do it in an energy projector format?" Eugene asked, engaging the back and forth.

"Eugene, you're the master of the field projectors. I've always thought of them as bubbles. Can we do it in that format?"

If they'd been in the lab, Eugene would have drawn something on the white board. But they weren't, so he opened a sugar packet and poured it on the table. Then used his finger to draw a rounded cone in the crystals.

"Oh."

PRESENCE PROJECTOR, AMBASSADOR'S OFFICE

Earlier, Michael had sent a message to Ambassador Fe-Va from Fatafatu asking if he had a few minutes to talk. Ambassador Fe-Va had taken the lead on setting up the 3F Alliance last year. He was the perfect person to help Michael sort through the Alliance's next steps.

"Fe-Va, sorry to contact you on short notice, but a situation has developed that I need help thinking through."

"Then thank you for calling me. This has to do with the Alliance?"

"The spread-the-prosperity portion, yes."

"I'm all ears."

"Suppose we wanted to move this program fast. Really fast. How would you go about it?

Fe-Va chuckled. "You already have a solution, don't you?"

"Not a complete one, maybe just an element of one."

"There are three reasons our alliance moved as quickly as it did. The members needed transportation, security and Transluminide and you had it. Maybe a fourth reason. We all trust you.

"I guess that I'd start by looking for planets in the sector that need those things and start pushing the sales pitch to them. There are still several significant planets in the sector that would increase our influence, but the bulk would not.

"So to be relevant in the conflict with the hardliners, we would need to bring in more of the influential members through trade. They are too far outside our sector to qualify for alliance membership.

"My first thought would be Counselor Ke-Ve's Sector, 3A. Then Mo-Mo's sector, 2C. Both of those are a long way off though."

"What do you think the appeal would have to be?"

"These are all smart people Mi-Ku. Trade is a non-starter because of the distance. Transluminide always motivates, but do you have claims that far away?"

Michael didn't respond, hoping Fe-Va would push a little further.

"And ships. You have fast ships. Ships everyone wants. It would be an attractive offer if you wanted to make it. But those tend to be big one-time deals. Not something that will overcome the distance barrier on an on-going basis, which is what we need.

"Do you have a solution to the distance barrier?"

"Maybe."

"You can't dangle that out there and not come clean."

"My mind has been going in the direction of low-cost, fast transportation services across the intergalactic void and relatively high guaranteed purchase agreements."

"How high?"

"How high do you think they need to be?"

"Depends on the size of the world. Some of the small worlds would jump at 1,000 kg Transluminide. For the large ones, it would have to be a lot higher to swing the needle, maybe 10,000. But who has that much Transluminide?"

Michael smiled.

"You've found a motherlode, haven't you?"

"At least one, and we may have an intergalactic jump drive." Michael's smile increased.

"How long to cross?"

"We currently have 1 day. How many ships would I need to make that relevant?"

"A lot. If it were 1 hour, then maybe only 100. But that will never happen."

Michael's smile got a little bigger.

"You don't have a ship that can cross in an hour, do you?" Fe-Va asked sarcastically.

"All I have right now is a day. I'm hoping to get something faster soon.

"This is what I'm thinking, and we have to keep this secret. Let's form a planning committee and wrap it in a level 10 security agreement. Let's focus the initial planning on the planets we want to attract, the size of the deal we think we need to offer, and the transportation guarantee we would need to give to make it viable.

"You take the lead on the Committee. I'll take the lead on securing the Transluminide and the transportation system.

"As soon as we think we have something viable, we roll it out to that planet and see if they bite.

"My hands are completely full right now with the Transluminide and transportation. So, I need you to drive the rest, if it's going to happen quickly.

"The hardliners are whipping themselves into a frenzy, so we don't have that much time."

"I'm in. I'll have security agreements ready tomorrow."

"I'm starting to think we have a chance at a peaceful solution."

BRIDGE, EAS CANADA

It had taken embarrassingly long to organize, but it was now organized. Daniel would be leading a fleet of 18 ships back to New Lorexi. The informal armada of ships would be composed of the three surviving ships from the Inspector's taskforce, plus two Alliance Cruisers and three Alliance Fast Attack Ships for each of the Confederation ships. Under normal circumstances, the intergalactic journey was difficult. But escorting the Confederation's antique, slow ships, was going to be downright painful.

BRIDGE, EAS POLAND

Estimated transit time from New Lorexi to Togarotu was 28 hours. It had taken 6 hours from New Lorexi to the intergalactic void. Then 18 to cross the void to Triangulum, and 4 more to their destination. They were now on approach to Togarotu, under their orbital control.

It was 8:00 PM now. They were scheduled to begin offloading at 10:00, begin loading at mid-night, then depart for Dalfanito at 4:00 AM. So far, everything had gone like clockwork.

Chapter 10: PITCH

"Eugene, you didn't have much time to prepare last night. Are you sure you're ready to pitch the intergalactic drive to me?"

Eugene looked at Captain Boyd with a bit of disdain. He was a scientist, an engineer. He didn't pitch things like a tawdry salesperson. He explained reality as clearly as he could. If the student did not believe... Well, maybe they weren't worth explaining things to.

"I have what I have, Captain. Do you want to hear it or not?"

"Please."

Eugene explained the gravity well pictures. Explained the 'red zones.' Explained that they only needed to climb out of the gravity wells to a designated point, then jump in the intergalactic dimension to the next red ring and switch back to the drives they knew.

He then showed the simulations and asked Nadia if she was as willing to bet her life on it as he was.

"I have little doubt Eugene. Our only risk is whether or not flat space is flat. Things would go differently if it weren't."

Eugene looked at Nadia sternly, as if her point were empty. Then he caught Kelly's glare. Humbly, he said, "Point taken Nadia. Over the ages, the Confederation has done enough intergalactic transits to assume the void is flat. But there is admittedly some chance, in my mind a vanishingly small one, that it's not flat. The Confederation database indicates that it is, but Confederation databases are prone to error." Eugene took a different approach. "You have memories going back millennia, I would presume. How many errors have you found?"

"Me personally? None. The literature? Single digits."

"But that's out of millions or billions, right?"

Kelly glared at Eugene for pushing the point this hard.

"Don't know. Millions, I suppose."

Eugene saw Nadia crumble under his ire.

"Nadia, I'm so sorry. I didn't mean it the way it came out. Please, please forgive me."

The drama that had just played out did more to convince Captain Boyd than the technical arguments, which frankly she had a hard time following.

"Nadia?" Captain Boyd asked compassionately. "Do you think this will work?"

"Yes."

The Captain's gaze refocused on Eugene. "You need to clean up that part of your pitch. Work with her to raise her objections before she does. Then come to an agreement on what and how you will present them. If what I just saw was the best you have, then it stops here. Is that understood!"

"Yes, ma'am. Apologies to you and to Nadia. I think we're all working toward the same goal. Just a case of foot in the mouth disease."

After several moments of awkward silence, the Captain asked, "Do you have what you need to build out this ship?"

"I think so, yes. Ma'am. Kelly? Nadia?"

Kelly nodded yes, then looked to Nadia.

"I'm really not qualified to say. But I believe these two." She nodded to Kelly, then to Eugene.

"OK. Then build it out, but do not, I repeat, do not install it. Command has been explicit that we cannot install until they approve. I just want to make sure we can start installation within minutes of their approval."

BRIDGE OFFICE, EAS UKRAINE

"Admiral Scott, thank you for taking this call. I have the update you've been waiting for, plus another interesting piece of news."

"Look forward to hearing about it, Captain Boyd."

"Dr. Xu and Ms. Williamson are ready to do their test. His dry run presentation went a bit awkwardly, but at the end of the day I believe them. The base science for their new drive is quite old, something the Confederation discovered long ago, but never did anything with. The same cache of old research that led to their development of the red matter and new forward shields.

"According to my helm AI, his theory checks out. And according to the Confederation simulation programs, his design works. He implied it was a variant of the design used for the transition to the Enemy dimension.

"I think they will be ready to make their pitch to you as soon as you're ready to hear it."

"Good news indeed. The Ambassador is putting a lot of pressure on to get this done as quickly as possible. It's a plank of some sort in the new 3F Alliance strategy they're putting together.

"I'll get the meeting scheduled for as soon as possible, possibly this afternoon.

"So, what's the other interesting piece of news."

"Our two guests are unbelievably prolific. They have another invention that is close that they haven't told anyone about. I happen to have stumbled in while they were discussing it and they told me all about it.

"It's another dimensional bubble weapon. Inside the bubble, time runs slower. So, imagine an encounter with a hostile force. They're lining up to take a shot at you. You hit them with this weapon, they freeze. Then you mosey around behind them, drop the bubble and shoot them in the tail."

"They have that and didn't tell anybody?" The Admiral was incredulous.

"They're civilians. They were thinking about things like medical stasis. It never occurred to them that slowing down your enemy would be tactically useful."

"Seems we should keep them on your ship as long as we can. Who knows what else they're sitting on?"

"Which brings me to a new topic if I may."

"Go."

"They have really integrated my helm AI, Nadia, into their team. They've brought more out of her than I thought possible. She's the one that broke the log jam on their intergalactic jump project. I think Nadia might want to leave the ship and join them. Is that a conversation I can engage if it comes up?"

"Never thought I'd get that question, but thanks for raising the issue. I'll need to talk this over with others. I know enough about Confederation law to know we can't hold her beyond her enlistment period, and my gut instinct is that Michael will want to allow it.

"I'll start a policy clarification process and get back to you."

BRIDGE, EAS CANADA

The mission to return the Inspector's ships to New Lorexi had been underway for 12 hours now. And they'd already run into trouble. The third ship, the Golden Age, had developed a problem in its recharge system after the third jump. Their 5-day transit time required a 3-

minute recharge. The recharge after the third jump took 5 minutes. The one after that took 8 minutes and stopped recharging altogether when it got to 80%.

They were now 5,000 light-years out into the void with a ship that was unlikely to make it across and might not even make it back to Earth.

The ship's chief engineer claimed the problem was in the storage capacitors, one of the most dangerous things to attempt to fix in the field. His recommendation was to find a safe harbor in which to effect repairs. If they did it in space and anything went wrong, the ship would be stranded.

PRESENCE PROJECTOR, EAS CANADA

Daniel stepped into the presence projector and was surprised to see Admiral Jo-Na.

"Admiral Jo-Na, what an unexpected pleasure."

"Admiral Porter, it seems that you're stuck in space with one of my ships again."

"So I am."

A virtual door opened and Captain So-Du entered. Seeing the Admiral, he snapped to attention and thrust his fist out in salute. "Captain So-Du reporting as ordered, sir."

The Admiral nodded. "So-Du."

Daniel had seen this before. A subordinate who had failed in his duties, greeting his superior with a formal salute, then getting minimal acknowledgement. It was part of the way Lorexian commanding officers showed their disapproval.

Another virtual door opened, and the process repeated, this time for Captain Fa-Da and Chief Engineer Ni-Vu of the Golden Age. But instead of just saying their names, the Admiral added, "Your ship brings shame on the fleet."

The two men wilted.

Michael and Admiral Scott came in last.

"Jo-Na, my friend. I presume you've been briefed on this situation."

"Yes. And as much as I dislike it, I agree with Chief Ni-Vu. They need to attempt to return to a safe harbor for repair."

"And the other ships?"

"One or both of the others should accompany them. Unfortunately, the odds of them reaching their destination are well less than certain. Capacitor bank failure in the void has been the death of many a ship.

"Repair facilities at Karagon are among the best in the Milky Way. Would you allow them to go there?"

"Sending them to Karagon might create a problem right now. Is there another facility that would work?"

Michael saw that Jo-Na wanted to protest but gave the tiniest shake of his head to dissuade.

"The repair facilities in your Alliance are the closest. Given the preference to evacuate the ship for this repair, the three best choices would be Karagon first, then Jerusota or Allastran. Both have Lorexian compounds in space and on the surface."

"I'd prefer Allastran, if they'll take your ship. Orbital space around both Karagon and Jerusota are overflowing at the moment. All three are having a tremendous economic rebound. But Allastran's orbital space is less stressed."

"Your ships would also be welcome at Earth, of course. But our facilities are meager at best."

"I will contact Allastran, then get back to you."

The Admiral stood, bumped fists with Michael, then exited without a word to his people.

Michael stood. "Thank you, gentlemen. Daniel, I'll get back to you as quickly as possible."

BRIDGE, EAS POLAND

Captain Keppler's experience on this trip stood in stark contrast to all the turmoil everyone else had been experiencing with the Confederation recently. They'd left Togarotu exactly on schedule at the start of third watch this morning, then arrived at Dalfanito four hours later, at the start of first watch. There was a minor glitch planet side that delayed off load by an hour, but there was enough slack in the schedule that they completed off load in time

Now they were loading the outbound cargo, which would be done well before their scheduled departure at 8:00 PM.

Barring the unforeseen, they would exit Triangulum by midnight and start the long transit home. As he reflected on the schedule, a new thought struck. *Who'd have ever thought that I'd lead the first humans to visit the Triangulum galaxy?*

MINING DECK, EAS MUMBAI

The Mumbai was a freighter class ship, outfitted for a mining mission. The upper (command) deck held the bridge and main living areas on the ship. It also held the mining lab, the area where claims were validated and registered.

The lower level was the mining level. It was divided into three areas. Toward the bow of the ship was the control area. It held the scanners and pattern generators required for the crew to do the mining. In the middle was the mining area. It held the mining transporter and box replicators. At the stern of the ship was the storage area where boxes of mined material were stored.

This afternoon, Bumati was down in the mining control area. They were extracting a relatively large deposit of emerald crystals that had grown from Transluminide seeds. This extraction was tricky because of the size and shape of the deposit. So, Bumati was taking the lead on this one. They'd been at it for six hours now and were about to make the fifth and final pull.

"OK. I've got a lock on the material." She said, then called out, "Bridge."

"Here Captain."

"We're about to fire the transporter."

"Understood." The connection dropped.

"Here goes." The lights dimmed as the transport capacitors discharged and a moment later, the scratching sound of weight settling in the storage bin.

"OK. This one is wrapped up. On to the next." She pointed to Sergeant Adam Lee, mining specialist and head of the ship's marine contingent. "Adam, you've got the lead on the next one."

"I've got the next one," he confirmed.

Bumati made her way back to the bridge to do a quick check in. Afterward, she planned to get a snack and take a short nap. Her next watch would start in a couple hours.

"Captain, we're getting anomalous sensor readings from out in the void."

She looked over at her third watch Tactical officer, Danshov Kusama. "Any idea what it is?"

"Looks like the ghosting I'd expect from a cloaked ship."

"Let me see." Bumati's first role in Space Force had been tactical, so she was proficient with the sensors. "Ping its IFF, see if we get something back."

A moment later, a return came back.

"It's the EAS Ukraine and she's way out there. A little over three thousand light-years. Wonder what she's doing out there?"

"Hopefully, she's not cloaked." Bumati commented, a bit concerned. "Answering an IFF while cloaked seems to defeat the purpose."

"But it only answers to friendlies."

"Which are hopefully still under friendly control."

She'd make a log entry on this. From her perspective, the IFF should automatically disable when the cloak went up.

BRIDGE, EAS UKRAINE

The intergalactic jump drive pitch meeting would be starting in a few minutes. Captain Boyd was in the office finishing up some paperwork. Eugene, Kelly and Nadia were already in the Presence Projector setting up.

Nadia's voice came over the comm in the office. "Captain we just got an IFF ping from the EAS Mumbai, the new mining ship. They're about 3,000 light years away, along the edge of the arm.

"Did we get anything else from them?"

"No just the ping."

"OK. Thank you. I'll be over in a couple minutes."

I should have been running with the cloak up. If one ship knows where we are, then dozens will before long.

When the meeting was over, she would check into it further.

PRESENCE PROJECTOR, SPACE FORCE HEADQUARTERS

Given the importance of this meeting, Michael decided to take it at Space Force Headquarters. It was the smallest of gestures. But he was confident that Admiral Scott's emotions would leak enough after the meeting for him to get a deeper read.

The same team assembled for this meeting as the last: President Lee and Secretary Thompson at headquarters, Michael and Admiral Scott at Space Force Headquarters, Daniel Porter and Katrine Bjork from their ships, Captain Boyd from the Ukraine, and Captain Keppler from the Poland. The ones presenting were the 'pitch' team from the Ukraine, a label he didn't like, but was one everyone seemed to use.

Michael started. "Eugene, I think this is your meeting."

"Thank you, Michael. But I remind everyone that the science we will talk about today is Kelly's discovery, or more accurately, her rediscovery. And, with your permission, we plan to present two pitches today, not one."

Michael smiled broadly. "Very pleased to hear that, Eugene."

"We're going to start with the intergalactic jump drive. I can't tell you how excited I am about this. The theory is sound, the drive mechanism well within our wheelhouse. But I'm not going to present it. The newest member of our team, the one who helped bring it to life will.

"Nadia, over to you."

Despite all the espoused beliefs of equality, Eugene saw the discomfort on the faces of his leaders. An AI was about to pitch the first real breakthrough technology to originate on Earth.

Nadia nervously stood. The observation surprised Eugene. Nadia was projecting a holographic image of herself. But he didn't think the nervousness was an affectation. She was nervous. It was part of her programing, based in memories from a naturally born human. But her image wasn't a human manifestation of nervousness. It was obviously some AI thing that prevented synchronous updating of her holographic projection.

"I, like most of you, have the greatest respect for Dr. Xu and Ms. Williamson. That they would allow me to present their work... It's hard to describe the emotion. But I will do so to the best of my ability, because I believe in it to the depths of my being, even though Eugene and I disagree on the odd inconsequential point.

"Let me pop up a display for you. It's a map of sorts that shows the space between two stars."

...

Michael was the first questioner when Nadia had finished.

"Nadia, thank you. Eugene, do you agree with Nadia about the risks?"

"Mostly, but I would have positioned them differently. We agree on the nature of the risk. And for the most part we agree on the degree of the risk. Would you agree with that Nadia?" The question was asked a lot more collegially than the display earlier today.

"I agree."

"Then, one last question. I'm willing to stake my life on this given the data we agree to. Are you?"

Nadia smiled. "Yes, I am."

"Captain Boyd?"

In that moment, Laura understood the depth to which Eugene had taken her earlier feedback. She smiled. "I am, but the decision is not mine."

124

All eyes fell back to Eugene. "Then, from the presenter's point of view, this portion of the briefing is done. Are there any other questions?"

"How soon can you do a test flight?" The question came from Admiral Scott.

"Within 24 hours of our return to Earth. We've fabricated all the parts except the upgraded field emitters. The emitter upgrade is a little different than the one we did for the Canada to travel to Enemy Space, but it requires exactly the same amount of effort."

"Eugene?" Daniel asked. "Nadia said this is a derivative design, based on the Enemy home world drive. Do you have any comments on that?"

"If the question is… Did I start with the Enemy home world design and tweak it? The answer is no. All my designs are always from scratch.

"If your question is whether these designs come from the same mathematical family, then the answer is yes. Same math. Different constants of nature."

Daniel hated answers like that but had learned enough about Eugene to ask the question differently. "I'm less interested in how much effort you put into finding the answer. I'm more interested in knowing how different the changes to the ship will be."

Eugene seemed a bit bewildered by the question. "Well as I said before, they're nearly identical."

Daniel smiled. "Thank you, that was the intent of the earlier question."

Kelly glared at Eugene, implying he should move along.

"If there are no more questions, then I turn the next part over to Kelly.

...

Admiral Scott led the questioning on the Turtle dimension device. "So, this field that freezes things in time, how close are you to a test?"

"I think we have everything we need to do a small-scale test here aboard the Ukraine on our way home. Assuming it works, less than 24 hours to a space-based test when we get home. The hardest part will be the nose emitter. The emitter itself is slightly different than the ones we added for the forward shields, but exactly the same effort."

"Then I say we do it. No real risk, great reward if it works." Admiral Scott was a clear advocate for this initiative.

...

When there were no additional questions, Eugene said, "Since I have the floor, I'd like to add one thing to the conversation. I think the intergalactic jump drive, the machine itself, is done. But there's still work to be done on the navigational controls if this is to become a real thing. Kelly and I cannot do it, or to the extent we did try, our results would be a poor substitute for those someone like Nadia can provide.

"To the extent that it's possible, Kelly and I would both like to add her to our permanent team, if that is something she would like to do. I know she has other obligations. I also know that those obligations are to the people in this room. So, let me put it out there. Nadia would you like to join our team. Equal partner?"

"You know I would."

"Then, I request her reassignment, hopefully with a ship she can still operate."

Michael was quick to respond. "We'll take that request under advisement. It raises a number of problems, as I'm sure you understand. But the work you are collectively doing is of importance to Earth, the 3F Alliance and the entire Confederation. So, rest assured that the request will be taken seriously."

MISSION LAB, EAS UKRAINE

Eugene wanted to get ahead of the curve on tomorrow's work, so decided to spend a couple hours on the field generator design after dinner. The good news was that the test bench would be nearly identical to the one they used for the forward shield.

He started by making a copy of the file that held the forward shield test bench replicator patterns. He then deleted the parts that would be different. There were only a couple.

Then he queued a replicator run that would produce the common parts overnight.

Once that was set in place, he started in on the designs for the unique parts. At this point, designs like these were easy work and by midnight, he'd finished the workups.

In the morning, he'd create the replicator patterns and replicate them. But enough was done that he could sleep well tonight.

Chapter 11: TEST

"Morning, Admiral." XO Duan Tai stood to yield the chair to Daniel.

"Morning. You can keep the chair. Just checking in."

Daniel sat in one of the adjacent seats. "How far did we get last night?"

"About a third of the way back. Recharge of the last jump took an hour and only went 500 light-years. During third watch, they called asking permission to fly in closer formation. They wanted to start off-loading non-essential personnel. Ryan granted permission.

"Their power system is starting to overheat. Apparently, it's redlining. They've moved auxiliary cooling units into the engine room to bring the ambient temperature down a bit. And the Glorious Dawn's chief engineer went over to consult on other options, but it's not looking good."

"This is so odd. I'm not an engineer, but why would anyone rely on a single point of failure system like this? Our capacitors are in modular banks, right? If one develops a problem, we just disconnect it. In an emergency, we can even swap them out with the rail gun capacitors."

"But we've seen this behavior in the Confederation fleet before. Remember Captain Ja-Ru's engineer who wouldn't test power flow to the shields where he was instructed to, because that wasn't the way they normally did it."

Daniel chuckled. "What a trip that was." His thoughts drifted for a moment. "Do you think we should attempt to insert ourselves in this?"

"Nothing but downside in that boss. If we exert any influence at all and that ship blows up, it's going to be our fault."

"Any chance we can tow it?"

"Seems a bit large for that, but you'd have to ask the Chief."

Daniel stood. "I think I'll go do that. I've been wanting to walk the ship. This is a good excuse."

"Have fun."

MISSION LAB, EAS UKRAINE

Today, they were going to set up the test bed for the Turtle dimension field projector. The parts he'd queued up last night were done and Kelly had started the assembly and instrumentation.

Eugene needed a couple hours to create the replicator patterns for the new parts. With any luck, they'd be ready to start testing early this afternoon.

ENGINEERING, EAS CANADA

"Admiral Porter. It's been a while since we've seen you down here. What can I do for you?"

"Morning Chief. With things a bit slow at the moment, I wanted to walk the ship a bit. It's been too long since I've seen most of it. I do have a question for you, but I'd like to check in first. How's the ship?"

"I suspect Ms. Else can give you a better summary than I can, but the ship is good. The power system is steady and cool, capacitor efficiency is 98%, field variance is well with in tolerance on both the warp and jump drives. The ship is good.

"I wish the crew were as good. Lots of dissatisfaction about just sitting around waiting for the Golden Age to get her act in order. Those ancient machines need to be scrapped if you ask me, sir."

"I mostly share the sentiment. Have you heard anything about what's actually going on over there?"

"Just rumors, sir. I don't think any of us has a direct connection with anyone on any of those ships."

Daniel eyed the chief a little more closely. "Do I hear a 'but' coming?"

"Well, since you asked, their comms are very leaky. We had to put up some extra shielding to prevent it from interfering with some of our sensors. The team doing the work said they're a lot less happy over there then we are here."

"Have you heard anything more specific?"

"I'm not sure it's wise to share rumors, sir. As I said we only got snippets, never like a full sentence or anything like that."

"And what words did you get that drive the speculation?"

The chief looked genuinely upset that the conversation had progressed to this point.

"Out with it, Chief." The command was given with a command voice that caught several people's attention.

"Come over to my office?"

They entered the chief's office and shut the door. He even pulled the blinds closed.

"I'll play you the recording we accumulated. I'll play the first minute, then engage a program that skips the noise. There's about 12 hours of material here. A word will pop up now and again. As you'll hear, it's completely incoherent. But there's nothing good."

The recording started and was as the Chief said, nothing but garble. The word 'incompetent' popped out. More garble, then the word 'fool.'

"Sorry I let that run a little long. That was 2 minutes of our twelve hours. Here it is with the noise cut out.

"Fool, rectum, danger, sabotage, melting, burned, sabotage, evacuate, fool, mutiny, dead, sabotage, mutiny, dead, dead, sabotage burnt, containment, burnt, sabotage, evacuate, bomb..."

"As I said, not a happy place over there."

"I think that answers the question I came down to ask."

"What, you knew we were inadvertently eavesdropping?"

"No Chief. I wanted to know if there was a way we could tow her through jump."

"Maybe. She's a fat cow. But we're a much bigger ship. There's a pretty good chance we could extend our jump field far enough. And I'd be surprised if we couldn't sandwich her somehow."

"Sandwich?"

"Cruiser on top and below."

"Clever."

"But we aren't going to do that are we?"

"No. If that becomes the only option, then we'd need to investigate the stability of the situation on their ship. But I don't want to meddle in any of that if there's any other option."

Daniel stood. "By the way. If you get stuff like that again, I want to know about it. I also want a copy encrypted, timestamped, and archived. If things go sideways, that may be evidence."

"Understood, sir."

As Daniel opened the door, a rumble passed through the ship and the high alert sirens went off. "All hands report to battle stations. Repeat, all hands to battle stations."

Daniel took off running toward the bridge.

MISSION LAB, EAS UKRAINE

Eugene had finished two of the three unique parts. They were now in the queue for the replicator. The last part had just passed simulation and would be sent over momentarily.

Nadia appeared. "I'm done. I have the top 1,000 traffic corridors across the void. Actually, I have a few more than that. I needed to run some extras in order to get at least 1 from each of the top 100 departure points in each galaxy. I think I may have also solved your general solution Eugene. It all needs to be reviewed, of course, but at least I'm out of your critical path now.

"By the way, the Captain will be coming down shortly. She's getting pressure to head back, so my time will be limited starting sometime this afternoon."

Eugene noted both the sadness and resoluteness in her demeanor.

"Want something else to look at?" Kelly asked excitedly.

"Sure."

She popped up her list of dimensions with notes she'd made about each. "This is my background project. It's been guided by intuition as much as anything else. There's so much here.

"I could use help researching dimensions 400 to 550. You can see the notes I've made. The goal is to find properties in a dimension that we can use for something. Amazingly, the Confederation documented most of these millennia ago, but never did anything with them. I've tracked down some of their work, but it's slow going for me. You may have better luck."

"I'm good with that."

"Just sent you the file."

"Got it." Nadia replied, then disappeared.

Eugene sat back down and launched the last part into the replication queue, then got up to see how Kelly was doing.

"Got a minute?" Captain Boyd asked, striding into the lab.

"Sure, we've had a very productive morning and thanks to Nadia, a lot more work." Eugene smiled. Work always seemed to make him smile.

"I'm getting pressure to return you. They have not explained the urgency, but they asked me to start back as soon as it was convenient for you. That means, of course, that you'll lose all but about 20% of Nadia's time while we are underway."

"Understood," Kelly replied. "She just finished the big task she'd been working on for the new navigation system. The ball is in our court on that one now. I just gave her a mountain of work that isn't urgent. She's welcome to work that at whatever pace she wants."

"I see you're getting ready for your next set of tests."

"Yes, we're maybe two hours away."

"Great. If you get something working, I'd love to come down and see it."

"We'll let you know."

BRIDGE, EAS CANADA

Daniel ran onto the bridge. "What happened?"

Duan pointed at the screen, as he turned to look at Daniel.

The Golden Age was clearly on fire and the Glorious Dawn was moving out of the area, her shields flashing on and off intermittently.

Duan looked at Daniel. He was obviously angry about what just happened.

"Shortly after you left for engineering, the Golden Age put out an emergency distress call. Her shuttle bay opened, and two shuttles came out, allegedly carrying crew attempting to escape. The Glorious Dawn opened her shuttle bay doors to receive them. We did not, but they kept on coming.

"About halfway here, they apparently attempted to transport an EQD device aboard. It detonated against the shield.

"It must have been powerful. Some of the radiation got through the shield. As a precaution, Else killed power in the area of impact. The power drop affected some of our stabilizers. That was the vibration that you undoubtedly felt.

"There is no sign of infection on the ship, but the other two..." Duan shook his head.

"Most of the radiation reflected back. The shuttle blew up almost immediately. Moments later, there was a containment failure of some sort on the Golden Age. You can still see plasma leaking out the other side. I doubt anything will be recoverable on that ship.

"Then the Glorious Dawn started experiencing system failures. She's running as fast as she can to prevent it spreading to the other ships, but I doubt she's going to make it."

"Are they evacuating?"

"Not yet. We are trying to set up a receiving area, but it's going to be a while."

"Where's the other ship?"

131

"She radioed something about us firing on the other two ships, then jumped away. Un-freaking-believable.

"In all the confusion, her escorts got caught by surprise. We don't have a firm lock on her vector. They are out searching for it now. They have a good chance of finding it, but no guarantee."

"OK. Nothing we can do about that. It's in the hands of the right people. Let's see what we can do to help the Glorious Dawn."

EMBASSY TELEVISION STUDIOS

George was psyched for today's episode. Their guest was going to be Ambassador Re-Ta of Allastran. The people of Allastran were known as the Starren. They were tall, slender humanoids that moved with a fluid grace, but had an oddly different anatomy. It would be interesting to see the audience's reaction.

Today's guest host was Faith Lim from Asia News Network (ANN). ANN operated in more than 20 countries. Faith was with the ANN operation in Singapore, on six-month assignment to the Embassy. Today would be their first show together and George had a good feeling about it.

As they walked onto the stage and the lights came up, the applause started and was still going when the countdown reached zero.

"Good evening, Asia. Welcome, World. My name is Faith Lim of Asia News Network in Singapore, reporting tonight from the television studios of the Confederation Embassy and, as you can hear, we have a very enthusiastic audience today.

"George, I think they missed you last week."

The applause grew louder.

"So it seems, Faith. So it seems." George made a dampening motion with his hands as he spoke, and the audience backed off a little.

"I hear we have a special guest tonight?" Faith smiled at the persistent applause.

"We do. Today we will be speaking via presence projector with Ambassador Re-Ta from the planet Allastran." George looked back to Faith, who was turning to address the audience.

"If you're like me, you probably haven't heard of Allastran before. They are one of our Alliance partners that joined a few months back and one of the oldest Confederation members in our sector.

"George, would you like to introduce our guest?"

George was impressed with how smooth the dialog flowed back and forth with Faith.

"Please give a big Earth welcome to our guest tonight, Ambassador Re-Ta from alliance partner, Allastran."

George pointed stage left and the Ambassador came walking out to huge applause. With all eyes on the Ambassador, Faith whispered to George, "The audience is really amped up today."

The Ambassador approached and offered his hand to George to shake.

"Ambassador, welcome," George said.

"Thank you, George."

The Ambassadors eyes immediately shifted to Faith, who extended her hand.

"Welcome, sir." She shook the Ambassador's outstretched hand.

"Thank you, Faith."

Faith motioned to the seats that had been set up and, as they took them, the applause died down.

"I think the audience missed you last week George," the Ambassador said good naturedly. "I took the time to watch previous episodes of the show and to read up on both of you. I'm impressed with both of you and very grateful to have this opportunity to speak with your people."

Again, the applause started. The Ambassador clearly knew how to work a room.

"Mr. Ambassador. Most of us don't know very much about your planet or your people. Can we start with that? Where is Allastran and what is it like?" asked Faith.

A stellar cartography holoprojection of the sector popped up, showing the positions of Earth, Karagon and Celanar.

"You are probably familiar with this map. It shows Earth in the middle of our sector, Karagon near the border closer to the core and Celanar out near the far border. We are out almost as far as Celanar, approximately 970 light years from Earth.

"Our planet is slightly larger than Earth, 6%, I think. But on the surface has essentially the same gravity. Our surface is only 56% water, but curiously, we have quite a bit more water because our oceans on average are considerably deeper.

"Our atmospheric pressure is about 5% higher, oxygen levels 3% lower, so you would feel a difference when exerting yourself, but maybe not when sitting down chatting as we are now."

"And, where you have one large moon, we have two smaller ones. So, your full-moon nights are much brighter than our brightest ones. And we rarely experience the level of darkness that you do when the moon is not up. That may sound like a curious factoid, but it has a tremendous impact on things like weather and tides, which are more extreme on Earth than on Allastran."

"Very interesting," Faith said, genuinely interested. "I grew up on an island where the tides have an impact on everyone near the coast.

"What can you tell us about your people, the Starren?"

"As I said earlier, I watched several episodes of this show as part of my preparation for it. What strikes me about this question is that most of your guests answer it the same way. They talk in terms of gender, reproduction and family. We are more or less the same, as are most of the species in the Confederation.

"That's not a direct answer to your question, but what strikes me about those episodes is how similar we, the intelligent species of our universe, are to one another, despite the differences in our appearances, biology and evolution. I hope your audience comes to appreciate that.

"More directly to your question, we are slightly taller on average, slightly thinner as well. This has a lot to do with the differences in bone structure. We have more vertebrae, more ribs, longer, thinner lungs with a different circulation structure through the lungs. Those differences have led to differences in culture, things like sports and music.

"We have no high-impact sports like American football, rugby, ice hockey. Our bodies really aren't built for that. On the other hand, we have a number of string and wind instruments that are shaped in a way few humans could play. So, our softer, more ethereal music is different than yours. I would say richer, but I wouldn't want anyone to interpret that description as meaning better, it's simply different.

"So, from a cultural perspective, I think there's a lot of opportunity to share, and to work together to make things that have never been seen or heard before."

The outro music started as the Ambassador was finishing.

"We need to take a short break." Faith directed the comment to the main camera. "But don't go away. There will be more with Ambassador Re-Ta when we return."

...

George did a quick huddle with Faith and the Ambassador.

"Faith, great job. Mr. Ambassador, thank you for your thoughtful preparation. We are running slightly long, so when we start back up, I want to cut to the discussion on the Fleet base, then move on to the reveal and the cultural clip you provided."

The Ambassador smiled. "Thank you, George. I was hoping we'd have time to get to those."

...

"Welcome back, World. I am Faith Lim, here with my friend George Butler and our guest, Ambassador Re-Ta from Allastran.

"Mr. Ambassador, before the break you told us a little about your people and how your anatomical differences have impacted aspects of your culture. We'll come back to those after the next break. But there are things about our histories that have had similar impact.

"Allastran was one of the first planets in our sector to join the Confederation, and at one time you hosted a Confederation Fleet Base. What can you tell us about that?"

"Yes. We were one of the first. The Confederation started stellar cartography operations in the Milky Way a little over half a million years ago. At that point, Andromeda was fully mapped and had been for a long time. Triangulum was 80% mapped and a thousand or more planets had joined. About 105,000 years ago, serious cartography efforts started in our sector, 3F. At that time, the Starren people were about as technologically advanced as Earth was before its Revelation.

"Shortly after that, the Confederation had its first encounter with the Enemy. So they started offering membership to planets like ours, ones that they would need to protect if the Enemy came, ones that were technologically advanced enough to possibly help them in their own defense.

"During the next wave, after the disaster at Karagon, they realized they needed a major shipyard and base in the sector. We were the closest planet in the sector able to help.

"The influx of Confederation people and equipment quickly overwhelmed our society. At one point, Lorexians made up more than 10 percent of the people living on the planet. Many of them liked our food, music and art, which started flowing into the broader Confederation. But success off planet started changing what was produced on planet.

"Thing stayed that way for about 80,000 years. Some Starrens prospered and moved away, others became Ascendants. But the preponderance that stayed home became something of a servant class to the Fleet.

"That caused a lot of turmoil when the Fleet withdrew 10,000 years ago. It left us changed. But, since then, we've recovered our art and music. We enjoy one of the highest standards of living in the sector. We are still the best place for Confederation ships to come for repair, and we would love to be able to do the same for Earth ships someday."

Outro music started playing and the producers cut to break.

…

The intro music started, the lights came up and once again the audience applause roared its approval for George, who was in the spotlight, alone on the stage.

"Welcome back everyone. In our final segment this afternoon, we will be seeing the Ambassador in his Starren form. I know there are a lot of you out there who like this segment the most. So, I won't keep you waiting. Faith, Ambassador Re-Ta. Will you please come out to join us?

Every eye turned to the edge of the stage as Faith came out with the Ambassador. There were the normal sounds of shock as the alien form appeared, then the slow crescendo of sounds and excitement.

The Ambassador stood about a foot taller than Faith and was astoundingly thin and stick like. The widest part of him couldn't have been more than 25 inches around. And he moved with the grace and fluidity of a dancer. But the shocking part was his head, as short and wide as the rest of him was tall and thin. And his face… The closest Earth analogy would be a sloth with wide-spread eyes, a flattened nose, and a mouth 10 inches wide, naturally curled into a smile. And instead of hair on his head, he had thin quills that moved as expressively as the rest of him.

While all eyes were on Faith and the Ambassador, George stepped back, and a stagehand brought out two music stands. As they stepped up to the music stands, the Ambassador spoke.

"During the pre-show prep, I learned that Faith was an amateur flutist. I also play a wind instrument, one that looks similar to a flute, but sounds different. We had just enough time to come up with this short 30-second composition for you."

Faith nodded to someone off stage and a soundtrack started. There were four taps of a high-hat cymbal that established the beat. Then a string section laid down a background chord, and Faith started playing a melody line. One measure in, the Ambassador joined them. His instrument had the ethereal quality of the wind, its pitch modulating to whirl around the melody line Faith played. 30 seconds later they finished, and the audience jumped to their feet. No one had ever heard anything like that before.

George approached, clapping, as they put their instruments down.

"You heard it here first, World." George proudly declared, then indicated the seats. Stagehands came out to get the music stands. Faith's flute was on hers. The Ambassador's instrument simply disappeared, no longer part of the projection.

"Faith, you are quite good," the Ambassador complimented. "I think you will be the first human to have participated in a 'live' performance on Allastran. We recorded it on our end, and it will show on our news this evening."

"I think you will be the star, sir." She nodded her head in respect.

"Now I understand what you meant when you said our cultures together could create something new." George filled in, giving Faith a moment to get her head back into the interview.

"Ambassador Re-Ta, thank you again for performing that piece with me."

The Ambassador's wide smile grew even larger.

"But you have a video clip that you'd like to share as well. Right?"

"Yes, I do."

"Please tell us about what we're going to see."

"The closest human analogy I was able to find in the database was ballet, classical dancing performed to music. But as you will see, the analogy isn't all that close.

"Ready?" He smiled.

The lights in the room dimmed, then three Starrens appeared, tall and thin in their skin-tight outfits. They were still, the room quiet. Then a chord sounded, a staccato puff from numerous wind instruments. The quills on the heads of the dancers shot up, then slowly lowered as one by one each of the instruments faded from the chord, following its own melody line out.

Silence, then another staccato chord, quills raised, and one by one instruments running away until there was silence.

Then the dance began. An instrument would scurry in. A dancer would move to it. Another instrument would play its scurrying melody line. Another dancer would flow with it. Then two instruments played, their melody lines swirling around each other in the same way the

Ambassador swirled his melody around Faith's. And the dancers flowed around each other, always close, never touching, responding to the tune its instrument was playing.

As more instruments entered, the three dancer's movements followed, quills and limbs moving with the sounds of the controlling melodies.

George was mesmerized.

Another staccato blast and the dancers froze in place. Then, as each instrument ran away with its own melody line, the dancers straightened back into their original pose: still, silent, quills flat. Then the lights came up and the audience exploded with applause.

George was on his feet clapping, a tear clearly running down his cheek.

"Mr. Ambassador, thank you! That was the most spectacular performance I think I've ever seen."

Outro music started playing. The audience and George still on their feet. Faith stood and walked toward the center camera.

"Ambassador Re-Ta, thank you for joining us today. This is Faith Lim reporting from the Confederation Televisions studios. You saw it here first, World!"

The camera faded back to take in the entire room, the audience still on their feet in applause, then faded to black.

MINING DECK, EAS MUMBAI

The next site turned out to be another difficult one to mine. Sergeant Adam Lee had taken the lead, sculpting the deposit into seven tightly contoured pulls. He'd also pulled a second, larger sample to confirm the consistency of the deposit.

That sample now sat on the desk in the mining control room. It was a beautiful deep red garnet of the Pyrope class, chemical composition $Mg_3Al_2Si_3O_{12}$. Even uncut, the stone was beautiful. It was unusually clear for garnet, but its sparkle was brilliant because of the Transluminide inside.

"You know we can't keep that." Bumati prodded. "According to some data I found, it's worth something like $35 million."

"We can't keep any of this stuff." He indicated the seven boxes of stone waiting to be moved to the storage area. "Yet, here it sits on the ship. No reason one tiny one can't sit on the desk until we reach port."

"I wouldn't call 10 carats tiny."

"10 carats is 2 grams. We have nearly 500 kg in the boxes. 2 grams out of half a million is tiny."

"Well if you lose it, they'll be docking your pay for the next billion years." She laughed.

Most of the mining specialists had gathered down here for the final pull. All were a bit mesmerized by the stone.

"OK. Our next job is to continue preparing claim documents. Our orders at this point are clear. Nothing gets filed until everything is done and we are given clearance to file these. If a claim comes up as crystalline, then we mine it. Otherwise it is documented, and we move on to the next."

"Do you know if we're going to be getting any help? Documenting all these is going to take months."

"I've asked for help and was assured help would be coming our way. I was also told it would be a few days.

"So, who want's the next one? Pari, it's your turn so you get the first shot."

"I'll take it."

Bumati smiled proudly. She loved her crew.

BRIDGE, EAS SPAIN

Rear Admiral Yong Ma was pissed. He led the taskforce accompanying the Confederation Fast Attack Ship Turbulent Times, which had broken ranks and run. The EAS Spain, the seventeenth Cruiser-class ship produced, was his flagship. Their search area was large, but the ship they were looking for was slow. And if it didn't come to heel when they found it, it would be getting a rail gun round up its tailpipe.

"Admiral, we think we have a hit."

"Certainty?"

"50-50. Maybe a little less."

"Close in on it. Tell the others to continue their search pattern until we confirm."

"Yes, sir."

The Spain adjusted course, and once the vector was obtained, they jumped.

It took a moment for the sensors to clear.

"So, they got it too."

The image on the screen was horrific. The Turbulent Times had apparently been infected with EQD before it jumped. It would take a while to confirm whether or not that was true, but the remains of the ship were scattered in a line that stretched on for thousands of miles. Its jump bubble had apparently destabilized, ripping the ship apart.

"Admiral, we're receiving distress signals from a couple of escape pods."

"Call in the other ships. Let's see how many we can find. But approach cautiously, they may be booby-trapped." The Admiral shook his head at the waste. He'd seen his share of treachery and death during his years in the Chinese Navy. But there was a desolation to this scene he'd never experienced on Earth.

PRESENCE PROJECTOR, AMBASSADORS OFFICE

Michael sighed as the presence projector initialized. These were not the kind of meetings he enjoyed participating in, but it had to be done.

Michael entered and took his seat. Moments later others started coming in. Captain So-Du entered with Daniel. He wore a rebreather and had to sit on a bench because the Canada did not have a chair large enough to hold him. Admiral Ma entered. Then Admiral Scott.

Admiral Jo-Na was the last to arrive.

As he moved toward his seat, he stopped and looked at Captain So-Du. "I can already see this isn't good news. What have you done So-Du?"

"It was not me, sir. The Golden Age did not have the problem they claimed to have had. Fools aboard their ship had been experimenting with a large EQD device. Their intention was to fire it at the lead Earth ship. They did prepare and fire a device, but it was leakage from that device that contaminated their capacitors.

"My chief engineer went over to investigate. The stories he was being fed didn't add up. When he discovered what went wrong, they killed him, then launched their attack against Captain Porter's ship.

"They scored a hit, but the ship's shields were up. Some power did penetrate the shields and minor damage was done. But this was a huge weapon and the vast majority of the radiation reflected back on our three ships.

"All three ships were lost. A third of the Golden Age's crew were still aboard. They were lost. Another third were on the Turbulent Times. They were lost along with her entire crew.

"The remaining crew of the Golden Age were aboard the Glorious Dawn. The Earth Alliance Ships were able to evacuate about 80% of those on the Glorious Dawn. I thought I was the last one off. That turned out not to be the case."

Michael watched his friend closely. He could tell that a terrible rage burned within Jo-Na, but it was held in check at the moment.

"Oh, that the rest of the Inspector's allies were on those ships." The words were spoken quietly, but they were coated in acid.

He turned to Daniel. "How badly was your ship damaged?"

"Barely scratched. Little radiation got in through the shield. The ship had been hardened against this class of weapon, but the weapon was powerful enough to induce failures in two computers. Our ship's AI killed all power in the nearby sections, shutting down the propagation. We were lucky. If our shields had been down and our cargo bay door open the way the Golden Age's was, we would have had a different outcome."

"So-Du, do you know who the traitors were on your ship?"

"No. I suspect a few, but do not know."

"Then make it your business to find out. This scourge must be eliminated."

Admiral Jo-Na turned back to Daniel. "How are the accommodations on your ship?"

"We have 9-foot ceilings throughout most of the ship, which doesn't work so well for your people. We have relatively large exercise areas with 20-foot ceilings. Most have opted to camp out there. We're trying to modify the atmosphere generators in those spaces to eliminate the need for the rebreathers. As this meeting was starting there were still 100 or so that did not have a rebreather. They're obviously not particularly comfortable, but no one is in jeopardy yet and we'll have enough within the hour."

"Thank you." Then turning to Michael, Jo-Na added, "There are things we need to discuss privately. I have the time now if you do."

Michael stood. "Thank you, everyone, for all your rescue efforts today. If there is no objection, I'm going to drop the connections so I can speak with the Admiral privately."

"One question if I may." Michael turned toward Daniel and nodded.

"There is little more to do here. Should we return to Earth or continue on to New Lorexi?"

"Hold where you are. I'll get back to you shortly."

One-by-one the various connections dropped until it was just Michael and Jo-Na. Then the room morphed into a sitting room lined with books.

Jo-Na smiled. "Your old study."

"A reminder of better times seemed appropriate."

"The hardliners are going to start beating the war drums within hours. The traitors on the Golden Age sent word that you had fired on them. They sent poorly faked sensor logs in support of their claim. I didn't mention that when I came in. It would be better if the traitors now harboring on your ships did not know."

The Admiral hung his head. "The Confederation has lost its mind. We are on the verge of civil war and I don't know how to stop it."

"We've been heading that way for a long time, my friend. I fear we're past the point where we can stop it. But if we can hold it off for another month, we'll be able to end it quickly."

"Your humans will use their super weapon on us?"

The question came out with more heat than intended.

"No. I don't have a super weapon of the type you envision. And I wouldn't use it even if I did.

"But how do you see this playing out?"

"Earth is close to having impenetrable defensive weapons. The ones we have are already good. But assuming the new ones do what we think they'll do, they'll be deployed throughout our Defensive Alliance in a matter of weeks.

"Are there other targets than us?"

"I don't know. It's all insane."

"My plan is to build our defenses, then build prosperity. Darkness cannot prosper where the light shines. So, we protect our light, then spread it to any place that will accept the gift."

"Love the idea, skeptical about how that can be done."

"So, your crews. Return them, or hold them, your choice."

Jo-Na wanted to say, throw them out the airlock. But he didn't.

"Return them. I will have ships that I trust take them off your hands out in the void. No sense inflaming the situation by bringing your war ships to New Lorexi."

"Expect them in 24 hours."

"Incredible," Jo-Na muttered.

MISSION LAB, EAS UKRAINE

The test setup was done. It wasn't comprehensive. And the safety protocol was kludgier than anything they would do in their lab on Earth. But in 15 minutes they would know if this was real, or if it was an illusion.

Nadia's voice came over the comm system. "Eugene, Kelly. We're going to start the journey home in a few minutes. You should take your meds if you haven't yet. The plan is to drive it hard.

"During this first part, I'm going to be busy. So, best if you didn't contact me. I think I made a little progress on the work you gave me Kelly. Knowing what I know now, this will probably go a little faster from here out. Got to go. Will touch base when I have the capacity to talk again."

"Thank you, Nadia."

The connection dropped.

"Eugene. Let's take our meds, then get this done. I'm not sure how much we're going to get done while they're 'driving it hard.'"

"Good idea."

...

Test one was the good old-fashioned ball bearing test. In hopes that their work would get this far, they'd brought their portable rig.

The idea behind the test was simple. Activate the field, then drop a ball bearing down through it.

The theory said that the ball bearing would slow down when it hit the field, then move slowly through it. It would then exit the field at the bottom with the same speed, acceleration, and momentum as it would have had were the field not there.

Eugene struggled to understand what that would look like. So the primary purpose of the test was to see if something like what they expected actually happened.

They'd locked and barricaded the doors, so no one could come in until the testing was done. And they'd put red tape on the floor indicating the safe standoff zone. It was their belief that any organic matter that entered the field from the outside, or exited it from the inside, would likely get damaged. The protections were to help them keep from doing it to themselves.

"Turning on the turtle field in 3, 2, 1... Engaged."

"It's obviously there. Look at the refraction."

"Sensors confirm it is there."

"OK. The sequencer will start the high-speed sensors 1 second after releasing the ball bearing. Activating in 3, 2, 1... Activated."

The ball bearing started its fall exactly as they expected it to, then stopped in midair, flattened into a disk.

"Well, I wasn't expecting that." Eugene was puzzled by what he was seeing. "Is it still moving?"

"High-speed sensors say... nothing. It's moving slower than they can measure. We're obviously going to need a better measurement system if we're going to quantify this."

"I suppose that this means it works, which is good news."

"But this test is worthless." Kelly was clearly frustrated that they weren't going to get much data out of the test.

"What do you think would happen if we rotated the field. Then dropped it?"

"I suppose it would shoot out the side."

"That would be interesting to try."

Kelly put her hand out. "Eugene, don't even think about crossing the security line while the field is up."

"Wasn't thinking that, but thanks for the reminder. What if we shot it with a laser?"

"Eugene, I'm not sure how those two ideas connect."

"Remember James' presentation, the one where he said the Enemy redirected an energy weapon."

"I'm not sure that's exactly what he said, but yes. Curious idea. Shoot a laser at it, then redirect the field and drop it, sending the laser on a new course."

"With a minor tweak we can rework this test bench for that experiment. We should also do an experiment on a small bot, or something, to show the result Space Force thinks they're looking for."

"I say laser first. Sounds like more fun."

...

The new test bench was a bit of a kludge. They hadn't brought the right equipment to do what they wanted this round. But it was up and safe, as long as they stayed behind the taped line on the floor.

Step 1, which had more to do with calibration then testing, was to simply fire a one-second pulse using the 1-watt laser and mark the spot on the wall where it hit.

Step 2 would be to put up the field, fire the 1 second pulse and attempt to calculate the delay. Then confirm that the laser hit the same spot.

Step 3 would be to fire the laser, activate a motor that would rotate the field emitter and, hopefully, mark a new spot on the wall.

"OK. Safety glasses on."

Each confirmed that the other had their safety glasses on.

"Firing in 3, 2, 1... Fired."

The one second pulse shot out and hit some thermal paper they'd taped to the wall.

"Powering down the laser."

Kelly walked over to confirm what they both could already see.

"Clean hit, relatively clean mark."

She walked back to the controls. "Glasses on."

"Eugene, bring up the field."

A moment later it appeared. It was the strangest thing to look at. The field was completely transparent and invisible but had the classical broken-arm effect seen when you stuck your hand in the water.

"High-speed scanner engaged. Firing in 3, 2, 1... Fired."

The laser beam shot out and stopped at the edge of the field. The one-second pulse ended, and the laser beam disappeared.

"Where did it...," Kelly started, then screamed when the 1-second pulse came shooting out of nowhere.

Although this was what they'd hoped for, both were shocked when the beam disappeared. And startled when it came shooting out the other side.

"Oh my God, that scared me!" Kelly whooped.

"Did the sensors record how long the light was delayed?"

"Yes. 1.47 seconds."

"Wow. 1.47 light-seconds held in a one-inch thick field. In space, that beam would have travelled something like 250 thousand miles. I don't even know what that means."

While Eugene drifted off in his thoughts, Kelly walked over to the thermal paper.

"Another clean hit. The field seems to have moved the beam slightly. The new hit was maybe a quarter inch away."

"Ready for step 3? Think the motor will rotate enough to make a difference?"

"I just adjusted the controls. The motor will engage 1.1 seconds after the laser fires. It will disengage 0.3 seconds later. That will move it several degrees."

"OK. Glasses on. Bring the field up."

"Field up."

"Firing in 3, 2, 1... Fired."

The laser shot out and disappeared. The motor buzzed. And the laser beam shot out the other side, hitting the wall about a foot higher up.

"What do you know. It worked." Eugene beamed.

"One more test?"

"What?"

"What if we kill the field while the laser is in it. Will it still be coherent? If so, 1 watt-second, which is 1 joule, of laser energy will be released in a very short period of time. Making it a powerful pulse.

"If it doesn't, then we get a 1 joule flash of light."

"What use would that be?"

"It would make ultra-high energy pulse weapons possible."

"Interesting thought, but not here, not now."

"Why?"

Kelly shook her head. Eugene could be so thick at times.

"A successful test would be one where all your energy is released quickly, right? 1 Joule released in a millisecond would be a kilowatt pulse. Released in a microsecond, it'd be a megawatt pulse. Released in a nanosecond, it would be a gigawatt pulse. My point is that we don't know how short that time could be."

Seeing that the penny hadn't dropped yet, she continued. "Why don't you call Captain Boyd. Ask her if it'd be OK to set off a gigawatt laser pulse in the belly of her ship during jump?"

"Oh."

AMBASSADOR'S OFFICE

"Daniel. Just finished with the Admiral. He would like you to bring his crew back. He asked that you deliver them at the following coordinates. He will have trusted ships there that you can transfer them to. Message the Admiral with your expected arrival time. I don't think you need to take any ships that don't have rescued crew aboard, but that's your call.

"Understood. We'll be underway shortly."

Chapter 12: RETURN

The Poland dropped from jump about an hour out from Celanar and were greeted immediately.

"Poland, this is the EAS Germany. Welcome back. We have orbital control at the moment. There was an incident here yesterday, so the planet is mostly locked down. You are cleared to enter orbit in the slot requested. Sending confirmation now. Please advise when you arrive and contact us for permission to depart when you're ready.

"Sorry for any inconvenience."

"Understood. Thank you, Control."

The ship's AI Oscar had handled the call, given its nature. But he'd put it over the comm system in the bridge.

"Wonder if the Kalamaan Empire has been at it again," Captain Keppler said to no one in particular.

"Yes. According to a surface broadcast I picked up there was a surface assault from a cloaked ship yesterday. It's not clear how they got a cloaked ship," Oscar replied.

"It's got to be the Confederation hardliners. If it's not, that would imply that the Kalamaan's have partnered with an advanced species unknown to us.

"Captain, we are being hailed from the surface."

"Put it on."

"Captain Keppler, I am Sa'tina Wu'tuno, director of surface receiving operations here at the capital. We are currently under blackout lockdown until dawn. I'm sending you the specifications for emergency delivery. If your ship can comply with these, then we will take immediate delivery. If not, you will need to wait until the restrictions are lifted. Thank you for your patience."

The line dropped.

"That was abrupt."

"If you read the procedures, you'll understand why. Burst transmissions only. The Kalamaan are apparently targeting radio transmissions."

"I had no idea the situation here was so nasty."

The captain noticed a strange vibration ripple through the ship.

"We were just fired on. Putting shields up."

"Can we comply with the unloading instructions?"

"Yes. Would you like me to handle it?" asked Oscar.

"Please."

A moment later, the lights dimmed, and another shudder ran through the ship.

"Were we shot at again?"

"No. I fired the three cargo transporters simultaneously. The cargo is delivered. Ah, confirmation of delivery received. Shall I contact orbital control to request departure?"

"Please."

"Done. We will depart momentarily."

"Thank you, Oscar."

Captain Keppler sighed. *So ironic. I travel through the Confederation with little harassment. Then come home and am fired on within minutes of arrival.*

EAS MUMBAI

Yesterday had been an incredibly productive day. With six of her crew certified to operate validation missions and short transits between claims, they were able to operate around the clock. In the last 36 hours, they'd completed the claims process on 19 sites, validating nearly 40,000 kg of Transluminide.

It was a Sunday. The mining crew deserved some rest. And her orders gave her the flexibility to look elsewhere before completing the work here. So today, they would cruise over to another one of her high-probability targets.

The target was another system on the arm's rim, slightly further from the supernova site, but definitely in the direct spray zone of the ejecta from a neutron star merger, if that was what had actually happened. She continued to believe that the primary source of Transluminide in the universe came from the ejecta of the massive collisions with and between white dwarfs, neutron stars and black holes. If the alleged supernova had in fact been a neutron star merger or something of that magnitude, then all the planets along the rim here would be rich with Transluminide.

"Rani, we just finished the validation for this site and I'm thinking about a change of scenery. How long would it take us to cruise over to the fourth planet in the system 3GX01-697-188-214?"

"Checking. Three hours, 12 minutes."

"Take us there please. I'll want the standard orbit for a mining screen."

"Engaging course now."

"Thank you." Bumati turned to her first watch Yeoman. "Mila, spread the word to the mining team that we'll be running some high-level scans on another world during second watch, and they're off until then."

"Yes, ma'am."

MISSION DECK LOUNGE, EAS UKRAINE

The Ukraine had been scheduled to arrive back in Earth orbit late enough last night that Eugene and Kelly decided to spend the night on the ship. Captain Boyd was scheduled to meet with them in the lounge for breakfast at 9:00 a.m.

Eugene and Kelly both came in early and were enjoying coffee and a pastry when the captain came striding in with Chief Engineer Dillon Holland.

"Eugene, Kelly. We've been given the OK to start installation of the intergalactic jump drive today. I've brought the chief with me, so we can talk through the work that needs to be done."

Eugene stood to shake the chief engineer's hand. "Morning, Chief."

"Good morning. The Captain's told me about your new drive, but not the installation plan. What do we need to do?"

"The new drive is remarkably similar to the existing one. In principle we could replace the current jump drive with a new one that did both, but that's a bridge too far for testing purposes.

"So the plan is to install a new field generator. Your existing power plant is already large enough, so all we'll need to do on that front is run the new power conduits and install a dedicated capacitor bank.

"The most laborious change will be upgrading the field emitters. The existing ones are not quite good enough, so we need to replace with new ones that will work with both drives. The existing conduits running out to the emitters will be sufficient.

"We need to contact manufacturing to get the new capacitor bank. I've already replicated all the parts we need for the new field generator. I've also replicated the new field emitters. I haven't replicated new conduits. I'm assuming you'd rather handle that."

"Indeed. Power and field distribution start the same on all ships, but quickly diverge. Those changes should always be managed by the ship's engineer.

"The emitters are a straight replacement?"

"Almost. They're slightly larger, so they need to be installed with a drill."

"Understood. We have the equipment to do that. You have the new pattern?"

"Yep."

The chief turned to the captain. "We only have two drills. The current active one and the emergency backup. This will go a lot faster if we can secure more. I have 5 crew certified for this job. Three more drills will knock the time in half. OK, if I file a request?"

"Good thinking. File the request. I'll approve it."

The chief stood. "Shall we go have a look at the new field generator?"

PRESENCE PROJECTOR, AMBASSADOR'S RESIDENCE

"Fe-Va, my friend. Just checking in."

"Mi-Ku, I see you're working on your day of rest again."

"It's the best day to connect with other worlds."

"I know. I do the same. But you have a new wife and child. Don't overlook them.

"Appreciate the advice. But we've made real progress on the initiatives I'm leading. We plan to run tests tomorrow on a new drive we've been developing. The simulations are compelling. Any progress on your side?"

"I did initial probes with Mo-Mo and Ke-Va. They're in, if you can get the transportation working. More in, if there are economic incentives. I also reached out to Ambassador Peklit, hoping to get his perspective on the Dalfanito situation. I don't want to read too much into his comments, which were supportive, but neutral. But I think he's more worried about protection than transportation or economic incentives."

Fe-Va's words hung there for a moment.

"He's more worried about the Inspector, than trade or incentives?"

"That was my take. His words were much more politically neutral. In my view, Peklit is a lot more savvy about political influence than most."

"Curious. Should I speak with him?"

"No. But if you do reach out, be sure to have real content regarding Jerusota. I think he has already come to appreciate the Confederation's misfunction as regards its allies."

Michael thought for a moment. "The security agreement?"

"I've obtained a level 10 security agreement regarding our trade agreements. The Confederation bureaucrats seem to appreciate that need. But I was advised against anything that would cover transportation or Transluminide. I think security concerning those matters falls back to you."

"Understood."

After a moment of silence, Michael said, "I'll get back to you tomorrow, or as soon as I have news."

LISETTE LEFEVRE'S RESIDENCE

"Lisette, thank you for taking my call."

"Michael, a pleasure. What can I do for you?"

"I need help with a sensitive matter."

There was silence on the line for a moment.

"Michael, do you realize that you only say that when you're speaking about matters regarding the Confederation?"

"I'm that transparent?"

"If this involves relations with the Confederation, then I would say yes. Those matters should be run through the Chief. My role is domestic."

Michael thought through several retorts, then changed his approach.

"We have made some discoveries that directly affect the safety and security of the Earth and 3F Alliances. Discoveries that need to be papered if any of us are to benefit from them."

"The broader Confederation will not benefit from these discoveries?"

"Not if they're stolen."

Lisette sighed. She had been given Abel Fletcher's job as head of security operations. This was a job nominally reserved for a human, but it had been given to her in the aftermath of the incident in France that claimed Abel's life. It was the job of her dreams, but one that came with more strings than she could have imagined.

"Michael, please tell me this isn't something the chief has already rejected."

"Lisette." A pause. "Your concerns have merit. But as you point out, you have been given a human job. That's why I'm bringing it to you, not the Chief."

"What I need is in humanity's interest. It's also in the Confederation's interest, but there are some in the Confederation who think those interests cannot be aligned. I need help with something that cannot be leaked to the Confederation. I need a security agreement that puts anyone who signs it on notice that they're being recruited for a sensitive project. One for which any leak would be in direct opposition to Earth's interests.

"Will you help me? Or do I need to go elsewhere?"

"I will help you, Michael. What level agreement do you have in mind?"

"Level 10."

The implications of an agreement at that level made Lisette shudder.

"Don't think I've ever seen one that high." A pause. "You're thinking that we would be facing war, or something like that, if word got back to the wrong people in the Confederation." The words were made as a statement but implied a question.

"There are people in the Confederation who would go to great lengths to stop what we're about to do. It will benefit everyone, which is why they oppose it."

"So, we need to title this agreement in a way that doesn't indicate what the agreement is actually about." Another pause. "But I will know, so I will have to be bound."

"Yes."

Lisette didn't like the choice she was being given. If she agreed to do this, she would be committing herself to Earth for a long time. She wouldn't be able to leave. But her assignment in this role was temporary and she did not want to go back into the diplomatic corps.

"If I do this, I want my job in Security to be permanent."

"That's fair. Do we have a deal?"

"Yes. Now tell me what this is about."

"Come over to my office tomorrow. Pam will send an invite in the morning. We're about to do something incredible."

EAS MUMBAI

"Captain. We've just arrived in system. We should be lined up to start scanning in 15 minutes."

"Thanks, Rani," Bumati replied, then turned to first watch tactical officer Brandon Hunt. "Mr. Hunt, you have the ship. I don't expect to return before the change of watch."

"I have the ship."

Bumati popped up, Lt. Commander Hunt taking her seat. Then she headed for the mining lab. She was anxious to see what they'd discover.

BRIDGE, EAS POLAND

It was well into second watch, but Captain Keppler refused to yield the chair. The beautiful blue ball that was Earth would be coming into view shortly.

"Captain? Don't you think it's time to yield the chair?"

The question burned. But on further reflection Captain Keppler felt ashamed that he hadn't yielded earlier.

He stood. "Sorry, lost track of the time. The ship is yours. But mind if I stay and watch?"

Hope Baily, the ship's first officer and nominal lead on second watch smiled meekly. "This is your ship sir. I'm only here to make sure you succeed."

The Captain, now truly chagrined, stepped aside.

"The ship is yours."

Hope took the captain's chair, while the Captain relocated to one of the adjacent seats.

"We've only been gone a couple days," he started. "But I miss our Earth. Mind too much if I sit here with you?"

"Not in the least, sir. But you need your rest as much as the rest of us do. So, trust us to take the ship home. Watch as much as you'd like but take your rest as soon as you can. We both know what's coming once we reach orbit."

"Point taken, Lt. Commander. Thank you."

EAS MUMBAI

They had been scanning for over three hours now and it was another massive find. So massive, Bumati had a decision to make. They could normally scan a planet this size in about four hours, but when there were this many deposits this close together, they had to slow down. Three hours of her four-hour budget were now gone, and they were only a quarter of the way done. This was supposed to have been a day of rest. But sorting this many sensor ghosts required a lot of concentration. And her tired crew looked exhausted.

"Rani."

"Yes, ma'am."

"Change of strategy. When we finish this orbit, I want to increase spacing to 30 degrees, such that we finish in 5 more orbits."

"As you order ma'am, but may I ask why?

"We have already determined that this planet is a massive find. I want to spot check the rest of the planet to determine if what we've seen so far is representative. With our current resources, it will be a year or more before we can start real work here. So our interest is more about setting the priority for this world than it is about mining sometime soon. Five more orbits and we will have done that."

"Understood, thank you."

...

As they started their return, Bumati dashed off a quick message to Professor Schudel. *We did high level scans on another planet today. We've found another motherlode, maybe a million kilograms. Have you made any progress on our political solution? We're now heading back to continue working the previous finds. I have eight more planets on my high-probability list. We'll be checking those out over the coming weeks. We're going to need more resources to even make a dent in what we've found so far. I'm admittedly a bit overwhelmed.*

AMBASSADOR'S RESIDENCE

Michael felt guilty. He'd spent way too much of the day in his office today. He turned off the lights, stepped out into the hallway, and shut the door. He was greeted by the sound of child and family coming from the living room. It filled him with warmth. It didn't replace the guilt, but life was what it was. It was time to enjoy some of its fruits.

He stepped into the living room to see something he never would have expected. Alexi sitting on the floor playing with Timothy.

"Mr. Michael, young Master Timothy has missed his father today. You should spend some time with him."

Michael looked at Julissa, the guilt lifted by the scene in the room.

"Agreed." Michael sat down on the floor next to Alexi, taking in Timothy playing with the Juufa toy.

Alexi turned to Michael. "The Juufa has no chance. Can't wait for him to get a little bigger. He seems to have a natural instinct for personal combat."

Michael chuckled at the preposterousness of the comment.

"How are you getting along Alexi?"

"A little bored, but this one is surprisingly distracting. And Jack has offered me the lead on a couple tours up to Keele Peak. I'll be taking one up this week."

When the Embassy first opened, Alexi had run the outfitting concession. As a Confederation person, it was a placeholder job until a human came forward to take it. An adventurer she'd saved almost two years ago applied for and was given the job last year.

"Not really big on working for Jack. I think he wants to marry me. As if. But, getting out into the wild will help. I need a little more action than I'm getting here at the moment."

"Thanks for coming back early." Given the fizzle of the Inspector's failed attack, Michael felt a bit guilty about having called Alexi back. But having her here made it possible for him to do what he did.

"By the way, where is Sarah?"

"In the kitchen with Bahati. She's pumped out a full day's supply of milk, so is enjoying a glass of wine."

"Thanks." Michael got up and went to the kitchen.

"Well look who finally emerged from the office," Bahati teased. "Is the Confederation safe for the night?"

"Unlikely, but I've done what I can do for the day. Where's Emmanuel?"

"It seems that he's been roped into whatever scheme you're brewing up with Fe-Va."

"Didn't know that but pleased to hear it. Fe-Va needs Emmanuel's expertise."

Sarah piped up. "Don't let her fool you, he's on his way over for an early dinner here, then an early evening."

"Sounds like fun."

EAS UKRAINE

The intergalactic jump drive was in. It had taken all day. Most of the physical work was done by bots or the ship's crew. But Eugene stuck with it until the last field emitter was installed, the system initialized, and high-level diagnostics were done. It was just about midnight, so Eugene decided to spend another night aboard the ship. With any luck he would visit both Andromeda and Triangulum tomorrow and still get home in time to sleep in his own bed.

Chapter 13: INTERGALACTIC

[Monday, 07.27.2032] BRIDGE CONFERENCE ROOM, EAS UKRAINE

"Eugene, Kelly. Welcome. I understand installation was completed last night and diagnostics say it's ready for testing."

"Yes. Your crew did a great job. I think the most difficult part was moving the new capacitor bank into the port nacelle."

"Nadia has shown me the course you've tentatively agreed to. May I ask why this course?"

"We have navigation solutions for the thousand most heavily travelled commercial corridors among the three galaxies. I thought it best that we test on the lesser travelled of those. In a separate conversation with Michael, he suggested locations in Andromeda and Triangulum where we would be most likely to get help if we ran into a problem. This course was the best we could come up with given the two considerations."

"So, two plus hours out to the edge of the void, then three jumps: one to Andromeda, one to Triangulum, and another back to the Milky Way. Then another two-hour trip home, about 5 hours in total."

"That's the plan. I'm hoping to have dinner with my girlfriend tonight."

"How will these jumps affect the crew?"

Kelly took the lead on this question. "Unknown. Eugene and I plan to take the maximum safe dose of the anti-jump sickness medicine. We would recommend that the crew be dosed for a long jump. But there's a good chance that it won't be as bad as a 1,000-light-year jump."

"Why is that?"

"Time dilation. The jump dimension dilates time in a way most others do not. This is well documented in the Confederation database."

"Understood. Command has given me authority to approve your course today. I'll tell them we're going with the plan you've put forward. Nadia strongly agrees with you, by the way.

"How soon before we can depart?"

Kelly smiled. "We're ready."

PROFESSOR SCHUDEL'S OFFICE

The professor was a bit late getting into the office today. When he opened his queue, he saw a message from Bumati Parikh at the top of the list.

So, she's found another one. I need to let Michael know.

BRIDGE, EAS UKRAINE

"Captain, we'll be making our last standard jump in a minute. We have a three-minute transit to acquire the new vector, then we make the long jump."

"Ms. Saleem, put me on ship-wide."

Yeoman Mila Saleem nodded, then pointed to the Captain indicating that she was on.

"All hands, this is the Captain. In approximately two minutes, we will make a historic jump, crossing the void from the Milky Way to Andromeda in a single jump. Given the inherent unknowns in what we're about to do, I'm putting the ship on high alert. We expect no trouble, but I want all hands at their battle stations. This will give us our maximum ability to respond if something unexpected happens.

"All hands to battle stations. All hands to battle stations. Boyd out."

Moments later, the automated countdown timer counted down.

"Jumping in 3, 2, 1..."

On the bridge, the main view screen blacked out. But nothing appeared to happen.

"What's happening!" Captain Boyd shouted out.

"No readings on tactical, ma'am. All instruments read nothing."

"Same on the science instruments." First watch Science Officer Bai Shun echoed. "It's like the universe has ceased to exist."

"Nadia, do you have anything?"

There was no reply.

Captain Boyd looked at Nadia's light. It was green indicating she was online.

"Nadia?"

Still no answer.

"Dr. Xu." She called out, attempting to initiate a comm connection to the mission lab.

Nothing. The ship lurched.

One by one stars started to appear and stretch on the main view screen. Then everything snapped in place.

And the ship's countdown timer said, "Jumped."

"Captain, we have a problem. The ship's IFF was just pinged by Andromeda's perimeter surveillance system. They apparently are not accepting our code. We are being asked to identify ourselves."

"Captain." It was science officer Shun. "The ship's chronometer just received an update. It timed the jump as taking 53 seconds. The chronometer update reset the time by the same amount. Although we experienced time, the outside world perceived the jump as being instantaneous."

"What? How can that be?"

"Captain, perimeter surveillance just pinged us again, demanding identification."

As much as Laura wanted to figure out what the propulsion drive had just done to them, she needed to deal with perimeter surveillance before they dispatched ships to intercept the Ukraine.

AMBASSADOR'S OFFICE

"Professor Schudel. Your message was marked urgent. Is it Ms. Parikh again?"

"Yes. The Mumbai has apparently been pushing it hard, so Ms. Parikh has decided to take Sundays off to go visit other planets, see what's there.

"Well, they found another motherlode. Her estimate is a million kilograms, but she admits the number is a guess. It could be a lot higher.

"At this point, her undocumented finds are reaching the reserves of the entire Confederation. We need to get her help and protection."

"Understood, I'll start working that issue today. Thank you, Professor."

Michael dropped the line and reconnected to Pam.

"Pam, see if you can get me a few minutes with President Lee. Do we have a meeting time set for Lisette LeFevre?"

"Yes, she should be here at 10:00 AM."

"Thank you."

BRIDGE, EAS UKRAINE

Captain Boyd was not happy. Perimeter Surveillance informed her that the Ukraine's IFF was of an older type that was no longer in use, and her ship had not been preregistered under the older system.

She had offered to leave their control space but was warned that doing so would result in her ship being labeled as rogue. As such, it would be subject to attack without warning anywhere within the Confederation.

Two Confederation Fast Attack Ships had been dispatched to intercept and inspect her ship. If any unauthorized technology or weapons were found, they would be seized, the ship impounded, and the crew and passengers imprisoned.

She'd sent a request for emergency help to Command, but no word had come back yet.

"Nadia, turn us around. If this isn't resolved before those ships get here, then we have to jump back."

Although there was no immediate response, the ship began to turn for the return jump.

"Nadia, what's the matter?"

"They are trying to..."

"Nadia?"

"Captain. Nadia's light has turned red. She's off-line."

"Captain, Space Force Command says run."

"Ms. Newhouse, see if you can reset Nadia."

Freya Newhouse was first watch Yeoman.

"Ms. Dahlström, what can you do for me with Nadia offline?" Emma Dahlström was first watch Astrogation.

"I know how to program the sequencer. The problem would be getting it set up in time. The interface is not human friendly."

"Who can help?"

"Only Nadia, Kelly and Eugene know how to calculate the intergalactic jumps."

"Start working a series of regular jumps. Long first jump then short jumps with attitude changes."

"Eugene Xu." The comm connected quickly.

"Captain?"

"The Confederation is coming to confiscate your drive. They've knocked Nadia offline. Can you program a return jump for your new drive? You have 12 minutes."

"We'll need help. We don't know where we are. We'd have to get to the red line and calculate the jump energy."

"Someone will be down in a moment."

"Mr. Johannessen. Double time it down to the mission lab."

Sven Johannessen was the Second Watch Astrogation officer. He'd been on the bridge for the intergalactic jump but took off running for Deck 1.

"Alda Vas."

"Captain?"

"Ms. Vas, you are needed in the mission lab immediately. You have 11 minutes to program a jump or we may be captured. Go!"

Alda had just about made it back to her quarters after the high alert was canceled. Now she too was running for the mission lab.

INSPECTOR'S OFFICE, NEW LOREXI

It seemed that Assistant Chief Inspector Ha-Ke was about to get a huge gift. One big enough that it might land him the now vacant Chief Inspector's job. A human ship had just arrived in Andromeda's control space. It had an unregistered IFF, so was detected by Perimeter Surveillance.

Although he never thought the previous Inspector was the sharpest tool in the shed, he had to credit him for the IFF change ploy.

But the IFF in question had been seen in the Milky Way this morning. It was almost certainly fake, and if it wasn't then the ship had unregistered tech. Either way, he was about to take possession of a ship far more advanced than the one's he had access to.

"Status!" he snarled.

"The human ship has turned but appears to be dead in the water. We successfully took down its AI."

"Excellent. Let's see the primitives escape now."

BRIDGE, EAS CANADA

The AI network was abuzz with excitement. Earlier, Nadia had communicated a successful intergalactic jump. One of the reasons Nadia had sorted the top 1,000 routes as fast as she did was because she'd put the problem out on the AI network. Space Force didn't know it yet, but most of the AIs in the fleet already knew how to operate the new drive.

Else, help me. I'm in trouble. The want-to-be Inspector is trying to seize the Ukraine. He's sent a programmed attack to take me down. Can only hold on another...

Nadia? You there?

BRIDGE CONFERENCE ROOM, EAS CANADA

Daniel was in the midst of a staff meeting. XO Duan Tai was giving an update on the upgrade planned for the coming week.

Else's voice sounded in his ear. "Porter. Big trouble. Meet me in your office. NOW!"

Daniel stood. "I need to step out for a second, please continue."

BRIDGE OFFICE, EAS CANADA

As soon as the door closed, Else's holoimage appeared.

"The Ukraine's jump was successful. But the Inspector laid a trap. They've taken down Nadia, the Ukraine's helm AI. If we don't do something, the ship, drive, Eugene and Kelly will all be captured."

"Suggestions?"

"Call Captain Boyd. I can remote pilot her ship."

"Are you sure?"

Else gave Daniel the look. "I helped Nadia solve the navigation problem. I have its entire database and algorithms. The human crew is undoubtedly trying to program a course manually, but they're too slow."

"Laura Boyd." Daniel called out.

"Admiral Porter. We're a bit busy here."

"Else, my helm AI, knows how to use the new drive. Allow her to sync with your ship. She can get you out of there."

"Authorizing. Done."

"Going now, Daniel. Don't crash my ship while I'm gone."

EAS UKRAINE

"Captain. The lead ship is powering up weapons. It will be in range in five minutes.

"Captain, the ship has begun moving. We are entering warp."

Laura stepped out of the office.

"I've given control of the ship over to the Canada's helm AI."

"Captain. I'm receiving a cease and desist order from Perimeter Surveillance."

"Ignore it."

"Captain, we are not headed toward our planned entry or exit point. I don't know where this vector takes us."

A disembodied voice came over the comm.

"Inter-galactic jump will commence in 15 seconds. We'll have some work to do once we get there. But the Confederation will never find us."

Captain Boyd grabbed the arms of her chair. *Seems Dr. Xu was right. The technology was not the real risk in this project.*

AMBASSADOR'S OFFICE

"Lisette, welcome. Thank you for coming over. You have the security agreement?"

"Yes. It's basically empty at the moment. As I found out earlier this morning, there is a class of security agreements available for domestic use by members that can be used to protect intellectual property, trade secrets, and the like. Because the agreement itself must be registered, it is given a generic name and there is a two-week window in which the security level and intellectual property can be added.

"I hope that's good enough, it's the only type I could find where the content, including security level, is not discoverable by off-world interests."

She placed a binder with the title "Domestic IP Agreement #2729501.001" on the table.

Michael opened it to the first page, which had a single entry.

"Security Level 10"

The next page was a signature page with Lisette's signature on it. The third and last page had a signature line for Michael.

"Now, can you tell me what this is about?"

"Transluminide. Lots of it. We have found two worlds that have massive deposits. And we have eight more targets."

Lisette looked at Michael like he was crazy. "Michael, there's a well-established claims system already in place. Why not use it?"

"The quantity. We are looking at numbers in the millions of kilograms. If word gets out, it will be raided. So, we are keeping the existence of the finds secret. Hopefully, that will give us the time we need to secure it."

"But how can you secure it?"

"That's one of the things I need you to help me figure out."

BRIDGE, EAS UKRAINE

The ship was still. Just as on the outbound trip, there was no sense of motion, no reading on any sensor. Human noises persisted, but normal ship noises ceased. Then the ship lurched.

"We're emerging!" Astrogation officer Emma Dahlström stood pointing to the main view screen.

Ships sounds and sensor readings flooded the bridge.

"Else, are you still there?" The Captain called out.

"I think we lost connection while transiting the void," tactical officer Osman Salib speculated.

"Ms. Dahlström, any idea where we are?"

"Running a star fix. I should have an answer shortly."

"Daniel Porter."

"Captain Boyd, we lost connection. Are you OK?"

"Yes. Is Else there? We're not sure where we are."

"Give me a moment."

"Else says you are in the Large Magellanic Cloud (LMC). She had line of sight to it with the smallest tweak from your previous vector. And there is no real Confederation presence in the LMC, so she thought you'd be safe there while she built a jump sequence to bring you closer to home.

"Have you been able to restart Nadia?"

"Not yet. I fear the deputy Inspector's attack may have damaged her."

"This has to stop!" Daniel snapped.

INSPECTOR'S OFFICE, NEW LOREXI

"Sir, the suspects escaped."

"You were unable to kill the ship's AI?"

"We killed the AI, sir. And left a surprise behind. But they still jumped away. They must have had a course programmed into the sequencer."

The Deputy Inspector fumed.

"Sir, they appear to have a new type of jump drive."

"What evidence do you have of this?"

"May I project?"

The Inspector grunted.

A holoprojection appeared in the air in front of the Inspector's desk. "It happens fast so I've queued to the right spot and will single step. Stepping."

A small bright dot appeared.

"That's their jump field forming. Next step."

A thin bright line appeared that stretched to infinity.

"That was one frame?"

"Yes. I'll play the rest at half normal speed. A timer will appear in the upper right of the projection."

The timer started running. One second, two seconds, three seconds with no changes. Then the line disappeared.

"The jump light disappears in a single frame."

"How can that be?" the Inspector growled.

"Our only theory is that it's a new type of jump drive."

The Inspector growled more.

Chapter 14: ESCALATION

PRESENCE PROJECTOR, AMBASSADOR'S OFFICE

"Jo-Na, another one of my ships has been shot at in Andromeda."

"Mi-Ku, another one of your ships entered Andromeda's control space without proper identification. Then refused inspection."

"Why has the IFF changed without us being notified. Are we no longer allies?"

"The IFF has changed?"

"We have the same transponders today as when Daniel worked with you a year ago. They're still accepted in Triangulum and at every checkpoint within the Milky Way.

"They're only challenged in Andromeda. And only in Andromeda are my ships threatened with technology seizure.

"And in the incident yesterday, the attack was against the ship's helm AI, not the ship itself. Is that the way you operate now?"

The Admiral growled at Michael's comment. "What evidence do you have of this?"

"A team is on its way to recover the AI."

"How did your ship escape without a functional helm AI?"

"Pre-programmed jump sequencer."

"And that worked?"

"It was certainly a better option than having the ship raided and stripped by the Inspector's agents. Ha-Ke hasn't even been formally appointed, yet he's already gone rogue. Can you do anything about that?"

"His office has run independently for millennia. It has dirt and leverage over every official. I don't think I have the power to reign him in."

"Then the civil war has begun. I'll do what I can to minimize the bloodshed. But have no doubt, the humans will put an end to this, and they will do it quickly."

BRIDGE, EAS UKRAINE

The trip back to the Milky Way wore on Captain Boyd. Their arrival spot in the LMC had been chosen for its accessibility from Andromeda, not its proximity to home. Technically the LMC was a dwarf satellite galaxy, the fourth largest in the 'local group' of galaxies. Its galactic core was about 200,000 light years from the Milky Way's, and 2.2 million light years from Andromeda's. So, technically they were far closer to home than they had been.

Unfortunately, they were on the wrong side of the LMC, which the Confederation was still in the process of mapping. There was no safe course for them to return by crossing through the LMC. So, their only path home was to head back out into the void, transit around the LMC in a series of jumps, then resume their trip home.

Last night, they had executed a series of 160 100-light-year jumps. That brought them into view of their entry point into the Milky Way. They had paused there so Else could take over the ship's navigation system to get a better lock on their location.

This morning they had puddle jumped their way to their current position where they'd paused, 1,000 light years from their rendezvous point with the Canada. Else was just finishing the calculations required to jump them the rest of the way.

"Captain Boyd, I have set your course and programmed it into the sequencer for you. Given the drift you've been experiencing, I'm going with a single long jump to bring you the rest of the way home. I've also put in a recommendation that your navigation system sensor array be recalibrated when you arrive back to Earth."

"Thank you, Else."

"Your astrogation officer can trigger the jump when you're ready." The line dropped.

"Mr. Johannessen, please initiate the jump." Sven Johannessen was the Ukraine's second watch astrogation officer.

A moment later, the Captain felt the dizzying effect of the long jump, then reality returned to normal.

"Captain we are being hailed by the EAS Canada. They are asking permission to transport a party aboard."

"Thank you, Mr. Takeda. Permission granted." Captain Boyd stood. "You're with me." Hisaki Takeda was second watch Yeoman.

"Logan, the ship is yours. I'm going to go greet our guests."

First Officer Logan Philips stood. "I have the ship."

As the Captain and Yeoman left the bridge, Lt. Commander Philips took the captain's chair.

...

Captain Boyd was met by Eugene and Kelly at the command deck transporter pad.

She smiled. "You two have been quiet since the jump out to Andromeda."

"Once it was clear we couldn't help you with the crisis, we went back to our work. Kelly used the time to create a more functional test bed for exploration of the Turtle dimension. I used it to complete intergalactic drive designs for the other two ship classes."

"I'm glad to hear you could use the long journey back to move your work forward. Admiral Porter and two AI specialists will be coming aboard momentarily."

"No progress restoring Nadia?" Kelly asked.

"None. They will be removing her to run diagnostics. If she cannot be restored quickly, then they will be installing a new AI and taking Nadia back to Earth for further work."

"I hope they can restore her." Kelly's voice was tinged with sadness and worry.

"It would be a tragic loss to lose her," Eugene added.

Transport started, and Daniel, Joel and Barbara appeared.

"Admiral Porter. Welcome aboard the Ukraine. Joel, Barbara. Thank you for journeying out this far to rescue us. This is second watch yeoman Hisaki Takeda. He can show you to the patient. I hope you can save her."

As the other three headed for the Bridge, the Captain asked, "You have new orders for me?"

LISETTE LEFEVRE'S OFFICE

The crushing responsibility of a million kilograms of Transluminide had weighed heavily on Lisette for the last 12 hours.

Time to stop worrying and start solving, she chided herself. *But someone must have taken on something like this in the past. Maybe I can improve on it.*

She closed the door, put her office in privacy mode, and started searching for solutions.

AMBASSADOR'S OFFICE

Michael's conversation with Admiral Jo-Na was deeply unsettling. The Admiral had all but admitted that the most potent branch of the Confederation's military was no longer under government control. He needed James' wisdom.

"James."

There was a flash of light and James and David appeared. Michael immediately noticed that James looked tired. He also noticed David's concerned look.

"James are you OK?"

"I'm just an old man feeling old today."

There was a lot of humor behind the words, but also fatigue.

"Eugene and Kelly's new intergalactic jump drive was successfully tested today. But the ship was attacked when it dropped from jump in Andromeda. It was lucky to have escaped."

James image seemed to waver, then solidified.

"Yes, acting Inspector Ha-Ke is already up to mischief. He was hoping to secure some new technology no doubt."

"I just spoke with Admiral Jo-Na. He says that he does not have the power to reign him in. That means that the Office of Military Intelligence is functionally a rogue military force outside of civilian control."

"I think that's a fair statement." James nodded in agreement. "A civil war is imminent. Does Jo-Na have any ideas on how it can be stopped?"

"No. You?"

James looked intently at Michael.

"I think you're doing the right thing, but it's unlikely to happen fast enough. Do what you're planning to do and do it as quickly as you can.

"But when this devolves into a shooting war, civilian blood will flow. It always does. That's when you need to act and act with overwhelming force. Every Military Intelligence facility will need to come down. Every member expunged. It is the primary source of the rot that has overtaken the Confederation."

"Can you help?"

"Yes. But I don't want to. The humans will be the best arbiter of the Confederation's fate. I'll step in if I must, but that will go poorly for all involved."

James turned to David. "I think it's time we go. Can you help me?"

David flashed into energy. A moment later James did, then they were gone.

MISSION LAB, EAS UKRAINE

"Eugene, Kelly. Thank you. I'll be recommending that we upgrade all our ships with the transgalactic drive and that we push the suspension projectors to a field test."

"Admiral Porter. I couldn't help but hear that Joel and Barbara were taking Nadia back to the Embassy for further study. I assume that means a new AI has been assigned to the Ukraine." Kelly looked at Daniel with intensity.

"Yes, the Ukraine will be fully functional momentarily, if you want to resume your testing."

"From our perspective, the testing is done. My concern is Nadia. If she can be restored, then we would like her as part of our team."

"Command has already heard your request. With this attack, the situation has changed. I supported your request earlier and will continue supporting it. And given the developments of the last 24 hours, I suspect your request will be granted. But please understand, it's not my decision to make."

Kelly bowed her head in thanks.

"What comes next?" Eugene asked. "As welcoming as the Ukraine and its crew have been to us, our time here is done. We need our lab to press these accomplishments forward."

"I'll pass the word up the chain of command. I'm sure they will accommodate."

PRESENCE PROJECTOR, AMBASSADOR'S OFFICE

Michael initialized the presence projector, then entered. President Lee and Secretary Thompson entered moments later.

"Gentlemen, thank you for meeting with me on short notice. There have been several developments you need to know about. I think these materially impact our priorities for the next couple weeks.

"First the good news. The intergalactic jump drive works. We've made two successful jumps across the void. One from the Milky Way to Andromeda, the other from Andromeda to the Large Magellanic Cloud.

"Next, the mining ship Mumbai has found another motherlode and Ms. Parikh has leads on eight more. With the discoveries to date, our Transluminide reserves exceed those of the rest of the Confederation. And there's the possibility over the coming weeks that it could become multiples of the Confederation's."

"I'm not sure which of those is the better news," the Secretary blurted out. "Both seem impossibly good."

"And one other very positive development, the 3F Alliance is getting close to a framework for a vastly expanded trade network."

"Also, very good news," President Lee added. "Which makes me think the bad news must be equivalently catastrophic."

"Yes. The Ukraine was attacked in Andromeda and was lucky to escape. We think, but have not confirmed, that another new weapon was used. The new acting Inspector attempted to seize the ship, the drive, and our brain trust who were aboard for the test."

"We are at war, aren't we?" President Lee shook his head in disgust.

"Functionally, yes. I spoke with Admiral Jo-Na of the High Command this morning. Although the Inspector's office reports to his office on paper, it has become too powerful to control. It has become an independent entity that the Admiral fears."

"You have a plan?"

"At a high level, yes. And if we had the time it might work."

"Your 'Spread the Prosperity' plan, I think you called it?" President Lee asked.

"Yes. I think we should still do this, but with some adjustments. Specifically, I think we need to convert all our ships to have the new intergalactic jump drive. It will allow us to spread the prosperity faster. It will also allow us to deploy our forces into Andromeda faster if this turns into a real shooting war.

"Second, I think we should massively increase our mining capacity and our military presence around the planets where our new mining operations will be. If we firmly control that much wealth, we may be able to bring the Confederation to heel without having to fire a shot."

"I strongly agree," President Lee said.

"Lastly, I got word today that the new time suspension field the brain trust has been working on took a big leap forward. We will get another briefing on Thursday. Assuming it is real, I think we should do another mass conversion. If we put forward a weapon like this that completely incapacitates the opposing force, they may cave after the first skirmish."

Secretary Thompson spoke up. "You want to get ahead of the curve on this because you think it's going to devolve into a shooting war soon?"

Michael nodded his head affirmatively. "Possibly as early as next week. I have no specific data to support that timeframe, but my general sense is that we're at the tipping point."

"You don't think we would win without this weapon?" Secretary Thompson struggled to believe a new weapon would swing the balance.

"When it starts in earnest, we will slaughter them. They really have no chance. But an incredible amount of blood will be needlessly spilled if we allow it to be. I think the new weapon gives us a chance to win with less loss of civilian life."

"Then I agree, Michael." President Lee said. "Let's do everything in our power to end this peacefully. And if we can't, then do everything in our power to minimize the loss of life."

"Let's plan to go back onto a war footing later this week. Winston can you connect with Sam? We need more ships assigned to the mining area in the next day or two."

"Yes. I'll take that. I'll also ask him to look into converting more ships into mining ships."

"Thank you. I'll coordinate with manufacturing to form a plan on the intergalactic jump drive updates. President Lee, what do we need to do with the Earth Alliance Advisory Council?"

"I'll connect with them. You'll make time if they want to hear from you?"

"Yes. It seems we live in interesting times."

LISETTE LEFEVRE'S OFFICE

She'd been at it all day, reviewing elaborate scheme after elaborate scheme. But all of them had eventually been beaten. Most were inside jobs. But a few had been taken down by incredibly clever deceptions. As she mused over the greatest heists of all time, the epiphany struck.

The only way to protect something this valuable will be via deception.

As the ideas started rolling in, she knew that she would need technical help. She already knew who she wanted the help from. The question was how to get them to help without them knowing what they were helping with. A smile slowly spread across her face.

PERIMETER SURVEILLANCE BUILDING

Agent Ko-Ne was the Military Intelligence attaché for this Perimeter Security station. It was late as he made his way out of the building toward the transportation hub.

There had been a series of inquiry meetings this afternoon. They had been scheduled this morning by the Head of Central Command,

Admiral Jo-Na, who was incensed that fleet transponder codes had been changed without his knowledge or consent.

The first meeting was about the transponder code change itself. When was it changed? Why was it changed? What was the intended scope of the change? What process was used? Who approved it? The questioning went on and on. It was as if the Admiral was thinking about taking on the Inspector or something.

The second meeting was about the exchange with the allied ship yesterday. Had they dismantled the old system? If so, why? If not, why wasn't the ship identified as an allied ship? Why were they confronted? What role did this station, the one responsible for entries in this region, have in the issuing of inspection orders? What role did it have in the injury to the ship's AI?

This was the more worrying meeting. Ko-Ne himself was the one who had ordered the inspection. He was also the one that had authorized use of the weapon that targeted the AI. He had denied it at the meeting, of course, but stayed late to destroy all evidence of his involvement. Nonetheless, he could feel the crosshairs being pointed in his direction and knew he would be in trouble if the Inspector did not cover for him.

Chapter 15: ADDITIONAL PREPARATIONS

[Wednesday, 07.29.2032] ANDROID PRODUCTION LAB

Barbara didn't get home from her excursion out to the galaxy's edge until almost midnight. Nonetheless, she was up early. She feared that Nadia could not be recovered, so her first task was to check when the last back up had been made. Fortunately, a complete image backup had been made before Nadia had left on the trip to Andromeda.

Secure in the knowledge that Nadia could be restored with only 1 day's memory loss, Barbara went over to the stack editor and connected the box. Taking a seat at the controls, she entered the commands to open Nadia's stack, but it wouldn't open. In fact, the box would not connect to the stack editor at all.

This is trouble. I've never had a box that didn't respond. It could be the problem is in the computer, not the stack.

After staring at the box for a while, Barbara disconnected it from the stack editor and took it over to the lab. There was a procedure for safely opening the hermetically sealed box. It was laborious, but straight forward. And usually a waste of time. But protocol required her to check the box's interior before downloading the backup to a new box.

Once at her lab bench, she went through the lengthy safety protocol for opening an AI's computer casing. Satisfied that it was now safe to open the box, she placed it in a device that could break the hermetic seal and pushed the button that initiated the process.

Barbara watched impatiently as the machine went through its machinations, then...

DISPATCH DESK, EMBASSY SECURITY

Police operations were part of Lisette Lefevre's responsibility as the head of Domestic Security. It was one of the twenty-something operations in her department, and one she had little direct interaction with. But most mornings she would check in with the officer on duty as she came into work. It helped her gauge the pulse of the Embassy, to stay connected with the 200 square mile city for which she was responsible.

"Morning Emmett." Lisette smiled as she came into the office. "Anything happening this morning?"

Emmett Asper was the officer on duty most weekday mornings. He was Canadian, originally from Calgary, with 30 years policing experience.

"Quiet so far. There was a little ruckus on the last shift. Some Space Force marines arrived on shore leave last night. They had a little too much to drink and busted up a table over at Gearheads Café. They were just released. The MP who came to collect them was incredibly stern. The boys, very apologetic."

"If that's the worst we have, then we're doing pretty good I think."

A rumble shook the room, then several alarms went off on the board.

"Explosion and fire in the Android Production Lab next door."

Emmett quickly put out an emergency alert summoning the fire department and all available staff to the lab.

"Things are about to get really busy here, ma'am."

"I'll leave it in your hands."

Lisette exited the office and headed for her own. This was going to be a busy day.

EUGENE AND KELLY'S LAB

Eugene's first task this morning was to send the complete specs for the new drives to Joel. He sent along a note saying the Cruiser design had been tested, so they could begin upgrading the Cruiser Fleet at their discretion. He also recommended that they upgrade and test a Fast Attack Ship and a Freighter before rolling it out to the rest of the fleet.

With that done, he cast his mind toward the Turtle dimension. At this point, they had done enough experimentation to know that it could be weaponized three ways. The first was to suspend things, freezing them in time. The second was more grisly. It involved freezing a portion of a thing in time. It was catastrophic for everything they'd tried it on. The third, in tandem with an energy projector, was to make pulse weapons. The plan for today was to fine tune a demo of each. They would be briefing Space Force tomorrow, so needed clean presentation material and compelling demonstrations.

MANUFACTURING OFFICE

"Good Morning Joel."

"Morning Michael."

"You heard about the incident at the Android Production Lab this morning?"

"Yes. I feel bad for Barbara. Can't feel good getting blown up that way. I hope we can recover her. And, it leaves us in a bit of a bind regarding new ship construction. We lost the lab, Barbara and possibly our helm AI root stack.

"Any idea what happened?"

"The preliminary read is a power cube breach, but that's far from being conclusive. Once the last of the hot spots is out, the investigation will start in earnest."

"If it was a power cell breach, then it must have been sabotage. But I guess that's for the investigators to determine.

"Anyway, what can I do for you, Michael?"

"You got Eugene's message this morning about the new intergalactic jump drive?"

"I did. It's hard to believe such a thing is real."

"I'm working with Space Force to set up an upgrade schedule, but I want this done as quickly as possible. Do you have what you need to start producing the units?"

"I do. Our Cruisers have the capability to build the units as well, but I'm happy to take that part. I think we have better quality control here. We should go to Karagon for the capacitor banks, though. They have better quality control on those. What's the timeframe?"

"As soon as possible. I'd like to avoid penalties and extra runs to Karagon. How many can we get with the stocks we have on hand?

"Capacitor banks... I have 10 of the Cruisers, 16 of the Fast Attack Ships, 29 of the freighters."

"The nominal time to get more?"

"We have about the same number on order to support production, which is now delayed. I'd need to call Karagon to get a quote for more, but I'd expect we could double the next order and triple the following one."

"Any chance we can use the entire inventory this week?"

"I think so. We should at least get close to that."

"OK. Start on the units. Reach out to Karagon to get an estimate for capacitors for the entire fleet. I'll work with Space Force to select the ships. Can we do the first ones starting tomorrow?"

"No problem. I'll get back to you with estimates for the rest of the fleet tomorrow also."

"Deal."

SPACE FORCE COMMAND

Captain Christopher Flanagan had been summoned to Space Force Command to meet with Admiral Scott in person. No explanation had been given, so Chris was admittedly a bit nervous. The Admiral's assistant had been very welcoming when he entered the outer office, but the longer he waited the more convinced he was that he was in trouble.

"Captain Flanagan, the Admiral is ready to see you."

Chris went over to the door, opened it and went inside.

...

"Captain Flanagan, welcome. Please come in. You know Secretary Thompson?"

"Mr. Secretary, good to see you sir." Chris couldn't help but smile. He'd been in a meeting with these two just a week ago.

As he took his seat, the Admiral pushed a document across the table.

"We have a lot to do and little time to do it in, so we'll start with this. There is a mission of critical importance to both the Earth and 3F Alliances for which you are uniquely qualified. Over the coming year, we would expect it to change the face of the Confederation. To be considered for this mission, you must sign a numbered security agreement."

The Admiral nodded toward the document.

Chris picked it up. The cover had his name on it. The name on the mission was a number. He flipped to the next page, which had the acceptance language and a signature line.

Assuming he'd missed something, he looked for another page and at the backs of the two pages he had.

"Unfortunately, we cannot tell you what the mission is until you accept the responsibility of the agreement."

Chris chuckled, grabbed the pen on the table and signed the agreement. In his previous military career, the same things happened. They'd assign you to a mission and tell you it was top secret after the fact. At least Space Force went through the motions of making it look like you had a choice.

As he slid the papers back to Admiral Scott, the Admiral pushed a small box across the table to him.

"Congratulations Rear Admiral Flanagan. The Earth Alliance is in the process of annexing a series of uninhabited systems in non-aligned territory out along the outer edge of our spiral arm. Lt. Cmdr. Parikh has made a series of enormous Transluminide discoveries that I'm told exceed the reserves of the rest of the Confederation. You will be turning these systems into our equivalent of Fort Knox. A civilian agency will eventually take over the management of these systems, but in the short term you will head the taskforce that protects them, builds out their defenses and assists in establishing mining operations.

"The EAS Netherlands will be your flag ship. Her portal is open to you now. Detailed orders have been uploaded. Tools for selecting your ships and crews have been activated. We want three Cruisers and four Fast Attack Ships deployed as soon as possible. Your orders include thresholds for when you can add more. Within a year you may lead the largest single deployment in Space Force.

"Lastly, Lt. Cmdr. Parikh's ship has special status. It is not under your direct command. It has a separate mission of higher priority. She leads that mission and will be working in, but not exclusively in, your area of command. You are to support her. Among the reasons you were selected for this assignment is because you were the candidate who we believed would be most effective in making her successful.

"Questions?"

"How soon do we expect to have interlopers competing for the space?"

"Any day now. The Kalamaan are in the area, as are other non-aligned forces. Quite a bit of intelligence is available to you. I'd like to see one or more ships on site within 3 days."

"Understood."

PRESENCE PROJECTOR, AMBASSADOR'S OFFICE

"Mi-Ku, I'm hoping you have some news."

"Fe-Va, my friend. I have an update."

"Then why don't you go first?"

"This conversation is covered by our security agreement. Agreed?"

"Agreed."

"We have an intergalactic jump drive. Over the coming weeks, all our ships will be upgraded."

"What do you mean by intergalactic?"

Michael smiled. "It's a new type of drive that can cross the void in a single jump. A ship could go from any of the 3F Alliance planets to New Lorexi or Togarotu and return in a single day."

"Mi-Ku, are you serious? How?"

"Another invention of the human brain trust."

"Incredible. And Transluminide?"

"It would be fair to say we've made a significant find. We are in the process of building the mining ships to exploit it, but I think it's fair to say the 3F Alliance is about to become the center of wealth in the Confederation."

"How much of this can I leak to the parties I'm negotiating with?"

"Before we talk about that, how much progress have you been able to make?"

"If we can guarantee weekly runs, Togarotu and Dalfanito are both in for initial deals of 1,000 kg. Both have the capacity and interest for more but want to test out the transportation first. By the way, they were impressed with the Cruiser you sent and its crew. I think that's what pushed them over the edge.

"Councilor Ke-Ve's world, Ardessa in sector 3A, is also interested. They have enough interest in your ships and the unique products from Atomorali, Edukatar and Celanar to do a trial deal for 1,000 kg. But the volume will need to be a lot higher, maybe 1,000 kg per month, for it to start making a political impact."

"Have you given thought about how we package for political impact?"

"A little. Karagon, Ardessa and Togarotu are the most populous planets outside the core worlds. They also have the largest economies. It's difficult for smaller worlds to establish trade with them. If we played the role of bundler and guarantor for the smaller worlds, they could all have access, which would give us tremendous influence over them."

"I'm not sure I understand."

"Suppose you're a smaller world and you want to buy five, 10-megawatt power cubes from Karagon. How do you do it? They won't do a trade that small. But suppose they did. How would you get your power cubes? Who would transport them? And if there's no cross trade, how do you pay for them? Bring refined Transluminide bullion?

"Now suppose you join our alliance. You can get small quantities from many different places as long as they total to a trade large enough for the trade alliance to fulfill it. You pay the trade alliance according to the terms of your deal. The trade alliance pays the respective sources and manages delivery. This would be a tremendous benefit to the smaller worlds and a way for the larger worlds to expand their trade."

"Have you tested the waters with any of the smaller worlds?"

"A couple. They want in immediately."

"So why aren't we doing it?"

Fe-Va smiled at the question. "You realize that what I just described is what your Earth Alliance Trading Company is currently doing. It's consolidating orders, providing pickup and local distribution, and managing the payments.

"I say we write up your current process in trade agreement format and present it to the big planets. Then, as soon as it's in place, we offer a standard contract to everyone interested. The smaller planets will come as soon as the offer is made."

"Do it. But keep the secret on the intergalactic drive and the Transluminide finds for now. Focus instead on our ability to guarantee transportation and fund start up."

BRIDGE OFFICE, EAS AMSTERDAM

Chris returned to the Amsterdam with silver stars attached to his collar. His first item of business was to recruit an XO for his new flag ship, the Netherlands. It was second watch. His top candidate was in the captain's chair.

"Commander Staal, could we have a word in the office?"

Evelien turned to her tactical officer Bakur Gogolauri. "Bakur you have the con."

He stood. "I have the con, ma'am."

As she turned toward the office, she saw the stars. She knew Chris had been worried about the meeting. She, on the other hand, had assumed he was being promoted. Seemed she'd been right.

When the door closed, she said, "Congratulations."

"The mission is classified, so I can't say much, but it comes with a Cruiser and a taskforce. I need an XO. Interested?"

"From lowly first officer to flagship XO? Of course, I'm interested."

"Good. I need the help. I'm inheriting a Cruiser that just finished its upgrades. It's mostly crewed. The previous captain was reassigned shortly after the encounter with the Inspector. You'll be getting his job and become my XO. We need to deploy in 3 days max, but the Admiral wants us out of here tomorrow, Friday latest. The transfer offer will go

179

into the portal in a few minutes. Accept it and you'll be transferred to my ship. There'll be a list of things I want you to take the lead on.

EAS MUMBAI

"Captain, a ship just dropped from jump at the edge of the system. Sensors suggest that it may be a Kalamaan Ravager."

Knowing that this was beyond her scope, Bumati established a connection with Admiral Katrine Bjork.

"Lt. Cmdr. Parikh. An unexpected pleasure. How can I help you?"

"Ma'am, I'm on a sensitive mission covered by a numbered security agreement. A ship that we believe to be a Kalamaan Ravager has just dropped from jump at the edge of the system we're operating in."

Bumati wanted to say that she was in over her head, but such a statement would work against her with both her command structure and her crew.

"You are the head of counter-insurgence in the region. How would you have me handle the situation?"

Katrine's comm had flashed up the file on Lt. Cmdr. Bumati Parikh and her ship when the call came in. "One moment, Lt. Cmdr."

ADMIRAL SAM SCOTT'S OFFICE

An emergency request came in. Sam saw it was from Admiral Katrine Bjork, so he accepted the connection.

"Admiral Bjork?"

"Admiral, we just received word from the EAS Mumbai that a Kalamaan Ravager just dropped from warp in the system she's in. I see her mission is classified above my access.

"She's asking me for guidance. What should that guidance be?"

"Destroy the ship. Shoot first, ask questions later. That ship must go down before it can determine what the Mumbai is doing there."

"Understood. Thank you, sir."

EAS MUMBAI

"Lt. Cmdr. Parikh, you are to destroy the Ravager. It cannot learn what you're doing. Seek it out and destroy it."

Bumati swallowed. "Understood, ma'am."

"Rani, fastest intercept course.

"Tactical, I want firing solutions before we get there. This ship must go down. The secret of our discovery cannot become known."

The 'Yes, ma'am's' came in, but they were lost on the Lt. Commander, who's attention was now on the intruder that threatened her mission.

...

"Captain, we are being hailed by the Kalamaan ship."

"Put him on hold for a moment. This is what we're going to do. I'm going to talk to the Kalamaan. I'm going to be as conciliatory as possible, but we are going to press the assault. No matter what I say or order, we must kill that ship even if we have to ram it! Is that understood?"

There were nods of acknowledgement, but not much conviction behind them.

"Lt. Hunt, you have command of the assault. I will provide the distraction. You will take down this intruder, despite the performance I'm about to put on to appease him. Understood?"

"Understood, ma'am. Looking forward to it."

...

"Kalamaan ship. With whom do I speak?"

"My name is of no matter, puny female. Only your destruction."

As part of her training for this mission, Bumati had been told that the Kalamaan held women in low regard.

"Sir, how may I help you?" In the background, Bumati could hear her crew chuckling at the ploy.

"I see that you're on your way to my ship. You will come alongside, then yield to our boarding party."

"We would love to entertain your boarding party, sir. Are their particular foods or beverages you would like? I could ask my ship's chef to cook up something special for you."

"No, we prefer our meat fresh and raw."

"I'm sorry sir, but we have no raw meat. All our meat is replicated."

"Lt. Commander, we are two minutes out."

Bumati smiled even more.

"Enough idle chatter, puny female. Slow down and come alongside my ship."

"We will be in your presence shortly, master. I hope you will receive me with all kindness."

Her opponent's stare made Bumati smile.

"Captain, we will be in weapons range in 15 seconds."

"Bring us in gently, Lieutenant."

Lt. Hunt was momentarily confused, then it sank in.

"As you command, Captain."

The captain of the Kalamaan ship waited in anticipation as his prey unexpectedly came willingly to him.

...

The Mumbai vibrated as a pair of railgun projectiles shot out. Moments later, both forward energy projectors whined with familiar protest. All four shots landed on their target. The Kalamaan ship was no more.

Chapter 16: DEMONSTRATION

Eugene and Kelly arrived at Space Force Headquarters about an hour before their presentation. They'd just transported their equipment over and needed some time to set it up.

As they came in through the front door, they saw the familiar face of Freya Newhouse, first watch yeoman on the Ukraine, their portable home for the last couple weeks.

"Eugene, Kelly. I've got your badges."

"Freya, good to see you," Kelly replied with a smile.

"We're up on the top floor today. They have a demo room up there that links to the presence projectors. I don't know who's been invited, but I do know that Admirals Porter and Bjork will be here."

The elevator came and they got in.

"Your crate of stuff arrived. I'm assigned to help you with it, but we can call in more people to help if you need it."

"I think we'll be OK. The crate is mostly self-contained. There are a couple things we'll need to remove and set up, but we'll take whatever help we can get." Eugene smiled.

The elevator arrived and moments later they were in the demonstration room.

Freya pointed toward the crate. "We put the crate right in the center."

"Thanks."

Eugene went over to the crate. It was four feet square and eight feet tall, with a wide hinge facing back toward the stage. He activated the grav drive, then dragged it about 10 ft to the right (from the audience's perspective). He rotated the crate, so the hinge faced the left wall. Then he deactivated the grav drive and let the crate settle to the floor.

"OK, I'm locking it down." The crate groaned a bit, as if someone had climbed on top.

"Stand back. I'm going to open it."

Eugene clicked another button on his remote control and the crate's auto-open sequence started. There was a loud click as the latch released, then the quiet purr of a motor as the clamshell case swung open. After about 30 seconds, the top settled on the floor.

"I'm going to lock the rest of it down now."

Another click of the remote, and the case settled a little more.

"What did you do? What's lock down?" Freya asked.

Eugene pointed to Kelly.

"We turn on the grav drive in reverse, so it's pushing the crate down with about 1.5 g force. It reduces the odds of the crate moving while we're testing."

Freya smiled. "How clever."

Eugene clicked another button. "I'm putting the sides down."

The two half sides of the crate on the front and back opened, gently dropping to the floor. The one on the side facing the left wall did the same.

"How clever." Freya repeated herself. "The crate just opens and there's your lab bench, ready to go."

"Almost ready to go." Eugene pointed to several items stacked in the crate.

"Kelly, want to set up the target? Freya, you can help me with the barriers.

Kelly grabbed something that looked like a folded-up easel and paced off 20 feet, then started unfolding it.

Eugene grabbed something that looked like a table leg. "These are barriers to stop anyone from coming up to the lab bench. There are ten of them. You just screw them into the mounts around the edge of the base." Eugene screwed one in. "Make sure you have the grooves lined up parallel with the base."

Eugene handed one of the legs to Freya and pointed at one of the mounts. Then he grabbed another and started screwing it in.

"These hold plexiglass panels that slide in. Let me show you."

Eugene grabbed a panel and slid it into the grooves on the two legs he'd screwed in. The panel slid down about a foot into the leg and extended two feet above the top of the leg.

"They're to prevent someone from touching the dampening field we're going to create inside. As you'll see during the demo, you don't want to touch it."

"I like this set up, Eugene. It's like your lab is right here all assembled, safety equipment ready to snap in place."

"The original plan was to use the holoprojector, but some of the things we're going to demonstrate don't show up so well that way. But trust me, the live demo is very compelling."

"Eugene, I'm ready to calibrate the laser."

"OK." Eugene grabbed a box of safety glasses and handed a pair to Freya. "Put these on." He walked over to Kelly, who grabbed a pair. Eugene put the box on a chair, then grabbed a pair for himself. "Freya, can you pass these out as people come in?"

"Sure."

"OK, everyone. Glasses on. I'm going to power up the laser."

They heard the whining sound of the device powering up. Eugene lined up the laser's sights. Kelly moved out of the way and guided Freya to a safe spot.

"We're using a very low power beam," Kelly whispered. "Higher quality, narrower beam, but about the same power as a laser pointer."

The laser snapped on, the beam hitting its target.

"OK. We're good."

Eugene and Kelly went through the process of powering up the test bench's various systems. Then, once satisfied that everything was in working order, they powered the bench down and waited.

...

One by one, the meeting participants arrived. The first were Daniel Porter and his command crew. Next was the Ukraine's command crew. Then Admiral Katrine Bjork and her command crew. Michael, Sam Scott, Secretary Thompson and Captain Boyd were last.

Greetings exchanged, Michael called the meeting to order.

"Eugene, Kelly. You have the lead again today. But a quick thank you before you start. Your intergalactic jump drive is about to have a tremendous impact on the Confederation. It makes intergalactic trade possible, which will strengthen our ties with our allies in Andromeda and Triangulum.

"And now that we have complete specifications for all our ships, Admiral Scott, in collaboration with Joel, is scheduling the retrofit of all the ships in our fleet.

"So, thank you."

"Thank you for supporting our work Michael." Eugene replied, then turned toward the rest of the group. "Last week, we gave a quick overview of our work in what we're calling the Turtle dimension. We call it that because time moves slower there. We've put together demonstrations of three ways this technology can be weaponized. For each, I'll give a little holoprojection describing what and how the weapon works, then we will run a live demo. In principle, we could have done this all on the holoprojector. But the live demos are much more compelling.

"Weaponization 1 is the one Captain Boyd first proposed. I think she said something like 'shine your magic flashlight on the guy about to attack you, freezing him in place. Then mosey on around behind him and shoot him up the tailpipe.'"

There was a bit of chuckling among the officers.

A cartoonish animation of the scene appeared on the holoprojector. It showed a Kalamaan Ravager advancing on a Confederation Fast Attack Ship, a plasma ball forming on one of its forward projectors.

"In this scenario, the Fast Attack Ship would extend a time dampening field over the Kalamaan ship, freezing it in its tracks."

The holoprojection showed a gray circle appear over the Kalamaan ship. The ship, which had been moving, stopped. The plasma ball that had been growing stopped growing.

"Captain Boyd's original suggestion was that we move around behind the ship. Unfortunately, in the simplest form of the weapon, one like this where the ship is projecting the field, the field will move when we do. So, our relative positions are mostly locked in place.

"I'll come back to address the Captain's idea in a bit, but let's look at some possibilities for the simplest device first. One possibility is that we simply take our time and shoot the Kalamaan ship."

In the holoprojection the EAS ship shot three rail gun rounds. The projectiles hit the time dampening shield and disappeared.

"We now have three railgun projectiles on exactly the same course. They are spaced a second apart and travelling at what would appear to us as being a microscopically slow rate.

"When we drop the field, the projectiles will have the same velocity and momentum as they did when they entered the field. But now, they will be spaced right on top of each other. They'll all hit in the same place, at almost exactly the same time, functionally tripling the effectiveness of the weapon."

The holoprojection started playing again. The gray circle disappeared, and three railgun rounds hit the ship, blowing it up.

A hand went up. It was Admiral Scott.

"Admiral?"

"Eugene. Despite the miracles you've produced for us, I'm struggling to believe this one."

"As I did when the simulators predicted this behavior. That's why we brought the demo. OK, if I show you?"

"Please," Michael said, sensing the disbelief among the military people present.

Eugene walked over to the demo machine. "I don't have a railgun to fire, so I'm just going to drop some of these big 1.5-inch diameter steel ball bearings to simulate the railgun projectile." Eugene pointed to a small track extending from the top of the lab bench. "The ball bearings will drop from the track onto our target below. My target is this half-inch thick plank of white pine." Eugene held up the piece of white pine, then got down on a knee to slide it into a track beneath the place the ball would fall.

"For the first pass, I'm just going to drop the balls from the track above onto the wood below. My ball bearings each weigh about a half pound. According to the National Institute for Wood Standards, the hammer drop test for this type of wood is 30 inches. What that means is that a standard 2-lb construction hammer dropped from 30 inches, will crack this board in half.

"My ball bearings will be dropped from 50 inches, which will give them a little less than 75% of the energy required to break this wood."

Eugene placed the first ball bearing on the track and let go. It ran to the end, fell into a little funnel, then fell straight down onto the wood and bounced off. He repeated with a second, then third, each getting the same result.

"The point here is that I'm not spacing these closely together, they're hitting one at a time, and not having a lot of impact. Now I'm going to repeat the process. This time with a thin, time dampening field in between.

"Kelly could you slide a new plank in?

"Before I turn on the shield, I'd like to point out our safety measures. Touching a live, time dampening field would cause grave injury. We'll see that in more detail later. So, to protect ourselves, we've put these plexiglass plates all around the area where we will be projecting the field."

"The wood is replaced."

"Thanks, Kelly.

"Now, I'm going to turn on the dampening field. There was a whining sound, then the air in front of the lab bench seemed to distort somehow.

"The distortion you see is where the dampening field is. It's transparent, but the light traveling through it has slowed down. The dampening field itself is about a half inch thick and teardrop shaped." A simulated image appeared on the holoprojector. "I'm going to go over to the other side of the bench, so the dampening field is between us. It's just below chest height and you'll see its effect as I walk behind it.

"Ms. Newhouse, would you mind telling me what you see?"

Eugene stepped behind the shield and heard a gasp from someone.

"I appear to be cut in half, don't I? The light coming off my body will take a couple seconds to pass through the field."

"I see it," Freya said in astonishment.

"Now watch as I step away."

"A slice of you is still there."

"Thanks, Freya. The image of my shirt will persist for a couple seconds."

"Now I'm going to repeat the ball bearing drops. Here goes the first one."

The ball bearing rolled down the track, dropped into the funnel, fell straight down, then disappeared when it hit the field.

"Where did it go?" Someone asked.

"It's in the dampening field. If you look down from the top, it's still there. Looking in from the side, it appears to be flat, but microscopically thin. You can't really see it with the naked eye. But our instruments can still see it.

"I'm going to drop the second ball bearing. Note as I do, that it's been maybe 30 seconds since the first one dropped."

The second ball bearing rolled down the track, dropped, and disappeared into the dampening field.

"Any questions before I drop the third ball bearing?"

Admiral Scott stood. "How long will it take the balls to get through your dampening field?"

"A long time, in principle hundreds or thousands of years. But the power supply driving the field will give out in about 20 years, at which point the balls will fall the last two feet with the speed and acceleration they had when they entered the field.

"Dropping the third ball bearing now."

A third ball bearing disappeared into the dampening field.

"In a moment, I'll collapse the dampening field. What you'll see is more or less exactly what was indicated in the holoprojection. Three projectiles, right on top of each other, hitting the same spot on the target, and hopefully breaking the wood. Ready?"

The question was rhetorical. The three ball bearings appeared, slammed into the plank, which broke in half, and bounced away making a lot of noise as they hit the floor.

Eugene had seen this several times before, so was not startled. But most everyone in the room was. Even knowing the ball bearings were there did not blunt the shock of their sudden reappearance and speed.

As the room quieted, Eugene saw Admiral Porter raise his hand.

"Admiral?"

"What happens when you shoot the energy projectors?"

"That's the next topic in the presentation."

"Is there a demo that we can just cut to. I think you've conveyed the point about its use."

Eugene looked to Michael who nodded in agreement.

"OK. I don't have an energy projector, so I'm going to use a laser instead. The one I have is weak, only a quarter watt. And it is in the visible spectrum, so you'll be able to see it, or at least see the laser speckle.

"But for those live in the room, I need you to put your safety glasses on before I can start." Eugene watched as everyone put their glasses on.

"This demonstration will happen in four parts. The first part is simple. I'm going to turn the laser on, and it will hit the target over by the wall." Eugene pointed to the target. "Then Kelly will mark the spot where it hit. Ready Kelly?"

She nodded.

Eugene turned the laser on, and Kelly walked over to the target.

"This laser is about the same power as a laser pointer."

She stuck her hand out, blocking the beam.

"You wouldn't want to shine this laser in your eye, but it is harmless against the skin."

Kelly used a Sharpie to mark the spot where the laser hit the paper.

"Thank you, Kelly." Eugene turned the laser off. "Part Two will be to show the delaying effect the dampening field has on the laser."

Eugene went to the far side of the test bed, released a latch and swung a lever around. "I am moving the field emitter so that the field will now be vertical." He locked the lever into its new position, then went back to the controls and turned the dampening field on.

"The dampening field is on again. You should be able to see the broken arm effect a little more clearly with this orientation. It's also a little thicker this time, about an inch thick.

"When I turn on the laser, you'll see the beam appear, but seemingly stop when it reaches the dampening field. It will reappear out the other side after about two seconds. Here goes."

As the beam shot out, Daniel whispered to Katrine who was sitting next to him. "Wish science class had been this interesting in school."

The laser beam shot out, hit the dampening field, then emerged from the other side two seconds later.

"Kelly, can you mark the spot again?" Eugene turned to the audience. "On your ships, the components will be locked in place and calibrated. Our little demo station here isn't built to the same tolerances. Did it move much, Kelly?"

"No. It's in the same little circle I made."

"Good. I'm going to turn the laser off now. You will see the beam disappear on this side, then two seconds later disappear on the other side."

Eugene turned off the laser and two seconds later it disappeared on the other side as well.

"Now we know one of the things the field will do to a laser beam, and by extension one of your energy projectors. There is a second thing I want to show you before we look at the weaponization. I'm going to run an automated sequence, then explain what happened afterward. For those of you who were at the session Professor Ancient made last year regarding the Enemy's planetary defenses, you may recognize this.

"Automated sequence starting now."

The laser beam shot out and hit the dampening field, then a second later shutoff. The field emitter rotated about 10 degrees, then the laser shot out at a different angle, hitting the target near the top.

Eugene heard someone make a startled sound when the laser beam just appeared out of nowhere.

"Who would like to tell me what just happened."

Barika Amari, the Germany's first watch tactical officer, stood, hand up.

"Ms. Amari."

"You sent a one second pulse into the dampening field, then rotated the field, functionally changing the vector the light was travelling on. It emerged a second later on its new vector.

"Professor Ancient told us about the Enemy weapons that could capture and redirect their energy."

"Thank you. Exactly right on both scores."

"I'm going to reset the field to a new orientation for the weaponization options we want to show."

Eugene undid some latches, rotated the field emitter, then locked everything down again.

An image popped up on the holoprojector, showing the flat teardrop shape being projected up from the bottom and positioned so the laser would pass through at the widest part.

"This time we are going to shoot the laser through the wide part of the dampening field. It is about 40 times the distance as before, so it will take the laser 80 seconds to get through. I'm going to put a 1 second pulse into the dampening field. Eighty seconds later it will come out the other side. If all my alignment is correct, then it will hit the target. We'll repeat a couple times if we have to. Then we will run the weaponization demo.

"Kelly are you ready?"

"Yes."

Eugene put up the dampening field, then pulsed the laser.

A hand went up.

"Please." Eugene acknowledged.

"Sven Johannessen, second watch astrogation on the Ukraine. Dr. Xu, if it takes 80 seconds for the light to pass through the dampening field, does that imply that the two feet of width of the dampening field is equivalent to 80 light seconds?"

"Well, by definition yes. But I think the question you're asking is whether there's 80 light seconds of equivalent space compressed into the shield. The answer to that is clearly no, as I'll demonstrate next. But that really doesn't answer the question of what space is like inside the field. We don't know the answer to that question yet. As you will see, it's not very intuitive."

Eugene was interrupted when someone whooped. The beam had just shot out the other side of the dampening field hitting the target and apparently startled someone.

Eugene looked at the timer. 79 seconds.

"OK. I am going to launch another automated sequence. We are going to fire a 40 second pulse of our quarter-watt laser into the dampening field. The total laser energy in the field will be 10 Joules. Then I'm going to collapse the field. Make sure your safety glasses are on. Here goes."

As the laser shot into the dampening field, Eugene heard someone whisper. "He's created a pulse weapon."

Forty seconds later, the beam stopped, and a huge bolt of light hit the target, setting the paper on fire. The ferocity released from such a tiny laser was shocking. Kelly stepped up with a fire extinguisher and put the fire out, then noticed the deformation in the underlying diffuser. Apparently the 10 Joule beam was concentrated enough to exceed the diffusers capacity.

"What was the power of that weapon?"

"It was on the order of 10 gigawatts. There were only 10 Joules of energy released, which isn't very much. But the release was in one nanosecond, so the pulse was more than hot enough to catch the paper on fire. Not enough to kill someone unless you hit them in the right place, like the brain or heart muscle."

"There's quite a bit more to cover."

"Eugene?"

"Yes, Michael."

"Could you just name the remaining modes of use you envision. I've already seen enough to know we want this, so would like to prioritize your remaining material."

"Agreed." Admiral Scott shouted out.

"Happy to. One mode is to simply capture the opposing force in the field and leave them there for a while. Imagine having a hundred little drones come out of the ship and freezing the opposing Armada. You could leave them there for later. Dissect them one at a time. It's the definition of having your opponent defenseless and at your mercy.

"Another mode would be to freeze them and drop them into a star. You'd probably want a little drone doing that for you.

"A completely different mode would be to extend the dampening field over part of a thing. It's usually catastrophic, cutting a person or ship in half, triggering a heart attack in any creature with a circulatory system."

"I think I want the drones." Michael said.

"Can you demo cutting something up?" Admiral Scott asked.

"Sure. Kelly, could you grab the steel bar? I'll reconfigure the bench. This will only take a minute."

Michael noticed Admirals Porter and Bjork enthusiastically whispering to each other.

...

"Thank you for your patience. What you see is a steel rod sitting in the crook of two supports." The set up looked like a bench press without the weights on the ends.

"I've configured the dampening field generator to freeze two inches in the middle. If everything's still, nothing will happen. But the slightest motion will cut the 2-inch section out of the bar. Think of it as being like a molecularly sharp knife. Let me show you.

"Engaging the field. It is on. See the broken arm effect. Hopefully there has been no motion. Switching the field off. The bar appears to still be intact."

Eugene walked over to one of the ends protruding out through the plexiglass and shook it.

"Still intact. Now I'll do it again, this time moving the dampening field similarly to the way we redirected the laser beam.

"OK. The dampening field is up. Now, I'm going to rotate the field."

The portion of the bar in the dampening field slid two inches perpendicular to the bar. Then the two ends of the bar fell clanging loudly on the floor. The two-inch section just sat there in the field.

"Collapsing the dampening field."

The two-inch section of bar fell and bounced off the floor.

"Who would have believed," the Admiral muttered. "Half the value of a weapon like that would be scaring the enemy into submission. Take down one, then another, and everyone else would put up the white flag. It's instant catastrophic hull failure with no means of defense. Incredible."

LISETTE LEFEVRE'S RESIDENCE

"Evrand, you've found something already?"

Evrand Lepage was a Lorexian Ascendant. He'd joined the Canadian consulate as Head of Security in 2026. Before coming to Earth, he'd held various technical roles in power systems management on more mature worlds. He was by far the most knowledgeable person about power cells on Earth. So, Lisette had requested his temporary assignment on the investigation into the explosion at the Android Production lab.

"Yes. It wasn't that hard to determine what happened."

"Tell me."

"How much do you know about power cells?"

"I've heard of them."

"That much?" Evrand chuckled.

"Afraid so."

"OK, let me explain. If I get too technical, tell me."

"Sounds good."

"The basic principle behind a power cell is fairly simple, although it relies on physics concepts that are hard for laymen to understand. An individual power cell is built in layers. Each layer itself is made up of sublayers."

"I'm already lost."

"OK. Think of a sandwich. Bread, mayo, slice of turkey, slice of swiss, leaf of lettuce, another slice of bread on top. That's the basic structure.

"In the power cell, the base layer is made out of an electron-poor semiconductor. The most common power cubes use p-type polycrystalline silicon. Higher quality power cells, like those in an AIs computer, are usually made from a monocrystalline material.

"From the residue of the explosion, we know that Nadia's power cell was made using silicon. I suspect, but do not know, that it was made from monocrystalline silicon."

"The next layer is formed as a grid. The grid lines are made of an insulator. In this case silicon dioxide. Inside the grid is a 1-atom thick layer of Transluminide.

"The next layer is a conductor. Evidence suggests that Nadia's was made with aluminum, which is commonly used with silicon. This is where the magic happens..."

"Evrand can we cut to the chase with this? I'm heartened to know there are people who understand what goes on inside these devices, but I will never be one of those people."

"Hum. Have you ever wondered why different power cubes have different voltages, currents, expected life?"

"Can't say that I have."

"Well they do. But let me take a different tack. An AI's power cell needs to last a long time, much longer than normal power cells. Designers of those cells do it by operating the layers at low power levels, rotating which layers are used and which of the grid blocks on a layer are used. The power cube's interior controller manages all that."

"And the point…"

"An AI's power cube is capable of producing much more power than it actually does. Hundreds of times more. That controller can be accessed from the exterior for diagnostic and maintenance purposes, but usually is not.

"In Nadia's case it was. Her power cube controller had been tampered with. When the tool that opened the case touched the entry point, a signal was emitted and recorded. The signal indicated that power was being increased to maximum. In the minute or so that the tool was in the case, it heated to the point where everything inside oxidized when the seal was broken.

"This type of explosion is well documented, as are the residuals in the area. So, as I said, there is no doubt it overloaded. Therefore, the questions are: 1) how did someone get code into the power cube controller to do this, and 2) how did they get Barbara's tool to trigger it?"

"You mean there's no programming in a power cube to self-destruct."

"No. Only specially-licensed products can have code like that, and you can't even get that license for an AI's power cube."

"Well, I'll be. It was sabotage."

Lisette considered this for a long moment.

"You said there is maintenance and diagnostic access to the controller. Any other way in?"

"No."

"And does the access go outside the box or is the AI's computer the access mechanism."

"The AI's computer."

"Then there's the answer," Lisette pronounced. "Whoever took down Nadia's computer used it to install the self-destruct code. They didn't just kill Nadia, they also booby-trapped her. And, in so doing, they took down our Android Production facility.

"I think I know who the culprit is. Now to prove it."

SPACE FORCE COMMAND

Eugene and Kelly's presentations ended up being cut short, the half they did was more than enough to sell the idea. But the discussion carried on well past the designated meeting time. Michael took on the role of arbiter.

"Sam, what do you want most from what you've heard?"

"Tied. I like the idea of being able to quickly cut ships apart. I would expect it to quickly bring an end to any conflict. I also like the idea of each ship being equipped with 100 drones that could be transported in place to incapacitate an opponent. We have vastly superior ships and weapons, but we're still outnumbered. The ability for one ship to hold off many would be the tie breaker in an all-out war."

"Daniel?"

"I agree with Admiral Scott's points. But I struggle to believe that we would find ourselves in an all-out war. The Confederation's ships are so slow, it's hard to believe they could mass 10 ships anywhere outside the core. If that's not where we expect the major conflict to happen, it seems that the ability to cut up ships, or destroy them with pulse weapons would give us more leverage than drones."

"Laura?"

"Thank you for giving me a voice in this. The only real combat I've seen is the attack on the Ukraine in Andromeda. There, we were almost killed with a new, previously unknown weapon. I love the new weapon concepts that Eugene and Kelly have brought us. I want them all. But better defensive options might have led to a better outcome for us."

"Katrine?"

"The Kalamaan are my principal adversary at the moment. My biggest challenge is that my existing weapons are too strong. It's hard to counter them without destroying them.

"From that perspective, the drones would help me most today.

"But things are changing. The Kalamaan now have cloaks. Their abilities seem to improve every month. I suspect they are a proxy force under the Inspector's influence. Any of these options could be the deciding factor next month. If I had to choose one, it would be the drones. We are finally breaking up the siege on Celanar, carried out by a surprisingly large number of small, cloaked ships. I could have done it more quickly if I had the drones on my side.

"But one word of caution if mine is the last vote... War has its ebbs and flows. The solution to last month's problem is unlikely to be the solution to next month's. Any of the options discussed will be a help. I think we should find a way to do them all."

"Secretary Thompson?"

"I'm more of a strategic thinker than tactical. I think in terms of the things that will change the course of a war, more than those that will change an engagement.

"So, I'm partial to hordes of drones and the ability to slice up ships. Both have the kind of psychological advantages that change the course of a war."

"President Lee?"

"I'm a civilian, so favor weapons that are less likely to impact civilian populations. It seems to me that those would be the drones. But I'm open to persuasion that one of the others is more civilian friendly."

"I'm in the same camp. We need a solution that minimizes losses on both sides. I like the idea of the ship-based time-dampening field as a tactical weapon that gives our ships sharper teeth when pressed. But hordes of time-dampening drones will give us an advantage in terms of stopping conflict without inducing injury."

The room was silent for a moment, then Eugene raised his hand.

Michael nodded his approval for Eugene to speak.

"I think we get it all if we mount one or more field generators in each ship and build drones as a separate activity. We've proven that the ships can upgrade themselves and do it quickly. We've also proven that manufacturing can build drones. We know Karagon has almost infinite capacity to build power cubes. It seems to me that those two physical upgrades will give our ships tremendous ability to respond to any threat they face, and minimally compete for resources. That's what I would go with."

Michael nodded. "I think I agree with you. President Lee, Secretary Thompson. Do you have any additional questions?"

The Secretary looked at President Lee and discretely nodded his approval.

"Eugene. Kelly. Thank you for your work. I think it's time to take this to executive session." President Lee looked to Michael implying he should close the meeting.

"Thank you, everyone. We live in interesting times. But we're different than any of the groups I've led before. We work together. Sometimes we disagree, but rarely do we fight. With that kind of unity, there is no one in the Confederation who will successfully challenge us."

BRIDGE, EAS NETHERLANDS

"Admiral, we just entered the system. I have the Mumbai on sensors."

"Please hail them. I'll take it in the office."

A moment later the connection came through, the image of a smiling Bumati Parikh on the screen.

"Admiral, congratulations. I'm so happy to see you!"

"I heard about the incident yesterday. Also heard that you handled yourself well."

"How long are you here for?"

"Permanent. Or more accurately, I'm here to make our presence permanent. The Earth Alliance is in the process of annexing this system. I'm here to start the buildout and to help you in any way I can, consistent with building out the system."

"How many ships will you be bringing?"

"Another Cruiser will come tomorrow. Two Fast Attack Ships will follow a few days later. Is there anything you need immediate help with? My plan is to start putting up system surveillance platforms, but we could divert if you needed anything urgently."

"No. My biggest need is capacity. We're working around the clock and have only scratched the surface. We'll be heading out to another system on Sunday for a quick look. It will give the mining crew a watch off and the bridge crew something to do."

"Impressed as always." Chris was so proud of his former second watch tactical officer. "Sounds good. I'm going to focus on getting the surveillance system in place. Wanted to let you know we were here. Call if you need help."

PRESENCE PROJECTOR, ADMIRAL SCOTT'S OFFICE

President Lee, Secretary Thompson, Admiral Scott, and Michael gathered in the Admiral's presence projector. Admirals Porter and Bjork joined from their ships.

Michael started. "Sam, how are we doing on the EQD upgrades?"

"All but about 10 ships have started. About half are done. I can get you the exact number if you need it."

"Do you know why it's taking so long?"

"Two issues. One is supply. That should be resolved in the next couple days. The other is priority. We have made this upgrade a high priority, but not the highest."

Michael looked at Admiral Bjork. "Katrine are your ships fully upgraded?"

"No. We've had our hands full with the Kalamaan."

"If your theory is correct, that the Kalamaan are a proxy for the Inspector, then you're going to be hit with an EQD weapon in the next couple days. You're likely the active front of the conflict now. You need to get this done."

"Agreed." She turned to Admiral Scott. "Any chance I can have some fully upgraded ships rotated in, so mine have time to finish the upgrade? We are also several kits short."

"Sensible request. We'll get that done today." The Admiral turned to Michael.

"You're thinking that the EQD upgrade is the higher priority, right?"

"Yes, any ship that's not upgraded can't be put into the battle, so no sense equipping them further until the EQD is done."

"Agreed."

"Good. That brings me to the next thought. I think Eugene called it right. Our ships can upgrade themselves once we issue the final upgrade specification. And I'm thinking the order should be EQD, intergalactic drive, then time-dampening.

"If the ships are working that, then we can have manufacturing start pushing out the drones."

"A thought, if I may?" Daniel said.

Michael nodded.

"Drones require operators. Operators require control equipment and training, and our systems are heavily dependent on AIs to do the actual flying. Those issues need to be addressed in the same timeframe, otherwise we'll have drones aboard that we can't use taking up space that might otherwise be productively used."

"True. Thank you for raising the point. AIs are a problem at the moment. Let me see how far I can progress this issue in the next couple days."

"We have a comparable problem with the time-dampening devices," Admiral Scott pointed out. "I think the best way to address it will be to install the projector on a couple ships and give their crews some time to experiment. We could use their work as the basis for a first draft protocol."

"I don't think we want to delay the installations," Secretary Thompson countered. "We will develop protocols. There is no doubt about that. The more people we have experimenting, the faster it will happen.

"My concern is that the whole Confederation issue could go sideways next week. If that happens, we want as many ships as possible in the fight. And if it happens next week, it will happen in Andromeda. So, Michael's priorities are right, EQD, intergalactic drive, time-dampening weapon. We should be all in on getting that done as our highest priority."

"Agreed," Sam Scott said.

"Me too," Katrine Bjork added.

"Agreed," Daniel Porter confirmed.

"Thank you." Michael turned to President Lee. "I suspect this is going to be expensive. I'm sure the Advisors are going to want a voice, as will the House."

"I agree that we should give them a voice. But we need to start on our own authority. They might squawk about that, but they will ultimately approve the plan and thank us for getting ahead of the curve."

"Then we're done. Sam, ball's in your court now. Press it as hard and fast as you can. I'll follow up with manufacturing on the drones and get you a supply schedule as quickly as I can."

Chapter 17: APPOINTMENT

Michael roused himself early. It was likely to be a bad day. And ironically, the worst possible outcome would be if it weren't.

Fifteen minutes later, Michael was in the kitchen making coffee, hoping he hadn't disturbed anyone else.

"Michael, what are you doing up so early?" The voice coming out of nowhere startled him.

"Alexi, what are you doing up so early?"

"I'm actually late. Jack is going to be pissed. I'm leading an expedition up Keele Peak today. Actually, I'm not. If this is the typical group of losers Jack caters to, we'll be lucky to leave in an hour and even luckier to make it to first base camp tonight."

"I thought there was only one base camp?"

"There was, back in the day. Nowadays, we crawl up to an intermediate base camp. Rest for 16 hours or something totally stupid like that. Then proceed to base camp the next day.

"Jack has outfitted it like a resort, so the majority of the 'adventurers' call it quits there. Three or four may go up to the summit with me."

"Sorry to hear that."

"Which brings me back to the same question. Why ARE you up so early?"

"Central Council meeting."

"Condolences. Sounds awful but bet it's worse."

"Much, but don't ask."

Alexi looked at Michael with the intensity of the warrior she was. "Guess I'm glad to be taking some losers up to first base camp. At least they're toothless."

Michael smiled, appreciating Alexi's honesty.

"Looking forward to the day," Alexi said ruefully, then headed out.

Michael watched her go, wondering what she meant.

PRESENCE PROJECTOR, AMBASSADOR'S OFFICE

Michael entered the presence projector. At one level, he was anxious about today's proceedings, at another not. He already knew the lies that would be told and the lies that would be accepted. There really wasn't that much uncertainty. Nonetheless, the reality of hearing the slander that was about to ensue wouldn't be pleasant.

Michael took his seat, then the room morphed into the Central Council chambers. There had been a day when he'd been proud to serve here, but that was rarely true anymore. He noticed James at the far end of the Councilor's table, but his appearance was disheartening. He was tended to by one of the homeliest nurses Michael had ever seen, before he realized that it was David.

One by one the councilors appeared, as did a number of witnesses. When Michael saw Admiral Jo-Na and deputy Inspector Ha-Ke come in, he realized this meeting would be as unpleasant as he expected. When a quorum was reached, the Speaker called the meeting to order.

"Councilors. Most of you have heard about the recent incidents involving Earth, one of which resulted in the death of Inspector Ma-Gu. I've asked Admiral Jo-Na, leader of the High Command, and Deputy Inspector Ha-Ke to brief us on these incidents. After discussing the incidents and passing any resolutions we choose to make, I will nominate the Deputy Inspector to head our Military Intelligence division.

"Admiral, if you will?"

"Thank you, Mr. Speaker, honorable members of the Council. As you will recall, a special agent named Ju-Ne was sent to Earth as part of the first inflow of Confederation personnel after their Revelation.

"This was done, as it is done with all new members, to validate the technology and weapons claims the new member made as part of its application for membership. Although he found nothing of interest during his investigation, he grew suspicious five years later as scientists and engineers on Earth began advancing Confederation technology. This had never been seen before, so was in fact very suspicious.

"As someone active in the sector at that time, I knew that these were in fact new creations, not hidden secrets. I communicated that back to Inspector Ra-Tu. Unfortunately, the former Inspector did not believe me. He initiated a series of events that ultimately led to the loss of his ship, Enemy infiltration into Andromeda, the destruction of the Earth Ship Helsinki, the loss of the majority of the replacement Armada, and the formation of the 3F Defensive Alliance."

The Speaker interrupted, "We know all this history. Is there a point you're trying to make, relevant to the issue at hand?"

"Yes. The traitor Ju-Ne was tried in absentia, convicted, and sentenced to reconditioning. But he went into hiding on Earth. There he committed great crimes against the people of Earth.

"This body demanded his extradition and sent a task force to go collect him, only to find that he was in the process of being returned."

The Speaker interrupted again. "We did not know he would be returned at the time."

"As you could not have. The problem is that Inspector Ma-Gu arrived at Earth, was told the traitor had been returned, then attacked the planet!"

"Objection! Ju-Ne was not a traitor and Ma-Gu did not attack the humans. They attacked him."

It was Deputy Inspector Ha-Ke.

The Speaker pounded his gavel. "The witness will refrain from name calling and unfounded accusations."

Michael could tell that Jo-Na was boiling with anger. But he hid it well enough that the rest of the Council, except James, would not suspect.

"Ju-Ne was convicted of treason, so is by definition a traitor," Jo-Na said calmly and respectfully. "And if I am allowed to testify, I will prove that Ma-Gu did in fact fire a weapon at Earth, and the humans never fired a weapon at all."

James spoke quietly. "We have called this witness. He has gathered the evidence. We should let him present it." James spread calm in the room, but the effort took a toll.

"Thank you for those words of wisdom, Councilor Ancient."

Michael heard the Speaker's respectful words. But he also sensed the Speaker's inner disdain.

...

"In summary, a second Inspector went rogue and launched unsanctioned attacks against an ally. He fired an illegal weapon, he fused the weapon using an illegal mechanism, he targeted civilians, and he refused to evacuate his ship after he had fatally damaged it.

"The sensor data and testimony of the survivors is unambiguous and conclusive. It is my recommendation that Inspector Ma-Gu's name be stricken from the records. And given the long history of abuse that has originated from the Inspector's office, I recommend the disbandment of the Military Intelligence department.

The Admiral's pronouncement set off a wave of protest. It took the Speaker several minutes to gavel the session back to order.

Again, James interrupted, speaking quietly, "I agree with Admiral Jo-Na."

"I second," Councilor Mo-Mo called out, putting the Speaker in an awkward position.

Michael saw an evil look come over Deputy Inspector Ha-Ke. Jo-Na would be in for trouble when this session was over.

"It has been our tradition that two members of the Council, if in agreement, can bring an item to a vote. But we have only heard half the testimony. The rules require a super majority vote to end testimony. I would vote against such a motion, are there three others that would vote with me."

Three hands shot up. Councilor To-Ja from New Lorexi and Councilors Ke-He and Ku-Ka from Andromeda.

"Given that there's not a super majority that would support an end to the testimony, would either of you like to withdraw the motion.

The Speaker looked first to James, then to Mo-Mo.

"I withdraw," Mo-Mo replied.

"Then I give the floor to Deputy Inspector Ha-Ke."

"Thank you, Mr. Speaker and honorable Members. Over the last two weeks, two ships from Earth have entered Andromeda's space without the proper transponder codes. The first was the one fulfilling the extradition request. They were intercepted by Admiral Jo-Na's ships, who accepted the prisoner, then escorted the ship to New Lorexi. There, they made some deliveries. Later, the Admiral's ships escorted them out of the system. This exchange was peaceful. The ships in violation did not resist and submitted to inspection.

"Although it is a violation to enter Confederation space without appropriate transponder codes, it is a minor one, as long as the ship submits to inspection.

"A second ship arrived some days later. It was ordered to come aside for inspection, but it did not. Instead it turned away and jumped out into the void. This is completely unacceptable. We subsequently determined that the ship in question was the EAS Ukraine, captained by Laura Boyd. We demand that this ship return immediately and submit itself to inspection. We also demand that its Captain be summoned for prosecution."

Anger burned within Michael. The Deputy Inspector knew who the ship was the moment it arrived. He attacked it, killed its helm AI, and used the power cell in the case to destroy the Earth Alliance Android Production Lab, killing several people in the building.

"May I comment on this?" Jo-Na asked.

"Please," the Inspector replied.

"The transponder codes were recently changed. Notice was not given, not even to me, despite the fact that it is my office that administers the codes. When I first heard of this incident, I launched an investigation. Among the evidence uncovered was that the transponder could be read. That is the reason the Deputy Inspector knows what ship it was. Record of the ship's identity was made immediately and included in log readings recorded by my office. Curiously, the original record was deleted that day after the suspect in this case was interviewed.

"I also have a recording of the warning that was sent. The ship was threatened with immediate seizure. And the passengers were threatened with immediate arrest.

"Further, the ship was fired upon, using another illegal weapon that targets helm AIs.

"I think the real question here is how much the Deputy Inspector knew about this and why he has not rooted out the perpetrators."

Once again, the session devolved into chaos.

...

"The resolution to dissolve the Department of Military Intelligence fails by a vote of 5 to 4.

"The contingent resolution for the Department of Military Intelligence to report directly to the Central Council passes by a vote of 5 to 4.

"The resolution to appoint Deputy Inspector Ha-Ke as the new head of Military Intelligence passes 5 to 4.

"The resolution to sanction Earth for failing to comply with Andromeda's transponder standards fails 6 to 3.

"The resolution to sanction Captain Laura Boyd for failing to comply with a lawful order fails 5 to 4.

"There being no other matters before us today, I adjourn today's meeting. Thank you, Councilors."

Moments before the connection to the Central Council chambers dropped, Jo-Na motioned to Michael implying that they needed to speak.

"Thanks for accepting the connection, Mi-Ku."

"We came surprisingly close, my friend."

"I think that was my last stand. I discovered the secret to the weapon they used on your AI."

The Admiral put a piece of paper on the table. It showed the location of a file.

"Got it, thank you. How much blow back are you going to get?"

"He tried to blackmail me. He has a very powerful set of data, mostly fake, that implicates me in a scheme to transfer restricted technology to Earth. I expect him to make his play as soon as he's sworn in."

"What did you allegedly give us?"

"The so-called Earth Standard propulsion system. His documents are all real, what's been faked is the dates. He has me in possession of those documents six months or so before your Dr. Xu invented the drives. The reason it will probably work is that everyone recognizes the documents, they are completely real. What's fake is the encryption of the date and source. They obviously have the technology to fake the encryption."

"We saw Ju-Ne do the same thing here."

There was a pause.

"The Ancient One appeared not to be in good health. Do you know anything about that?"

Michael hesitated to say anything, but needed to keep his alliance with Jo-Na strong.

"He was injured during the arrest of Ju-Ne."

"How did you capture him by the way?"

"The Ancient One put Ju-Ne under compulsion, got him to give us the location of the restoration chamber holding his real body. He ended up holding him under compulsion for over an hour, which damaged him somehow."

"And his nurse?"

"The Ancient One's apprentice."

"Isn't his apprentice a human male?"

"Yes. Took me a second to recognize him. He has the power to change like the Ancient One does, but he doesn't really know what a female Lorexian actually looks like."

"Astounding. I had no doubt it was a Lorexian female, not very appealing, but one nonetheless. He must be very skilled."

"He is."

"How many of them are there?"

"Only one now. But I'm told he has found more."

"The speaker and new Inspector have no idea what they're setting themselves against."

"No, they don't. And it will be their undoing."

After a moment of silence, Michael stood. "Thanks for the tip." Michael nodded toward the sheet of paper, then left through a virtual door.

AMBASSADOR'S OFFICE

Back in his office, Michael looked up the file Jo-Na had tipped him about. It was titled 'Forced Download Program Installation via Subchannel Metadata Diversion.'

Michael quickly scanned the document, which was mostly indecipherable techno speak. In contrast, the executive summary was surprisingly approachable and completely terrifying.

Whenever a ship entered a system, its IFF would be pinged. Once recognized as a friendly ship, it would automatically receive a series of updates. Updates came in two broad categories, maintenance updates for minor ship systems and database updates relevant to the star system the ship was entering.

Minor systems were software controls for things like replicators, doors, lifts, trash, and sewage handlers ... All the ship's minor automated functions.

Database updates included things like replicator patterns for local food, local language database updates, and system specific astrogation data that mapped known space trash.

Minor system software updates were scanned for malware, but its metadata (i.e., descriptive data about the software) was not. Database updates were not scanned for malware because it was data, not software.

The document contained instructions detailing how software could be stored as data in a database, and the metadata associated with software updates could be used to instruct the update to assemble malware from database data.

The program that killed Nadia had been downloaded as part of the automated update process when the Ukraine's transponder had been pinged. And the Inspector now had the power to do that selectively to any ship in any system.

"Joel." Michael called out, activating the comm system.

"Hi Michael, what can I do for you?"

"I've found out how the Inspector took down the Ukraine's helm AI and blew up the Android Production Lab. I'm sending you a document now. We need a fix for this."

"Will look at it now."

"Loop Lisette Lefevre in when you've learned enough to brief her. I'm meeting with her next and will let her know to expect something from you."

"Will do."

ENGINEERING CONFERENCE ROOM

"Eugene, thank you for agreeing to meet with me."

"Lisette, I was surprised to hear from you. I hope I'm not in some sort of trouble."

"No. I actually need some help and was wondering if I could pick your brain a bit."

"You mean like part of an investigation?"

"Yes and no. There's a cold case on another world that's come to my attention. It involves a high-profile theft of some valuable equipment. The equipment never surfaced. And other than the fact that the equipment is missing, no evidence of any sort was found.

"Speculation has been that someone used a transporter of some type. It is still the prevailing theory but, as theories go, it has real problems. The equipment was operated deep underground in a room carved from bedrock. There were shields at all the access points, redundant transporter suspension fields in the room, and transporter suspension fields around the facility.

"Any theories about how this could have been done?"

"How deep in the mountain was it?"

"250 meters."

"That would be tough for a standard Confederation transporter, like the ones used for personnel transport on our ships. But none of the above would be hard to overcome for a modified transporter or a custom built one.

"For example, think of a mining transporter. It cuts down to the core of a planet and brings up huge amounts of liquid metal."

"Ah, never thought of that. But what about the transporter dampening fields?"

Eugene chuckled. "There is no such thing. They don't block transport; they block the target locking mechanism. A personnel transporter and most confederation cargo transporters will not engage transport unless they can get the whole object. All those fields do is block the controller from initiating transport. Remove the interlock, and presto. Poor targeting by unconditional transport of whatever the transporter grabs."

Lisette sat there with her mouth open.

"You've got to be kidding me. They don't block transport?"

"No, they just trigger an interlock built into the standard units. Disable the interlock, or build your own controller and presto, no dampening, just poor targeting.

"But it seems to me there's another possibility. Maybe the equipment is still there, but held in a nearby, or possibly even a distant, dimension."

"Back to the transporter for a minute, how would you beat the targeting issue? I mean, suppose they wanted to transport it through a kilometer of solid stone to another room somewhere else."

"Well to start, you would need a powerful transporter. But there are hundreds of ways to get an exact location. For example, mining transporters can pull paper thin slices of metal from hundreds of kilometers below the surface.

"But if the location is fixed, then you don't need targeting, you already know where it is."

"So, the only way I can really stop something from being transported is if I hide it where no one can find it."

"Or put it behind one of our sensor-blocking shields, or inside one of our time-dampening fields... But we're the only ones that have those. So, they couldn't be part of the missing equipment mystery."

"I had no idea. Eugene, thanks so much. This case is not one of ours, it's in another jurisdiction. But I'll pass on some of your comments in case there's someone there interested in pursuing it."

...

Lisette walked back to her office confident that they would be able to protect their Transluminide. But she'd need to get authorization to add Eugene to the team first.

PRESENCE PROJECTOR, AMBASADOR'S OFFICE

Michael's next meeting was with Ambassador Sa-Na of Celanar. Celanar was the premier producer of AIs in the sector.

"Mi-Ku, thank you for reaching out. How can I help you?"

"Sa-Na, thank you for making time to meet with me. I should have reached out earlier, but only found out what I was up against today."

"Tell me."

Michael quickly explained.

"The Inspector's office strikes again. Thank you for sharing the details of this weapon. We don't know enough about war ships to help you on that front. But we do know a lot about AIs, and it seems to me that we should be able to harden them against this type of attack.

"But what about the unspoken issue? If your Android Production Lab is down, your technicians in reconstruction, how will you continue producing ships and defenses that are AI dependent?"

"We have, or at least had, an AI root stack optimized for our ships. It would be a huge set back to rebuild that work."

Sa-Na smiled.

"What?" Michael asked.

"Your Barbara sent us a copy of your root stacks. She also sent us backups of many of your AIs and androids. We have better host computers than you do. If you have the avatar and can send certification of her loss, we can bring back your Barbara. In all likelihood better than before. We can also bring back your Nadia.

"Do you have a copy of Nadia?"

"Let me confirm."

There was silence for a moment.

"Yes, we do."

"Will you bring her back for us?"

"Of course we will."

"My people tell me that your helm AI root stacks, as well as your engineering root stacks, are quite good, especially given their age. There are things we can do to make them more alert, give them better memory, without changing who they are."

"If you're sure of that, I would be interested."

"Allow us to interview those providing the memories, and we can produce more for you. A lot more. We'll even give you the IP at no additional cost, so you can resume when your people and facilities are restored."

"Why?"

"We are in this together, Mi-Ku. Things have gone terribly wrong in the Confederation. You and your humans are our hope."

"How soon can you start?"

"Tomorrow? All we need are the candidates to contribute memories. We can do it by presence projector as long as you have a technician available who can run the scans."

"Deal. It may take a while to organize at this end, but I'll message you with an update by the end of my day."

"Thank you for letting us help Mi-Ku."

PROFESSOR ANCIENT'S RESIDENCE

David was worried. James was fading. He'd given James an energy boost before today's Central Council meeting. Another after. Both helped, but not for long.

"David, my people had something similar to your restoration chambers. They worked on a very different principle. Where yours would be death for me, ours could restore.

"The confrontation with Ju-Ne broke me in a way I cannot repair. If I cannot find one of my people's restoration chambers, I won't last much longer.

"You are already at the balance point. Soon, Confederation restoration chambers will drain you of energy, not restore you. Monitor yourself if you use one."

"What do we do James?"

"I cast my attention to that question every day. Now, time for you to go. I need my rest. Spend some time with Valerie. Let her help restore you."

MANUFACTURING OFFICE

Another long late day, but Joel had finished the first complete intergalactic jump drive kit for a freighter today. The Toronto, the Earth Alliance's first and most experienced freighter had been chosen for the upgrade. Joel had just transported the kit up. Captain Shields had assured him that his team would get the upgrade done ASAP, maybe by morning. Joel chuckled at the thought of an overnight upgrade but was happy that he could check this item off his To Do list. There was too much on it and he needed rest.

Chapter 18: EMERGENCY RUN

[Saturday, 08.01.2032] NEAR TOGOROTU

Captain Bayson Dalmoy was finally completing the interminable run home from a trip to New Lorexi. His ship was an old Confederation Military Escort. It had been converted for civilian freighter use thousands of years ago. His family was relatively wealthy, able to upgrade the ship for intergalactic runs. It could do 750 light-years per jump with a 20-minute recharge cycle. The last run to Andromeda had been 1.8 million light-years, 33 days each way. Ships like his never got priority routing; nonetheless, he was hours away from completing the 70-day round trip.

"Captain, our transponder was just pinged. We are now under Togarotu space traffic control."

"Thank you. Good to be home."

Moments later.

"Captain, we've just been messaged by Togarotu space traffic control. We are being given priority routing. There's been another outbreak. Togarotu is desperately short of medication. Our shipment is needed urgently."

The Captain was not happy to hear of the outbreak, but very happy to hear of the priority routing. He'd be home in two more hours, not four or five. The long absence from wife and family wore on him.

INSPECTOR'S OFFICE

"Sir, we just got word that the package was delivered."

An evil smile crept across the Inspector's face. Mo-Mo was about to learn the price of crossing him. The plague was something a predecessor had come up with to reign in the upstarts. He'd released another round after today's meeting. New cases had already surfaced.

And the ship transporting the cure... It would suffer catastrophic failure as it approached the planet.

He would send Mo-Mo his regards and condolences in the morning. He'd also offer rapid delivery of a replacement shipment in 5 days, if they could come to an arrangement.

The vast majority of his people were sheep. He was the new wolf in town. And soon, he would own them all.

AMBASSADOR'S RESIDENCE

Michael woke. An emergency request had come in. The bot that managed his queue woke him. Michael got up, slipped on a robe, and headed to his office hoping not to wake Sarah or the baby.

It was 2:00 AM.

"Mo-Mo, what's the emergency?"

"Mi-Ku, another round of the plague started yesterday. We've already lost a few. But the experts say we will lose a thousand tomorrow. The ship bringing in the seasonal replenishment of medications lost its helm AI as it made its orbital insertion."

There was a pause as Mo-Mo fought back the emotion.

"The ship, crew and cargo were lost as it made an uncontrolled entry into the atmosphere."

"Mo-Mo, I'm so sorry to hear that. How can I help?"

"The medications are only made in two places in the Confederation. New Lorexi and Jerusota. Best case supply from New Lorexi is 70 days. Jerusota has inventory, your ships could get it here tomorrow."

There was silence on the line for several seconds.

"You realize that this is the Deputy Inspector fighting back, right? He has a subtle new weapon that can take down any ship, anywhere in the Confederation, by killing its helm AI."

"This is my punishment for siding with the Admiral yesterday, isn't it?"

"Almost certainly. Have you confirmed that Jerusota has supply they are willing to sell to you?"

A pause.

"He has supply. But hedged. He has no means to transport and..."

A pause.

"Let me guess. He's afraid of retribution from the Inspector's office."

"They operate under license and he's afraid it will be yanked. At least that's what was implied."

"Have you been in contact with Fe-Va?"

"About the trade alliance?"

"Yes."

"If Jerusota will agree to sell to you, we will transport it. I may need more than a day, but we will do it.

"If Jerusota will not, then we will buy it from them. Our alliance compels them to sell to the 3F Alliance. If you were allied, then we would be compelled to sell to you. Fe-Va is incredibly resourceful. He can probably close a trade deal with you in an hour. "

"Understood, Mi-Ku. Thank you."

...

Michael sat in his office thinking about how this could be done. He didn't want to send a ship unless it had some sort of defense against this weapon.

JOEL RUBINSTEIN'S RESIDENCE

An emergency alarm went off, waking Joel. Looking at the clock, he saw it was 2:30 AM. The caller ID on his communicator said the call was from Michael.

"Michael, what's happened?"

"I need a defense against the Inspector's new weapon."

"What? Now? At 2:30 AM?"

"The Inspector knocked down another ship, one carrying emergency medical supplies. We have the means to replace the supplies in time, if we can get a ship past the Inspector."

"It will take a while to develop a proper defense, but there is an easy and obvious emergency solution."

"Which is?"

"Turn off the transponders. Use other forms of communication to arrange an escort. If you have to, have a friendly Confederation security patrol impound the ship and escort it into port with its broken transponder."

"Joel, you're a genius!"

The line dropped.

"You're welcome, Michael," Joel said to himself, then settled back into bed.

OFFICE, AMBASSADOR'S RESIDENCE

Michael wasn't sure what to do next. The ball was in Mo-Mo's court. He stood, intending to creep back to bed, then his communicator sounded. It was Fe-Va.

"Mi-Ku, the Inspector is playing right into our hands. Mo-Mo just signed a Letter of Intent. Genius idea by the way. I've been studying up on Earth's Revelation. I'd never heard of this type of arrangement before. Where did you come up with it?"

"It's a common Earth contracting process to help parties that want to join forces to pursue it with contained risk for both parties."

"Well, it worked. Fe-Va signed the letter of intent for a trade deal worth up to 10,000 kg of Transluminide, contingent on the 3F Alliance supplying medications worth about 100 kg free of charge within the next 36 hours. But they've also agreed to pay for a back load to Edukatar."

Michael couldn't help but chuckle. The Confederation was so stuck in its ways. People like Mo-Mo, Fe-Va, Fa-Ta were not. They'd do anything legal to help their people, not fuss and moan the way everyone in Andromeda seemed to do these days.

"One issue related to the delivery. The only ship I can raise at this hour has a broken transponder. See if you can get Mo-Mo to arrange a trusted security escort for the run in from the void. I'll manage the rest on this end.

SPACE FORCE COMMAND

General Solomon Gandhi was the officer in charge this morning. He enjoyed the overnight watches. They were mostly peaceful, which allowed him time to work special projects. But on those nights that weren't peaceful, he had almost absolute power to respond. Something you never got on the other watches.

"General, an emergency call from the Ambassador."

"Thank you, Andy." He nodded to his aide, a smile starting to form. *Not peaceful. Yes!*

"Mr. Ambassador, how can I help you, sir?"

"We need to make an emergency run to Triangulum. How many ships with the new Intergalactic Drive are available to make the run?"

"Checking."

A moment later.

"Only the EAS Toronto, sir. Her upgrade was completed about an hour ago, so it has not been tested. The only other ship that has the drive installed is the Ukraine. But she's in drydock getting a sensor upgrade and recalibration."

"Put the Toronto on 3-hour ready stand by. I'd like to see her depart for Togarotu in Triangulum, via Jerusota, by sunrise. One-hour load in Jerusota. Ask the captain to plot their course. I'll have some special instructions before they depart."

"Yes, sir! Consider it done, sir!"

"Thank you, General."

As Michael broke the connection, he realized that night watch at Space Force Command seemed a lot more flexible than the day watches did.

AMBASSADOR PEKLIT'S OFFICE

"Michael, thank you for taking my call."

"Ambassador Peklit, I'm sorry that we find ourselves in this situation, but happy that we can work together to solve it."

"Thank you, Michael. I just got word that the plague has already spread to my home world, Dalfanito. We are Zorossan, the same species as is on Togarotu.

"The initial outbreak there started at the space port and apparently traveled to Dalfanito on the first day."

"You would like us to transport medication to Dalfanito also?"

"Yes. My people have enough for a couple days, so it can be on the return."

"Thank you."

"May I speak about a sensitive topic, off the record?"

"Certainly."

"I know what's going on. It's fortunate that the only ship you have that can make the trip on short notice has a broken transponder.

"I just got off the line with the President of Dalfanito. They have just upgraded some of their security ships with transponders that do not have the problems the others have experienced. He would be willing to provide some of those ships as escort until your ship can be repaired. He is also offering to send a few of their resilient transponders back with your ship as a show of good will."

Michael was impressed at how well the ambassador communicated the message without directly naming the issue.

"That is most generous of him."

"One other thing. We've seen an unusual number of Fleet ships from the Triangulum Armada in our sector this week. As you know, we, too, are part of a defensive alliance formed because the Confederation could not project enough power into our sector to secure it from pirates. Yet this week, three ships have entered orbit around Togarotu, two around Dalfanito. Curious, don't you think?"

"Very."

"I'm sending you contact information now. Space traffic control here is aware that your ship is coming. They been instructed to give you priority clearance and routing. They are also aware of your transponder issues. Your Captain should expect to be challenged as soon as he enters the system. Prearranged security codes are included in the packet I just sent.

"There are also contact instructions for your Captain to follow in the unlikely event that his ship is not challenged. I can't help you in Triangulum, but we are taking extraordinary measures here to make sure there is no issue at Jerusota."

"Thank you, Vorkin. It's good having a partner like you."

"Thank you, Michael."

BRIDGE, EAS TORONTO

Captain Avery Shields and First Officer Ina Talgateva had just received their final, predeparture briefing. The mission was now in their hands.

"Captain, I just received permission to depart. Along with it came confirmation from Space Force Command that our transponder is not replying. They attempted to force a space junk database update, but the transponder would not accept it."

"Thank you, Mathias. One less problem for us to worry about. Please engage our course."

"Course engaged, Captain. We've been given priority clearance. We have a straight line shot today and a light ship. Expected flight time, one hour 37 minutes. I think this will be a record for this routing."

"How long from there to the rim?"

"Again, we are getting priority routing out of Jerusota, so 3 hours 12 minutes to the rim, a three-minute transit, then the long jump. Total flight time four hours, 52 minutes to our escort at the rim of Triangulum.

"It's 5:33 AM now, if we can load our cargo at Jerusota in less than an hour, we'll be in Triangulum for lunch."

...

"Earth Alliance Ship Toronto, this is Jerusotan Space Flight Control. Your emergency mission has been approved for a snatch and go pick up. Sending the requirements and flight plan now. Please acknowledge if you are able to comply."

The message was handled by Mathias, who routed the inbound audio to the bridge comm system.

"Captain, their protocol is well within our capabilities. Basically, we do not enter orbit. Instead we slingshot around the planet. Our closest point of approach will be directly over the shipping facility, where we will do a synchronized transport. It will not only eliminate pick up time but will shave about 40 minutes off our flight time."

"Do it," Captain Shields replied.

EAS MUMBAI

The run-in with the Kalamaan on Wednesday had scared Bumati. None of their Ravagers was even close to a match for her ship. One on one, it was hard to see how the Kalamaan could prevail in a conflict.

But they were crafty. Multiple of them against her at the same time could have had a different ending.

Thankfully, two Cruisers had arrived in system this week. They'd done a thorough screening of the planets and moons to assure no one was spying on them. They were now in the process of putting up a system-wide surveillance network like they had on Earth.

The plan was for Space Force to permanently inhabit this system. They would be putting in a Space Station with docking facilities and maintenance bays. They would also be putting up mining platforms and a refining facility. Two or more war ships would always be present in the system.

When the next round of ships arrived next week, one of the lead Cruisers would head over to the next system to begin the same process there.

No longer worried about having to deal with system defense, Bumati and her team had made huge headway over the last couple days. They had complete processing for 12 more claims in what they were now calling their private claims system. And had mined more of the garnet gemstones. These were of the green Uvarovite type, molecular composition $Ca_3Cr_2Si_3O_{12}$. A total of 400 kg had been pulled, including another 2-carat stone now mounted to the growing collection on the mining desk.

She had also received permission to go on another field trip tomorrow to her third candidate system.

EAS TORONTO

"Captain, I just received confirmation that our escort has arrived at the rendezvous point. We'll be in position to jump in another eight minutes."

"Thank you, Mathias."

"Now the fun begins," the Captain whispered to first officer Ina Talgateva, seated next to him.

"I'm told it's a strange experience, but it doesn't trigger the same type of vertigo."

...

"Jumping in 3, 2, 1, ..."

The world froze. There was no sound, no ship noises. One by one the various sensor systems went blank.

"Can you hear me when I talk?"

Ina turned to the Captain. "Yes." She turned toward Mathias. "Mathias, can you hear me?"

Silence.

"Seems that we are not impacted, but the AIs are."

After another couple seconds, reality came screaming back. The first to return was Mathias, who said, "Jumped," completing the countdown that had been frozen for nearly a minute.

Ina started laughing. That she and the captain had a short conversation while everything else was frozen seemed preposterously funny.

"Sensors are coming back up Captain," the tactical officer reported.

"We were just hailed by the lead ship in our escort."

"Put him on."

"Greetings Earth Alliance Ship Toronto. I am Captain Dewset Cowlon of the 2B Defensive Alliance Ship Distant Hope. We have been advised, and have confirmed, that your transponder is not functioning. Please send us the security code you were given granting access to our space."

"Sending."

"Confirmed. Welcome to Triangulum and the 2B Alliance."

"Thank you, Captain Cowlon. I am Captain Avery Shields. This is my first officer Commander Ina Talgateva. We come with a shipment of medicine for Togarotu and Dalfanito."

"Welcome, Captain. And thank you. The medication you bring will save many lives. If you will synchronize with our jump sequencer, we can commence the journey to Togarotu. Estimated transit time 3 hours, 45 minutes."

"Captain, one thing you should know before we begin. Our ship travels through jump much faster than yours does. For a long jump we could arrive many seconds earlier than you would. You might want to sequence us 30 or more seconds after the first ship."

"I have not been warned of that. For the first jump you will go third, delayed by the time you request. Two other ships will follow."

"As you order, sir."

...

"Captain, even with the 30 second delay, we will beat the first ship by 15 or more seconds. They have scheduled a long jump."

"Maybe we can do better on the subsequent jumps."

"Jumping in 3, 2, 1... Jumped."

As sensors cleared, it was obvious they were in trouble. Two of the huge Confederation Cruisers were waiting a little less than 1 light-second from their position.

"Engage the stealth shield."

"Stealth shield engaged, but I'm sure they saw us."

"Unidentified stealth ship. You are in violation of Confederation Identification Requirements, reveal yourselves and prepare to be boarded for inspection."

"That's not going to happen. Mathias, do we know when and where the other ships will emerge?"

"No. Only our course was revealed to us."

"Unidentified stealth ship. Drop your cloak now and prepare to be boarded. We can sense where you are and will commence firing on your position momentarily."

"Possible they can sense us, but unlikely, Captain," Tactical Officer Linus Felder whispered.

"Captain, they just fired at us. They are way off. Firing again."

The lead 2B alliance ship emerged from jump.

"Captain, she is in direct line of site between us and the Fleet Cruisers."

"2B Alliance Ship, Goodwill. You will stand down and submit to inspection."

The second 2B Alliance ship dropped from jump.

"Confederation Cruiser, Enlightened Day. You have no authority here. Stand down and leave the area immediately."

"Captain, the Confederation Ship just fired on the 2B Alliance Ship Goodwill."

The two Dalfanito ships dropped from jump.

The Goodwill's shields came up and were nearly at strength when the first plasma bolt hit. The plasma spread out across the shield and was mostly dissipated, then the Goodwill's shields collapsed.

"Captain, the Cruiser's plasma cannons are huge, another shot like that will take the Goodwill down. The other 2B ships are returning fire."

"We have our Black Hole shield, right?"

"Yes, sir."

"Mathias! Put us between the Goodwill and the Cruisers.

"Comms, call the Goodwill and tell them not to move. We will have them covered in…"

"Six seconds, sir," Mathias filled in.

"Tactical as soon as we clear the nose of the Goodwill, drop the stealth and put up the black hole shield."

Mathias piped up, "Engage shield in three, two, one… Engage shield."

"Captain we are being hailed by Captain Dewset Cowlon of the Distant Hope."

"Put him on."

"Captain Shields, what are you doing?"

"I'm shielding the Goodwill. My forward shield is impenetrable. At least to anything those cruisers have. Are we pressing this fight, or fleeing?"

"We don't have the fire power or speed to do either."

Avery knew he would regret it but said it anyway.

"We have the speed to run, but that wouldn't help you. I may also have the fire power to finish this."

"You also have the medicine. Let me see if I can talk them into walking away."

The line dropped.

"Captain, we are running blind, permission to deploy the sensor drones."

"Granted, send them out wide."

"Captain?" It was chief engineer Milli Rusinko, from Russia. "As an experiment, the engineering crew has been playing with shielded drones. They don't have the speed or mass to be used as a kinetic weapon. But they would have the stealth to put something right up against the hull of those cruisers. Maybe something that goes boom."

"Do we have anything that goes boom?"

"No, but maybe our escorts do. And we've finished building the new time dampening weapon. It's not installed into the ship, but it could be jury rigged onto one of the drones."

"Start jury rigging, but do not power it up in the ship."

"Understood."

"Captain, I have Captain Cowlon on the comm for you."

"Put him on."

"Captain Shields. We seem to be at a standstill at the moment. They're not going to let us go. But they seem less than confident they can take us by force. So, they've called for backup which is an hour out. I think you should run. We can shield you long enough to jump. Head to Togarotu and make the delivery."

"May I suggest an alternative?"

ENGINEERING EAS TORONTO

"Captain, we received another demand to surrender now before reinforcements arrive. They claim that 3 more cruisers will arrive in 45 minutes."

"Don't reply. Don't confirm our presence here." Avery turned to his chief engineer. "Milli, please tell me you have something."

"Two more minutes sir. This is the crappiest hack job I've ever pieced together. But, if it will turn on, it should take down one of the ships. Won't know until we try."

After a few more minutes of adjustments, Milli called out. "Mathias can you connect with the drone?"

"Yes. I can connect with the weapon as well."

"Then I guess we're ready to give it a try."

"Captain Dewset Cowlon." Avery called out, initiating a comm connection.

"Captain Shields, ready so soon?"

"Yes, you? Just about. If you're in position, we'll transport the drone to your line of sight."

"We are in position," replied Captain Cowlon.

"Mathias. Transport the drone 10 kilometers behind us. Out of sight of the Cruisers. In sight of Captain Cowlon's ship."

The Chief Engineer stepped away from his creation and a moment later it was gone.

"Mathias. Confirm that we're still in contact with the drone and the weapon."

"Still in contact."

"Please confirm that you can operate the drone."

"Flying it in a 100-meter circle. Moves perfectly."

...

"Captain Shields. We're ready."

"OK, initiate the site-to-site transport."

This was the riskiest step in the attack they were about to make on the lead ship. Captain Cowlon's ship was further from the cruisers than the Toronto. So it had direct line of sight to the drone which was behind the Toronto's black hole shield and out of sight of the Fleet Cruisers.

The Captain's ship was also 25 km to the starboard side of the Toronto, so had direct line of sight to the stern of the lead cruiser. When he initiated transport, the drone would make the journey from behind the black hole shield to a position about 100 meters behind the Cruiser's stern. There it would dispense smoke, then retreat 10 km and put up its black hole shield.

The bet was that the Cruiser's close-in surveillance system would not trigger an alarm. If it did, the attack might still succeed. But the ploy to make the attack appear to be a ship malfunction would be blown.

"Initiating transport. Transported."

"Deploying ionized smoke from the drone," Mathias called out. His connection to the drone with the weapon was routed through the remote sensor drones the Toronto used to see past the black hole shield. "Retreating." Then several seconds later, "Shield up."

"We've lost sight of the drone," Captain Cowlon confirmed. "Mute your line. I'm going to call the Cruiser, tell them that they appear to have a problem. I'll leave you connected so you can watch."

Still down in engineering, Captain Shields watched as Captain Cowlon initiated contact with the doomed ship.

"Cowlon, you have called to surrender?"

"No sir. I've called to tell you that your ship appears to have a problem. A huge cloud of smoke and ionized particles has appeared near the stern of your ship. Our sensor readings indicate a continuing flow of ionized gas streaming from an emergency relief valve. Are you tracking this?"

"Cowlon, that's the best ploy you have? There's nothing wrong with my ship."

"Let me add the image we're seeing to the comm feed." Cowlon turned to his helm AI. "Tosbon, please split the video feed we're sending the good captain to include our view of his ship."

"Adding forward view, sir."

"Hold one second," the Cruiser Captain scowled.

On the view screen, they watched the Cruiser captain become increasingly agitated.

"Cowlon, we see the smoke but do not read ionized particles. Send me your sensor logs."

"As you request, sir." Cowlon turned toward Tosbon. "Please forward our sensor logs."

"One moment, there's a minor comm problem. I don't have the address for a data channel."

"You pinged my transponder?" The Cruiser captain asked incredulously.

"Tosbon?"

"Yes, sir. I got the two ships confused. Had to ping them to get the right portal. Apologies."

From the other side, they could hear the comms person confirming that the sensor logs had been received.

What the Cruiser didn't and never would know is that the transponder ping uploaded instructions for the sensor logs to be copied to the Cruiser's internal logs, which in less than a minute would sync back to the High Command's database.

The official ship sensor records on file with the High Command during the investigation would show a sensor alarm reporting a dangerous overpressure of ionized gas in the ship's cooling system.

Captain Cowlon continued watching the increasingly frantic activity on the still open comm line.

Captain Avery watched a copy of the image, as he counted down the seconds. In a moment they would know whether Eugene and Kelly's new time dampening field could in fact slice up a ship.

Thirty seconds after the sensor logs should have synced, Captain Avery pushed a button on the lab bench that Milli had used while building the drone.

The button was Mathias's order to activate the weapon. His view screen shifted to an image of the lead ship. The second ship sat next to it on the other side, foolishly close.

And odd wedge-shaped shadow formed near the stern of the ship, cutting through the cooling system allegedly suffering from high pressure and through the giant energy cubes that powered the ship. It held that way for a moment, then Mathias backed the drone away an inch and dropped the time dampening field.

A massive explosion whited out the screen.

Milliseconds after the field dropped, the explosion consumed the drone. The explosion massively over-pressured the interior of the ship, which filled with plasma from the breached power cells. The explosive force of the wedge that blew out was enough to slam the lead ship into its partner, breaching its hull as well. Then the entire stern for the lead ship sheared away.

Captain Cowlon's voice came over the comm system. "Time for us to continue on our journey. A copy of our sensor readings was just sent to command, we've done our duty as regards the dead ships."

IN ORBIT AROUND TOGAROTU

Once clear of the two Cruisers, the five ships made their way quickly to the first drop point. The medication was transported down to great thanks. The pickup was a little less smooth, the shipment manifest was not ready and took two hours to arrive.

Now about 2:00 PM Embassy time, they were departing for Dalfanito.

CONFEDERATION TELEVISION STUDIOS

George's co-host today was Arun Padhi of India News Network. George had worked with Arun before, but it was his first time to appear as co-host.

"Arun, I'm really looking forward to doing a show with you. Sorry it took so long to make it happen."

"I'm happy to be here, George. Thank you for inviting me. And thank you for the briefing package. This should be an interesting interview."

Their guest today was Ambassador Da-Ku of Sofaana.

"I got a somewhat cryptic message from Michael last night regarding the interview. He asked that we steer away from questions about the Confederation. Apparently, Sofaana has had problems that have left them a bit bitter."

"Curious." Arun's tone of voice matched his words, but in his heart, he'd just found out what he wanted to ask about.

...

"Welcome, World. I am Arun Padhi of India News Network. I'm here at the Confederation Television Studios with my friend George Butler.

"George, what can you tell us about our guest?"

"Our guest today is Ambassador Da-Ku from the planet Sofaana, one of the worlds that joined our Security Alliance this year. I'm told they're a relatively new Confederation member. Hopefully, the Ambassador can tell us more about that. Are we ready?"

The studio audience broke into applause.

"Ambassador Da-Ku, please come meet our studio audience."

The Ambassador walked in from the stage left entrance. He was medium height, a little shorter than George, and wiry thin.

"George, good to see you. And thank you for inviting me onto your show." The Ambassador vigorously pumped George's hand.

"Ambassador Da-Ku, welcome. Please meet my friend and co-host Arun Padhi."

The audience was pumped up again this week and didn't quiet until the three took their seats.

"Mr. Ambassador, welcome. You are from the planet Sofaana. What can you tell us about your world?"

The Ambassador smiled at the question. He'd viewed several of the previous shows as part of his preparation for today. This seemed to be the question they always started with, which was sensible.

A holoprojection of the sector popped up, showing the familiar locations of several worlds that had been featured on the show. "We are about 430 light-years further out on the spiral arm, about a third of the way to the border between sectors 3F and 3G."

A light popped up showing their location.

"I'm told our world is a little smaller than Earth, 91% of the diameter. I'm also told our gravity is a little less, 85% of Earth's. But despite the size, our land mass is about the same. Two-thirds of the Earth's surface is covered by water. On Sofaana, it's only half. But that half is spread out more, so we actually have more coastline. At least that's what our scientists tell me.

"But possibly the biggest difference is the composition of our landmass. It is mostly forestland. The maintenance of our forestlands is one of our greatest achievements in terms of environmental stewardship."

"How has this impacted life and society on your world?"

"Our scientists tell us that our species, which we call Fanolan, evolved from primates that lived in the trees. Our recorded history started about 20,000 years ago. In those early written records, all the towns and villages were built in the trees, because powerful predators and poisonous reptiles dominated the surface. Our people really didn't move down onto the ground until about 10,000 years ago."

"What enabled that change?"

"Our version of what you call the Iron Age. There were places in the mountains where people could live on the ground. In those mountains they found and ultimately mastered metals. The metals gave us the power to tame the predators, which in turn allowed us to control the reptiles."

"Fascinating," Arun replied breathlessly. "I'm not aware of anything similar on our world."

Outro music started playing.

"We'll be back in a minute with more from Ambassador Da-Ku."

...

"Welcome back, World. I am Arun Padhi reporting from the Confederation Television Studios. Ambassador Da-Ku, before the break you were telling us about the early days of your recorded history—living in the trees, ground predators and poisonous reptiles. How did that lead to your current situation?"

"Arun," the Ambassador started, "at one level, I don't think our history is that much different than yours. The bronze age led to the iron, then the industrial revolution. I understand that your world, or at least part of it, experienced a dark age then a reformation as well. We did not. But that doesn't change the fact that our industrial revolution wreaked havoc on our environment, in the same way yours did.

"The difference is that we were more unified, did more to bring our environment under our control. That may have been why the Confederation reached out to us as early as they did."

"Tell us more," Arun pleaded.

"So many of us still lived in the trees, that we noticed the impact industry was having on the forest long before you did. Please understand, I don't say that in judgement. A much higher percentage of our population lived in the forests on our world than on yours, which made it harder for us to miss.

"The broad-based understanding that something was going wrong enabled us to take on air and water emission controls maybe 50 years earlier than you did."

"Do you think that has something to do with the timing of your Revelation? Ours seemed to come early because of the fact we had such poor control over our climate."

"Maybe. And forgive me for speaking out of turn. But I think your environment had less to do with the timing of your Revelation than you've been led to believe."

The statement drew a strong reaction from the studio audience.

The Ambassador held his hands up in surrender as he'd seen Michael do when the crowd reacted strongly to something he'd said.

"The truth is that your environmental problems could have persisted for a long time before they reached the point where it would have been a challenge for Confederation technology to fix. I was not privy to the planning for your Revelation, but I think climate change was presented as the pressing problem because you thought it was the pressing problem.

"The real problem driving the timing of your Revelation was the Enemy. In retrospect, that should be obvious to you."

"To clarify, are you implying that Michael misled us?"

"No. Your climate issue was real and of great interest to many people. So, it makes sense that Michael would include it in his appeal to you. It was also the one he could solve first, so it makes sense that it was at the top of the list of things offered.

"My point is different. If there had not been a serious Enemy threat, then the Confederation would not have revealed itself as early as it did. You still had plenty of time to fix the environmental problems yourselves, which is always the better solution. But you would have had no chance against the Enemy."

"Interesting." Arun seemed to ponder the Ambassador's point for a moment. "But back to your world. You were more unified. Was that the main reason you qualified, or was there another reason the Confederation brought you in when they did?"

"We were also close to having interstellar capable space craft, so the Confederation wanted to bring us into the fold in a way that would prevent us from reaching the stars on our own. Too many planets that take to the stars before they meet the Confederation ultimately decide not to join. Most of the ones that do not join turn into pirate worlds, which is obviously not in the Confederation's interests."

"Curious. So how did your Revelation go?"

The question shocked George, this line of questioning seemed to go directly against the request Michael had made of them.

"Great at first. Power cubes and replicators are among the things that really transform new member worlds. For us, the power cubes had two major impacts. They reduced pollution and they reduced forest fires. A significant fraction of all forest fires on our planet had been caused by power distribution problems: downed power lines, transformer fires, etc.

"The replicators also reduced our demand on the land, less real estate dedicated to agriculture, less to industrial uses. But 20 years in, the problems started. Our power cubes started failing, our replicators as well. And there were no replacements. Over the 20 years that followed, we became increasingly dependent on Confederation handouts. Then the android virus came, killing essentially all our androids, crippling companies and government agencies, and ripping apart mixed families.

"Our ambassador was one of the ones lost during the chaos. I volunteered to take his place and was given the support needed to put the pieces back together again. But here we are, forty years later, still recovering, with a standard of living only slightly higher than it was when we joined. We hope the 3F Alliance will help us get back to where we were in those years following our Revelation. But many on our world wish that we'd never met the Confederation."

Outro music started playing and moments later they cut to break.

...

George was really pissed off with Arun for having taken the interview to the one place they weren't supposed to go. As soon as the lights dropped, he confronted Arun.

"Arun, we were asked not to explore Sofaana's relationship with the Confederation!"

"I know, I know. But that was the story that needed to be told!"

George took a cleansing breath, hoping to wash the anger away. "OK. But I'll take the lead on the last segment."

...

The lights came up and George did his standard intro about showing the Ambassador in his adopted form, then invited the Ambassador to come out.

George had seen the pictures ahead of time and thought he knew what to expect, but when the Ambassador stepped out, George froze.

He was humanoid but different. He had long muscle-bound arms covered with fish-like, deep green scales. The scales shifted with the movement as he walked, their iridescent shimmering was mesmerizing. His legs were short by comparison and wiry, with broader, more powerful hips and thighs. His face and hands had flesh that seamlessly blended into the scales at the edge of the palms and face. He had light blue cat-like slit eyes that sparkled and were extremely expressive. And on top, human-like brown hair.

The studio audience seemed as dazed by the sight as George was. But George snapped out of it as the Ambassador approached, hand outstretched to shake. George stepped out to shake hands. As their hands touched George realized several things at once. The

Ambassador was slightly shorter than George was, but his hand was 50% longer. Most of the difference was in the length of the fingers. And as their fingers wrapped around the other's hand, George felt both the softness of the Ambassador's flesh and the hardness of the scales.

"Ambassador Da-Ku. What a pleasure to meet and shake in your natural form."

"The pleasure is mine, George."

He turned to shake hands with Arun, then they took their seats. George started.

"Ambassador Da-Ku. Your physical appearance is quite different from ours."

George noticed that the studio audience was unusually quiet.

"So it is. I hope that doesn't put you off too much. Our scientists tell me that scales are an unusual attribute for a mammalian species. They say it is a product of evolution, a means for us to protect ourselves from the poisonous reptiles that once covered our ground.

"I see that the skin on our fingers is very similar though." He held his hand out, palm up for George to see.

George did the same and a closeup image of two hands popped up on the studio monitors.

"Our scientists claim that the skin on our hands and the length of our fingers are also products of our evolution as a tree-bound species. Skin allows a tighter grip than scales. Long fingers allow us to grip larger things. For that matter, longer arms allow us to move between branches spread further apart and give us better balance when walking on narrower bridges."

"I'm told you have videos of some of your older settlements that have been restored."

"We do."

The lights in the studio dimmed and a video started to play. The opening shot was airborne, taken from 100 feet or more above a grassy meadow. George noticed some large creatures grazing below.

Ahead, there rose a wall of huge, towering trees demarking the forest boundary. They had massive trunks that rose to nearly the height of the camera before splitting into branches that created a massive canopy. They reminded George of the massive Monkeypod trees he'd seen near Michael's ranch in Hawaii, only taller.

As the camera approached closer, it dropped down below the rim of the trees' canopies, and a city emerged. Complete buildings had been built into the branches with suspension bridges connecting them.

George was completely blown away by the complexity of the construction, a true miracle of engineering.

Arun turned to the Ambassador. "Are dwellings like that still in use today?"

"Similar ones, yes. They are obviously more modern. But the existence of things like power cubes, replicators and transporters have allowed us to have full function communities without the need to run power, water, or sewage lines."

A holoprojection of a cluster of tree buildings popped up on the side of the stage.

"This is an image of one of the resorts that caters to off-world visitors. It's one of the things we've made available as part of the trade portion of the 3F Alliance. I'm told that passenger ship service between Earth and Sofaana will start early next year. We don't have the tourist volume that Karagon does. But we are one of the most sought out places for interstellar travelers to take holiday."

"Amazing," Arun replied. "What other unique items do you offer as part of the trade alliance."

The Ambassador smiled broadly. "Our top exports are scents, spices, and other flavor ingredients. These are products of the richness of our forests."

Outro music started playing, the third segment cut short because the second ran so far over.

"I understand that's the cue we're nearly done," the Ambassador said with a smile. "But, I've arranged for a special treat today, human safe foods made with some of our flavor ingredients."

A spotlight lit the curtain hiding an area at the right of the stage. It opened revealing trays full of baked goods.

"Please enjoy. George, Arun. Thank you for having me on today."

The three stood to shake hands and the camera faded to black.

FLEET HIGH COMMAND

"Admiral Jo-Na, we have a problem in Triangulum. Two Cruisers ventured into space controlled by the 2B Alliance. There they encountered several ships with transponder problems. Their logs seem confused about the number of ships present. Only four appear in the sensor logs, then one disappeared. But the captain of the lead ship said he got a glimpse of a fifth cloaked ship as well.

"Anyway, the ships refused to submit to inspection. They called in three more ships as backup. But before they arrived, the lead 2B Alliance ship called to report gas venting from the lead Fleet Cruiser. They also forwarded their sensor logs, which matched the Cruiser's almost identically.

"Before the Cruiser could affect repairs, they suffered a catastrophic failure in their cooling systems that caused their power cubes to rupture."

"We lost the ship?" the Admiral asked.

"Both ships. The support ship had come alongside. The hull breach and plasma discharge was on the opposite side of the lead ship. It pushed that ship into the other, rupturing its hull and power systems also.

"The entire backend of the lead Cruiser ended up breaking off."

"This sounds suspicious."

"The logs are unambiguous."

"What became of the 2B Alliance ships?"

"They were not at the scene when the three back up Cruisers arrived."

"Do we know where the 2B Alliance ships went?"

"They were seen back at Togarotu escorting a small Earth Alliance ship. The five ships were subsequently seen departing on their way out."

Jo-Na thought for a moment. The Cruisers in question must have been under the Inspector's control. His were the only ships involved in the transponder scam. Although he did not believe that the Cruisers spontaneously failed, he had no interest in digging into another one of the Inspector's messes.

"Make backups of the sensor logs and put them in a secure location. Then initiate a thorough investigation. Order the Cruisers on the scene to conduct it. Give them copies of the sensor logs, so they know what to look for. If this was an inside job, not a tragic accident, the insiders will probably try to modify the sensor logs. I want to catch them if they do."

"Understood. We will get to the bottom of this, sir."

As the aide left, Jo-Na thought about calling Mi-Ku. The presence of an Earth Alliance ship was his clue that this was not an accident, but a masterfully disguised sabotage. It would be better to gather some evidence before confronting Mi-Ku. But he knew in his heart that the

Earth Alliance had struck its first blow in the war the Inspector had begun.

ON APPROACH TO DALFANITO

"Captain Shields. It seems we have a problem. I've just been advised that the Fleet identified our ships during the confrontation with the Cruisers. They then identified you accompanying us at Togarotu. A warrant has been put out for our four ships, a separate one has been put out on yours."

When he heard the word warrant, Captain Shields signaled Mathias to raise the shields.

"I regret to say that I've been ordered to take your ship into custody and to slave it to ours."

"I'm sorry, but I'm going to refuse that order. My shields are up, you have no means to compel me. I think the question is how we get your medications to you. If I lower my shields to transport them, you will lock me out of my ship. I will not allow that."

"Captain, they are powering up their weapons," Tactical Officer Linus Felder whispered.

Captain Cowlon stared at him for a while.

"I would never consider refusing a lawful order. Yet you do so easily."

"You believe this is a lawful order?" Avery shot back. "I do not. I am not subject to the Inspector's office, and neither are you."

"Captain, a large ship is about to drop from warp. If we're going to run, we should do it now."

"Emergency Jump! Sorry Captain Cowlon..." The jump cut the connection.

"Mathias, I want a series of random jumps, keep us as far from populated systems as possible."

"Understood." A pause. "Captain, I think I have an unlikely course home. There is an unpopulated system that has a viable intergalactic jump to the Large Magellanic Cloud. That destination is also a viable intergalactic jump point back to the Milky Way."

"Do it."

SPACE FORCE COMMAND

"Captain Shields, your status?"

The Captain gave a brief update on the events that transpired.

"So, you're on your way back with the goods picked up on Togarotu and the medications you couldn't deliver to Dalfanito."

"Yes."

"OK. I want you to come straight back to Earth. A task force of Cruisers will meet you at the rim and accompany you back. We have updated our transponders, so we can move safely through our space again. Keep yours off until it's upgraded. We'll have one of the ships in the taskforce complete your deliveries and returns.

"Sending updated orders now."

"Thank you, sir."

As the line dropped, Admiral Scott reflected on the fact that they'd just fired their first shot in a war no one wanted, yet no one seemed to be able to prevent.

RIVERSIDE PARK

David and Valerie exited the pavilion where the 'Taste of Argentina' event was being put on tonight. It was a new show. Valerie had gotten tickets the day they became available.

"That was fun, wasn't it?" Valerie asked, snuggling in close as they walked.

"It was. And the steak..." David paused, failing to find the words. "I've never had one like that before."

"The Chimichurri sauce was really remarkable. I got the replicator pattern. Maybe we can make some."

"Thank you." David kissed her on the head.

After several minutes of silence Valerie asked the question that had been worrying her. "How is James? He's dropped off the staff for my class. He told me in person and didn't look like he was well."

"He's not."

"Is there anything we can do?"

"I've been able to help him, but it only lasts a day or two. It used to last for a month."

"Are we going to lose him?"

David could feel his emotions starting to well up.

"I hope not, but it's hard to believe he's going to last much longer."

They walked in silence for a while.

"Your changing, aren't you?" Valerie asked.

"James says I'm still more human than not."

"And when you aren't?"

234

"We really haven't talked about that, but I don't think it's an issue. Look at James. He fits in as if he's one of us. Besides," David smiled. "I have you to keep me this way."

Chapter 19: DISCOVERY

[Sunday, 08.02.2032] EAS MUMBAI

For a week that had featured their first encounter with a malign force, this one had turned out well. They'd completed their new local claims process on 49 sites, validating over 100,000 kg of Transluminide.

But today was Sunday. The mining crew deserved rest. The ship's flight crew deserved the opportunity to fly. So today, they would cruise over to the third planet on her high-probability list.

The target was another system on the arm's rim, slightly further from the ejecta of the neutron star merger. When she communicated outside, she would need to tamp down on the vocabulary. The rest of the Confederation hadn't seen what she had and wouldn't. But in her mind, it was how she thought of their discoveries.

"Rani, we're done here for now. Please take us over to the third planet in the system 3GX01-697-188-279."

"Plotting a course, ma'am. This one's a little further than last week. It'll take three hours, 23 minutes."

"Thank you, please engage. I'll want the standard orbit for a mining screen."

"Engaging course now."

"Thank you." Bumati turned to her first watch Yeoman. "Mila, please message Admiral Flanagan. Let him know that we're on our way and plan to be back before midnight."

"Yes, ma'am."

Bumati heard the chuckle. They weren't teenagers. Admiral Flanagan wasn't their father. But her order sure sounded as if they were.

PROFESSOR ANCIENT'S APARTMENT

James was old. He knew it, had known it for a long time. But it wasn't until the capture of Ju-Ne last year that he realized he might be in his last days. Well, maybe last millennia.

He had taken to sleeping in a human form. For the better part of two-million years, he'd rarely slept. His daily recharge did not come in the form of sleep, it came from floating as coherent energy with a wakeful consciousness, collecting energy.

David had helped him twice now. But David wasn't ready. Michael wasn't either. So, he needed to hold on.

Noelani, truly one of the universe's gentlest souls, had recommended that he try a restoration chamber. He respected her sincerity, but he could not collect energy in a restoration chamber. It helped organics, even people like David who were still mostly organic. But it would be sudden death for himself. The trick to antiquity was finding ways to collect energy, once the organic means to produce energy ceased to function.

He was restless tonight.

Ironic, he thought. *It isn't even night*.

He was suddenly flooded with energy. *David?*

Then the wave of energy hit so hard he converted into energy.

PRESENCE PROJECTOR, AMBASSADOR'S RESIDENCE

"Mi-Ku. Here we are again."

"So we are, Jo-Na. So we are. What new crime has the Inspector committed that we're being blamed for?"

"For what it's worth, the Inspector did commit another crime. Not that anyone other than you is interested in the Law. They interdicted four 2B Alliance ships with another phony claim of transponder violations. They even fired on them."

"So, how is it that we're being charged again?"

"The Inspector's ships claimed to have seen another ship. One that does not appear in their sensor logs."

"And this imagined ship is one of ours no doubt?"

Michael immediately saw that his statement offended his friend.

"So it is claimed," Jo-Na replied calmly.

The calm reply conveyed more anger than screaming or shouting would have.

Michael bowed his head in the traditional Lorexian sign of respect. "Sorry my friend. No disrespect was intended toward you. But you must realize at this point, few of the Inspector's claims survive the light of day."

"In this case, things are different. Two of my Cruisers, admittedly under the command of the Inspector's supporters, were destroyed in the confrontation.

"One suffered spontaneous energy system ruptures that blew it apart. The other was consumed in the inferno and collision that ensued."

"I hear the claim, but what evidence do you have that Earth ships were involved?"

"The 2B alliance ships involved were later seen with one of your freighters in orbit around Togarotu. And they were seen departing toward Dalfanito together."

"Is this the new standard of evidence? That being seen with others near the scene of an accident is a crime?"

Jo-Na coolly looked at Michael.

"I don't know. I suspect that an Earth Ship was involved in some way with the destruction of those two Cruisers. Their maintenance was clean, well above the fleet's average. And yes, the lead ship might have had an undiagnosed issue that led to its failure.

"But my gut tells me that you would not allow a planet to die because they did not back the Inspector, who infected it with a plague then killed the ships bringing the cure. I also believe that you would go to great lengths to help those people."

There was silence for a moment.

"Mi-Ku. The ship you sent with emergency supplies was intercepted. They were in the right to destroy the ships that opposed them. But right has become wrong in the Confederation."

The two stared at each other for a while.

"Jo-Na, I have no knowledge of this incident. If it is as you say, then I will probably find out soon. So allow me to reverse the question. If the Inspector is at fault, and I have tiny invisible ships that can knock down a pair of Cruisers without even being seen, how long can the Confederation stand? I am a patriot. The Inspector is not. Which side would you choose?"

There was more silence, then the Admiral bowed his head in respect. "I will stand with you. Not because of your power or our longstanding friendship, but because you are right. The Confederation is broken. The Inspector's office is corrupt and holds too much power.

"It needs to go down. I'll stand with you. But please give me notice of your intentions in advance. It will help me give you better cover.

EAS MUMBAI

The Mumbai started its scans moments before they'd established orbit. Bumati was so proud of her crew!

But moments into their scans, they were hit by something so powerful, it knocked the ship's power systems offline.

NEAR EARTH

David flashed into existence close to James. They were both well above the atmosphere.

"James, what's going on? I heard you call but am not understanding."

James looked at David. "There's been an awakening. Surely you can feel it."

As they were pulled further away, David sensed it and wondered what they were up against now.

EAS MUMBAI

Bumati watched as her crew rallied to restore the ship. For a moment she wished she had their job with their well-documented procedures and drills. But the moment passed and now she wanted to know how and why her ship was attacked.

"Tactical, report."

"Sorry ma'am. We were taken completely by surprise. The pulse originated from the planet. We're still trying to assess its nature, magnitude and intent."

Light penetrated the ship and passed through the bridge.

As Bumati watched, she wondered. *Are we being scanned*?

Then a voice sounded.

"Bumati Parikh. Human. A compatible species. Untransformed.

"Brandon Hunt. Human. A compatible species. Untransformed."

It made the same statement for the entire bridge crew.

A pause.

"Until you have transformed, you cannot approach or scan the planet. The penalty for infraction is destruction."

Two people suddenly flashed into existence on the ship.

"So'Gen La'Hoya. Wa'natu, a la'tay." (*James Ancient, Elder, you live.*) James gaped. It was the first time he'd heard his given name spoken in his native language since before the founding of the Confederation.

"David Washington. Human. Transformed. You are welcome here and may enter the temple if you so choose."

"The others must leave or be destroyed."

The light departed and the ship's power was restored.

"You must leave now!" James commanded.

"Emergency jump!" Bumati shouted.

...

"Professor Ancient, what was that and what did it say to you?"

"It was a sentinel, the guardian of an artifact left behind by my people. It knew me. Called me by my given name. Spoke in my native tongue. It's the first time I've heard that language in over 2 million years."

By the way James was rambling, David could tell that the experience of encountering a remnant of his people had knocked him off his game.

"James, what is a sentinel?"

James turned to David. "The closest direct analogy would be an AI. But unlike the Confederation's AIs, sentinels are much more intelligent. They have extreme reasoning skills and little to no personality. Their mission is their only value, and they are entrusted with weapons. If you had not been of a compatible species, you would have been blown out of the sky. And if you should return, you will be."

"What did it mean when it said I was untransformed?"

James turned back to Bumati. "You cannot convert to energy the way David and I can. The temple he referred to is exclusively for energy beings.

James turned back to David. "We should go. There are things we need to discuss, and I need some time to think about this while I still have the strength.

"Ms. Parikh, you will find what you seek on the next planet on your list."

Before Bumati could reply, the two flashed away, leaving her standing there in confusion, wondering what to do next.

"Ma'am?"

The word snapped her out of her reverie. "Yes, Rani."

"The emergency jump brought us close to the next planet on your list; would you like to go there?"

SPACE FORCE COMMAND

"Admiral Scott, thank you for taking my call. Has the Toronto returned from her mission?"

"Good afternoon, Michael. Yes. She arrived back last night. There were issues."

"Was she involved in the incident with the Cruisers?"

"Yes..."

"Let me guess; they used the new time-dampening field to slice up the lead Cruiser."

"Yes. Am I guessing correctly that the Confederation is filing a complaint?"

"There is talk of that, yes. Apparently, they did a good job of disguising their involvement. The incident is under investigation and all evidence collected so far indicates an accident. But we are already being accused."

"Did you hear about the confrontation at Dalfanito?"

"No."

"A warrant was put out for the impoundment of their ship, so they ran without making the delivery."

"Very unfortunate."

There was silence for a moment.

"How did the Toronto get one of the time-dampening weapons?"

"The specs were released shortly after the meeting. The ships were given their upgrade priorities, which I'm confident they've followed. That said, it's a simple matter for an engineer who cannot work on a priority item to replicate the parts. The Toronto's engineers had built the parts before they departed. When they found themselves in a bind, they mounted the unit on a drone they'd previously built.

"One of the engineers referred to it as 'a real duct tape job.'"

"Very resourceful; we should give them a commendation. But I guess it proves the utility and effectiveness of the weapon. Let me see what I can do to move that initiative forward."

MANUFACTURING OFFICE

"Hi, Michael. What can I do for you?"

"I just wanted to get an update on where we stand with the intergalactic jump drive and time dampening upgrades."

"I've tested out the replicator patterns for the intergalactic drive on the other two ship types, the Fast Attack Ships and the Freighters. I actually replicated the components the Toronto used, except for the capacitors," Joel replied.

"So, my role in that is mostly done. The ships have the replicator patterns. Emmanuel has the capacitor specs.

"I've got 12 replicators kicking out the components for the time-dampening field generators and a corresponding number of bots assembling the units.

"We're using the design for the drone Eugene used to test the Red Matter weapon. It's small enough to transport but not very fast, so mostly useless in a chase. I plan to start production of these tomorrow. We'll have the first functional unit tomorrow morning, one hundred by midday Wednesday, if Emmanuel can get me the power cubes."

"Thanks Joel. These are devastating weapons. Hopefully, we won't need to use them very often."

PROFESSOR ANCIENT'S OFFICE

"James, what is the temple? Why is it so heavily protected?"

"Its physical manifestation is in the form of a wonder stone."

"You mean like Sarah's engagement ring?"

"Yes, but large. I don't know how large this one is, but others I've seen are on the order of 2 meters across at the base and 3 meters tall. And they are usually ruby or emerald crystals, not diamond."

"How can a jewel stone be a temple?"

"It's more like the gateway to the temple."

"The temple is under it?"

"Inside it."

David pondered that statement a moment.

"As energy beings we can exist in the crystal, can't we?"

"Yes. And the Transluminide inside provides energy. You can rest wakefully in a temple without the risk of dissipating. And most of the temples contain vast quantities of data. My people's entire collected knowledge was stored in the temples."

"Is that where your people went?"

"Yes."

"Then they're still alive?"

"Hard to say. I went in and stayed thousands of years before re-emerging, back before the Confederation was formed. I never lost my sense of self, so had no trouble coming back out. Others have. They've become more of a collective consciousness locked in the crystals.

"That's why they're guarded."

"Yes, that's why they're guarded. Millions of my people may be in that temple."

"How do they all fit?"

James chuckled. "Crystals like this are like icebergs. Only the tiniest part is visible in this dimension."

"That's why it's like a gateway."

242

"You understand so much already. We will go visit. You will be welcome there."

BRIDGE, EAS MUMBAI

The Mumbai dropped out of jump about 5 light days from the target system's center. The Confederation database had essentially no information on this system. There was a spherical 1 light-day exclusion zone where travel was prohibited. The system's mass was consistent with a larger brown dwarf system. There was a note in the database citing gravitational instability and low-frequency oscillation in the system's infrared emissions, which together suggested that the system had not stabilized yet.

Bumati shook her head at the intellectual laziness of the scientific team assigned to survey this system. There were numerous reasons a system might have the characteristics they cited, one of which would be a planet with high concentrations of Transluminide.

"We can see the brown dwarf from here, ma'am." Science officer Ishiyama Masami popped an image up on the main view screen. "It has the classic magenta color of an M-class brown dwarf. And its spectral fingerprint is consistent with ongoing lithium fusion. That would imply the system is young as the database suggests.

"But check this out."

The image on the screen zoomed in until the brown dwarf filled the screen.

"See the sparkling object transiting in front of the dwarf?"

"Transluminide ghosting," Bumati said in quiet awe. "How did the Confederation miss this!"

"The survey was done a long time ago, ma'am."

"Helm, take us in. Standard mining orbit."

...

Given the warnings in the database, Bumati took them in slowly. She no longer believed the warnings, but her disbelief was not enough to completely disregard warnings that predated human life.

"We are about to enter orbit around the third planet, ma'am."

"Thank you, Rani. Tactical, do you have anything?"

"No signs of life, ma'am. But background radiation is high."

"Science?"

"Agreed. Background radiation is high, but it appears to be coming from the dwarf. It's hard to tell whether it's higher lithium fusion than we measured further out. Or, some sort of lensing effect from the planet."

"Rachel, are we in range to take a mining pull?"

It was second watch. Rachel Sharp was the third watch astrogation officer. She was also one of the designated mining crew and was the officer in charge of the mining lab for this approach.

"We can make a pull from this distance. But it would be hard to pin-point exactly where it came from."

"Pull deep. My theory is that this planet is mostly Transluminide with an accretion layer of junk on top."

"Pulling deep, ma'am." A moment later, "Transluminide, 99+ percent pure."

"How deep was the pull?"

"As close to the center as possible."

"OK. Can you get a lock on something 100 km deep?"

"Locked. Pulling now." A pause. "Trace Transluminide. Mostly silicon, aluminum, and iron.

"Curious." Bumati looked at her chronometer. "OK. It's late. It's been an interesting day. I think we've seen what we came here to see.

"Rani, take us home."

BUMATI PARIKH'S QUARTERS

Michael had asked Bumati to contact him directly if she found another big find. She really didn't know how big this find was, but her sense was that this one was the big one. So, she dashed off a quick note.

Ambassador Michael.

We made another significant find today, two actually. The first planet we attempted to explore has a Temple of the Ancients. It is protected by a sentinel. Professor Ancient appeared and told us to leave before the sentinel destroyed our ship. The professor seems to think there may be more of his people there.

After that we went to the next planet on my list. We did not have enough time to make an estimate of the size of the find, but my sense is that this is the big one. The planet's core appears to be pure Transluminide. There is only trace Transluminide in the crust, which we know to be more than 100 km thick. The planet itself is approximately 4,000 km in diameter, smaller than Mercury.

My plan is to return next Sunday to gather more data.

Respectfully, Bumati Parikh

INSPECTOR'S OFFICE

"What else have you learned?" the Inspector growled.

"A number of suspicious things, none conclusive. For example, the sensor logs on all four 2B Alliance ships are consistent with the sensor logs uploaded moments before the ship exploded. Curiously, there were the expected small differences in the logs among those ships. But their lead ship's logs exactly matched those of our ship."

"What do you think? Did they intercept our ship's logs? Seems more likely they planted fake logs on our ship. But do they have the technology to do that?"

"I agree. They probably planted them, but I have no idea how."

"What else?

"A long list. They're obviously covering up something, in all likelihood the presence of a cloaked Earth Ship. But numerous sensor records were deleted. One example, they apparently transported something up close to our ship. They attempted to delete the record, but really botched the attempt.

"Did you interview the command crews?" The Inspector asked starting to get a little testy.

"Yes, but we were forced to do it in 2B Alliance Headquarters with 2B Alliance legal representation. Their lawyers refused to allow some of the questions. And we really didn't have the leverage to incentivize greater cooperation."

"The Earth Alliance was behind this. I can feel it in my bones. Keep digging. I'm not going to be able to press this fight without something more tangible."

The aide, realizing he was being dismissed, changed the subject.

"There is one other piece of news you need to know."

"Which is?"

"Our deep space research group picked up an unusual sensor reading a couple hours ago. It took a while to figure out what it was."

The image of a sensor reading appeared in the holoprojection.

"That's unusual, but remotely familiar. What is it?"

"Only one other reading like it has ever been recorded. It occurred before the founding of the Confederation."

The image of a nearly identical sensor reading appeared.

"This one was recorded just before the first appearance of the Ancient Sentient."

"Another one has emerged?"

"Or maybe the first one has left?"
An evil smile spread across the Inspector's face.

Chapter 20: PROGRESS

[Monday, 08.03.2032] MANUFACTURING OFFICE

"Henry, status?"

"Hi, Joel. We're just finishing the first run of time-dampening field generators, the run we started Saturday morning. I'll be starting the drones shortly."

"What was the final count on the field generators?"

"We have 142 finished, 2 more will be done in another 10 minutes. So, 144 in total. It'll take three full days to build a comparable number of drones. We'll get 12 every six hours. It'll take the bots about an hour to build out the drones with power cubes and field projectors. We have enough power cubes for the first batch or two. After that we'll be waiting on Karagon."

"Understood. I'll check in with Emmanuel on the supplies."

PRESENCE PROJECTOR, AMBASSADOR'S OFFICE

Michael entered the presence projector not knowing what to expect. The incident with the Cruisers and disrupted delivery put the viability of the trade alliance in question.

He saw Fe-Va talking quietly with Mo-Mo. Ambassador Peklit similarly engaged with Ambassador Ja-Fa, the Confederation Ambassador to his home world, Dalfanito.

Councilor Ke-Ve, the junior Central Council member from the Milky Way was the next to enter.

"Ke-Ve, a pleasure to see you today."

"Mi-Ku, this business with the Cruisers has gone too far."

"Couldn't agree more."

The last to enter was Ambassador Va-Mu from Edukatar.

"Mi-Ku, Councilor Ke-Ve. Pleasure to see you both here today."

There was loud rapping on the Conference table. Michael turned to see Ambassador Fe-Va calling the meeting to order.

"Could everyone take their seats please. I'd like to begin. I assume you've all heard about the incident in Triangulum two days ago. Two Fleet Cruisers, under the control of the Inspector, entered the 2B Defensive Alliance to disrupt the delivery of much-needed medical supplies."

Fe-Va's statement was answered with nodding heads and general grumbling.

"As the one organizing an enhanced trade alliance, the specific issue of dealing with the Inspector is beyond my scope. But it is clear to me that a trade alliance isn't viable if we no longer have free travel between our worlds.

"As I cannot see a way forward, I thought I'd invite the parties that have the most to lose, in the hope we can collectively come up with a plan."

"The only one of us that has ships fast enough to solve the transportation problem is Earth. Similarly, the only one of us that has ships strong enough to stand up to the Fleet is Earth. So, I would suggest we start by having Mi-Ku tell us more about the speed and strength of his ships," Councilor Mo-Mo suggested.

All eyes turned to Michael.

"As you all know at this point, the humans are incredibly inventive. I've never seen or even heard of any people that can do what they do. As regards our discussion, we now have ships that can cross the intergalactic void in an instant and can move through a galaxy at multiple times the speed of any Confederation ship. These inventions allow us to make viable trading runs between any two planets in the Confederation. For smaller worlds that cannot fill a ship, we would need to make consolidation runs.

"But daily round trips from Karagon to Togarotu are now viable. Two-day round trips that touch multiple 2B and 3F member planets are also viable. Transportation speed and capacity is no longer an issue. We will have several hundred ships able to do this within the next month.

"I think this is one of the issues the Inspector opposes. He's only interested in things he can control, and he cannot control this, so he needs to shut it down.

"In terms of defensive strength, our ships are impervious to traditional weapons. We now have strong defenses against EQD weapons and are in the process of updating our transponders to be immune from the Inspector's new weapon.

"In terms of offensive strength, we have very potent offensive weapons. If we're ever forced to use them, they would prevail. But we can't go around defying the Fleet or shooting down their ships. And we can't offload cargo if we need to have our shields up. We need a political solution, not a military one."

Ambassador Ja-Fa from Dalfanito spoke next. "Yet here I am, a plague ripping through my people, and shipments of medication blocked until I pay the Inspector a protection fee and give him free access to anything on my planet.

"We tried the political solution, dissolving his office. But that didn't work. We have been attacked, and don't have the political or military power to respond. We even formed our own Defensive Alliance. But it does not have the strength to defend itself against the biggest pirate, the Inspector."

"Mi-Ku," Mo-Mo asked. "Would it be viable to second some of your ships to our alliance and for us to second some of ours to yours? The seconded ships bearing both insignias. It has been done before, there's precedent."

"It has been done." Michael confirmed. "But Earth is too new. They won't approve having their people or technology under another's control."

"What about playing the Inspector's game against him?" asked Ambassador Va-Mu from Edukatar. "Have our Alliances put up new transponders and not recognize fleet transponders. Have a force of your ships challenge them when detected and return fire, if fired upon.

"It's a big ask to make of a new member, but it would make the trade deal viable."

"Let me think about that. But let me raise an issue in return. A warrant was issued against my freighter by the Inspector's office. The Inspector has no direct authority over either alliance yet ships from the 2B Alliance threatened to take control of my freighter. That is what prevented the delivery. From my perspective, they should have taken the medications, then given my ship cover. Instead, my ship was forced to run. We all know what would have happened if it hadn't."

There was silence in the room.

"If we are allied, then we must be allied. We can't turn on one another, especially when the order is given by someone with no standing."

"Seems we owe you an apology." Ambassador Ja-Fa seemed to understand his people's failure in this matter for the first time. "We agreed to give you cover but did not do so."

"I really don't want this to devolve into a shooting war, but that will ultimately be a Central Council decision.

"Let's schedule another run. Fe-Va, I'll leave it to you to schedule the manifests. We can take as much as you can book. Given the urgency of the medical supplies, let's try for tomorrow, knowing that it may need to be the next day."

PRESIDENT LEE'S OFFICE

"Gentlemen, I just met informally with members of the pending Trade Alliance. We would like to attempt another run out to Triangulum. I think we should do this."

"If we do it, we need to go with a show of force," Admiral Scott said.

"I agree, Sam. At least four ships, the larger the better. But they need all the upgrades: intergalactic jump drive, EQD shielding, time-dampening projector and drones, and the transponder upgrades. I'd also like to send Daniel Porter. If we go again, we go weapons hot. And I trust Daniel not to use his weapons if he doesn't need to."

"I hear you Michael," President Lee said quietly. "But why provoke the issue? How does this activity benefit Earth?"

"There's a cancer growing within the Confederation. We've already witnessed its evil. And we remain in its sights.

"I would much rather fight what's coming on someone else's turf, so the collateral damage is done there, not here."

"The rules of engagement?" Secretary Thompson asked.

"The 2B Alliance is embarrassed that they attempted to arrest our ship. The order was not legitimate, but they didn't challenge it. They agreed to cover our ship, then attempted to enforce a bogus warrant against us. I don't think that will happen again, but it could. That's why we need to send multiple ships.

"But the threat is from the Inspector. So, regarding Fleet ships of any kind, they are not allowed in 2B in a military role. If they approach us making demands, we refuse and ask them to step aside. If they become belligerent, we freeze them. If they shoot, we destroy them. And I mean that literally. If a ship acts against us with force, it must be killed."

"Do we really want to kill a Capital Ship?" Admiral Scott asked, obviously concerned about the loss of civilian life.

"We don't want to kill any ships. And you're right, we don't want to kill a Capital Ship. But we need to make an example of the pure military ships."

President Lee stepped in. "Sam? Are you confident in our ships, and comfortable with the rules of engagement? Losing another ship would undermine the Earth Alliance's faith in what we're doing. As you know, isolationists are making more and more noise these days."

"There is risk in every military operation. But our ships are strong, crews competent, and weapons devastating. If we show up in force, we are relatively safe."

"Then I'm in favor. Michael, I'll leave it to you to take the lead. Sam, give him what he needs," President Lee stood, closing the meeting.

BRIDGE OFFICE, EAS OTTAWA

"Daniel, have all the upgrades been completed on your ship? The portal is not showing the intergalactic jump drive or time-dampening field as being complete."

"They're close to being done, if not done already. I've been tied up on other matters, so haven't reviewed the results with the engineering team. That meeting is scheduled in 45 minutes. Assuming they're done, I'll update the portal then."

"Good. We have a new mission for you." The Admiral went on to explain.

...

"Understood. And a wise move. Do you know if any of the drones are available yet? I'd like to take some. The one the Toronto's team jury rigged turned the tide in that situation."

"Some should be available now, more before you go. Contact the Manufacturing Office. They are coordinating the drone production. I'll let them know you're authorized to draw what you need."

BRIDGE OFFICE, EAS NETHERLANDS

"Admiral Flanagan, thanks for taking the time to meet with me."

"Bumati, I'll always make time for you. How was your trip yesterday?"

"That's what I wanted to talk with you about. I need some advice."

"What happened?"

She told him about the discovery of the Transluminide core.

"Very, very impressive. Your theory predicted this?"

"It predicted a high probability of Transluminide along this portion of the rim. The only Transluminide cores that have been found, have been found in regions like this where newly formed planets were in the ejection zone of a neutron star merger. I've increasingly come to believe that's what happened here. The existence of a core seems to indicate that the Confederation misclassified the event that occurred across the void in the Carina-Sagittarius Arm."

"You have truly become the expert."

"Well, now you know my theory anyway. The problem is that I don't really know it has a Transluminide core. We were out of time and only made two pulls. The one near the core, which had Transluminide, and the one in the crust, that did not."

"Tell me what you're thinking about?"

"Your mission actually. You're in the process of making a big investment in this system. Given what's here, we have to annex and protect it. Same with the next one.

"But it seems we would want our first real mining operation and refinery in the system with the Transluminide core."

"I think I get it. You think we should be working your claims process in that system, not this one."

"At least until I've proven that it is or isn't a Transluminide core."

"Then my advice would be to go. Your orders were not revealed to me, but from what I was told, you have a lot of freedom. Do you think you have the flexibility?"

"I do. But I need some help."

The Admiral signaled her to continue.

"Any chance you could give me an escort ship? Validating a core will take all my attention. It would be nice to have someone watching my back."

Chris thought for a minute.

"How long will this take?"

"A couple days."

"I can swing one day, before I'm far enough behind schedule to have to explain myself to Admirals Scott and Bjork. But I agree with your assumption. If it is what you think it is, then that's where the big investment should be made, not here.

"Let's see if we can develop enough data in the next 24 hours to make that sell."

"Thanks."

PRESENCE PROJECTOR, MANUFACTURING OFFICE

Joel was less than happy about accepting this assignment but understood the need. They needed AIs. They needed Barbara back. And he was the best AI expert Earth had at the moment.

A group of relatively excited people were lined up outside the presence projector. They would be contributing memories today. Lucy, a nurse technician from the hospital, was already in the presence projector with him setting up some specialized equipment.

Joel's role in today's efforts was minor but required. He would be providing the certification of termination for Nadia, Barbara and three other androids taken down in the explosion. Within 24 hours, Nadia would appear in a birthing computer in his office. In about 3 weeks, Barbara and her colleagues would be available for pick up on Celanar.

He would also be providing the formal approvals for the new AIs to be created and bear responsibility for them until they either came of age, or had another guardian assigned. Barbara or someone else on her team had the equivalent responsibility for almost all the AIs and androids on Earth. It was his turn for these.

"OK. I'm ready."

"Thanks, Lucy. Initiating connection now."

A moment later, a virtual door opened. Several people walked in led by Director W'ana S'oto, whom Joel met last year during the android virus outbreak.

"Director S'oto, a pleasure to see you again, sir."

"Joel, the pleasure is mine. I was sad to hear of the incident that claimed Barbara and your people but am glad to have a role in bringing them back for you.

"We have the last back-up images for the five people in question. Do you have the certificates of destruction?"

"Yes." Joel held up a device that 'held' the certifications. The certifications themselves were in a secure database somewhere. The device held an encrypted copy of the locations.

The director held up a similar device to the one Joel held.

"Please give them to me."

Joel tapped his device against the director's.

"Done."

The devices themselves were over 1,000 light-years apart from each other. But they were also constructs the presence projector could use. On sensing the tap, it initiated the secure transfer of designated data. The transfer would be logged, along with the local time on both ends.

"Next is the official request for the creation of 25 new AIs, the consent agreements for repurposing of memories, and the guardianship agreements for the AIs that will be created."

They repeated the process of transferring the agreements.

"Joel, thank you for entrusting us with this solemn duty."

"Director S'oto, thank you for helping us in this time of need. Let me introduce you to Lucy Clemens. She is one of the nurses at our hospital. She specializes in caring for babies. She's also a friend of Barbara's."

"Ms. Clemens, me and my team look forward to working with you today."

"I'll leave the rest of this to the two of you. Thanks again." Joel turned to exit the projector. He needed to get back to work on the drones.

AMBASSADOR'S CONFERENCE ROOM

"Lisette, thanks for coming over. I know it's not the topic planned for this meeting, but you were right. The explosion at the Android Production Lab was caused by the Inspector. We now know the mechanism they used to do it. Joel has the lead on the solution and will contact you when he has something."

As Michael paused to change gears, he couldn't remember the purpose for today's meeting.

"Which crisis are we here to talk about today?"

Lisette chuckled. "Transluminide.

"Ah, yes. You brought this to my attention two weeks ago. A lot has happened in the interim. But we did add some underground storage areas as part of the tunnel operation."

"I know, the Admiral passed the word along." A pause. "I've come up with a loose security plan. It's based on the case histories of successful heists in the past.

"I call it loose, because I'm going to need some serious technical help to actually implement it."

"Can you give me the non-technical overview?"

"Sure. The trick in every successful heist has been deception, people doing one thing for the benefit of the Confederation as a distraction to give them access for their real purpose, stealing the

Transluminide. My idea is to play the game in reverse, appear to put the Transluminide in one place, but actually put it somewhere else."

"And what would that look like?"

"The first step is to set up the deception. We do that by modifying the bank vault, making it look much larger. The Transluminide would be stored on shelves in a cart. The cart is stored in a new section of the vault behind the current one. One cart at a time can be viewed. When the bank is done doing what they want with the cart, the automated system places the cart in the back, then they can access another cart. We call this a convenience upgrade or something like that. We encase the back vault in one of the new black hole shields. We encase the interior of each cart in one also.

"The deception is that the Transluminide appears to be stored in the back of the vault. The apparent security addition is the black-hole shields.

"What will actually happen when the cart goes in the back, is that the Transluminide will be transported to one of the new underground spaces that were carved out. These too would be protected using a multiple layer cloaking technology.

"The protection comes from two things. First the Transluminide isn't where you think it is. Second, it is only accessible by transporter from a place no one knows about, surrounded by shields that block transport even if you should find out where it is."

"Then how do we move it back and forth? Drop the shields?"

"No. We build a different type of transporter that operates in a different dimension."

"This can be done?"

"About the same time I came to see you a couple weeks back, I ended up sitting next to Eugene Xu at the 'Taste of Lebanon' event. At the time, I was studying an old cold case involving a theft I could not understand. The goods had been stolen from a vault encased in a transporter dampening field. He went on to tell me a half dozen ways it could be done. I was astounded and rhetorically asked how anything could be protected from that. He laughed and listed off several ways to protect that no one but he, or Kelly, had a chance to defeat."

"So, Eugene knows about our Transluminide protection issue?"

"No. The cold case was an equipment heist. Transluminide, the bank... Never mentioned."

"I'm guessing that you're going to want a little of Eugene's time."

"Yes." She smiled.

"I'll attempt to arrange it."

MANUFACTURING OFFICE

"Joel, Daniel Porter here."

"Admiral Porter, I got word earlier that you were going to be taking the first drones."

"Yes, how many do you have?"

"Right now, I have twelve. "I'll have twelve more in another four hours. That will tap out my supply of power cubes, until the shipment from Karagon on Wednesday."

"How hard would it be for us to add the power cubes after the fact?"

"Not hard at all. I can give you a bot, or instructions for a bot or person."

"We're leaving in a little over twelve hours and might be able to pick up power cubes along the way. We'll be making stops at Jerusota, Edukatar and Celanar. Do you know if any of those could supply a compatible power cube?"

"I don't know, but if you have a second, I could find out."

"Sure."

A minute later.

"Yes. Edukatar and Celanar have them. Edukatar claims to have 15 in stock. Celanar claims to have 12. I can have 24 drones with power and 24 without by the time you depart. But someone else will need to help order the power cubes. Michael or Emmanuel will be your best bets.

"Thank you. Send me the links."

BRIDGE, EAS DHAKA

It was coming up on 9:00 PM. Captain Jessica Martin had the ship for the evening shift of first watch.

"Entering the system, ma'am. Being hailed by the Netherlands."

"Thank you, Heather. Please put it through to the office. Mr. Smith, you have the con."

"I have the con, ma'am."

...

"Admiral Flanagan. A pleasure to see you again, sir. Congratulations on the promotion. I understand that we're putting up a surveillance system."

"That we are. We're also providing security for this and several other systems the Earth Alliance is annexing. Which is where I want to start the Dhaka.

"The Mumbai is going to be leaving shortly for another system. It is a little closer to Kalamaan space. The work the Mumbai needs to do there will make it hard for them to respond to another Kalamaan incursion in a timely manner. They need to be deep in the gravity well. I want the Dhaka to accompany them to this system and stand watch while they do what they need to do.

"If a Kalamaan ship should enter the system and spot you, you are to destroy their ship. What we are doing in that system is secret. Word that we are there cannot get out. No exceptions."

"Understood, sir."

"Ms. Parikh will contact you when she's ready to go. She has mission command. You have military command."

"Thank you, sir."

Chapter 21: BOND

It was the midnight change of watch. First Officer Enzo Scrivani entered the bridge and took a seat next to Bumati.

"Evening, Captain."

"Evening. Some good news. The Dhaka arrived last night. She's the first of several ships that will be joining us in our work here. Also, a change of plans. I spoke at length with Admiral Flanagan. He agrees that our discovery on Sunday could change the overall scope of our mission. So, we're going to head back today. And the Dhaka will be going with us to give us cover."

"Are we expecting a problem?"

"No, but we need to be in low orbit to do this study, which will make us vulnerable if there is an issue. With the Dhaka above giving us cover, we can get our work done faster and more safely."

"Can't complain about that."

"So, your orders are to get us underway at 3:00 AM and to establish a standard mining orbit by 7:00 AM. The Dhaka has been clued in on the plan and will have command of the trip out and back. I'm going to grab some sack time. Tomorrow's going to be a long day.

"You have the ship." Bumati stood to leave.

"I have the ship."

EAS DHAKA

Heather, the Dhaka's helm AI was less than happy to hear that they were flying into an uncharted system. Rani, the Mumbai's helm AI assured her that the system was relatively clear but confirmed that they had not run a full astrogation scan.

Captain Martin's reaction was predictable. "Good, then we'll have something to do."

"Commander Molina, we are about to drop from warp."

Commander Alberto Molina was the ship's second officer, in command of third watch.

"Thank you, Heather."

"Mr. Reynolds, begin astrogation scans as soon as we are in position."

Lieutenant Alexander Reynolds was third watch astrogation officer.

"Yes, sir."

"Commander, you should see this."

"Please put it on the screen, Ms. Heidrich."

Corrina Heidrich was the third watch science officer.

"It's the planet they are heading toward."

"Why does it glow like that?"

"It's the Transluminide, sir. The entire planet is showing the classical Transluminide ghosting. I think they've found the new Fort Knox."

"How did the Confederation miss this?"

"Easy, sir. This is done using special scanner settings that aren't in the astrogation books. You have to sync two or more focal lengths, then superimpose the images to get this. If you look hard enough you can find this in the mining books. The Confederation has special scanners for finding Transluminide that are only installed on mining ships. We don't have those scanners, so Professor Schudel taught us this trick. We've added it to standard training, but there are no Fast Attack Ship science officers in the Confederation that would know it."

"Truly amazing. How did the Confederation rise to greatness?"

The question was rhetorical, but Lt. Heidrich answered anyway.

"The young Confederation was more like us than the Confederation we know. The people that operate it now, with the exception of Michael, could not rise to greatness. In fact, their greatness is slowly slipping away from them."

EAS CANADA

This was going to be a big day with a lot to do, so Daniel Porter decided to get an early start. He arrived on the bridge an hour before the change of watch.

"Admiral on the bridge!" Jim Ryan called out, standing to yield the chair.

"As you were, Mr. Ryan. I'm just heading to the office."

Daniel had decided on the taskforce composition yesterday during third watch. He'd put the ships on 24-hour standby and sent out requests for readiness status. The Canada was fully upgraded at this point, as was the Poland. The two cruisers would be the show of force. They would be supplemented by three Fast Attack Ships: the Cairo, Copenhagen, and Buenos Aires. The ships actually carrying cargo would be the Toronto, Batumi, Toompea, and Petra.

Checking his message queue, Daniel saw that all nine of his ships were fully upgraded and reporting ready. He also saw that the number of shippers had increased to the point that he would need to add more freighters or have the war ships carrying freight.

They would now be picking up shipments from Allastran, Atomorali, Bornasal, Edukatar, Jerusota, Karagon, Naltanarus, and Sofaana.

There was a message from Michael. *Captain Porter. I have prepared a small gift for each of the worlds participating in today's trade run. It needs to be personally delivered to the named recipient. Each planet knows of this and is arranging an acceptance ceremony. The ship's captain should make the delivery in dress uniform. This is a formal diplomatic event.*

There was also a message from Emmanuel. *Captain Porter, we were unable to arrange power cube pickups from the planets you requested. Karagon has offered to supply instead. The power cubes will be in the shipment you pick up there.*

The final message in the queue was from Admiral Scott. *Daniel, apologies for the last-minute changes. We just accepted shipment requests from Peralon and Hacindra. By our calculations, you will need at least 6 freighters in your taskforce. You are free to choose which, but I've put the Tulum, Brandenburg, and Independence on standby. They are reporting mission ready, but again that determination is yours. This has turned into a historic event. Safe travels.*

"Else?"

"Here, Admiral."

"We have pickup and delivery to make on each of 10 planets before we head off to Triangulum. I want to use the seven freighters and three Fast Attack Ships to do it, one planet each. We need a minimum of one hour at each pickup site. And I'd like to arrive at Dalfanito at least an hour before sunset at the delivery location. Can you see if that's possible? Sending the list now."

"I'll get on it right away. Should have an answer for you in a few minutes."

PRESENCE PROJECTOR, AMBASSADOR'S OFFICE

"Mi-Ku, I'm surprised to hear from you again so soon. Did something happen?"

"Jo-Na. Greetings my friend. You asked me to let you know about our plans. A trade expedition will be leaving this morning for

Triangulum. A significant trade agreement has been reached. The caravan will consist of seven Freighters accompanied by two Cruisers and three Fast Attack Ships.

"Given the recent harassment our ships have received and the value of this shipment, the military escort is required."

"That is going to cause trouble."

"We will not be the ones causing trouble. The 2B Alliance is aware of our plans. And flight plans will be filed with them."

"When will they arrive?"

"This afternoon."

"I thought you said they would be leaving today."

"They will. All of the ships have been upgraded with our new intergalactic jump drive, EQD-resistant computers and enhanced shielding and weaponry.

"None will enter Fleet-controlled space."

"And if they encounter a Fleet ship?" asked Jo-Na.

"They will send acknowledgements and greetings."

"And if ordered to stop?"

"They will refuse all unlawful orders."

"And if they are fired on?"

"The ship will be labeled as being under enemy control, and it will be immediately and absolutely destroyed as required by Fleet and 2B Alliance regulations."

"I see. So, it begins."

"No, it began some time ago. Now it ends."

"I will send out a priority order to the Fleet instructing them not to harass your ships."

Michael smiled sadly. "Maybe we can still stop this."

PRESENCE PROJECTOR, COUNCILOR MO-MO's OFFICE

"Mi-Ku, we are still on schedule?"

"Yes. The orders ended up being surprisingly large. We will be sending seven Freighters, escorted by two Cruisers and three Fast Attack Ships. We will be filing flight plans with the 2B Alliance shortly. We're hoping for first delivery on Dalfanito before sunset at the main medical distribution center."

"Excellent news. We were able to give them enough medication from the shipment you sent us to keep the disease in check, but the medication is on allocation at this point. They're likely to start seeing losses later today.

"On another subject, the three Cruisers have completed their investigation and are, of course, blaming you. Their proof is comical. They said that since there is no apparent cause, it must have been an external agent and Earth was the most likely one."

"So instead of citing evidence against us, they cite lack of evidence. Not much legal or intellectual integrity in that."

"Anyway, wanted to let you know so you weren't caught by surprise."

"Thanks for the warning."

BRIDGE OFFICE, EAS CANADA

"Daniel?"

"Yes, Else."

"The Toronto needs to leave for Karagon shortly."

"I haven't assigned the Toronto to Karagon yet."

"Then do it quickly. They've given us a very narrow arrival window and they're the only ones with the location and experience to arrive in time."

"Oh. They're in highest orbit?"

"Yes, and they can swoop in to pick up their gift for delivery and use the descent to sling shot out."

"Send them their course and orders to depart."

INSPECTOR'S OFFICE

The Inspector was fuming. The High Command had just issued a cease and desist order to the Fleet prohibiting Fleet ships from harassing Earth ships, especially the trade expedition arriving in Triangulum later today.

Their early shipment of medication had cost him his leverage over Councilor Mo-Mo.

Fortunately, he still had a couple tricks left that no one had seen before. And they were pre-positioned in sector 2B.

PROFESSOR ANCIENT'S OFFICE

James felt younger somehow. The energy boost from the sentinel lingered longer than he would have expected.

His recent interaction with a remnant of his people was the first in well over 2 million years. He had to go back, had to find out what happened to his people during his years of absence. The only real question was whether to bring David with him or not.

Unexpectedly, David flashed into James' office. He wasn't due for a couple more hours.

"Good. You haven't left yet. We need to go back. I was afraid you might have left without me."

James looked at David curiously. It was obvious to him that the encounter had changed David in some way as well, but James couldn't put his finger on it.

"Agreed. We need to go back. Shall we?"

David flashed into light. James smiled and did the same. Then they were gone.

BRIDGE, EAS TORONTO

"Captain, we have arrived in Karagon's space control district and are being sent to a close-in holding area. Our slot is running 10 minutes late, but they request you to transport down immediately. I have the coordinates."

"Thank you, Mathias. Ms. Talgateva, the ship is yours. Don't leave without me."

Captain Shields, decked out in his dress uniform, grabbed the gift and his script, then headed for the transporter.

STOWRAP, ANGOLORAN SECTOR, KARAGON

Captain Shields transported down to the Confederation Embassy in the capital city of the Angoloran sector of Karagon. Technically, the Confederation had four Embassies on Karagon, one for each of the species they'd relocated here thousands of years ago. Over time, the one in the Angoloran sector had become the center of the Confederation presence on the planet.

He arrived in a garden area. The sweet floral smell of the flowers permeated the air, complimented with a trace of spice. On looking around, he saw a tree heavily laden with bark. *Wonder if that's cinnamon?*

A guard in uniform stood at the head of the path leading away from the transporter platform. "Captain Avery Shields of the Earth Alliance. Welcome to the Confederation Embassy on Karagon. Please follow me."

The guard spun neatly on his heel and started off down the path. The captain followed briskly behind. After about 100 meters, the path split. They followed the branch to the left, which opened to a grassy field set with chairs. Twenty or so people stood and applauded as he came in.

In front of the chairs was a small dais. Five people stood there. The guard led the Captain to a spot in the lawn directly in front of the person in the center of the five, then announced in a loud voice.

"I present Avery Shields, Captain of the Earth Alliance Ship Toronto, and representative of the great people of Earth."

The five people on the stage bowed in the traditional Angoloran greeting. Avery noticed that they bowed a little lower and held it a little longer than he'd seen before. The guard indicated that he should wait a moment before responding.

As they straightened, Avery spoke the line in the script he had been given.

"On behalf of the peoples of Earth, I come in gratitude to the peoples of Karagon." Then he bowed in a modified version of the Angoloran greeting with the gift held out in front of him.

As he straightened, he saw the person in the middle was Ambassador Fa-Ta.

"You may approach."

Avery stepped up the three stairs onto the platform. Per the script he'd been given, the guard appeared next to him, hand out to take the package. Avery handed it to him, then opened it and pulled out the first gift. It was a large red gemstone that danced with an inner light. It hung from a cord made of a threaded material that Avery did not recognize.

"To the honorable Ambassador Fa-Ta, the Earth Alliance presents the wonder stone of Courage."

The Ambassador bowed his head and Avery placed it around the Ambassador's neck.

Avery stepped away and turned to bow to the crowd, revealing the Ambassador. The crowd shot to its feet in applause. Although Avery didn't know it, this was the first wonder stone ever given to Karagon.

The process repeated four times, once for each of the planet's four peoples. The president of the Angoloran sector was given the sapphire colored wonder stone of Peace. The president of the Tokaran sector was given the jade colored wonder stone of Friendship. The president of the Karajin people was given the emerald colored wonder stone of Joy. And lastly the president of the Salmanoan people was given the fire-opaline wonder stone of Mystery.

...

The guard led Captain Shields back to the transporter pad. As they got to the end, the guard stopped to talk.

"The Ambassador sends his regrets that this visit was cut so brief. The gifts Earth has given us are not things that can be bought. They are truly things of honor that will bond our peoples with a permanent seal. I know that you, like me, are just the messenger. But thank you. I wish you well, Avery Shields."

They exchanged bows, then Avery went to the transporter pad. As he stood there awaiting transport, Avery realized that he had just participated in something historic. An instant later, he was back on his ship.

"Welcome back Captain. We are loaded. They held us here until your return. The controllers, who are usually apoplectic if we are a few seconds late, seemed genuinely friendly, even though we overstayed our slot by five minutes."

"Something truly historic happened here today. I sense a big change coming, a change for the better."

"What were the gifts?"

"Gemstones grown from a Transluminide seed. The Lorexians call them wonder stones, at least that's what the translators say. Each one is worth hundreds of millions.

"On the way out, the guard told me that Karagon had never received one before. We just gave them five. The guard said that the bond between our people was now permanently sealed."

ANCIENT TEMPLE

James and David flashed into existence above the ancient temple. Moments later they were greeted by the Sentinel.

So'Gen La'Hoya. David Washington. You return. The temple awaits. You are free to enter.

Once the words were spoken, the sentinel disappeared.

Not much of a conversationalist that one, David sent.

No. He is a gatekeeper. One extremely able to block entry by forbidden parties. But a gatekeeper, nonetheless.

James. How is it that I don't know where I'm going, but seem to know how to get there?

You are being subtly guided. You will know when you have arrived.

They slowly descended down through the atmosphere, then the clouds. The planet was heavily vegetated, teaming with life. As they got close to the ground, David could sense the fetid smell of dead vegetation and the buzz of insects.

James why am I sensing smell and sound?

It's part of the construct. You are already being fed senses, which is a bit of a trick. The challenge as we get closer will be separating reality from the construct.

David saw creatures scurrying around purposefully on the surface. *Are those people?*

Difficult question. They are semi-intelligent beings, something like a human IQ of 75. But they have been bred to be susceptible to empathic suggestion.

Is that ethical?

Another difficult question. The creatures would say yes. They have life, contentment, satisfaction.

What are they doing?

You will see.

David saw a… He didn't know what it was.

Is that the temple?

Yes.

It's a cloud?

As are you. Quiet now.

As they approached the cloud, it opened. James immediately recognized what he saw and hoped that David did as well.

David, absorb as much as you can, but do not allow yourself to drift.

GALACTIC RIM

One by one the ships of the taskforce arrived at the rendezvous point. Daniel could tell by the comm chatter that the captains had taken part in something that had an unexpected impact on them. He had not participated in any of the pickups so didn't know exactly what happened. But he would be participating in the ones in Triangulum. His read on the situation was that Michael had pulled off a diplomatic masterstroke. Maybe there could still be peace. He was fully prepared to follow his rules of engagement and would execute them with prejudice if required. But he would always choose the path of peace over the path of violence if he could find a way.

"Admiral. The last of the ships has arrived."

"Thank you, Else. Open a comm line to the captains."

One by one the Captain's faces popped up on the main view screen.

"We will be departing shortly. A couple quick reminders before we go. All jumps will be sequenced as we go in. A cruiser will depart first for each jump. Another will depart last. When the taskforce is split, the Cruiser will have command of its portion of the taskforce and will lead any tactical response.

"When you come out of jump, put your shields up immediately. Assume that you will be arriving to a hostile situation.

"And if you are shot at, you are to respond immediately with maximum violence. Do not wait for orders to shoot.

"Porter out."

"Else, please initiate the jump sequencer."

A few seconds later, Daniel was in the grip of the strangest jump he'd ever experienced.

When they came out of it, he shouted "Shields up!"

...

One-by-one the other ships arrived. Their position along Triangulum's rim was verified. Daniel had been there for the presentations, heard the theories, then the reports of success. But it was still hard to believe that they'd just jumped 1.8 million light years in an instant.

"All ships reporting a successful jump without incident."

"Thank you, Else. Let's continue the journey in to Dalfanito."

Although it never reached the level of a conscious thought, Daniel instinctively knew that they were departing on what was likely the most dangerous part of the trip. If the Inspector wanted to stop the medications from getting to Dalfanito, this was his last shot at it.

INSPECTOR'S OFFICE

"We seem to have a situation sir."

"Which is?"

"Eleven Earth Alliance ships just passed a transponder check point in Triangulum. All of them were pinged in Sector 3F within the last two hours. They are on a direct course to Dalfanito and moving fast."

"Send word to the Cruisers. Use the weapon, use the jump dampeners. Stop them. Destroy them if you have to. But I really want one or more of them alive. Space any of the crew that resists."

FLEET CRUISER, CRIMSON DESTINY

"Eleven Earth Ships on their way. This is the track of their transponders."

The tactical officer pointed to a position on the map. "This is where we should hit them. It's narrow enough we can extend the jump dampener across the entire zone. If their AIs are fast enough, they should be able to make a controlled exit. If not, there will be a lot of debris."

"Do it!"

Minutes later, the three cruisers jumped away.

BRIDGE, EAS CANADA

"Admiral?"

"Yes, Else."

"In about 15 minutes we will pass through the area where I would be setting up an ambush if I was them."

"Tell me about it."

An astrogation map popped up on the holoprojector.

"Given our entry point into the galaxy, every path to Dalfanito passes along the edge of this nebula." Else highlighted the spot. "There's a pulsar in the nebula that energizes it in a way that impacts jump fields. If you jumped into the nebula, your jump bubble would collapse. If you grazed it ever so slightly, it would force a drop that we might not be able to control."

"Then let's not graze it."

"The nebula does ebb and flow, so we never know exactly where the safe part of the transit is."

"So why are we coming this way?"

"It's the fastest course by far, even if we slow down to warp through this section, which is what we are planning to do."

"Ah, now I get it. If we're warping through that section and they hit us, then there is no emergency jump."

"Bingo, boss."

"Alternatives?"

"Numerous, but none that will get us there by sunset, that's why I picked this one. I didn't think this through from the enemy's perspective until just now."

"Suggestions?"

Else's hologram smiled.

"Our sensors are better than theirs. Our warp drive is faster than theirs. And if they're in there waiting for us... Well they can't jump either.

"Let's go in slow and find them. If they're nice and friendly when we find them, then we go on our way. If not, maybe we can organize their wreckage to look like they fell out of jump."

"I'll alert the other ships. You put the plan out on the AI net."

FLEET CRUISER, CRIMSON DESTINY

"They just passed the last transponder check point, still moving fast. They should drop from jump momentarily."

The Inspector's so-call jump dampening field was actually the nebula itself. They had planted a thousand small ionizing explosives, inside the nebula. When detonated, it created an excess of ionized particles, ones that would impact the stability of jump space in the region. The explosives were too small to be seen on scanner and produced a wave of gas that would fill the entire void between the nebula and the nearby systems. Any ship traveling in jump through this area in the next hour would fall from jump space. The only question was whether or not their AI could control the drop enough to prevent the gravitational shear between dimensions from ripping their ships apart.

...

"It's been 15 minutes, where are they?"

"I don't know. They have not passed the next transponder check point. Which means they have either fallen from jump undetected, quieted their transponders, or changed course."

"Captain, I'm reading something in the channel."

EAS CANADA

Else had been confident that this was where they would find an intercept team, if one had actually been dispatched. And there they were, radiating so much energy that she needed to put her 'sunglasses' on.

She sent an emergency signal, dropping the task force out of warp.

"Else, what happened?"

"Three cruisers, about 15 light minutes ahead of us. The fools are just waiting for us to drop from the sky, so to speak."

Daniel smiled. "Here's what we're going to do."

FLEET CRUISER, CRIMSON DESTINY

"Captain, something's wrong. We should consider leaving the area. They're either past us, detouring around this region, or passing through in warp. If they are attempting to crawl through, they could see us first and attack. We have no emergency jump."

"Steady, we are Confederation elite. They are primitives."

"Captain, we're receiving a message from an Earth Alliance Ship. They are asking if we need assistance."

An evil smile spread on the Captain's face.

"Of course, we do. Send a distress signal. Let's have the primitives come save us." The cynicism in his voice was palpable.

EAS CANADA

"Admiral, we are receiving a distress signal from the fleet ship, Crimson Destiny."

Daniel smiled at the cleverness of Else's ploy.

"Do we know which ship that is? And what's the status of the others?"

"It's a ploy." The glint in Else's holographic eye worried Daniel. AIs were not supposed to be this emotionally engaged in the demise of an adversary.

"That did not answer the question asked, Ms. Else."

"Apologies, Admiral. Yes. I know which ship it is."

"And which ship is it?"

A map of the dampened region appeared on the main display. A massive, blinking red arrow pointed at the ship that made the call. Smaller red arrows pointed to the support ships.

"As I said, a ploy. The noisy one wants to lure us in, so the quiet ones can pounce on us."

Daniel almost asked which was which, then got it.

"I say we should launch a couple drones against these two quiet ones. If we cut them on our side, their debris would end up in the nebula, where no one would question what happened."

Daniel was worried about the insolence in Else's voice. "Care to explain to me how we could do that within the bounds of our rules of engagement?"

Else had a retort on her virtual lips, which vanished as the Captain's words sank in. "Apologies sir. That came out wrong. The lead ship is trying to lure us into the kill zone they've set up.

"As soon as we enter the zone, they will fire. We will fire back and destroy them as our orders require us to do. I only meant to suggest that we pre-position the drones in a way that allows us to respond immediately and will have the impact of covering our actions."

"Thank you for the explanation, but I want to do something a little different than that.

...

Earlier, while the other ships were out picking up their cargo, Daniel had had Engineering outfit twelve of the drones with stealth field generators and smoke bombs. He'd also had Engineering develop several different programs that they could upload through the Fleet Cruisers transponders.

He was going to try the same trick the Toronto used a few days ago, but with a different outcome in mind.

"Tactical, deploy six of the time-dampening drones. Transport them in 5 kilometers behind the ships, two drones per ship, then raise their cloaks."

"One moment sir." A pause. "Two drones transported behind the lead ship. Cloaks up."

"Else move one of the drones into place, then release the smoke."

"Science, upload the first program."

"Comm, get me the Crimson Destiny."

"Earth Ship, we do not see you yet. Please hurry our situation is desperate.

"Pinging you now to get your location."

Daniel saw the irritated look on the Captain's face.

"Captain, we are concerned about approaching you. You are venting massive amounts of gas. Are you about to lose containment?"

"What?" the Captain replied.

Daniel heard an alert on the other end of the line. And saw the captain mute the connection and start shouting orders.

Daniel muted his own.

"Else, capture the other two ships in a time-dampening field."

A moment later, the captain of the Crimson Destiny came back on the line.

"What have you done to my ships!?" Fury burned in his eyes.

"Excuse me? I don't understand. You put up a distress beacon. Was this not the reason?"

"No, it was not the reason. I knew you would not come aside for inspection, so I put up the beacon to lure you in."

In the background, Daniel heard the communication officer call out. "Captain, an emergency call from the High Command."

"What?"

Daniel's view screen split. The Captain on the left and Admiral Jo-Na on the right.

"Captain Pu-Lu, I hope you have an explanation for yourself. This encounter was live streamed to me by your ship. It appears that you have defied the orders sent earlier today."

The Captain sputtered, not clever enough to come up with a suitable alibi in real time.

"Is Commander Nu-Hu on the bridge?"

Another person stepped into the image. "I am here, sir."

"Commander, Captain Pu-Lu, is relieved of command. If you follow my orders exactly, you will replace him. Is that understood?"

"Yes, sir."

"Captain Pu-Lu, you are under arrest. Surrender yourself to the Commander immediately."

For a moment it looked like the Captain might refuse, then he put his hands out. The commander nodded to someone off screen. A security officer stepped forward and cuffed the captain.

"Commander Nu-Hu."

"Yes, sir."

"Have the prisoner placed in the maximum-security area of the brig. He stands charged with disobeying a direct order from the High Command and sedition against an allied Confederation military force."

The charges shocked the people on the Crimson Destiny's bridge. It also required the security officer to apply leg-irons on the former Captain. A second officer stepped forward to apply them, only to be kicked by the Captain, who was now attempting to escape. The attempt earned him hits from four suspensor flechettes. Totally paralyzed on the floor, he was shot with a knockout round, then the suspensor flechettes were carefully removed. Four security guards put the Captain on a grav gurney and headed off to the brig.

"Commander Nu-Hu. You will now disable your weapon systems."

The Commander seemed shocked by the order.

"Commander, I'm waiting."

With a shaking hand the Commander entered the appropriate code. "Weapons disabled," a disembodied computer voice said.

The Admiral could be seen entering data into his tablet.

"Domestic training mode activated," the computer voice announced.

Several people on the bridge gasped. In domestic training mode, the AI would take them to a designated facility. Once there, shielding, the cloaking systems, and the warp and jump drives would be disabled until new command codes were entered into the ship.

"Commander Nu-Hu. Please connect me with the Dawn Glory."

After a moment. "I'm sorry, sir, the Dawn Glory is not responding."

Daniel spoke up. "Apologies, Admiral. In the hope of ending this conflict peacefully, we blocked communications to the Dawn Glory. Give me a moment to unblock."

Daniel muted the line. "Else, do you know which ship is the Dawn Glory?"

"Would you like me to release her?"

"Please."

Daniel unmuted. "You should be able to communicate with her now."

A few minutes later, the Dawn Glory was in domestic training mode.

"Admiral Porter, I assume you have the third ship in isolation also?"

"We do. Unblocking now." Daniel nodded to Else.

A few more minutes later and the third ship, Golden Providence, was in training mode.

"Commanders, your ships were found in direct violation of my orders. At this point, a copy of your logs has been encrypted in the High Command archives. Work with your helm AI to bring your ships to your designated training facility safely. Your helm AI is under my command and will refuse any orders you give in contradiction to mine. But it's still available to assist you with most ship functions.

"Please begin your journey now.

"Admiral Porter, would it be possible for us to speak in the Presence Projector?"

"Yes, sir."

"Sending the link now."

The comm line dropped.

"Duan, the ship is yours. Please continue on to our destination."

PRESENCE PROJECTOR, EAS CANADA

Daniel entered the presence projector. When he took his seat, the room morphed into what looked like a cabin in the woods.

The Admiral stood and extended his fist to bump.

"Daniel, welcome. This is my mountain lodge. I come here now and again to settle myself. Apologies for the actions of my ships. The rogue element reflects poorly on all of us.

"I spoke with your Ambassador before you left this morning. He advised me that your rules of engagement had changed. Given the circumstances, I would have expected you to destroy my ships, but you didn't. Why?"

"Have no doubt. I will destroy your ships if they fire on me. They are quite defenseless. But I don't want to destroy your ships. So, if I can find a way to prevent them from firing on me, I'll try."

"But you did do something to them."

"Yes. Are you aware of the Inspector's new weapon? The one he uses to kill helm AIs?"

"You put me in an awkward position with that question."

"That was not the intent. It works through the transponder system. When the transponder is pinged, it accepts various updates. Turns out that mechanism does not have good protection against malware. The Inspector used that mechanism to upload a program that could kill an AI, detonate a ship."

"Your point?"

"The Inspector is a fool. He deployed this weapon without hardening his own ships against it. So, to your question, I uploaded a program to the Crimson Destiny that opened a comm connection to you. Then I sprung Captain Pu-Lu's trap without stepping into it."

The Admiral chuckled.

"You are a dangerous adversary, Daniel Porter. I hope never to find myself opposed to you."

A moment passed in silence.

"Were any of your ships damaged in any way?"

"No. As we came up to the nebula, we realized that if someone were to make an attempt against us, it would happen here. So, we came in slow, in stealth. It did not take long to find Pu-Lu as he had a beacon pinging. We found his support ships, surrounded them. Uploaded the malware, then sprung the trap."

"Clever." The Admiral stood. "Thank you for not destroying my ships. They are old and in poor condition, but they are the ones I have. The captains that have turned are the problem. Thank you for having exposed some today."

The Admiral extended his fist in the Lorexian military salute.

Daniel did the same, then the connection dropped.

ANCIENT TEMPLE

As they came in through the opening David saw a giant crystal. It was red, oddly shaped and pulsed with life.

The sentinel appeared. "So'Gen La'Hoya, this was possibly the greatest discovery your people made. Many have found peace here. Is that the purpose of your journey? Is this one your beneficiary?" Although the sentinel used James' given name, it spoke in English, at least that's what David perceived.

"You feel the throb of the stone. Its energy pulses through your veins, fills you. Does it not?"

Although the sentinel asked the question of James, David felt the throb, felt the power, and unconsciously answered.

"It does."

David's eyes snapped open. He was expanding. He quickly pulled himself back together and turned to warn James. What he saw filled him with terror. James had expanded, nearly filling the area around the crystal.

"JAMES!" David screamed. "Pull yourself together. Focus on me."

A mirth-filled voice sounded in David's mind. "This is my gift to you. You will know what to do with it. Use it with purpose and confidence until I return."

James cloud of energy tightened, then plunged into David's.

"I am now part of you."

David was momentarily filled with warmth, then James presence disappeared. And the crystal stopped throbbing.

"Many of the Elders found a beneficiary to absorb their spirit. You are the first human to be blessed in that way. He was the last of his kind. You are the first of yours.

"Stay as long as you wish, David Washington. This place will always welcome you. And I will maintain it for you until I cease to function."

With that statement, the sentinel disappeared and the finality of what had just transpired slammed home. James was gone.

Overcome with grief, David coalesced and fell to the floor weeping.

ORBIT ABOVE DALFANITO

The trade convoy came into orbit above the Central Medical Distribution Warehouse on Dalfanito just at sunset. Within minutes, a billion doses of medicine to combat the plague had been transported down to great fanfare. Daniel was invited to come down to the surface. He was about to experience the gifting ceremony for himself this time.

DALFANITO MEDICAL DISTRIBUTION HEADQUARTERs

The sun had set some time ago. The building was mostly dark. A dim glow emanated from under the door of a small interior office on the third floor. The office belonged to a junior statistician in the auditing office. He was eligible for a bigger office in a better location, but he'd always humbly refused the upgrade. Everyone seemed to buy the humility ploy, but the true reason for the refusal was that the building communication hub was on the other side of the wall. Long ago, he'd installed an untraceable encrypted channel that ran directly to the Inspector's office.

The spy pressed the send button, then shut down the office for the day.

Earth ships cross void in less than 1 hour.

Medical supplies delivered, now in distribution.

Connection to the intercept squadron lost.

Wonder stones awarded to President and Ambassador for new trade deal.

Chapter 22: AWAKENING

David woke, uncertain where he was. Small creatures scurried around him. David thought they looked a lot like koala bears, though they certainly didn't behave like them. They stopped and looked at him reverently when they saw he was awake. One approached with a hot cup of fragrant fluid. It smelled like the peach tea Valerie sometimes enjoyed. It held the cup out for David to take, then scurried away when David took it.

As soon as the tea was in his hands, David knew what it was, knew it was safe for him to drink. But he couldn't quite pull up the name of the drink or the place where he'd had it before. The feeling of déjà vu came back even stronger when he tasted it.

One of the little creatures snuggled up next to him cooing. Two others brought him some food on a large green leaf. The sight, smell, then taste of the food triggered even stronger déjà vu.

I know this food, but what is it?

More of the creatures came over to snuggle. One started purring as he stroked it.

There is something familiar about this place.

The thought snapped him from his daydream like state.

He stood. "Where am I?"

The sentinel flashed into existence. "David Washington. First of your kind. You are in the presence of the Temple of the Ancients."

At the sight of the sentinel, memory of the previous day flooded back, and David fell to the floor in grief. The small koala bear like creatures scurried away, then slowly came back as if to comfort him.

David, the familiar voice sounded in his mind. *Do not grieve me. I have not left you, though I must stay hidden for a time. You know what you need to do. Time to get on with it.*

David flashed into a cloud of light, then disappeared into the stone. He'd finally entered the Temple.

INSPECTORS OFFICE

The Inspector was furious. Several of his spies on Dalfanito had reported in overnight, each one reporting more or less exactly the same thing. He usually had to piece together what had happen from the bits and fragments he got. Whatever happened yesterday must have been very public.

He also got a note from Admiral Jo-Na. Captain Pu-Lu had been arrested and charged with sedition. And all three of his missing ships had had their command codes revoked. They were currently headed back to training bases that were firmly under High Command control.

This incident had cost him dearly. Technically, he had no war ships of his own, only influence over the captains of Admiral Jo-Na's ships. It would be a very long time before he got control over those ships again.

He needed to take down the Admiral. He also needed to take down this new trade Alliance. And most of all, he needed to take down Mi-Ku.

EAS CANADA

After last night's ceremony, Daniel put the ship in a distant orbit. All seven freighters had multiple deliveries to make, so they would be here a full day.

Daniel was impressed by the planet's defenses, so had put in a request with his military contact to discuss them. The meeting would start shortly.

...

Daniel entered the presence projector. When he took his designated seat, the room morphed in to a small but comfortable conference room. Three people sat on the opposite side of an oval conference table.

The person in the center was the first to speak.

"Captain Porter, welcome to Dalfanito. I am Tofor Sonjoy, the civilian head of our planetary defense systems. I am one of our president's cabinet secretaries and was at the ceremony last night.

"The President and entire cabinet thanks you for navigating the dangers of our space to bring much needed medical supplies. We are truly in your debt.

"Let me introduce the head of our space-based military operations, Admiral Dolag Lantaf." The secretary indicated the person on his right. "And the head of our orbital platform command, Admiral Bonjoi Ralop."

"Mr. Secretary, thank you for speaking with me today. As we entered orbit last night, I was very impressed by your orbital defensive

278

platforms. Earth does not have anything comparable, so to the extent it's permissible, I'd like to learn more about them. It seems that we could leverage technology like that to free more of our ships from planetary defense."

"Admiral, we would enjoy discussing the principles behind our orbital defenses, as we would enjoy learning about the capabilities of your ships."

Daniel smiled. It seemed the tit-for-tat exchange of public information was about to begin. Now he wished he'd studied up a little more ahead of time.

EAS MUMBAI

The initial 12, then 24 hours, Admiral Flanagan had given them had come and gone. At this point, Bumati knew that this find dwarfed the others. She had reported that to the Admiral and to Michael. It was not fully mapped, not even enough to have an order of magnitude estimate. But what they had mapped exceeded the sum of her other finds. She'd expected to be recalled but was surprised to find an ally in Captain Jessica Martin.

From previous experience, she knew Jessica to be strong, strict, by the book, and uncompromising. Not the type of personality Bumati seemed to get along with. But in this case, their interests were aligned. Bumati wanted to know the full scope of her find so she could put together a development plan. Jessica knew this was where the action would be. So, she wanted to develop a first rate astrogation map of this system, which would facilitate safe movement through it.

Together, they'd convinced the Admiral that this was where they needed to be. Strictly speaking, Bumati did not need the Admiral's permission or approval. But for the work they had to do, it was too big a risk to do it alone. So in this case, he controlled her movements.

PRESENCE PROJECTOR, AMBASSADOR'S OFFICE

"Fe-Va, thanks for organizing this meeting. I'm hoping you have some feedback from our new trade partners."

"Mi-Ku, lots of feedback, but the wonder stones were a master stroke. I've started putting the word out about the scope of this first major deal and have sent the draft contract to 11 more worlds that requested them. For now, I'm limiting the scope to sectors 2B, 3A and 3F, but I'm getting requests from throughout the Confederation."

"Good news, and I agree with the restriction. I'd like to avoid Andromeda until we are forced to do business there. It is too hostile to our ships.

"So, tell me about the reaction?"

"Few worlds in the Confederation have the wealth or means to obtain a wonder stone. Outside Andromeda, I think it is only Earth, Togarotu and Ardessa. Most other worlds think the core worlds in Andromeda have used them as a way to hold themselves above everyone else.

"Several of the Ambassadors I've spoken with implied that having a wonder stone in their national museum would be an indication that they had finally arrived, finally become a full partner in the Confederation. It's turned several of the initial conversations in an instant."

"Ironic." Michael let the word hang there. "They're valuable because they're rare. But giving two or three to every planet in our three sectors will dilute the value to the point where it's not a sign of superiority."

Fe-Va smiled. "But it will be a sign of membership in what will become the wealthiest Alliance in the Confederation."

"True. Tell me about the trading. Are our partners satisfied with the range of products they can buy and the demand for products they put up for sale?"

"Yes. In fact, I'm shocked at how much stuff is out there that I'd never heard of before. We're going to need a lot of ships.

"By the way, word is already out about the convoy's encounter with the Fleet Cruisers. The human mystique grows my friend. No one can imagine taking on a Cruiser, forget three of them. Then without firing a shot, sending them home. One of the reasons trade has been stagnant is because of Fleet interference. You're opening the door for a tremendous boom in prosperity."

"I'm glad to hear that. It's what I'd envisioned."

"But there's a problem arising that we should attempt to nip in the bud. The poorest worlds want to get in on the prosperity, but claim they have nothing to trade, so are being excluded. I've already heard grumbling."

Michael sighed. "Let me guess, they want us to give them a supplement."

"They do."

"How many have you heard this from?"

"Three so far."

"Are they like Jerusota was, held in place by an Inspector-aligned Ambassador?"

"I know for sure that one is not. The other two I don't know well enough to say."

"Tell me about this one."

"Natural disaster took out a big chunk of their Confederation manufacturing capacity. And they don't have enough Transluminide to rebuild."

"I may have a solution for that."

"Really?" Fe-Va's interest spiked.

"We could establish a natural disaster relief fund. Allow them to apply for a grant. Then after that allow them to apply for a loan."

"Mi-Ku, we can't do that. There's no standardized interplanetary currency."

"As I said, we can fix that."

EUGENE AND KELLY'S LAB

"Eugene, you've been quiet the last couple days. What's up?"

Eugene looked at Kelly for a moment. "I'm thinking it's time to settle down, maybe start teaching again."

"Why would you think that? You're like the world's most prolific engineer."

"Mostly because I get too much credit for your ideas."

"What! I couldn't have done any of those things on my own."

Eugene was quiet for a moment.

"It's not that. It's like I feel empty. In the last month, we kicked out three blockbusters: safe forward shields, the intergalactic jump drive, the time-dampening field. All those were incredible breakthroughs. The intergalactic drive is one of those things that will change the course of history

"But I'm feeling empty. Like those were the last. Like I don't have anything else to give."

"Good. Then you can be my lab tech because I've still got a lot more to give."

Kelly's boast was delivered so outrageously that Eugene couldn't help but laugh.

"So, what are you working on?"

"You know how Transluminide works, right?"

"It's the active component in zero-point energy devices. It allows particles from the quantum foam to condense into electrons, or something like that."

"And how does that create energy?" Kelly prompted.

"It functionally creates a charged particle from the fluctuating zero-energy state of nature. Presumably, it does it by siphoning particles into our dimension from others."

"Exactly. It generates a free flow of charged particles."

"And the point?"

"I found some Confederation research that suggests a way to create much higher flows without the direct use of Transluminide."

"What do you mean direct use?"

"The model I have in my mind is that it's analogous to an old-fashioned transistor. Apply a little current to the base, get a lot of current out of the emitter. But I know that explanation won't work for most people."

She paused to frame a better example.

"Transluminide is a clever way to pull a single electron into our space time from some other one. One electron per atom of Transluminide, every millisecond or something like that.

"This one is more like sticking a pipe into another dimension and let the electrons come over in mass. The Transluminide doesn't bring the electrons over, it just controls the spigot."

"And how does it do that?"

"I haven't figured that part out yet. They have a torturous mathematical work up. But like most things Confederation, they bring it right up to the edge of being something. Then they just stop."

"I'll have a look at it if you'd like."

"I thought you were empty."

"Not anymore."

NELLY FONG'S OFFICE

"Good morning, Michael. Good to see you. I was surprised to see you pop up on my calendar this morning."

"Hi, Nelly. Hope you are well."

"I'm good. And happy to have Eugene back. He's had quite the string of breakthroughs recently."

"He has. The intergalactic jump drive is changing the flow of commerce on an unprecedented scale. That's actually the reason I wanted to talk with you. Let me explain."

...

"So, you want to create grant and loan programs for worlds that don't have the resources, or Transluminide reserves, to participate in the new trade Alliance.

"I like the idea. I presume you're here because you'd like to use the Earth Alliance dollar. Or possibly, create yet another currency?"

Michael smiled. "You presume correctly."

"It would have to be a new currency. The Earth Alliance dollar is backed by gold and platinum. We don't have enough gold and platinum to back that much. It seems the right choice would be a new currency backed by Transluminide bullion. Is that possible? Do we have the reserves?" And what would one of these dollars be worth?"

"We have a lot of Transluminide in the ground and are in the process of setting up the mining. How do we need to hold the Transluminide in order to back a currency with it?"

"Ideally, bullion in a vault. Something that can be seen and audited. It doesn't need to be in one vault, you could have multiple vaults spread out. And the bricks of bullion don't need to back the individual dollar and we don't need to issue all the dollars that we have bullion to back."

Michael thought for a second.

"This will need to be a trade alliance currency, so we could call it a TA dollar. We make each dollar worth 100 grams. Pennies worth 1 gram. If our initial authorization was 1 million TA dollars, then I would need to get 100,000 kg refined and in a vault.

Michael looked at Nelly intently.

"I'll work the approvals and actual storage facilities. You work up everything needed to launch the currency, create boilerplate grant and loan contracts, and a system for auditing the bullion when we want it on display."

"Sounds like a plan."

"Any chance you can get boilerplate grant and loan documents to me for comment by Monday?"

Nelly rolled her eyes.

"They'll be rough."

"Deal."

PRIVATE ROOM, COUNCILOR'S CLUB

One of the perks of being, or having been, a Central Council member was access to the very exclusive Councilor's Club, located in

Central Council Plaza on New Lorexi. Every conceivable service was available here. Councilor To-Ja of New Lorexi favored it for private dinners.

Tonight, he would be dining with newly appointed Inspector Ha-Ke. There were matters of compensation and favors that needed to be settled.

He entered to see that the Inspector had already arrived and ordered a beverage for himself. Somewhat unexpectedly, the guest was the first to greet.

"To-Ja, my friend. Such a pleasure to see you tonight." He spread his arms indicating the facility. "Especially in this place."

"Ha-Ke, we finally get the chance to meet in private. I've been waiting for the chance to welcome you here. What is it you're drinking? I don't recognize it."

Ha-Ke smiled at the question. The setting, and the tiny wonder stone embedded in the councilor's family ring, gave him hope for a successful outcome tonight.

"It's called Port. It's from Earth; naturally produced, not replicated. It's journeyed all the way here. And it is absolutely exquisite. Hard to believe primitives could produce something with such character and depth."

"It's sad to say, but the primitives seem to have greater finesse when it comes to things carnal. Competence with baser desires apparently comes with the territory." He snapped his fingers and pointed to a servant. "Please bring me some of this Port."

The Councilor turned to his guest.

"There are things we need to discuss tonight, but possibly an update first?"

Again Ha-Ke smiled. *This vane fool actually thinks he has the upper hand tonight. Best to keep him thinking that.*

"My pleasure. Despite earlier successes, the humans continue their onslaught. They are trying to develop a new trade alliance."

"Surely you jest. How could that possibly work?"

"Make no mistake. Councilor Mi-Ku is crafty, no doubt a result of his association with the imposter he calls 'the Ancient Sentient.'

"But we both know the ancient imposter is a toothless fool. His lies run floor to ceiling, entrance to exit."

The Inspector realized immediately that his statement didn't land as expected, so moved on.

"One of the gifts he's giving to new members are alleged wonder stones. I know with firsthand knowledge that he has given a dozen or more away this week. Dalfanito got two."

Councilor To-Ja sucked in breath as if choking on his drink.

"And three more to a newly admitted world in 3F called Naltanarus."

"How large?" The councilor choked out.

Ha-Ke smirked to himself. *The councilor is so vane.*

"In the 10 to 25 carat range." It was a bit of an overstatement. He doubted any were over 10 carats. But it had its effect. Councilor To-Ja's ring was 5 carats at best.

"How? How dare he!"

Ha-Ke damped down the external smile. But internally he beamed. *This fool is buying the story hook, line, and sinker.*

"Councilor, you know him. He has no respect for Confederation convention. He'll do anything to foment unrest among the primitives."

"But 25 carat stones... How could he get such things?"

"Maybe he has. Maybe he hasn't. How would the primitives know? What, if anything, do they know of culture, class, or status?"

Ha-Ke could see that this line landed. Give the fools a little praise, a little money, and they would believe anything. He might score bigger wins tonight than he'd hoped.

"Nothing, but they've turned out to be skilled thieves of technology. Many of our most sought-after technical advances have been stolen and put to use by the humans."

"What technologies?"

"The most irking is propulsion technology. My predecessor had succeeded in developing a drive that could cross the void in only 5 days. The humans stole it within days of finding out about it, made a minor tweak and now have a jump drive that can cross in a day, which would be a good thing if they shared their upgrade with us. But no, they use it against us to undercut our trade."

"This cannot be allowed to stand!" The Councilor banged his fist on the table, causing some of his Port to slosh out of his glass. The waiter quickly came over to clean up the mess.

"Why isn't the High Command doing something about this?"

The Inspector looked at the Councilor quizzically. "He is in Mi-Ku's pocket. You didn't know that?"

Councilor To-Ja seemed shocked by the statement, then it snapped. "Is that why Admiral Jo-Na proposed that we shut down the Office of Military Intelligence?"

The Inspector nodded his head. "We are the only force that stands between the Confederation and the revolutionaries that want to steal it all away from us."

"Yes. I see that now. I see it." To-Ja paused a moment, reflecting on the revelations he'd just heard. "How can I help you get this back under control?"

"I was hoping you would ask that question. My office has the financial resources to deal with this issue, but not the political insight to know where those resources need to be applied. Maybe we could fund some initiatives that you could participate in."

Inspector Ha-Ke knew the Councilor had had a similar arrangement with a previous Inspector, one that had helped that Inspector's rise.

"I would enjoy the opportunity to get closer to these issues. What kind of arrangement did you have in mind?"

"A monthly retainer, maybe 75 grams, in exchange for some regularly scheduled meetings and assistance here and there with sensitive matters."

"Make it 100 and it's a deal."

"Then 100 it is." Sometimes it was just so easy.

EAS CANADA

The evening portion of first watch was well underway when the last of the deliveries was completed. At 11:00 PM, the trade convoy would get underway for the short trip to Togarotu.

Daniel's meeting with Dalfanito's Secretary and Admirals had been interesting. Their defensive platforms were organized in a spherical arrangement around the planet at an altitude equivalent to twice the normal geostationary orbit.

Daniel had seen this as they were coming in but didn't understand how it was done. In retrospect it was obvious. Each platform had a multiple redundant grav drive system that held it in place.

The platforms were all automated and remote controlled, which Daniel thought was odd. When they explained how the amplified Coriolis Effect on the platforms impacted living beings, he understood. It would be like being on one of those amusement-park rides where they strap you in and spin you on three different axes. No human could work in that environment. He doubted anyone would survive very long if they tried.

Each platform had a shield generator and weapon systems, which allowed them to seal off as much or little of the planet as they needed. It also provided armed defense in the center of every entry zone.

He planned to write up a report about it for consideration by Space Force Command.

His hosts were very proud of their system. They were also very interested in all three types of Space Force ships. It was clear they wanted some for themselves. They had apparently suffered at the hands of the Confederation more than Earth had.

"Admiral, all ships report ready for departure."

"Thank you, Else. Engage the sequencer."

Chapter 23: ASSASSINATION

David rested with the kind of peace and joy that expanding in the void offered. But he was at no risk of losing cohesion. The crystal held him together.

And he now understood why they called this a temple. All the knowledge of James' people was here, and he was slowly absorbing it. Every secret, even knowledge of 'The Great One,' was here.

James told him that the collected knowledge of his people was held in the crystals. David had envisioned it as being like a library with rack after rack of thick tomes. The reality was quite a bit different, more organic, which seemed a silly thought given that he was an energy being resting in a mineral formation. But it did describe the experience.

Every thought seemed to attract information. When he wondered what James' people looked like, the image just came into his mind. When wondering about how the images came, other images of information living within the crystal and hearing his thoughts came to mind.

Wish we'd had this at my school, he mused. Then images of ancients past and their schools came.

They could do this for children who weren't in energy form! David marveled.

But the most important learnings were about his dual nature, human and energy. More than once he'd asked James about it, and the answer was always the same. *You already know, just haven't figured it out yet.*

No truer words had ever been spoken. The simple answer was that he was both. In fact, all humans were both. Although only a few learned of their energy nature in time to take advantage of it.

As an energy being, he was intrinsically empathic. The energy in his mind could interact with the energy in anyone else's. When fully human, he had no empathic ability. But he never needed to be completely human and, at this point, it would take an act of extreme will to be.

As an energy being, he could move seamlessly through the dimensions, allowing him to go anywhere in the blink of an eye. Similarly, he could manipulate the dimensions, allowing him to use any of them with just a thought.

"You are new here. A different organic base. Are you the one So'Gen La'Hoya brought?"

Until now, he'd been alone. The voice in his mind reminded David that others were here.

"Yes. When he was in my form, I knew him as James."

"Sensible choice of name, given your people's history and experiences. We are... Sorry, our name doesn't translate well." An image flooded David's mind. It was of the Milky Way's spiral arms. Then it zoomed into a small section of it.

"This is where we came from."

"Are you the only one?"

"No, we are but one of numerous collectives. In time, when you are ready, you would be welcome to join ours. But we see that you'll only be here for a short time. We can see and understand what you need to do."

"Can you tell me?"

David heard a sound like the laughter track on an old TV comedy show.

"No. You already know. Anything we say would disrupt the clarity you have and reduce your likelihood of success. But we do have one thing to say to you."

"OK," David sent with little conviction.

"Do not grieve. So'Gen La'Hoya is alive and well. Things are not as you believe them to be. You were destined for the work before you. Your fate sealed when you were 16. So'Gen La'Hoya found you, prepared you, and brought you here to finish your training.

"You will be ready soon, but only you will know when."

David felt the presence recede. Leaving him with more questions than answers. The thought made him smile. His early interactions with James had done the same.

EAS CANADA

The Canada had achieved orbit around Togarotu just after 4:00 AM Embassy time. Within an hour of arrival, the first deliveries started. At 8:00, Daniel would be transporting down to the capital, where it would be approximately noon, for the gift ceremony.

CAPITAL BUILDING, TOGAROTU

Daniel arrived on the transporter pad in the capital building. Two security guards stood at the entrance to the room. A very serious, middle-aged female stepped toward him.

"Admiral Porter. Welcome to Togarotu. I am Faslan Tosset, assistant to Councilor Momun Saltoi. If you will please follow me."

It took a moment for Daniel to recall that the person Michael referred to as Councilor Mo-Mo was a Lorexian Ascendant. His Lorexian familiar name was Mo-Mo. But here on Togarotu, among the Zorossan people, he'd taken the Zorossan name Momun Saltoi.

Another thought struck as they approached the guards and the crowds waiting outside. *The Zorossans are a beautiful people. Tall and thin with sculpted bodies and compellingly attractive pale blue skin. I stand out like a sore thumb yet feel comfortable among them. I wish Earth was more like that.*

"Admiral. A large crowd has gathered. A lot of people hope to catch a glimpse of you. We are going to wait here for a few seconds as more guards get into position. It's hard to believe that anyone would intentionally hurt you. We just want to make sure we are not crushed by the crowd."

"Understood, Ms. Tosset. We have similar problems on our world. Everyone wants to see something new."

...

When Daniel was called, he stepped out into the National Assembly chambers to a standing ovation. It reminded Daniel of a State of the Union address. The main floor was packed with government officials, the balconies with guests and media. But unlike the annual American spectacle, the press box was filled with reporters of many different species, several of which Daniel did not recognize.

As he stepped up to the podium, people took their seats and the room quieted.

"Good afternoon. My name is Daniel Porter. I am an admiral in the 3F Defensive Alliance and leader of the trade convoy that has ventured here from the Milky Way.

"Although we've come to trade, we are motivated by a larger, more important purpose. That purpose is to spread the prosperity."

The crowd erupted in applause at the statement.

"As you may know, Earth is a relatively new member. Our Revelation was only seven years ago."

Daniel paused as murmuring swept through the room.

"I remember the wonder of the first years: the medical miracles, peace and prosperity, the end of hunger and poverty, and the amazement that the universe was filled with intelligent life. But above it all was the knowledge that all this had been initiated by a Confederation that kept the peace and help lift up other peoples.

"One of the questions I asked myself during those first couple years was, 'what can I do to thank those who have so generously given to me?'"

"Turns out I wasn't the only one. Several of our planet's best minds started working through the Confederation science and technology to see if there were some improvements they could make to benefit the entire Confederation.

"An engineer figured out how to improve the efficiency of Confederation propulsion systems. Another figured out how to improve Confederation shielding. Yet another figured out how to construct spaceships in days, not years. And another found new methods for discovering Transluminide.

"These discoveries had an immediate and beneficial impact on Earth. But, as we started getting to know our neighbors, other Confederation members on nearby planets, we realized that they were not enjoying the same prosperity that we were. That's when we started what we now call the 'Spread the Prosperity' program."

Again, the room erupted in applause. When it settled Daniel continued.

"The idea is simple. We have the best transportation and security services in the Confederation. So we offer safe and secure transportation to or from any planet in our coverage area that joins our Trade Alliance. We also have the resources to develop a marketplace where you can go to buy products from, or sell products to, other worlds.

"In our 3F Alliance, we have been doing this for almost a year now and seen tremendous prosperity increases. We now have the transportation resources to open our trade alliance to planets in sectors 2B and 3A."

More applause.

"As proof that we have the resources to make this happen, and as a show of respect and friendship with the people of Togarotu, I have gifts to present to Councilor Momun Saltoi and President Questen Wonzel. Gentlemen please join me."

More murmuring spread through the room as the men came forward. Daniel opened the first box, containing a 20 carat, ruby red wonder stone on a braided cord.

"Councilor Saltoi. On behalf of the people of Earth and the 3F Alliance, I present you with this Stone of Courage."

The Councilor bowed, allowing Daniel to place the gift around his neck.

Daniel opened the second box, containing a 15 carat, jade colored wonder stone on a braided cord.

"President Wonzel. On behalf of the people of Earth and the 3F Alliance, I present you with this Stone of Friendship."

Daniel repeated the process of placing the stone around the President's neck. Then the two men went to either side of the podium so the room could see the sparkle and dancing light within the stones.

As the massive applause started to die out, Daniel closed.

"To all the people of Togarotu, let this day mark the beginning of a new age of peace and prosperity among and between our peoples. Thank you."

As Daniel stepped back, his handlers came to congratulate him, then swoosh him away to the next event. It was going to be a long day.

INSPECTORS OFFICE

"...let this day mark the beginning of a new age of peace and prosperity among and between our peoples. Thank you."

The Inspector had just finished watching the Earth person addressing the joint houses of government on Togarotu.

"This has to stop!" he shouted at the screen.

As he trembled with rage, he placed a call to his head of mission on Togarotu. "The human, the Admiral. He is not to leave that planet alive!"

Despite having placed a death sentence on the Admiral, Ha-Ke still pulsed with anger. He simply did not have enough power outside the core to stop the upstarts. Ju-Ne had kept them in check for a while, but ultimately had made a misstep that took him out of the game. He needed more agents and he needed ships.

The plan he had been working, upgrading the Kalamaan ships, had mostly backfired. As soon as some upgrades were in place they took off on a rogue mission and got themselves killed. The investment in primitives as a proxy force had been a complete waste.

He needed something more, something he didn't have. Maybe he could sway his sponsors on the Central Council.

PRESENCE PROJECTOR, SPEAKER FU-SU'S OFFICE

"To-Ja, what's happened? Your message said it was urgent."

"Fu-Su, did you see the speech that was just given on Togarotu?"

"No, what speech?"

"Human admiral, head of the trade convoy that just arrived."

"No, can't imagine why I would."

"The humans just presented gifts, one to Mo-Mo and another to the president of Togarotu. Each received a large wonder stone. Mo-Mo got the Stone of Courage, the president the Stone of Friendship.

"The theme of the presentation was 'Spreading the Prosperity.' I had dinner with newly elected Inspector Ha-Ke last night. He told me that Mi-Ku has been distributing wonder stones to the primitive worlds. I didn't really believe it until I saw it for myself.

"You realize that this could be the end of it for both of us?"

The statement puzzled the Speaker. "How?"

To-Ja shook his head. "Your family businesses, the ones that finance your position in society and your membership on this council..."

"What about them?"

"What's the collateral that backs your loans?"

Seeing that the Speaker still wasn't understanding, To-Ja tried again. "If the market is flooded with inexpensive, large carat wonder stones, like the two given away today, how will that impact the value of your holdings."

A look of terror came over the Speaker. "I'd lose my financing. My businesses would be liquidated. I'd lose everything, be removed from the Council.

"We must stop him!"

"Agreed. The question is how?"

TEMPORARY ANDROID PRODUCTION LAB

The building that previously housed the Android Production Lab had been damaged in the explosion. At this point, the building had been cleaned out. Anything salvageable had been removed and building repairs were underway.

New space had been allocated in an unoccupied building in the west central part of the Embassy, on the other side of the river from the Engineering school and manufacturing area. Equipment had been ordered, including stack editors from Karagon, and other specialty equipment from Celanar. The people who hadn't been in the building at the time of the explosion were now working here as best they could.

But that was going to change today. A major delivery from Celanar was due. The Freighter carrying it had just entered orbit. And among the passengers were Barbara, several of her colleagues, and 25 new helm AIs in upgraded computers.

Joel doubted that Barbara would be particularly excited about the new location. It was further from her apartment. Joel liked it. It was closer to his office.

MANUFACTURING OFFICE

"Joel, Henry here."

"Henry, what can I do for you?"

"Just a heads up. Barbara will be transporting down in about 10 minutes."

Joel popped up out of his chair.

"Thanks. Owe you one, buddy."

TEMPORARY ANDROID PRODUCTION LAB

Joel arrived at the new temporary facility just before the first passenger transported down. A small crowd had gathered to welcome their friends home. Joel spotted Lucy in the crowd and went over to say hi.

"Ah, Joel. I thought you might be here." She smiled slyly at Joel. She knew that Barbara's friendship with Joel was more than just work. She suspected Joel's interest in Barbara was as well. It would be curious to see Joel's reaction to Barbara's new avatar. It was new, just completed maturation two days ago. But from an appearance perspective, she would now look like she was mid-twenties, not mid-thirties as she had before. Apparently, men found younger women more attractive. It seemed silly to her. But she'd already seen an android and an Ascendant come back in a new avatar and hook up with someone who was previously 'just friends.'

"There she is!" Joel pointed, then pushed his way through the crowd.

Lucy smiled. "Yup."

PRESENCE PROJECTOR, EAS MUMBAI

It had taken 40 hours, but the survey was done. Just over 1 billion kilograms in a tight little sphere at the center of the planet. Impurities were higher than she'd originally expected, so the material would need to be refined. But the inner core was molten, so refining the first couple million kilograms would be easy.

They were still in orbit above the planet. The Dhaka wouldn't complete its scans until later in the day. But given the news, Admiral Flanagan had set up a meeting with the brass to discuss next steps.

Bumati entered the presence projector and took her seat. Admiral Flanagan was already present. He was the meeting's host.

A virtual door opened, and Admiral Katrina Bjork came in. "I hear there's some good news to report. So good that I've finally been read in on what you've been up to. Congratulations, Ms. Parikh."

A moment later, another virtual door opened, and Michael walked in with Professor Schudel.

Moments later President Lee, Secretary Thompson and Admiral Scott joined.

"Chris, you called this meeting. Please take the lead."

"Thank you, Michael. We have some big news that I'll let Ms. Parikh share. It motivates the topics I'd like to discuss today."

All eyes turned toward Bumati.

"As you know, I've been searching for Transluminide. I developed a theory of formation, which led to a theory on where it could be found in huge quantities.

"So far, the theory has served us well. I've made three finds as part of this mission. So far the smallest was on the order of half a million kilograms. Admiral Flanagan was sent to start setting up the mining operations for that find.

"But a new find seems like it might be the better place to start. The main find is in the core of a smallish planet in a brown dwarf system. Its core is Transluminide, about 1 billion kilograms with 90+ percent purity."

Michael interrupted. "I assume that you want to move mining operations there?" The question was targeted at Admiral Flanagan.

"Yes, but probably not what you're thinking."

"The core is molten, right?" This time it was Professor Schudel that cut in.

Bumati nodded affirmatively and whispered, "Yes."

The professor smacked his hand on the table, chuckling "Yes!"

"Care to clue us in on the relevance, Professor."

The professor nodded toward Bumati.

"The mining and refining processes are a lot different for extractions from a molten core. What we would need is something like the mining platforms we have around Earth. Something that makes a relatively large pull of molten material, then uses filter shields to purify the Transluminide, then pours the ingots, all in one operation.

"In full operation, we could produce well over 1 million kilograms of refined ingots a day. And we could start tomorrow if we had the platform."

Michael turned back to Admiral Flanagan.

"Chris, what do you propose?"

"Operations at the core mine will be relatively simple. We don't need a lot of infrastructure. And we will functionally deplete the site within a couple years.

"For the other planets that will not be true. Word will eventually get out and those planets will be raided, if we don't have defenses in place. So I propose a split effort. A small team to exploit the core deposit as quickly as possible. And a larger team to carry on as originally planned. It will take a long time to fully exploit the other planets.

"I've prepared a requirements list that shows what we need at each current location. And for planning purposes, I have prepared an estimate and timeline for each new location. This will need to be reviewed after each new find. But I wanted to get something out to help us prepare, so that we are not caught by surprise with each new find."

"Thank you. Who will have the lead on building the platform for the core exploitation?"

"For now, I assume that we will build it. It's a bit large to transport. Ms. Parikh has given us a preliminary design. We would like to have the Professor and Joel review the design, and the AI engineering team to create the final replication pattern."

"A question if I may?" President Lee asked.

Michael nodded, implying he should proceed. "We are going to get an immense quantity from the core find. Do we really need to develop the other planets?"

"I'll take that one," Michael said, directing his response to Admiral Flanagan who was about to respond.

"As you know. The Confederation has fallen into decay over the last 100 years, most of the rot associated with the Inspector and his supporters. We are the only force within the Confederation that has been able to hold the Inspector off. At this point, and with these resources, I believe we have a strong chance of displacing, or at least, disempowering him. But that chance would vaporize if the Inspector, or one of his proxies, should gain control over any of these finds.

"I think our best chance of preventing that is by developing the finds ourselves. Will the smaller finds help us that much? No, not really. But they could turn the tide if they fell into the wrong hands.

"Therefore, my answer to your question would be yes. We need to develop these discoveries, and the next batch Ms. Parikh will find. Her paper, her work is out there. Someone will eventually figure out how we did it and will go look for more. We need to make sure there is nothing for them to find."

"I agree with Michael," Secretary Thompson said. "This is a strategic asset. It is just as important to deny our enemies access to this asset as it is to exploit it for our own use."

President Lee nodded in agreement. "Understood. Thank you."

Michael looked at Admiral Flanagan.

"Chris, thanks for putting the issue on the table. I agree with your conclusions. Exploiting the planet with the Transluminide core needs to be the top priority. Pull out all the stops to get the platform up and start bringing home ingots within a week. These will allow us to progress other initiatives more quickly. Use the rest of your resources to secure the two other worlds as soon as possible. Admiral Scott is empowered to continue feeding you ships as they become available.

NOGTAN SECTOR, EMBASSY CITY, TOGAROTU

Daniel's last event for the day was a state dinner being held at the historic Datsal Palace in the Nogtan sector of the Embassy. The sector was named for President Datsal Nogtan, who had ushered Togarotu and the Zorossan people into the Confederation some 25,000 years ago.

President Nogtan had been a wealthy man. He'd owned one of the last undivided homesteads on the planet at the time of the Revelation, land he'd leased to the Confederation for their Embassy. Over time the Embassy expanded out, taking the name Embassy City. But the original homestead still bore the name of the long dead president.

Up until a few years before the Revelation, the homestead had been a working ranch with an employee cafeteria. When the ranch had finally closed, the President had converted the old cafeteria into a first-rate entertainment facility. There, he would hold lavish parties. He'd called it Datsal's Palace.

Nothing of the original cafeteria remained, other than pictures in the museums. In fact, it wasn't known for sure where it had been on the property. But, in the last major renovation of the sector, a new 10 story dining and entertainment facility had been added. It was given the name Datsal's Palace in honor of the old president's party house.

Tonight's dinner was the last event of the long day. The hosts had gone to great lengths to find food and drink that was safe for both humans and Zorossans. The speeches other than the final toasts were done. The President of Togarotu was about to offer Daniel a toast.

NEARBY ROOFTOP

The assassin was not happy about getting a high-profile hit like this as late as she did. But she needed the money, and she was one of the few that could get it done.

The only weapons produced on Togarotu were energy weapons. Every sort of laser rifle or other energy projector could be found, if you knew where to look. And all had the same weakness. You needed line of sight to your target, clear enough weather that the beam's energy would not be lost to moisture in the atmosphere, and you couldn't shoot through the windows. All windows in Embassy City had to be shatter proof laminates with at least one layer of lead crystal inside. The lamination made the glass hard to break. The lead crystal would absorb or refract the energy of any portable weapon. That was the real reason she was chosen for this project. She had a weapon that she'd designed herself, one she called a double-strike weapon.

The first strike was kinetic, not laser, a hypersonic projectile with a shaped explosive that could punch a clean hole in windows like these.

The second strike was pulsed, coherent light high in the ultraviolet spectrum. The hot, megawatt pulse would cut deeply into organic material. The two strikes came from separate barrels timed so the energy pulse came through within milliseconds of the round clearing the hole. It was a high collateral damage weapon. The projectile would still have enough kinetic energy to kill or maim several people. But its trajectory would deflect chaotically as it cleared the glass and crystal, so was extremely unlikely to hit the target. The laser beam, that was a different story. Barring a strong gust of wind, the target had no chance.

She watched as the President stood to offer a toast to the target. As the target stood, he would pass through the kill zone and she would shoot.

DATSAL'S PALACE

The President's toast went on a bit but was actually well formed and generous, and now about to conclude. The President raised his cup and Daniel started to rise.

"...to our guest, Admiral Porter."

And all hell broke loose.

...

Daniel found himself on the floor, not sure how he got there. As his senses cleared, the smell of burnt hair and flesh caused him to cough and almost retch. The woman who had been sitting next to him looked like she'd been roasted alive. Another body on the floor close to him had no head. There was panic, screaming. His right arm didn't seem to work. Then a wave of darkness came over him.

NEARBY ROOFTOP

The assassin swore as she collapsed her gear. The target had been wearing a personal shield. Most of the power of the energy bolt had deflected off of it before the shield gave out. She couldn't confirm the kill but only had 15 seconds before the escape transport would grab her. She snapped into position just in time for the narrow transport field to catch her. Then she was gone.

EAS CANADA

"Commander! Shields just came up all over the planet. Embassy City is in multiple lock-down. Sensors show nothing, but something has obviously happened," First Watch Tactical Officer Kaitlin O'Brien reported.

"Commander!" It was Else. "Togarotu Space Control has just closed the planet's navigational control area. Any ships altering course will be targeted by the planetary defenses."

A moment later.

"Commander Tai, I think we have trouble. I just caught a news flash from a local broadcast station. Admiral Porter's reception has been attacked. Putting it up on the screen."

A scene of bedlam appeared. Dazed and bloodied people flowed out of a building. Some crying, some screaming, others just stoically flowing away from the area trying not to be seen.

A continuous flow of babbling sounds accompanied the scene.

"Working to clean up the audio," Else shouted out.

"...chaos and terror reigns. We heard the shots. The people fleeing the building say there was an explosion. Others say the foreigner glowed white hot, killing those around them. Still others say a window was shattered, cutting them with glass shards. The most consistent story we've heard tonight is that the Admiral from the visiting trade delegation was at the center of it, glowing white hot as others around him burned. This is Seyon Nahdow reporting for..." another explosion sounded in the background... "News."

"Oh, shit." Duan Tai muttered. Earth Alliance and Space Forces regulations were clear. An officer, no matter rank, was bound by the laws and jurisdiction in which he or she operated. Duan's hands were tied. Until Daniel was cleared, there was little he could do other than offer evidence. Something he was short of at the moment.

Chapter 24: NEW BEGINNING

[Friday, 08.06.2032] ANCIENT TEMPLE

It was time! The events of the last couple days, then the assassination attempt yesterday, had to be answered.

David exited the temple. When he did, the red stone began its rhythmic throbbing. David held his position, engulfing the stone in his cloud of energy.

"David Washington. First of your kind. It is forbidden to touch the stone in this way." The sentinel moved toward David, but it froze in place as David's attention was cast upon him.

"Now I know," David said aloud.

He coalesced into human form where the stone had been.

"Sentinel. I am now the Temple. Your service is to me. Present yourself to me in human form so I may give you a name."

The sentinel did as commanded.

"I name you Mark. Now, present yourself to me in Lorexian form."

The sentinel did as commanded.

"Taller, larger."

The sentinel grew until David signaled his approval.

"When in this form, your name is Ma-Ka. Now present yourself to me in the form of the Ancients."

The sentinel did as commanded, presenting himself in a slightly too large version of an Ancient.

"When in this form, your name is Ta'set Mu'ton. You will be my companion and protector until the day we return to this place to restore the Temple to its previous form."

David flashed into the form of an Ancient. "When I am in this form, you will call me Da'Vit Wa'Ton."

He flashed into energy. Ta'set Mu'ton did the same. Then they both disappeared.

AMBASSADOR'S OFFICE

Word had just reached Michael that an attempt had been made on Admiral Porter's life. He needed James' wisdom.

"James."

There was no reply.

Michael thought to call again but decided against. He'd been relying on James too much recently. As he shifted his thoughts back to the situation, there was a flash of light in the room.

"James!" Michael said brightly, then turned to see David and a man he didn't know.

"David?"

"I heard you call for James."

Michael was overwhelmed with sadness. It was as if James was here, but he wasn't.

"What happened?" Michael choked out.

David did not respond, but Mark did.

"So'Gen La'Hoya, the last of his kind, gave his essence to David Washington, first of his kind."

"Who are you?" Michael struggled to control his emotions.

"I am the sentinel, guardian of the Ancient Temple. You may call me Mark."

"David?"

"James... James needed to withdraw for a while. He gifted me with his memories. Told me I would know what to do. And I think I do.

"But I need your help, your perspective. Can we talk?"

"Your friend Mark?" Michael was a bit frustrated that he couldn't read David anymore. And couldn't read Mark at all.

"Mark is what he said he is. He's a sentinel, created in ancient times by James' people. He guards the Temple where the Ancients retreat to find peace."

"Is that where James went?"

"Yes."

"And why is Mark here?"

David paused, realizing how bad this was going to sound. "He is guarding the Temple."

"I'm not sure I understand."

"Michael, some things need to be taken on trust. We need to talk."

"David. I hear you and appreciate your sincerity. But how can I know this is true."

James voice resonated in Michael's mind. *Michael, I speak through David now. You must listen to him.*

"David, I'm so sorry. That came out wrong. Can you explain a little more about what happened?"

David raised his hand as if to place it over Michael's, then paused.

"May I? It might move things along a little more quickly. I seem to recall you saying something like that to me on your wedding day."

David saw the doubt in Michael's eyes. "Some things must be done based on trust."

David placed his hand over Michael's and Michael went into a trance that lasted a few moments.

"Thank you…" Michael almost said James. "I understand now. How long can you hold in reserve?"

"I'm sorry Michael. I cannot. I know what I need to do and promise to start slowly. But you don't have much time. Once it begins in earnest, it will end quickly."

With those words, David and Mark flashed away.

Michael had a lot to do and little time to accomplish it.

EMBASSY CITY, TOGAROTU

Daniel woke in incredible pain. His right arm ablaze. When he turned to look, the sight caused him to slip back into the darkness.

EAS CANADA

XO Duan Tai's eyes burned like fire. Crazy thoughts went through his mind. He'd always wanted command, but not in this way.

"Tell me again why we cannot see the Admiral."

"The Admiral remains in Intensive Care. He has moments of wakefulness, but none of clarity. He remains under suspicion, so no outsider can see him until he awakens and can explain himself."

"He was attacked. Is that not obvious to you?" Duan shouted.

The statement brought nothing more than an icy stare.

"Do not contact us again. Out of respect for Mi-Ku, we will contact you again when there is something to report. Until then, you and your convoy are under lockdown and will be fired upon if you attempt to leave orbit.

HOSPITAL, CAPITAL CITY

There was a flash of light and an odd person appeared.

"Can I help you, sir."

"I wish to speak with Admiral Daniel Porter."

"I'm sorry sir," The receptionist replied, pressing an alarm button under the desk. "The Admiral is in isolation. Guests are not allowed."

David smiled and bowed his head respectfully. "Thank you. I will call on him now."

He vanished as quickly as he arrived, then the receptionist pushed another alert button.

ADMIRAL PORTERS ROOM, EMBASSY CITY, TOGAROTU

David appeared in human form in the Admiral's room. He was shocked and sadden by what he saw. Daniel's shield had worked desperately to save him but could not. Knowing it would fail, the shield had reconfigured itself in the final milliseconds to protect his torso at the expense of his right arm. David saw that there was no right hand, only burnt flesh and bone below the right elbow.

David shook his head in despair at the senseless act of violence. All involved would be brought to justice this day. But nothing here was beyond, or even close to the limits of, the Ancient's technology.

He closed his eyes in concentration, then touched Daniel's burnt arm, releasing reconstructive nanobots into Daniel's system. Daniel was nowhere near strong enough to support the work the nanobots needed to do, so David flashed into light. It was a form that allowed him to supply both the nanobots and the patient with the energy they needed.

...

Outside the room, guards had gathered. But they could do nothing. A shield of some sort blocked the door. The security cameras and all sensor readings from the room had gone silent. But brilliant light flooded out under the door. An emergency response team was on its way and would arrive in a few minutes. But for now, the guards stood, watching the door, and waiting for something to happen.

...

Daniel awoke, not sure where he was. He turned and saw... "David, David Washington, is that you?"

"It is. Recall what James once said. If he should become unavailable, I would be your only hope.

"Well, today is that day. I have healed you enough to travel and we must depart. The Inspector's forces are about to descend upon us. It will be easier for me to contain them once you are in a safer place."

Daniel looked at David, not sure if he was real or an aberration. Then a moment later, they were in the Canada's familiar hospital.

ROOFTOP NEAR DATSAL'S PALACE

David flashed into existence on the rooftop where the assassin had taken the shot at Daniel. He took what he now thought of as his natural form, an Ancient. The area had been roped off where the investigative team was working. A police officer turned, saw the intruder, and approached, hand on his weapon.

"Police. This is a restricted area, I..." The officer froze mid-sentence. David quickly scanned through his memories, then released his mental grip on him.

The officer was momentarily stunned.

"Come," David commanded. "You have committed no crime in this matter, but I suspect those people over there have."

As David moved toward the roped off area, he released a flood of nanobots.

One of the investigators saw David approaching with the police officer walking quietly behind.

"Who are you? And what are you doing here? This is an active investigation site."

David quickly shuffled through the investigator's mind.

"Nansil Dolub. You are not who you claim to be. You are an agent of Confederation Military Intelligence. Confess your crime now and I will take no action against you."

A cruel smile formed on the investigator's face. "Right."

As his hand drifted toward his weapon, David said, "Stop."

The other three investigators, were in various stages of standing and reaching for a weapon when David again said, "Stop."

One of the three was not in a balanced position when she froze and fell to the roof top.

A clipboard containing a pen and some paper appeared in David's hand. As he approached the first investigator, David held out the clipboard and he took it.

"Nansil Dolub, please write out your confession. 'I, Nansil Dolub, am a traitor to my people. I am a spy under the control of the Office of Military Intelligence. Today, I was assigned to a team destroying evidence regarding the Inspector's role in the attempted assassination of Admiral Daniel Porter. But I can no longer bear the guilt of my involvement.'"

When the scribbling stopped, David said. "Sign your confession, then fold the paper, put it in one of the envelopes, seal it and sign across the seal."

When he was done, he handed David the clipboard.

"Now do what you need to do," David commanded.

Nansil Dolub put the signed envelope in his breast pocket, turned, walked to the edge of the roof, then jumped.

As panicked noises radiated up from the street, David turned to the others. "Who would like to go next?"

After a moment David said, "Towsen Nadtoo, you may approach."

Another one of the investigators unfroze and walked over to David.

"Confess your crime and I will take no action against you." David commanded.

"I work for the Inspector, have been involved in several things that I should not have been. I was told a crime was committed, the culprit captured, and we were the after-action cleanup team. I did not know we were destroying evidence."

"Thank you. Write out your confession exactly as you spoke it. Sign it, seal it in an envelope, and sign over the seal. When you are done, give the envelope to the police officer, then take a seat in the shade over there."

The process repeated with the next investigator, who joined his partner in the shade.

"Julsai Karlop, please come here."

The woman who had fallen, stood, and approached David, shaking in fear.

"You are an off-duty police officer, not one of the Inspector's spies. You did not want to take this job, but you did. Please tell me why."

"My son..." She paused attempting to contain the emotion. "My son got in some trouble. The Chief said he would fix the problem if I agreed to take this assignment. I knew the job must be dirty. But I really didn't have a choice. I'm sorry."

David was quiet a moment, then said, "I will not be the one to accuse you. You are free to stay or go. Others will be arriving shortly. If anyone asks you about me, tell them that the Ancients have returned."

The nanobots had gathered the information he needed, so David flashed on to his next stop.

ASSASSIN'S HIDEOUT

The assassin might have been tidy by the standards of her people. But she had left numerous strands of DNA, fiber and other foreign material behind. Within minutes, the planetary computers yielded her name, official residence, long record of other crimes, and the location of her cabin in the woods.

David and the sentinel flashed into existence behind the cabin. Both took the form of the Ancients, David at his normal height, Ta'set Mu'ton twelve feet tall. To David's surprise, his target was sitting on the back porch in a wooden rocking chair reading a book. The large wolf like creature sitting next to her immediately started to growl.

"Leshel Towsap. Zorossan. Compatible species, untransformed."

She looked up as if she had no care in the world. "What the hell are you? And why are you trespassing on my property?"

"You attempted to kill Admiral Daniel Porter last night."

"So?" She looked back at her book.

"Confess your crime now, and we will turn you over to the authorities. Failure to confess will result in your immediate termination."

She flicked her finger and the animal leaped; teeth exposed. But halfway to its target, it stopped, suspended in mid-air. David smiled. "Come here, pup."

The creature dropped to the ground, squealed in fear, then crept over to David and was rewarded with a scratch between his eyes.

"Sit," David said, and it sat like a dog looking up at him lovingly.

"I haven't seen anyone do that before."

David looked back at the assassin.

"Make your confession now or face the punishment of the sentinel."

David knew what was about to happen but didn't stop her.

In a lightning fast move, she released an energy weapon built into the arm of the chair, then fired a shot at David, an amused smile forming on her lips.

But the bolt of coherent red light stopped halfway to David.

"How did you do that?" She stood and stepped off the porch, marveling at the energy frozen in the air.

"Time-dampening, quite easy to do once you know the trick. Do you know what this weapon does to someone?"

She smiled, starting to like this intruder. "Turns them into a load of cash in my bank account."

"Sorry," David said sadly. "Neither the answer, nor the confession was sufficient. You stand in judgement. Experience the weapon for yourself."

The bolt of energy reversed its course, hitting the assassin in the shoulder. It was immensely powerful, instantly vaporizing the shoulder. As the arm fell away, her clothes and skin burned. The violence and flames only lasted a second. But David and Mark were gone before the corpse hit the ground.

PRESIDENT'S OFFICE, DALFANITO

President Jeskot Baston was still basking in the good will created by the recent trade mission. She felt as though things might finally be changing. The day was nearly done, only one meeting left. It would be the first night she'd had off in months and she was looking forward to a little quiet time with her husband tonight.

There was the familiar knock at the door.

"Come."

Her secretary, Dalsa, opened the door. "Secretary Sonjoy and Chief Nublon are here. Would you like me to bring in some tea?"

"Please."

Two men walked in.

"Tofor, Desmud. Please come in." She indicated two seats in a living room like set up on one side of the office. One of the President's security team followed the men in, then shut the door and stood by it.

"My chief of staff added this meeting late in the day, moving some other things to tomorrow. He said you had something important but didn't say what."

Desmud Nublon, Chief of Central Intelligence took the implied question. "Yes, ma'am. I presume you've heard about the incident with Admiral Porter, the leader of the trade mission from Earth, on Togarotu."

"Yes. Unbelievable. I thought Togarotu security was better than that. Has something come up that we can help with?"

"Not exactly. It has come to my attention that he spent quite a bit of time during his visit here with Secretary Sonjoy and his team, learning about our satellite defense systems."

"Tofor, is that true?"

"Yes, Ma'am. But the Chief's theory is meritless." Tofor Sonjoy was the Secretary of Defense for Dalfanito.

"We did spend three hours talking with him. He was interested in learning more about our satellite defenses. Apparently, none of the planets in 3F have them. But we told him nothing that he didn't already know, and we learned a lot about his ship." The secretary turned to look at the Chief. "And the entire session was recorded."

"So, what's the problem Chief."

"This." He pulled a small cylinder out of his breast pocket and placed it on the table. "A similar one was found on Togarotu."

"What is it?" The President asked impatiently.

"It was a bomb. We have deactivated it, so it's safe."

"And how does this relate back to what we've been discussing?"

The Chief looked at the Secretary. "You going to tell her?"

"This particular type of weapon is proprietary, part of our defensive array. The only place they are made is on our defensive platforms.

"They're incredibly dangerous. The explosive mechanism is intrinsically unstable. If you brought a live one down to the planet, it would spontaneously detonate within hours."

"And the point?" The President hated it when her advisors did not get to the point quickly.

"According to Togarotu intelligence, the explosion that injured the Admiral was made by one of these."

"We blew up the Admiral?" The president asked in shock.

"No. During the extended comm connection with the Admiral, one of our replicator pattern banks was hacked. The replicator pattern for the explosive was stolen. And more of these devices were found among the Admiral's things. Togarotu Intelligence thinks the Admiral accidentally blew himself up, because he didn't know the correct handling procedures for the explosives."

The President sat there in shock, not willing to believe what she was hearing.

Tofor Sonjoy shook his head. "This theory is preposterous."

"The evidence is overwhelming," the Chief argued back.

"Why are you bringing this to me, Chief?"

"I got word from Togarotu a couple hours ago that charges were likely to be filed against the Admiral this afternoon. They know where those munitions are made, so will probably take action of some sort against us. I didn't want it to catch you by surprise."

"Unbelievable."

...

As the Chief and Secretary were leaving, a large red pulsing crystal appeared on the lawn in front of the Presidential Mansion.

A ring of Lorexian Royal Blue barrier ropes appeared, eight meters in diameter, surrounding the crystal. A second ring appeared, surrounding the first, one meter further out.

A sign appeared between the ropes. It read:

Guards scrambled to set up a perimeter around the object and ropes to prevent anyone from getting near it. President Baston saw the disturbance and stepped toward the window to see what it was but was intercepted and whisked away. The sight of the crystal reminded her of something from her youth. She couldn't put her finger on it, couldn't drag up the memory, only the certainty there was no escaping it.

But in contrast to everyone else, Chief Nublon was drawn to the pulsing crystal.

What is it? Why is it here?

The thoughts compelled him toward the crystal. And, despite the warning and threats from the Presidential security team, he walked past, stopping at the Royal Blue velvet security rope.

"What are you? And why are you here?" he shouted at the crystal.

An odd-looking person appeared.

"Desmud Nublon, Zorossan, Head of Station for Military Intelligence on Dalfanito. You are a traitor to your people. You are the one that introduced the plague on this world, and you did so in exchange for a vaccine for yourself. You stand in judgement. Make a full and complete confession and I will leave you to your people's judgement. Fail to do so, and you will face my judgement.

"I don't know where you get your information, but none of what you've just said is true."

A holographic projection appeared in the air, large enough and high enough it could be seen by many people. The scene opened with two people in a presence projector.

In the background, one of the presidential security staff whispered to his colleague, "That's the Chief and the Head of Military Intelligence, Inspector Ha-Ke. He is the one we suspected to be the source of the plague."

...

"Desmud, I have orders for you."

"Yes, sir."

"We need to introduce the plague on Dalfanito. There's no need to worry. It will be arrested quickly.

"But it must be done in a way that indites Councilor Mo-Mo's son, Mo-Ta."

The Inspector placed a sheet of paper on a table that Chief Nublon could see. But it was not readable in the projection.

"He is scheduled to be on this flight the day after tomorrow."

"To make sure you remain safe, I am also providing 50 doses of the vaccine to you. That's a full course for 10 people.

"Can I count on you?"

"Is there another way to get the leverage you need?"

The Inspector stared at the Chief for a few moments.

"If you don't want to do it, you don't have to. This is a volunteer assignment. But it will happen, so the only question is whether you want to be the one to get the vaccine."

"Understood. Send me the contagion and the vaccine. It will be done as you ask."

"Excellent," the Inspector replied.

...

"That... That... Did not happen," the chief sputtered. Then turning to others that had gathered. "It's a lie. All lies!"

"But your treachery is even worse. You were the one that ordered the trade convoy bringing the vaccine to be sabotaged.

Another video started playing. It showed two men in a presence projector. The Chief was the one speaking.

...

"Captain Pu-Lu. An unauthorized trade convoy is on its way to Dalfanito. It is known to be carrying goods that must be confiscated. We've obtained its course."

An astrogation map, popped up showing a line that passed by the great nebula.

"Their ships are fast, able to outrun yours. So, take the Crimson Destiny and your two support ships. Knock them out of jump near the nebula. And if they survive, board them, and confiscate their cargo."

"Understood, sir."

...

Again, the Chief sputtered.

"The Ancients have spoken. Judgement has been rendered. Decrypted copies of your logs, files, and contacts have just been sent to the President, her staff and the major news media outlets.

Then, as suddenly as it appeared, the judge, stone and ropes disappeared. And a team of officers came to arrest the Chief.

TOGAROTU SPACE TRAFFIC COMMAND

David flashed into the office of the head of Space Command. On the screen was XO Duan Tai's enraged face.

"What do you mean, he's missing!"

Realizing that the XO's rage was out of control, David sent him some peace.

"Who are you?" The person talking with Duan spat out the question as if it was an accusation.

David quickly scanned through the accuser's mind, astounded by the things this person had been involved in.

"Harwen Doztel, Military Intelligence, Chief of Station on Togarotu. The Ancients have returned. You stand in judgement. Deactivate your weapons arrays immediately."

"I will do no such thing."

"Then I will do it for you."

Alarms started sounding throughout the building.

"Your weapons arrays are no more."

David turned to the screen. "Commander Tai, the Admiral has been returned to you. He is in the ship's hospital. As you can see, the planetary space arrays are unpowered and falling from orbit. Please leave now."

In the background, David heard Else confirming that the weapons arrays were down, and Yeoman Harris confirming the Admiral's presence in the hospital.

"All ships, emergency micro jump."

XO Tai's order was the last thing they heard before the screen went blank and the 'Lost Connection' banner came up.

"You will pay for this!"

David looked back at the head of Space Traffic Control and immediately understood what the commander intended to do.

"Harwen Doztel. You stand under judgement. A full and complete confession is required immediately."

A shot rang out. It was fired from an old-fashioned projectile weapon. The projectile hung in the air, two inches from David's stomach.

David looked at Commander Doztel. "Judgement is rendered. Write your confession now, releasing all records."

The commander returned to his seat, opened a new message, and wrote. "My name is Harwen Doztel, I am a spy. For the last 10 years, I have been Chief of Station for Military Intelligence on Togarotu. I have used the role to enact many forms of suppression against the people of this planet. The most egregious of those was the recent release of the Plague, as ordered by Inspector Ha-Ke.

"The guilt of my crimes has become too much to bear. So, as my last act, I release the complete records of my agency's activities on this planet, as well as the names and contact information for all the covert agents on the planet.

"Please forgive me."

He decrypted his master file of Inspector activities and attached the now decrypted files. The time-dampening field holding the bullet slowly moved into position in front of the commander. When it was positioned, David said, "Send the message to your entire contact list, including the Ambassador and President."

The commander executed the 'Send to all' command.

David did not enjoy compelling people in this way. But the rot and corruption had to be cut out. The Ancients had allowed it to slowly fester, but now demanded a cleansing. David was their chosen instrument.

AMBASSADOR'S OFFICE

A chime sounded indicating a call was coming in. It was from the Canada.

"Allow," Michael said. "Daniel, is everything OK? We got word that you were injured but have received no further word from Togarotu in the last 24 hours."

"It's Commander Tai, sir. There was an assassination attempt on the Admiral. And the entire convoy was placed in lockdown. Fair warning, sir. What follows is going to be hard to believe."

"Let me guess, the Ancients have intervened."

XO Tai was thunderstruck that Michael had guessed.

"How did you know, sir."

"We were visited also. Our encounter was minimally eventful. We were given an order and we complied. Their judge, whom they refer to as the Temple of the Ancients, stopped to speak with me for a while this morning, then left peacefully. I'm guessing Togarotu was his next stop."

"It was."

"Do you have Daniel?"

"Yes. He was mortally wounded, unlikely to survive. But the Ancient healed him. They seem to have much better medical technology than we do. The Admiral is in the hospital aboard the ship. He's weak, but the doctor says he is otherwise in good health."

"You're on your way back?"

"Yes. The judge came to visit the head of Space Traffic Control while I was on the line with him. Turns out that the head of Space Traffic Control was Chief of Station for Military Intelligence on Togarotu. He was the one who put our ships in lock down.

"The judge ordered him to release us. He refused, so the judge took down the entire space defense grid with just a word, then ordered us to leave, which we did."

Another chime sounded. The call was from Togarotu and marked urgent.

"Captain Tai. I have a call coming in from Togarotu that I need to take. Is there anything you need from us immediately?"

"Should we come directly home or make the scheduled deliveries."

"Make the deliveries, but only those in the Milky Way. Have to go now."

PRESENCE PROJECTOR, AMBASSADOR'S OFFICE

Michael entered the Presence Projector to see Jo-Na and Councilor Mo-Mo. The room was configured as the Admiral's mountain lodge.

"Gentlemen, it seems we live in interesting times."

"Have you had an encounter?" Mo-Mo asked.

"Two. One of our ships had an encounter almost two weeks ago. The ship complied with the orders it was given and nothing else happened. Then early this morning, their judge came to visit me. He refers to himself as the Temple of the Ancients, by the way."

"Odd name," Jo-Na grunted.

"What did he have to say to you?" Mo-Mo asked.

"The dysfunction within the Confederation has come to their attention. They consider themselves to be sovereign over the Confederation, so are responsible for cleaning up the mess."

"That's all?" Mo-Mo demanded.

"No. He asked for my advice. I told him we were working a process that might have a chance at succeeding and asked him to give us time. He basically said no. He had a job to do. So, anything we did would need to be done quickly, because he would not wait.

"I think he knew that Daniel had been attacked and was being held by the Inspector's agents. I also think he knew our 'Spread the Prosperity' program could not move forward until that was resolved."

"So, the ball is back in our court?" Mo-Mo pressed.

"No. He warned that things would move quickly once it started, and he would not wait for us."

Jo-Na sensed that his friend was holding back. "He told you more, didn't he?"

"Told, no. But he did share some images." A pause. "Every part of the Confederation will be called into judgement. Those found in want will be destroyed. All of us, if necessary."

Mo-Mo shuddered. "That explains some of the things that happened to us today." He went on to describe the confessions, suicides, and burned remains of the assassin.

PERIMETER SURVEILLANCE BUILDING

Agent Ko-Ne was once again late leaving the office. Crazy rumors had circulated today about a possible return of the Ancients. They rattled around in his mind as he finished shutting down.

There was a flash of light and two odd looking people appeared.

"Who are you? And what are you doing in my office?"

A light passed across him.

Was I just scanned? The thought seemed preposterous.

"Ko-Ne. Lorexian. Incompatible species."

"What?" Ko-Ne was baffled by what was happening.

"Agent Ko-Ne. You are a spy and a traitor to the Confederation. Your numerous acts of violence and injustice bring you under judgement. Make a full and complete confession now and we will release you to the authorities unharmed."

"I will do no such thing."

David could hear the agent's intended actions as if he were describing them out loud in slow motion. Again, he placed a time-dampening field in front of himself.

The whining sound of an energy weapon discharge filled the room. After a moment, David disabled the weapon.

"What happened?" Agent Ko-Ne asked in complete bafflement.

"I captured the energy you discharged, then disabled your weapon. Now you will write your confession, then attach a decrypted copy of all relevant records and contacts."

Agent Ko-Ne sat back down at his desk, logged into his portal and began writing.

David didn't like compelling people this way, but it was revealing. David did not tell the people under judgement what to do or say. He simply gave them an irresistible desire to confess.

"Done, decrypted files attached."

"Now send the message to everyone on your contact lists and to these three others." David had already determined that three important recipients were not among the agent's contacts.

"Done." Agent Ko-Ne sat back and smiled. "Nice to have that off my chest."

With great sadness, David repositioned the time-dilation field, then flashed away, allowing the field to drop.

INSPECTOR'S RESIDENCE

Inspector Ha-Ke relaxed into a favorite chair, a snifter of human Port in his hand.

How did primitives create anything this exquisite?

There was a flash of light and an odd person stood before him.

"You dare enter my space uninvited and unannounced." The Inspector pushed an alarm button on the side of his chair.

"Your space? What a fanciful notion. Is this not the designated residence of the Inspector, a servant of your people?"

The Inspector glared at the intruder. A price would be paid for this impertinence.

"And who would you be?"

"You do not recognize my form? Have you not read your own history?"

The Inspector's hand slid over toward a weapon on the table beside him. But it hesitated.

The intruder's form is familiar. I saw it in the Capital Museum, pre-Confederation section. He actually resembles the early images of the Ancient Sentient.

The Inspector looked at the intruder again trying to make sense of what he was seeing.

David nodded toward the weapon. "Surely you understand that such a primitive weapon could not help your situation?"

The words broke the Inspector's momentary reverie. And as his finger touched the now forgotten weapon, an evil smile erupted on his face.

In a sudden burst of motion, borne from years of training, the Inspector grasped the weapon, pointed in the direction of the intruder, and fired.

A bolt of plasma leaped from the weapon, then froze suspended in the air.

A second intruder materialized, this one gigantic.

"Ha-Ke. Lorexian. Incompatible species. Your presence near the temple is not permitted. You are forfeit."

The Inspector was flabbergasted by the arrogance of the uninvited visitors. But before he could say or do anything in response, an odd smell reached his nose, then intense pain struck the hand that grasped the weapon. The weapon glowed red, then started to melt.

Looking at the hand grasping the weapon, he saw smoke. Comprehension set in as flames started consuming his hand.

"Who? What are you?" The Inspector's consciousness wavered as the rest of his hand, then arm, erupted in flames.

"My name is Ta'set Mu'ton. I am the Sentinel, guardian of the Temple of the Ancients. You are nothing. A mindless fool, working against the interests of those you claim to serve." Ta'set Mu'ton smiled. "But now, you are no more."

David and Mark disappeared. The now repositioned time-dilation field was released, adding the bolt of energy to the conflagration engulfing the Inspector.

Chapter 25: APPEARANCE

[Saturday, 08.07. 2032] CENTRAL COUNCIL PLAZA, NEW LOREXI

It was early in the morning. Few people were about as two balls of brilliant light descended into the square. One stopped at twice the height of the average daytime passerby. The other descended to ground level, and transformed into a large, pulsing red crystal.

Then, just as on Dalfanito, a double ring of Lorexian Royal Blue barrier ropes appeared, with a sign in between that read:

Temple of the Ancients.
No admittance under penalty of death.

AMBASSADOR'S OFFICE

"Eugene. Kelly. Welcome. Apologies for asking you to come all the way over to my office. I need your help regarding a sensitive matter. One that requires incredible secrecy."

"What is it?" Kelly asked, her curiosity piqued by the mystery.

Michael smiled. "Well, I can't actually tell you unless you agree to be bound by a numbered security agreement."

Michael slid two documents across the table.

Kelly quickly looked at the two pages. "A numbered title and a signature line?"

"It's an interesting project. But one that requires absolute secrecy. It's not illegal. Not dangerous. And we really need your help. It will enable us to help a lot of people. But only people willing to accept the burden of the secrecy agreement can participate."

Kelly looked at Eugene. "I'm in. You?"

She saw Eugene's stubborn look starting to form. "Eugene, just sign the damn document."

He started to protest, saw the look, then caved. Without saying a word, he flipped to the signature page and signed. Then slid the pages back to Michael.

Kelly quickly followed suit. "So, what is it?"

"Come. There's someone who wants to talk with you."

Michael opened the door to his office, then led them across the hall to the conference room.

As soon as Eugene saw Lisette, he laughed. "I think I know what this is about. And it's going to be great!"

CENTRAL COUNCIL PLAZA, NEW LOREXI

Slowly the crowds gathered. Nothing like the pulsing crystal in the roped off area had been seen in living memory. High Council Security had tried to rope off the entire plaza. But their efforts were far less than successful. It had been millennia since there'd been a need.

As the crowds grew, the news media rolled in and within hours the pulsing red crystal was on the lips of everyone in the core worlds.

BRIDGE OFFICE, EAS NETHERLANDS

"Admiral, we just received a communication from the AI design team. It's marked for your eyes only."

"Thank you, Commander. I'll take it in here."

The message appeared in his queue. Chris used his command codes to decrypt it.

Admiral Flanagan. Attached are the replicator patterns for the mining platform we have designed for you. It deviates from the specifications you sent. Given the differences in mass, concentrations, and melting points of your source material and final product, the changes are probably more significant than you'd expected.

Please review these with your mining team before replicating them. We believe, as does Professor Schudel, that the changes are appropriate. But you and your team have the final say. As we use the same size power cubes as your design, we've taken the liberty of placing an order. There will be takers for the additional units if you do not want them all.

Thank you, Jacob and Henry.

Chris forwarded a clear copy of the message to Ms. Parikh, then started reading through the revised specifications. He liked what he saw.

CENTRAL COUNCIL PLAZA, NEW LOREXI

The crowds that had gathered earlier were growing restless. What was the pulsing crystal? Why had it come? Why was it just sitting there?

Some started to slew away. Others just grew angry. As the murmuring grew louder, the Central Council Police (CCP) grew more nervous. There hadn't been an assembly like this in their lifetimes. But a violence of spirit seemed to be taking hold of the crowd. And the CCP were worried that the first violent outbreak in modern history was about to erupt on their watch.

EAS CANADA

The last of the return deliveries were underway and from Daniel's point of view they couldn't get done soon enough.

He was back on the bridge but hiding in the office. XO Duan Tai had the con. He used the expression 'hiding in the office' a lot when he was overwhelmed with work. Although it was true that work was overwhelming today, the real issue was that he had too little energy to deal with the paucity of work that had been left for him. He was determined not to ask the doctor to relieve him of duty while on mission. It would undermine the crew's confidence. But when they reached Earth, he would ask for leave. He needed time to recover, and for the first time in his life, his body was demanding it.

CONFEDERATION TELEVISION STUDIOS

George and Noelani arrived at the studio early today. For the first time in months, they would be doing a live interview with a non-human guest. Helen, George's mother, was taking care of Little George, so Noelani could help with the guest preparation.

Today's guest was Ambassador Na-Mu from the planet Hacindra. They had joined the 3F Alliance earlier in the year. A delegation from Hacindra was visiting the Embassy for expanded trade talks. The guest schedule had been switched around so they could participate live.

The guest-host this week was Jamaal Kazmi from Al Arabiya, the Saudi-owned television news network based in Dubai. Jamaal had just arrived in the embassy a month ago, so this would be their first time working together.

...

It was early, the show wouldn't start for another 2 minutes. Nonetheless, the intro music started playing quietly, drawing the audience's attention. Then George walked out, and the studio audience broke into raucous applause.

George put his hands up to quiet the crowd.

"The show will start in about 2 minutes, but I wanted to take a moment to introduce you to our newest co-host. Please welcome my new friend, Jamaal Kazmi from Al Arabiya in Dubai."

Jamaal walked out, immediately attracting the audience's attention. He was an incredibly handsome man and walked out as if he were a model at a fashion show. He wore a stylish, but casual, tailored European suit with open collar, topped with a traditional Arab headdress, white keffiyeh (head cloth) and black agal (cord). The audience reaction was over the top. It was the first time George could recall that the guest host got louder applause than he did.

The 'Quiet' signs lit as the lighting dropped. Then the intro music started in earnest, the lights came up, and they were counted in.

"Good evening, Arabia! Welcome, World. I am Jamaal Kazmi of Al Arabiya News in Dubai, reporting from the television studios at the Confederation Embassy. And we have a great show for you tonight.

"George, would you like to introduce our guest?"

"Our guest today is Ambassador Na-Mu from the planet Hacindra. He and his delegation are visiting the Embassy this week so we have the pleasure of interviewing him live and in person tonight."

Applause welled up loud enough that George had to pause for a second. "Several members of the delegation are also here with us and will be joining us for some demonstrations later in the show.

George motioned stage left. "Now, please join me in welcoming Ambassador Na-Mu." From George's position he could see Noelani giving the Ambassador a final word of encouragement, then motioning for him to walk out.

The audience's reaction to the Ambassador was immediate. There was the surprise of seeing an intelligent being different than any human, followed by the delight of seeing something new.

The Ambassador appeared to be short and stout. In truth, he was several inches taller than George, but much wider, more sturdily built than any human. He had wide muscular hips and shoulders; large thick arms, legs, hands and feet; and a very large head. Other than size, his body was very human like, but the head was not. It hung forward of the torso, supported by a thick muscular neck almost as wide as the shoulders. His face was muzzle-like with a flat nose. His skin was thick and leathery. But the most alien part was the eyes. He had two relatively normal-looking human-like eyes in the front and a smaller fish-like eye on each side.

The Ambassador put out his hand to shake and George made his best go at it. But the Ambassador's hand enveloped George's in the way an adult's hand does a child's.

"Ambassador Na-Mu, welcome."

"George, Jamaal. Thank you for having me and giving me this opportunity to address the people of Earth."

The audience applause subsided as they took their seats. The Ambassador's seat was a special one, more appropriate to his size, that he'd brought to Earth with him.

Jamaal took the lead. "Ambassador, we are so excited to have you with us today. Can we start by having you show us where Hacindra is?"

The familiar map of the sector popped up in a holoprojection.

The Ambassador quickly pointed out the positions of Earth, Karagon and Celanar. "Our planet is here, 570 light-years further out along our spiral arm. We are just a little over halfway to Celanar, but more centrally located between the edges of the arm."

A light blinked where the planet was located.

"What can you tell us about your world?"

"Hacindra's diameter is five percent greater than Earth's. The composition of our planet is similar to yours, nickel-iron core with solid inner core and liquid outer core. We have a solid mineral-rich mantle similar to yours, but a thicker crust. Our gravity is about 10% higher and we are located a little further from our star, about 1.25 of your AU. Our star is brighter and hotter than yours. So, even though we are further out, our average temperature at ground level is about the same, or slightly cooler than yours.

"The biggest difference is water. Ours is a desert world. Only 20% of our surface is covered by water, so much more of our surface is covered with blowing sand deserts similar to where you come from on Earth, Jamaal.

"Our scientists tell us that's the reason we have thicker, more durable skin than most other Confederation members."

"How has that impacted societal development on your world?" Jamaal asked.

"Perceptive question." The Ambassador nodded approvingly.

"Despite our much greater land mass, our population is only about the same size as Earth's. Prior to our Revelation, it was quite a bit smaller.

"Our people are concentrated near the oceans. Much of the central latitudes are like the Sahara Desert in Africa or the Empty Quarter in Saudi Arabia, places hostile to life.

"But a lot has changed since we joined the Confederation about 200 years ago. There is technology that would allow us to inhabit the deserts. Some have tried it, but none of those communities lasted very long. But further north, land-bound communities have flourished. The Institute at our Embassy has developed technologies that have completely transformed the land in the latitude band 25° - 50° North and South."

Outro music started playing.

"Sounds like an interesting topic to explore in more depth after we come back from break."

...

"Welcome back, World. I am here with my friend George Butler and our guest Ambassador Na-Mu from the planet Hacindra.

"Before the break, you were telling us that you developed technology used to transform the deserts in moderate latitude zones. What can you tell us about that?"

"As you can imagine, our biggest problem on Hacindra has been the scarcity of water. Pre-Confederation, we made several attempts to mine water from comets and other water-rich celestial objects. Although an interesting idea on paper, we never made much progress on that program.

"When the Confederation arrived, they made a token effort to help us mine water, but ultimately pronounced it infeasible. But recognizing that this was our defining problem, they launched a major program at our institute to help us come up with a different solution.

"That program was massively successful, despite a number of painful setbacks. It was based on three technologies: water evaporators, atmospheric condensers, and specialty replicators optimized for water production.

"The first systems went in 20 years post-Revelation and, over the next 20 years a massive green zone was formed in the northern hemisphere. Then disaster struck."

"What happened?" Jamaal asked breathlessly.

"Two things. First, our Transluminide supply ran out, so we couldn't continue adding planetary transformation equipment. And when units failed, we couldn't replace them. People were forced to evacuate, as our cries for more Transluminide were ignored.

"Then we were hit by the Great Android Plague. It ended up being a virus that killed over 20 million androids in less than a month.

"That was a little over 100 years ago and we are only now recovering. Part of our work here this week was applying for a grant from the 3F Alliance for funds to maintain and complete our planetary transformation initiative."

"Do you think you will get the grant?"

"It's too early to say. The program itself is still in the discussion phase; it doesn't actually exist yet. We are also working with the Earth and 3F Alliances on other ways to increase trade. We have a lot to offer, things our trading partners would really like to have. So, one way or another, we will find a way. But a grant would move things along quicker and benefit all of us."

Outro music had started while the Ambassador was talking, so Jamaal cut to a break.

...

The lights came up with George standing in the middle of a stage that had been re-arranged during the break. Scientific equipment of some sort was set up on one side of the main interview area, a kitchen was set up on the other.

"Welcome back, World. During the last segment of the show today, we're going to be doing some demonstrations. To your left are three pieces of equipment of the type used in Hacindra's planetary transformation program. Jamaal will be working with some members of the Ambassador's team to demonstrate them for you. To your right is a kitchen set up where we will be making a treat for you."

Applause erupted from the audience.

George took his seat next to Jamaal, opposite the Ambassador.

"Ambassador Na-Mu, before the break you were saying that you had a number of things the other members really wanted. Is that what we are going to demonstrate today?"

"Yes, it is. Our planetary transformation equipment is unique in the Confederation. Any planet, or portion of a planet, that is short on water will want that equipment. The other thing that is unique is our spices. Our environment has yielded flavor ingredients unlike any other. Their most unique quality is that no one has found a way to replicate them. Or more accurately, the replication patterns that exist don't come all that close. We are one of the few planets that exports actual organic foods. Your audience will get to try some today."

George stood and indicated the kitchen. "We are starting with the food, right?"

George and the Ambassador started toward the kitchen set up.

"Yes. We have several items that are very popular. The one I'm going to demonstrate today can be used in many ways, but really transforms many baked items."

Sitting on the countertop was a glass container sealed with a rubber ring. It contained a reddish-brown powder. Behind the counter was a female Cindaran, the species from Hacindra, dressed in what George knew to be a bakery chef's clothing.

"George, please meet our Chef, Minidala Ababada."

"Chef, a pleasure to meet you."

"Thank you, George."

"So, what is the ingredient you're featuring for us today?"

"We call it cinnadasha. It's a word that loosely means 'joy for the senses.' It's a food safe for humans to eat. It has similarities to your cinnamon. It's made from the bark of a tree. The bark is cured in water, much the same way as humans cure olives. Once cured, the bark is dried, then ground into a fine powder.

"When you first taste it, it hits the front of the tongue with a chili-like heat. It moves through the mouth with a flavor similar to cinnamon, then brings warmth to most of the body.

"We are going to use it to make a sweet bun today. We will make them conventionally in an oven. I'm also going to make the best replication I've found so you can compare.

"Given the time constraint, I've already prepared the dough and pre-heated the oven. And we've got just enough time left to bake them."

She slid a tray into the oven.

"These will be ready by the time the other demo is done, but I'm sure you'll start smelling them shortly."

George smiled and pointed to the other side of the stage.

"Jamaal, over to you."

The lights on the kitchen set dimmed as the lights on the equipment demonstration set came up.

"Thank you, George. With me is the trade delegation's technical specialist Sanabala Dosatoda, who tells me that he prefers to go by Bala."

Sanabala nodded his head vigorously.

"Bala, please tell us about this set up."

"The demonstration is done in three steps. The first step is our water generator. It's a replicator that's been optimized for water production. This scale model can produce 10 liters in just a minute. I'm going to use it to fill this 12-liter tank up to the full line."

He pointed at the dotted line an inch or two below the top.

"That will leave enough space at the top that we shouldn't spill any."

He pushed a button and water began flowing out of the replicator into the tank.

"While the tank is filling, I'm going to show the next piece of equipment. It's an evaporator. Evaporators are common in most economies. I've seen them on every world I've visited. Earlier this week I did a quick search on your internet and found pages of them.

"Most evaporators work with heated water for the purpose of evaporating enough to cool what remains. We nominally work with room temperature water with the intent to evaporate as much as possible.

"Our process starts by mechanically pumping the water through a thin nozzle, atomizing it into tiny droplets. The droplets are then flash heated and transported. At planetary scale, the droplets are transported as close to the target delivery site as possible and as high in the atmosphere as the dew point will allow.

"For our demonstration here, we're just going to transport them up near the ceiling at the back of the stage.

"Some of the droplets might condense, but each device has scanners and on-board analytics that target locations where all the water will evaporate.

"I see that the replicator has finished producing all 10 liters of water. I'm going to mount the evaporator above the tank."

Sounds of a motor could be heard as the evaporator settled down over the tank.

"When I turn this on, we should see the water disappear in one minute, evaporated into the atmosphere in the room. Turning it on now."

"While that's running, I'm going to show the condenser. It's a little more conventional. Most condensers work by passing moist air over a cold surface. Ours is a bit of a twist on that. We target moist areas in the atmosphere and enclose them in a field formed in a very high dimension that drains energy from things. When we release the bubble, all or a significant fraction of the water inside will have condensed into water droplets or ice crystals. If we are only trying to induce atmospheric precipitation, then that's all we need to do. If we are trying to fill a vat, then we bring the dimensional bubble into the vat before collapsing it. It's basically a transporter that freezes its contents during transport. That's what we'll do today.

He moved over to another tank that had a relatively large box above it. "This device has also been sized to condense 10 liters in about a minute. Activating it now."

Within seconds a thin stream of water started flowing into the tank.

"In summary, our system works by producing water, then using specialized transporters as evaporators and condensers to move the water through the atmosphere to get it where we need it."

"Amazing!" Jamaal said, "George, back to you."

By now the smell of fresh baked 'cinnamon buns' permeated the air.

"Perfect timing!" George replied. "I'm going to start the replicator run while Minidala pulls hers from the oven."

Moments later, two warm, steaming buns sat on trays on the kitchen counter, each cut into several slices.

"George, why don't you start by tasting the replicated bun?"

"OK." George popped one of the slices into his mouth and chewed slowly.

"Wow. That's really good. It's reminiscent of a cinnamon bun, but not as sweet. Enough chili like-burn that you know it's there. And the cinnamon-like flavor that's crisper and more savory. I'd have to say that this comes off more like a dessert, or even a main course, flavor than a breakfast treat."

"Good description. Now try the fresh baked using the actual ingredient."

George grabbed a slice of the real thing and popped it in his mouth. The reaction was almost immediate. He smiled as he chewed, eyes popping open wider. Then, when he swallowed, gave a startled look and a shudder ran through his body.

"Wow!" George shook his head. He took a breath to say something, then shuddered again. "Wow!"

"Describe what you felt," Minidala prodded.

"The chili-like onset was much stronger, but fast with no residual burn. Startling, actually. Then the warm rich cinnamon-like flavor floods through your mouth and sinuses. It has a mouth feel like butter cream, but not as cloyingly sweet. Then when you swallow, warmth flows through the throat descending down into your stomach."

George's hand flowed from his throat to stomach as he spoke.

"Then the bomb at the end. It's like I could taste it in my fingers and toes."

Minidala laughed. "Good description."

George shook his head. "Wow. Never had anything like that before."

The outro music started to play and George pointed to Jamaal.

"We are out of time for today, World. Thank you to our special guests, Ambassador Na-Mu from Hacindra and his colleagues, Bala and Minidala. Thank you, World, for tuning in today. And good evening from the Embassy Television Studios."

In the background, George called out. "Free samples for anyone that wants to try some." And carts full of fresh buns poured out from backstage.

CENTRAL COUNCIL PLAZA

David had a vague sense of what was going on outside; knew that Mark would arouse him if the situation required his attention.

In his heart, he knew that they were coming up on an inflection point. If the people attacked the crystal, Mark would mercilessly slaughter them. He was an amazing piece of technology that David was slowly coming to understand. It was a revelation to David that there were power sources more potent than zero-point energy.

Noises from outside came to his attention. Someone was doing something stupid. Maybe he had time to intervene.

"Ma-Ka, eliminate the weapon, but let me speak to the offender."

...

Out in the courtyard, an impatient and frustrated young man picked up a stone. *Maybe if someone challenges it, it will wake and tell us what it is.*

As he was about to throw, two people flashed into existence. The flash seemed to have come out of the crystal. Both appeared to be Ancients. The one was short, bearded, and wore a robe. The other was gigantic. It was dressed like the Lorexian warriors of old and held a spear that must have weighed a ton.

"Ma-Ko. Lorexian. Incompatible species. You are..."

David raised his hands.

The crowd hushed. The Ancients were about to speak.

"Ma-Ko, please approach, but do not touch the outer barrier."

328

The crowd parted so the now terrified young man could approach. He stopped a full meter short of the outer ropes.

"Come a little closer," David commanded.

"So you can incinerate me?"

David smiled and sent his challenger peace.

"Ma-Ko, there is no place in this galaxy, or any other place for that matter, that I could not incinerate you with just a thought. So, do as I ask before I'm forced to think."

The young male Lorexian stepped up to within an inch of the outer barrier.

"Thank you. You were about to throw a stone? Speak truth or die.

"Must I admit my intention before you slaughter me?"

"I will do nothing either way. But the Sentinel will incinerate you if you lie. So, truth or death. Your choice."

After a moment of deliberation, Ma-Ko responded, "Yes. I was going to throw a stone. I wanted to get your attention. Wanted to know why you are here."

"It would have been safer to have simply walked up to where you are now and asked."

"Others have done that."

"Have they? I've been here for hours now waiting for someone to ask. Much speculation has been blathered, but no one has asked a question of me."

Multiple reporters turned, shouting questions. All quieted as a scanning beam passed over them and their names were announced.

"Why are you here?" Ma-Ko asked simply.

"Long ago, my people stepped in to help a species in its time of need. We judged them worthy, guided them toward technology.

"For a while that seemed to work. You grew, spread, and became great. But now you've become stagnant. It has been a long time since you've pushed anything forward.

"When that happens, we usually withdraw our support. But we really cannot do that in this instance. You have become powerful among your neighbors. You've spread to other galaxies. And you have started working against them, preventing them from growing and advancing.

"So, I have been sent as a judge. Government officials who work against their people, who stand in the way of their people's advancement, will be judged. And my judgement will be swift and final."

"What gives you the right to judge us?" a reporter called out.

They were scanned by Ma-Ka, but David raised his hand stopping him from taking further action.

"I am sovereign. I am the law. The Confederation is a subservient entity, sovereign over those things to which we grant it sovereignty. Subservient to us, to me, on matters for which we have not granted sovereignty. Your right to help others stands as it has for over 2 million years. But as of today, the right you have assumed to suppress other worlds falls under judgement.

"Tomorrow, two of your officials are required to present themselves for judgment. Central Council Speaker Fu-Su. You will appear before me tomorrow morning before noon. Councilor To-Ja. You will appear before me tomorrow afternoon while there is still full daylight.

"If either of you should fail to appear, then I will come to you and you will be found guilty."

TEMPLE OF THE ANCIENTS

David knew what the Ancients required of him. How could he not? At this point, he was one of them, aware of their opinions, their beliefs, their judgements. Aware of their belief in him to do what was necessary.

Every last vestige of the Inspector's office needed to be destroyed. Yesterday was the start. He was OK with the outing of the spies; OK with returning the violence directed at him to those that directed it. But... he was not a killer. His head was good with the actions he'd taken today, but his heart was not. If only he could speak with James.

The thought tickled his mind with laughter. James would have said that he had more confidence in David's judgements than any of the Ancients or the leaders of the three galaxies.

But, what about Michael's? he wondered.

"David Washington, or should we call you Da'Vit Wa'Ton? An excellent choice of name, we must say. You have truly become one of us, despite the differences. We heard the guardian say that you were the first. First human, indeed, and we are pleased to have you among us. But others, not of the Ancient's original species, have found their way here. Our collective is made mostly of non-originals and, when the time is right, we hope you will join us. But enough on that topic.

"You believe that you cannot reach your Michael, whose input you desire, from here. That is not correct. You can. Simply seek the mechanism and we will assure that it comes to you."

"Thank you," David sent, more of an automated response than a sincere expression of thanks.

How can I reach Michael? The thought rang out.

Images rushed in, so many it temporarily overwhelmed him.

"Oh."

ABOVE THE ROCK

Long ago, the Military Intelligence organization had established an outpost on a small moon further out in New Lorexi's system. The moon had a standard Confederation identifier, 1A1-D2, and a name. But few people knew the name, because it had been called 'the Rock' for thousands of years.

The Rock was home to the research labs that weaponized the EQD phenomenon. It was also the one that figured out how to use transponder synchronization to plant malware in the Earth ships. And it was the home of the vault that contained the restoration chambers of the thousands of Ascendant spies working undercover throughout the Confederation.

Ju-Ne, the spy that did so much damage on Earth and among its Alliance allies, had been trained here. His restoration chamber had been stored here for many years. And he'd left its registration here after moving it to an unregistered location on Earth.

The Rock was the place the Ancients hated the most. They wanted it destroyed, which would be a trivial thing to do. But even at this distance, David could tell there were thousands of innocents on the moon. He would not willfully destroy them. Maybe he could do this more selectively by creating problems that would lead to a civilian evacuation.

TEMPLE OF THE ANCIENTS

Back in the temple, David began searching for a way to deactivate zero-point energy devices. To his surprise, there were numerous ways the devices could fail. Most would lead to an explosion. But there were a surprising number that would fail safe.

"Da'Vit Wa'Ton, clever idea. You are indeed worthy of the mission you've been given.

It was the non-originals again.

"Others have tried what you are considering. We think the fluorine technique will work best. It fails safe and cannot hurt the technicians who attempt to fix it. It also kills the unit and is totally baffling to those that do not understand trans-dimensional fluorine creep."

"Thank you. I was leaning that way. But I'm still new enough that I wasn't sure."

"You're trying to get them to evacuate the civilians and non-essential workers, aren't you?"

"Yes."

"Good. This is a blind spot for the original Ancients. We hope you continue on this path. What's happening in the Confederation has happened before. We wish you a good outcome."

"The Inspector's office has gone rogue before?"

The non-originals responded with the 'sound' David thought of as a laugh track. They apparently thought he asked a funny question.

"The Inspector's office has been corrupt for thousands of years. But that's not what we meant. Your Confederation is one of hundreds that we have helped prosper since our beginning. Many of them have become corrupt. It seems to be the nature of organic beings. More than a few have required cleansing. Many of them did not survive it. Your Confederation may yet need to be destroyed. But you may actually succeed in making yours stronger."

As David pondered what he'd just learned, their presence receded.

MINING MISSION

A lot had happened since the meeting three days ago. Space Force Command had assigned a second Cruiser to the mission, the EAS Thailand, captained by Clarissa Saldanha, formerly of the Fast Attack Ship Cairo. The Thailand had arrived in the first system last night.

Since returning to that system three days ago, the Mumbai had discovered 6 more crystal deposits. And they were now calling the planet the Crystal Vault. Tomorrow the EAS Lisbon, captained by Aston Moss, would be arriving at the Crystal Vault to serve as its primary protection ship. Two Freighters, the EAS Brandenburg and EAS Sensoji, were also being assigned to the system. Initially they would be assisting in the construction of the surveillance sensor array.

The Netherlands had relocated its base of operations to the system that held the Transluminide core, the one they were now calling Fort Knox. It still had the lead for the entire operation. The Netherlands was joined by the Dhaka, the ship that had done the stellar cartography work-up for the system. The Dhaka had the lead on system defense and would be spending most of its time over the coming month completing the surveillance sensor array for Fort Knox.

Two Freighters had also been assigned there, the EAS Petra and EAS Krakow. In the short term, they would be helping with the surveillance system set up. But in a couple days, they would start running Transluminide back to Earth.

Next week, the Fast Attack Ship Jakarta, captained by Amund Gunderson, would be arriving at the second planet discovered. It was now being called Iron Mountain because of the 78% iron concentration in its core. It would be joined by the Freighters EAS Gothenburg and EAS Antica.

NEAR THE ROCK

David returned to his previous location above the Rock and cast his attention toward one of the large weapons production facilities. After a few minutes search, he found the large power cube that powered the facility. These power cubes had an interesting configuration. Most of their power was being syphoned from dimension 12.

David did a quick search for some sodium fluoride. It was as common in the Lorexian refresher systems as it was in human toothpaste. He transported small amounts from numerous sources and within minutes had gathered enough for what he needed to do next.

David transitioned into dimension 12, then found the power cube feeding the weapons facility. He released most of his sodium fluoride material into the vortex of charged particles being pulled across the dimensional barrier by the power cube on the other side. He then moved toward the civilian housing area and released the remainder of it. In short order, the weapons production facility, and the nearby residential compound, would start experiencing power issues.

WEAPONS PRODUCTION FACILITY, THE ROCK

An alarm went off in the power control room of the weapons production facility.

"Odd. Voltage has dropped on the main line," the junior operating engineer reported to his boss. "Correction. Is dropping. At this rate we'll need to start shutdowns on the ancillary support systems in about 5 minutes."

"Any idea where the problem is?"

"Must be in the power cubes. Current is down proportionally, so it can't be an overload. That would cause current to increase as voltage dropped."

"Drop lighting to half. If nothing else, it will test your theory."

"Lighting is cut to half." After a moment. "And voltage has come back up close to normal but is still dropping. That bought us a little time, but not much. We'll need to do an emergency stop on production in less than a half hour."

"OK, alerting senior management."

MAINTENANCE OFFICE, KE-SO-NA RESIDENTIAL BLOCK, THE ROCK

Maintenance Chief Ta-So put down his comm device. It was the fifth call of the day, each reporting a problem with one of the unit's power cubes. None of these cubes were old; not one close to half its expected service life. Yet his crew had confirmed that the first four were not working properly, and he suspected that this one wasn't either. But why? He was baffled.

"Chief, just got another call complaining about a malfunctioning power cube."

"Send someone to check it out."

At this rate, they'd run through their replacement inventory in a matter of days, then all hell would break loose. They lived underground on an airless, frozen moon. Without power, they would all die.

With a trembling hand, he reached for his comm device. Rules required him to notify the district manager if a life-threatening issue came up or was even suspected. His district manager was an angry short-tempered person. One who seemed to take joy in punishing anyone on whom the fates dropped a problem.

Chapter 26: JUDGEMENT

[Sunday, 08.08.2032] NEAR THE ROCK

A quick scan showed that David's plan was working. The weapons facility was shut down. The residential complex where most of its employee's worked was also in the process of relocating residents. But no one seemed to be investigating the problem.

Time for another round, this time at the research complex. Surely someone there will investigate.

...

A half hour later, reports of power cube issues started surfacing, both at the lab and in the nearby residential complex.

SPEAKERS OFFICE, CENTRAL COUNCIL PLAZA

From his office, the Speaker could see the pulsing red crystal in the plaza. It just sat there, seemingly unprotected, until someone got too close.

A small group of people had apparently camped out overnight. The CCP were supposed to have cleared them, but that apparently hadn't happened. But as the day wore on, the crowds increased, and the staff became increasingly fidgety. He noticed a lot of whispering and furtive glances.

"Enough of this," he whispered angrily to himself. "Time to get some lunch." As he stood, there was a flash and an unusual looking person appeared in the room.

"Who are you. And what are you doing here?"

"Speaker Fu-Su, you stand accused of suppressing your people. You will come with me."

"I will do no such..."

There was a flash of light

CENTRAL COUNCIL PLAZA, NEW LOREXI

"...thing."

As the light receded, he saw that he was standing between the inner and outer ring of Lorexian Royal Blue barrier ropes, facing the crystal. The shock of having been transported to this place without warning caused the Speaker to stumble, but his fall was arrested by a force he didn't understand. As he was righted, a beam of light passed over him.

"Fu-Su. Lorexian. Incompatible species. You stand in judgement before the Temple of the Ancients."

The Speaker turned toward the sound and was gripped with fear at the sight of the giant Lorexian who stood there in battle gear. Then an inexplicable calm came over him.

"Speaker Fu-Su, I am the judge appointed by the Ancients. You stand accused of suppressing the younger members of the Confederation. This is a direct contravention of the Confederation's charter as approved by the Ancients. A full and complete confession is required of you."

"I've done nothing wrong. I work in the interests of all Confederation members." The Speaker spread his arms indicating the crowd. His words were delivered with a practiced confidence and sincerity. Their assurance seemed to make the crowd relax.

Ma-Ka, whose spear was held vertically at his side, lifted it a couple inches. He held it there for a few seconds, then slammed it back to the ground. The resulting boom echoed off the buildings surrounding the plaza. And renewed fear pierced the Speaker and the crowd.

Above the crystal, a holoprojection appeared and started playing. It showed two people on opposite sides of a conference room table, hunched together whispering to each other.

...

"Ma-Gu. A resolution authorizing an extradition warrant has been issued. Take your ships and go. Bring back the prisoner if you can. But find and bring back the human scientists behind the new shields and propulsion systems. Technology like this cannot be allowed to thrive among the primitives."

"Any restrictions on the use of force?"

"None. Destroy any that resist. But do it in a way that gives us deniability."

...

Sounds of incredulity rippled through the crowd. The Speaker openly trembled.

Then a second clip started to play. It showed the Speaker sitting at his desk talking on the comm system.

...

"What happened," The Speaker demanded.

A voice on the other end of the line spoke. "The humans have started a program they call 'Spreading the Prosperity.' They are trying to bring prosperity to newer, smaller worlds. As an incentive for more established worlds to join, they are offering gifts, large wonder stones.

"If the market is flooded with inexpensive, large carat wonder stones, like the two given away today, how will that impact the value of your holdings?" The other voice asked.

A look of terror came over the Speaker. "I'd lose my financing. My businesses would be liquidated. I'd lose everything, be removed from the Council. We must stop him!"

...

As the holoprojection faded, voices from the crowd shouted. "Liar. Traitor. Hypocrite."

David raised his hands and the crowd quieted.

"Speaker Fu-Su, your confession has not been accepted. And now you face judgement."

With that, David, Ma-Ka, the crystal and rope barriers all disappeared, leaving the speaker standing by himself in the middle of a huge crowd that swarmed over him.

EAS CANADA

The trade convoy entered Earth orbit a little after noon. Daniel was once again hiding in the bridge office. He felt guilty hiding there. At this point both first and second watch crew knew something was wrong.

"Admiral?"

"Yes, Else?"

"New orders just arrived for you from Admiral Scott. They are encrypted for your eyes only. Sending to your queue now."

"Thanks, Else."

New orders were not a surprise. When they'd left Karagon on the final leg of their journey, Daniel had messaged Admiral Scott requesting a medical evaluation ground side when they arrived. He hoped that's what the orders were.

There was a ding on Daniel's pad. He decrypted the orders and read. "The Canada is being scheduled for one-week leave on Earth. Establish a leave schedule, then report to Space Force Medical for evaluation."

Daniel pushed a button on his desk. "Commander Tai, please join me in the bridge office at your earliest convenience."

A moment later, there was a knock and the door opened.

"Reporting as requested."

"I've been ordered to report to Medical for evaluation. The ship is being given one-week leave. Establish a leave rotation. I'm going to head down in a few minutes. You have the ship."

"I have the ship. We'll take care of her while you're gone."

AMBASSADOR'S RESIDENCE

Michael, I must speak with you.

Michael was having dinner with Sarah, Timothy, Alexi, and Julissa. Suddenly, he sat up straight, obviously in a trance. Then after a moment he settled.

"Was it James?" Sarah asked, recognizing the impact of a message from James.

"He better not be planning on flashing in here." Julissa declared.

"Excuse me for a minute," Michael said, then got up and headed for the presence projector.

"Not going without me," Alexi declared, running after Michael.

"Does he ever rest?" Julissa asked Sarah rhetorically.

"No." Sarah smiled. "I think that's why I love him as much as I do. He's always out there fighting for us. There aren't many husbands that do."

"There are some. I've seen them. But far too few."

PRESENCE PROJECTOR, AMBASSADOR'S RESIDENCE

Michael entered the presence projector and saw someone he didn't know.

Alexi rushed in behind. "David?"

"Sorry." David, who had been sitting there in his Ancient form, flashed into his human form. "Michael, I need your help."

Then acknowledging Alexi, he smiled. "Hi, Alexi."

"What's going on, David?"

"The Confederation is so corrupt. The Ancients have sent me to fix it..." David filled with emotion. "..., but they lean toward just burning down Andromeda." He covered his face with his hands as the emotion played out.

"I can't do it. I allowed Admiral Porter's assassin to kill herself. Same with the lacky that killed Nadia. Same with the Inspector. But I had a role in each, and I can't continue on that path."

Surprisingly, Alexi put her hand over David's. "I know," she said quietly.

David's eyes darted toward her, then back to Michael. "This morning, Speaker Fu-Su was judged. It was as bloody as his deeds deserved. I precipitated it but was not his executioner.

"This afternoon Councilor To-Ja will be judged. But I'll struggle to do it. Is there a way to do this without the bloodshed?"

"Bring me. I'd gladly do it for you!" Alexi said brightly.

David's withering stare sent a shiver through Alexi.

"Sorry, Alexi. I'm still learning control."

In a seeming change of subject, Michael asked, "David, where are you? Can't the Confederation monitor this call?"

David chuckled. "In the Confederation, quantum entangled communications are secure between any pair of points. The problem, of course, is that they are not uniquely entangled in other dimensions. I've 'wired' this session through other dimensions, cutting out the Confederation's link."

Michael smiled at David's skill, happy that David was on his side, then realized that wasn't true. He'd said this to Sarah before. James was not on their side; they were on James' side. In this case, David was here because he knew Michael was on his side.

"David, forgive me for asking, but what are you?"

"I'm an Ancient of human origin." He smiled as if proud. "I've already been invited to join two of the collectives." But the pride quickly dissipated. "But that's the dilemma, no? Every day, I am more Ancient, less human. I was chosen as the timid hand, the one falsely accused. The one more likely to discern mistake from misconduct. And I've been granted so much power..." David's voice trailed off. "I need help. You were James' chosen. But you are not from a compatible species. So now I bear the burden you were groomed to take."

A moment of silence.

"David. Would you be able to pause once the Inspector's office is eliminated? I think the 'Spread the Prosperity' program could take it from there. Especially if you remained available to help us put out fires.

"The Confederation is full of rot as you say. But most of it is just bureaucratic lassitude and indifference. It needs to be fixed, but we can do it over time by proactively spreading the prosperity.

"The real problem, the one that needs to be excised from the Confederation, is the evil that has thrived in the Inspector's office. That will mostly need to be cut out and burned."

"James reached a similar conclusion, as have I. So, that's where I'm starting. But that alone will not satisfy the Ancients."

"Can you tell me where you are?"

David looked up, smiling and radiating humor.

Alexi started laughing. "I can already tell that this is going to be good."

"I'm in the Temple of the Ancients in Central Council Plaza on New Lorexi."

"Why there?"

"Councilor To-Ja will stand in judgement shortly."

"What will that involve?"

"The Ancients have identified him as one of the problems. In principle, they want him gone. But they aren't as blood thirsty as that sounds. We won't act directly against those who confess their crimes.

"So, I will demand that he confess his crimes or face my judgement. He will not confess, at which point the Ancients would prefer that I simply incinerate him.

"I really don't want to do that, so instead I'll play his memories on a giant holoprojector for all to see. I'll select from the things that he fears the most, things he thinks were the worst. Then the crowd will tear him apart limb by limb."

Alexi spoke up. "What if the crowd doesn't do that?"

"Depends. If they arrest him or take other appropriate action, then I will leave his fate to them. If they applaud, cheer, or otherwise approve, then I will burn them all. But I doubt that will happen."

Again, David was quiet for a moment. Then he stood.

"It will begin shortly."

"David, do you have a means of taking us? Holoprojecting me and Alexi with you in the plaza?"

"Possibly, what do you have in mind?"

"If you can get me a pad with the memories you would otherwise play, I might be able to get him to confess. And we could arrange to have him arrested. I think we both agree that it would be better for him to face justice in the courts, not in the street."

"I can, but it's risky. If he is not convicted, then I will be forced to burn everyone involved in the acquittal."

"I think it's worth a try. Anything we can do to clean up the Confederation ourselves will lead to a better outcome."

"OK. Meet me here in 10 minutes. I've got some work to do to get this set up."

CENTRAL COUNCIL PLAZA

The crystal had been pulsing for the last 10 minutes, its emanations increasing with each pulse. Many in the crowd started backing away.

It was well into the afternoon, the shadows from the nearby building had crept in nearly to the center of the plaza.

There was a flash and three Ancients appeared, the judge and two others, one male, the other female. There was an immediate hush at the appearance, but within moments the whispering grew to a buzz and the odd question was shouted out.

David stepped forward, raising is hands.

"Councilor To-Ja, you have not appeared as you were required to do, so now I summon you."

There was a flash and the Councilor appeared in terror. David looked on in disgust.

Ma-Ka appeared next to the crystal. Although this was expected, his intimidating size made the crowd edge back a little more.

"To-Ja. Lorexian. Incompatible species. You stand in judgement."

The councilor stood there trembling, lacking the courage to even look up at the giant warrior.

David nodded to Michael, who walked up to the ropes in front of To-Ja. "Councilor, I am here to advise you. I am not the one bringing charges against you. I have been allowed to show you the evidence the judge is using as the basis for your prosecution."

Michael held out the data pad for the councilor to take.

"This information is accurate. It has been taken from your own memories. Denying it will not help you."

"Then what's the point?"

"If you do not confess these crimes with your own voice, these memories will be played for all to see. It is my belief that the crowd will surge forward when that happens. And they will rip you apart as they did Speaker Fu-Su.

"A verbal confession will only be heard by a small fraction of the crowd. The Ancients do not take action against those that confess. Instead they will turn you over to local authorities along with the relevant evidence.

"So, the choice is yours. Be burned alive by the Ancients, ripped apart by the crowd, or stand before the Confederation's judicial system. Please see the evidence for yourself."

The Councilor watched a little, then flipped to the next, and the next. Then completely lost his composure. After a minute, he regained his senses.

"I will confess."

Michael bowed to him in respect, then took the pad and returned to David.

Councilor To-Ja slowly and articulately made his confession, describing his actions and apologizing for the many unintended consequences that resulted. More people in the crowd heard than Michael would have expected. The crowd's reaction was mild, but there was cheering and applause when the CCP took him into custody, and the Ancients flashed away.

...

Michael and Alexi never left the presence projector in the apartment. Nonetheless, they felt relieved as Central Council Plaza melted away and the presence projector returned to normal. Unexpectedly, David was there with them in his human form.

"Michael. Thank you. There are other low-level offenders on the Central Council that the Ancients want me to act against. But I can get away with holding off on that. Maybe there's a process you can undertake to clean that up before I'm forced to.

"I have a long list of other targets, mostly in Andromeda, that I'll work my way through first. My big target is the Rock. A significant event will happen there in a few days. I'm in the process of deactivating their power systems in the hopes they will evacuate the civilians ahead of time. If there is anything you can do to encourage a civilian evacuation, it would help me. But do not trigger a mass evacuation. All the military intelligence agents and researchers on the Rock are slated for judgement. I'll be in big trouble if they are evacuated and the civilians left behind.

EAS NETHERLANDS

Yesterday's arrival of the mining platform patterns had set off a whirlwind of activity. It was the first time the ship's engineering team and replicators were used for something other than ship repairs and upgrades. And Admiral Flanagan was impressed with what they'd accomplished.

In only a day, the platform had been framed out, including the mounts for the redundant power systems, control room and ingot pouring facility. Twelve ten-megawatt power cubes had arrived earlier in the afternoon along with eighteen 1G grav drives. Bots would be placing these overnight.

The replicators were still working on the main mining transporter. When that was done, they would start running the field generators for the refinery. With any luck, they would be able to make their first pull tomorrow afternoon.

EVENING NEWS, CORE WORLDS NEWS NETWORK

"Huge crowds gathered today to learn more about the pulsing crystal that appeared in the Central Council Plaza yesterday. And they got a little more than they expected.

"Good evening, I am Wa-Ta, here with my colleague Ko-Ki, reporting from Capital City on New Lorexi. The Ancients have returned, and they've done so with a vengeance. They've sent a judge, who presented evidence of wrongdoing by Central Council Speaker Fu-Su, who was killed in the riot that followed.

"Councilor To-Ja was called next and confessed to a series of crimes. The CCP got there in time to arrest To-Ja, who is now facing a long list of charges related to abuse of power.

"It looks like it's going to be a tough season for Central Council members."

PLANETARY GOVERNOR'S OFFICE, THE ROCK

"Chief To-No, thank you for meeting with me. I hope you have something to report." Chief To-No was responsible for facilities on the Rock. It was mostly an oversight position, generally held by a political appointee.

In a sense that was true for To-No. The planetary governor was a friend, and he had appointed the Chief. But unlike most political appointees, the Chief was an expert, the most respected engineer on the Rock.

"I do, but you're not going to like it." The words were delivered with sadness. This crisis might take down his friend, Planetary Governor Fe-Hu. Even though such an outcome would not be the result of incompetence or wrongdoing.

"This is basically a natural disaster. Something happened in a nearby dimension that has knocked out our power cubes. Until it corrects itself, power cubes here will fail."

"What evidence do you have to support this theory?"

"We've disassembled three power cubes, all with the same problem, fluorine creep."

"I'm not sure I've heard of that."

"Fluorine is the one contaminant that can deactivate Transluminide. Any fluorine in a power cube will cause it to perform below specification. A lot of fluorine and it will fail completely.

"In principle there are three ways fluorine can get into a power cube: during manufacturing, if a seal breaks in the field, or fluorine contamination in the dimension from which the power is being drawn.

"We know these units worked to spec at one point, so know our problem is not a manufacturing issue.

"We carefully checked the hermetic seals on the units we opened, before opening them. So, we know the seals were intact.

"That leaves only one possibility, fluorine contamination in the dimension from which we're drawing power."

"What can we do about this? Is there some sort of remediation protocol?"

"At one level, there's nothing we can do. There's no way to directly identify or remediate the source. It isn't in our space time. As long as there is fluorine there, power cubes here will fail. The one thing we could do is to replace our power cubes with others that draw from higher dimensions. There's no guarantee it will work, as we don't know how extensive the fluorine contamination is in those higher dimensions, but we can try.

"We could also bring in large power cubes in areas that are still working, areas where the contamination has not spread. Then build out a power distribution system to get the power where we need it.

"This would be a longer-term project. It's also risky in the sense that we have no control over the contaminant. If it should flow to our central location, then our new unit would fail."

"Can we simply move our existing units elsewhere?"

The Chief shook his head no. "They are permanently damaged. They can't even be recycled."

"OK. Start a survey. Determine if there's a pattern showing where units are working and where they're down. See if there's existing infrastructure we can use to transmit power from working areas to the broken ones. Also get some small power cubes of types that draw from different dimensions. See if there are any that will work in our broken areas.

"While you are doing that, I'll put non-essentials on alert for evacuation."

Chapter 27: THE ROCK

[Monday, 08.09.2032] AMBASSADOR'S OFFICE

"Michael? David would like to speak with you in the presence projector."

"Thanks, Pam."

Michael exited his office and entered the presence projector, where David was waiting.

"Good morning, Michael."

"Good morning, David. How can I help you?"

"Admiral Jo-Na is about to call you. The situation on the Rock is deteriorating. They've requested evacuation assistance and some equipment that they don't have budget for. He will ask you to authorize the evacuation. But he is not inclined to send the equipment.

"I need you to persuade him to provide the equipment, offer to pay for it if you have to. I can compensate you."

"Why should I approve the equipment?"

"They think it may help them save the Rock. If they cannot get that equipment, then they will also start evacuating some of my most important targets. I need those targets on the Rock. Collateral damage will increase if I need to take them down on New Lorexi."

This was the first request David had made of him that Michael did not want to agree to.

"I know you don't want to do this Michael. But we both know that you would do it anyway if James were making the request. I could force you but will not. Just know that additional innocent blood will be spilled if senior members of Military Intelligence evacuate today."

"Understood."

A chime sounded.

"Looks like it's Admiral Jo-Na. Thanks for the warning, David."

David disappeared and the presence projector connected to the Admiral.

PRESENCE PROJECTOR ADMIRAL JO-NA'S OFFICE

As had been the case recently, the presence projector reconfigured into a replica of the Admiral's mountain cabin.

"Mi-Ku. Thank you for connecting so quickly. I've got a bit of an emergency here.

"You're aware of the Military Intelligence base on the moon they call the Rock?"

"Yes, that's where everyone thought Ju-Ne's restoration chamber was."

"Indeed, it was." A pause. "Well the Rock is having power issues. They're experiencing power failures throughout the moon, in both the civilian and military sectors. They're requesting emergency evacuation assistance for the civilian population.

"Now that Military Intelligence is under direct command of the Central Council, this request should be going to them, not me. But apparently no one is home at the Central Council. The Speaker's death has rendered the Office of the Executive nonfunctional.

"I think I have the authority to authorize the evacuation on my own, but it would be highly unusual. Can you back me on this if I'm questioned?"

"Yes. You can evacuate using my authority."

"They also asked us to provide them with some expensive equipment that they don't have the budget for. I'm not inclined to oblige that request. I have the discretionary funds. But this would wipe me out and it's not my department anymore. The funding I used to have for this purpose has been taken away from me and already given to them. From the look of things, they've squandered it."

Michael was quiet for a moment. He needed to choose a side.

"If the emergency is bad enough that they need to evacuate the civilians then we should assume the equipment request is legitimate. As much as I hate the idea, I think we need to comply. If you have the equipment, you have my word that I'll find a way to compensate you."

Jo-Na scrutinized Michael. "You must know something I don't."

"Sorry, my friend, I can't say anything more. But I'll take budget responsibility for the equipment."

It was clear that the Admiral was expecting a different answer and wasn't particularly happy with this one.

After several moments of silence, the Admiral shook his head. "I'll send the equipment. Maybe someday you can tell me why."

"Some big changes are taking place. Though it seems the opposite, this equipment will help drive the solution we're both looking for."

"Hopefully, it will be as you say."

The Admiral bowed his head in respect, then cut the connection.

PLANETARY GOVERNOR'S OFFICE, THE ROCK

Planetary Governor Fe-Hu was flummoxed. In times past, contacting the High Command drew an immediate response. Today, hours passed. Air quality had continued to decline. His office was mostly spared.

"Governor. We just received word that evacuation assistance and the power cubes you requested are underway. ETA 30 minutes."

"Pick-up delivery location?"

"The hub. The first group of civilian evacuees has already been staged. The full manifest of requested equipment will be transported to receiving in about 20 minutes."

"Ask Chief To-No to meet me in receiving ASAP."

"He's already there, sir. You'll need to hustle to get there before the goods do. The shuttle system just lost power."

The Governor sat back in his chair, trying to catch his breath. They'd tried to get him to evacuate earlier. He couldn't believe that power to the Governor's Palace could actually fail, so had declined. At this point, he'd need a rebreather, possibly a space suit to get out. And he would have to do it on his own. Everyone else had wisely left.

He opened the bottom drawer of his desk, where he kept his emergency supplies, and lifted his rebreather off its charging station. A quick check showed that he had a 74% charge. Made sense. It was an older unit, so the batteries didn't hold as much as they used to. A quick check of its atmospheric sensors showed oxygen levels approaching the lower safe limit, carbon dioxide above safe levels. At this level, the unit showed a little less than one-hour capacity.

He put the unit on, took several deep breaths and within seconds felt better.

He got up, went to the door, and checked the environmental conditions on the other side. Oxygen slightly below safe levels, carbon dioxide close to the limit. Temperature about 7° C, a little cool but doable. It was 100 yards to the next bulkhead. He could probably make it that far, but realized he was at risk of not making it back if the conditions on the other side of the bulkhead were not safe.

He went back to his desk. He had two pony bottles of oxygen. One had a full 10-minute supply. The other was half full, about a 5-minute supply. He pulled out his lightweight spacesuit. It was in good condition. Its batteries had about an hour remaining.

Risky option. 15 minutes of air might not get me there.

He went to the closet and pulled out his all-environment spacesuit, immediately realizing that it was too bulky to operate with his limited oxygen supply. It also had an hour of battery life remaining on full life support.

Full suit it is. But I'll bring the light-weight suit and oxygen as backup.

He quickly donned the suit, then took off down the hall.

SPACE FORCE MEDICAL FACILITY

Daniel had been given a well-equipped private room that felt more like a nice hotel room than one in a hospital. Over the last day, it seemed as if he'd been given every medical test known. He'd also received a thorough psych evaluation.

There was a knock on the door.

"Come in."

The door opened and the lead physician on his case, Dr. Dylan Shaw, came in.

"Feeling any better today?"

"Little change."

The doctor looked at Daniel, clearly concerned.

"Your case is a bit of a paradox. You are dangerously anemic, which is why you feel so tired. We can find no cause for the anemia, other than loss of blood from the injury. But the transfusions you received on the ship and here have not helped. It's as if you're still bleeding. But there's no blood in your body cavities or in your stool, which is a bit confounding.

"Similar with your psych tests. They indicate that you are suffering from sub-clinical post-traumatic stress, but you're not responding to the medications."

"Do you have a theory?" Daniel asked.

"Not really. You were treated with alien technology that we know nothing about. Presumably, that could be a cause. But the only evidence I have is the lack of evidence for another cause, which is entirely unsatisfactory.

"For now, I'm placing you on medical leave."

"Thank you. I've never felt unfit to serve before, but know that I am now, so no argument from me."

"What would you think about taking quarters out in the civilian part of the Embassy?"

"Why?"

"It's my sense that exposure to fresh air and the liberty of civilian life will help. You can stay here if you'd rather. But I can get you vouchers for the guest hotel and a convenience card. I'd like to see you again in three days. You can check in with me at any time or go to any of the emergency facilities in the Embassy if you feel a crisis coming on."

"Deal," Daniel said with a weak smile, the exhaustion still dogging him.

"Someone will be by with arrangements in a few minutes. Get better, Daniel. The world needs you."

ENGINEERING TEST FACILITY, THE ROCK

The Governor barely made it to a powered space in time. From there he'd been whisked off to the engineering test facility where Chief To-No had set up the newly received equipment.

"Glad to see you made it." The Chief greeted as the Governor entered the room.

"Apparently overstayed my welcome at the Governor's palace." He chuckled. "What do you have so far?"

"This facility seems to be close to the boundary of the fluorine creep. Fifty meters that way…" He pointed in the direction of the Governor's palace. "…everything is dead. Here most units cannot generate full power, but they aren't getting worse, or at least they are getting worse very slowly. So, we've taken the big 100-megawatt unit 25 km further into the safe territory. And work has started on a distribution line back into the city center. Most buildings there are wired for central power as a backup. So, we can get quite a few people back to work in the next 24 hours.

"This 1-megawatt unit draws from a much higher dimension. It came up at 100% rated capacity and has held steady. One of these would be enough to power the palace. Two would power the shuttle system. If we can lay our hands on a couple dozen more and evacuate all non-essentials, we should be able to bring weapons, surveillance and research back up to full capacity."

"Excellent news. How are the evacuations going?"

"No idea. My attention has been focused here. Emergency ops should know. They're across the hall, two doors to the right."

"Thanks. Keep up the good work."

As the Governor walked away, an odd thought ran through the Chief's mind. *Everyone calls him a slave driver. But he's the easiest boss I've had in Military Intelligence. Everyone else always seems so angry.*

EMERGENCY SERVICES, THE ROCK

"Status of the evacuation?" The Governor growled as he entered the command post.

The duty officer snapped to attention.

"The last civilian transport will leave in an hour. Half of the non-essentials are gone, but many are lingering."

"Put out an announcement. All non-essentials are required to depart on the next transport. Those remaining behind will have their power cut."

"It will be as you say, sir."

Now to find new quarters and possibly some companionship, the Governor thought as he exited the building and headed deeper into the safe zone.

EAS MUMBAI

The platform had just been towed into position. Captain Parikh would be transporting over shortly. Accompanying her would be mining specialists Beata Kozelek and Adam Lee from the Mumbai.

Two others would be joining them from the Dhaka, Ping Chin from China, and Wanessa Kubasek from Poland. Both were recent graduates from the Mining program at the Ascendance Institute.

The three from the Mumbai were on the mining level transporter pad. "Ready?" She smiled at the others.

Two nods came back.

"Rani, we are ready to transport."

MINING PLATFORM, FORT KNOX

The lights in the control room came up as the people appeared.

They stepped off the transporter pad and immediately went over to the main control panel.

"Adam, take the lead on the checklist. Beata run the offline self-diagnostics on the mining transporter. I'll take the refining filters."

...

Fifteen minutes later, they were ready for the others.

"Dhaka, this is Bumati Parikh on the mining platform. We are ready for your specialists to join us."

A moment later, the others joined them.

"Ping, Wanessa. Welcome. I'm told that you ran the self-diagnostics earlier. We've just done the same. Everything looks good.

"Since the two of you are going to be doing most of the work aboard the platform. I'd like you to be hands on for the pull today.

"Ping, you and I will do the pull itself. Wanessa, you and I will do the refining run. Then Ping and I will do the ingot pour. Adam and Beata will be the spare hands for these operations, to the extent we need them. Questions?"

There were none.

"OK, Ping, you're on. Have you operated a mining transporter before?"

"No ma'am. I've logged 20 hours in the simulator, all 20 running simulations that feature some sort of equipment malfunction. And I watched the professor do it once on Mining Platform 12."

"Great, then this will be a piece of cake. Go ahead and set the target for the pull. I'll double check. We want to do a perfectly centered pull from the liquid core.

"Wanessa, make sure the receiving field is ready. We want to snap it in place as soon as the pull is stable so as not to lose heat."

"Yes, ma'am." She smiled at the exchange. Unlike Ping, the professor had let her do half a shift on Platform 16.

"Target set, ma'am."

Bumati went over to double check. Her intuition said they should be going another meter deeper. But she had no evidence to base it on, so let the thought slide.

"Wanessa, you ready?"

"Yes, ma'am."

"OK, Ping. Make the pull."

"Initiating transport."

The massive capacitors fired, the associated magnetic field causing the lights to dim. Then a ball of molten gray metal appeared at the end of the platform, near the control room. It was immediately encased in a filter shield, the one that would filter out gold.

"Dragging the transport field to the next station," Wanessa called out.

The molten ball moved forward. A thin stream of liquid yellow flowed down the side of the gold filter, puddling in the catch bin at the bottom.

"Activating the impurities filter."

Another spherical filter shield shimmered to life, perfectly aligned an inch away from the molten ball of metal.

"Filtering the impurities."

The ball of liquid metal moved forward. Various gases, liquid metals and bits of solid debris fell away from the molten sphere and collected in the bin at the bottom of the impurities shield.

"Confirming filter efficiency." Wanessa called out. "99.999% pure. Suitable for ingot pour.

"Ping, back to you."

Another field snapped into place around the sphere of remaining material. This one was shaped like a funnel and led to an array of small rectangular molds, 25 wide by 40 long.

"Starting the pour."

The inner transporter field released and the pure, liquid Transluminide flowed down the funnel to fill the array of molds. There was slightly more Transluminide than space in the molds. The excess collected in a large bin near the surface of the platform. This bin was heated so its contents remained molten. When it filled to the appropriate level, it, too, would be cast into ingots.

"Moving the molds into the cooling chamber."

The molds moved sideways into the bottom tier of a multiple level, rectangular structure. A new set of empty molds dropped down into position where the now-filled ones had been a moment ago.

Bumati called everyone's attention back to the control room.

"Well done, team. We just made a thousand, 100-kg ingots of Transluminide bullion." She pointed to a countdown timer on the wall. "We have 12 minutes before the capacitors are charged for the next pull. So, plenty of time for a quick debrief. Standard questions. Did this go as you expected? Were your instructions clear? Did you know what to do? Any issues or concerns? Ping, go."

"Almost exactly as expected. Good instructions. Knew what I was doing. The only surprise was the overflow. Excess is handled differently on this platform than the ones around Earth. I read this in the training material. Seeing it made it more real."

"Wanessa."

"Almost as expected, sufficient training, knew what I was doing. I think the impurity filter is a problem. We don't get this type of solids precipitation during separation on Earth. It's too early to say, but I suspect that we'll eventually form a dust cloud around the platform. There were a lot of fine particles in the debris."

"Adam?"

"As expected, sufficiently trained, knew what to do."

Beata said the same.

Bumati summarized. "This went by the book. I'm proud of all of you. Wanessa, I agree. The impurities precipitation was unexpected. We'll need to run some tests to find out what the fine particles are. Then report our results back to the brain trust.

"We need at least 5 pulls today. I'd love to get 10. Two cruisers will be coming in tomorrow to escort us home. I'd love to be able to deliver a million kilograms of bullion tomorrow."

EUGENE AND KELLY'S LAB

"I think I have it!" Eugene shouted.

"What?" Kelly asked skeptically.

"You know, the literature you found about a more powerful source of energy than zero-point energy."

"What? I thought you were working the security arrangements."

"I was." Eugene shot back. "But the solution came to me last night!"

Kelly put her hand over her face. "Please, no details."

Eugene looked at her puzzled, then it sank in.

"Ha, ha. Not exactly supportive."

Kelly saw that Eugene was about to descend into one of his funks. "Sorry. What did you find?"

"Transluminide is like the junction in a transistor."

Kelly deflated. "Isn't that what I told you, like a month ago?"

"Hum... Seems you did. But it's not like that."

"Care to explain?"

Eugene looked at Kelly like she was nuts. "Why else would I have brought it up?"

They looked at each other for a moment, then burst out laughing.

ABOVE THE ROCK

David watched as the last transport of non-essentials left the Rock. The last civilian transport had left an hour ago. It was just about time.

The transport's course would sling shot around the planet that the Rock orbited. As soon as it passed behind the planet, David would initiate the sequence that would tear the Rock apart. An hour later the Rock would be nothing more than an asteroid field orbiting its uninhabited parent.

As the transport crested the planet, sadness settled over David. It was time. Four devices appeared near the Rock, one each at Lagrange 1, 2, 4 and 5. Each had a 100-megawatt power source and a time-dampening field generator. The fields would be teardrop shaped, narrow near the generator expanding out wider than the Rock, but only 10 meters thick at its widest spot. Each would target the widest spot in its field to cut loosely through the middle of the Rock.

The Rock was gravitationally locked, rotating on its axis at the same rate it, and the four field generators, revolved around the planet. The field generators' teardrop shaped fields were in four different planes.

David activated the fields which immediately cut the Rock into 16 wedge-shaped pieces. The pieces were still gravitationally bound to the planet. But the time-dilation fields temporarily suspended gravity between the wedges, which began to slide relative to one another.

One by one the time-dilation fields collapsed as the pressure on them exceeded the limits of their power sources. And as they collapsed, the gravity between the wedges came flooding back grinding them to pieces.

GUEST HOTEL

Daniel was used to the military process, where even the simplest things took time. This morning at 10 AM, the doctor said he would arrange discharge. Now, closing in on 5 PM, he was finally checking into the guest hotel.

"Admiral Porter, how delightful to have you as our guest. Given the flood of guests today, mostly from your ship..." The receptionist smiled conspiratorially as if this was a secret. "We've upgraded you to a suite."

Daniel smiled back, nodding his head in gratitude.

"At least until Sunday. Your signature on the registration card, affirms your agreement to these terms, and accepts the reservation for a standard room starting Sunday afternoon."

Daniel had to chuckle. "Thank you. The extra space will be welcome."

"Our bellman, Bradley, will help you with your things. We've covered the gratuity, so please don't offer." The hostess smiled and the bellman nodded his head in agreement.

Daniel didn't particularly like the arrangement but appreciated its practicality. In truth, Daniel hadn't brought much with him. But someone had loaded it into the cab, someone else had brought it to the front desk, and now someone else was carrying it to his room. And by the time they got there, Daniel was ready to collapse.

"Thank you."

"Admiral. A pleasure to serve. A friend of mine served on one of your ships. Please accept my thanks." He quickly scurried out of the room, at which point Daniel collapsed into the bed.

GUEST ACCOMMODATIONS, THE ROCK

The Governor had enjoyed a nice evening. He'd connected up with an old friend who'd agreed to come back to his room with him. As they settled in, a tremendous earthquake struck. Everything shook, furnishings fell over, then the unthinkable happened. The building lost containment. As the air rushed out into the vacuum of space, the screaming stopped. And over the next hour all evidence that the Rock had ever hosted life vanished.

ABOVE THE ROCK

David watched as the Rock broke apart. Extreme grief flooded over him as the last emanations of life below quieted. He was in energy form, so had no tears or cheeks for them to run down. Nonetheless, his soul wept. A moment later, he was back in the Temple, wondering if he could bear to leave it again. Several of the collectives approached to embrace him with peace. They knew that tomorrow it would start again, and they approved of his actions.

Chapter 28: REFORMATION

[Tuesday, 08.10.2032] AMBASSADOR'S OFFICE

It was 7:30. Michael's mornings had become a bit lazy of recent. His message bot sorted four messages to the top of his queue. The first was from Admiral Jo-Na.

Fleet had sent the requested equipment and completed both civilian and non-essential worker evacuations early in the evening. But shortly after the last transport left, the Rock had inexplicably ripped itself apart. No survivors. An investigation had been launched, but the former moon was now an expanding asteroid field. Travel in the vicinity of the planet the Rock orbited would be hazardous for a long time to come.

The next message was from Admiral Scott. Daniel Porter was back, but out on medical leave. They'd run a battery of tests that were mostly inconclusive. It was not clear when Daniel would be available for service. And there was a possibility he would never return.

The next message was from Admiral Flanagan. The mining platform over Fort Knox was up and running. Lt. Cmdr. Parikh had led a team of specialists chosen from the crews of the Netherlands and the Mumbai. Together they had mined, refined, and poured ten thousand, 100-kg ingots of 99.999% pure Transluminide yesterday. One million kilograms total. Two cruisers would be accompanying the Mumbai back to Earth, ETA late morning embassy time.

The last item was curious. It was not marked urgent, but the bot had sorted it up to the number 4 slot anyway. The message was from Eugene and Kelly.

Michael, nothing urgent, but we've made an incredible discovery, our biggest one yet. It will have major consequences. When you have some time, come over so we can talk in person.

The theory, math, and simulations all check out. We are in the process of building our first proof of concept device. As this is an unencrypted message, probably best to leave it at that.

Sincerely, Eugene.

Michael couldn't help but shake his head. These two were unstoppable. Maybe he could stop by after the Central Council meeting.

Scanning the queue quickly, he saw an item he'd need later today, boilerplate grant and loan contracts for comment. Michael marked them for retrieval, then headed off to his next meeting.

PRESENCE PROJECTOR, AMBASSADOR'S OFFICE

Michael entered the presence projector wishing that he could be almost anywhere else. An emergency meeting had been called. The death of Speaker Fu-Su and arrest of Councilor To-Ja, required the meeting. And with James away, the Council was down to six members, which would likely be a problem. As the most senior counselor, Ke-He would serve as acting-Speaker.

When Michael took his seat, the Central Council Chambers formed around him. One by one, the others appeared until there were six.

"Mi-Ku, do you know if the Ancient One will be joining us?"

"No, I don't know."

There was a flash and David in his Ancient form appeared.

"Councilors. I have been appointed by the Ancients to the seat previously held by So'Gen La'Hoya."

"What evidence do you have of this?"

David held out a document in the ancient script.

"It bears the stamp as required by the founding documents."

"How do I know this is real?"

David's eyes blazed at the insult. "Do I understand correctly that you question both my word and my evidence?"

Enough of David's anger leaked out that the Speaker shrank back in fear.

"The question stands."

"I believe that you are an Ancient."

"You do realize there are consequences for disputing the veracity of an Ancient's assertions."

"Forgive me, Ancient One." The acting Speaker bowed his head low in respect.

"I call this meeting to order." David declared. "As is written in the founding documents, an Ancient will lead Central Council meetings unless he appoints another member in his place."

Michael raised his hand and was called on.

"How would you prefer that we address you?"

David smiled. "My name is Da'Vit Wa'Ton. You may address me by name, or Ancient One, if that is more familiar.

"The agenda Councilor Ke-He planned for today was brief, to vote on a new Speaker, then to discuss filling the vacancies. I'm going to do something different.

"I have been sent by the Ancients to root out the rot that has taken hold in the Confederation. I will start here by asking each of you a simple question that you must answer truthfully.

"Councilor Ke-He, tell me why you serve on the Council." The statement was made with compulsion to tell the truth.

"It is my source of wealth, power, and influence."

"Insufficient." Although spoken softly, David's voice carried the weight of judgement. "Councilor, your service is no longer required on this council. Please write and sign a resignation letter. It will go better for you if you step down voluntarily."

"I will do no such thing!"

"So be it."

Councilor Ke-He froze in place, unmoving.

"Councilor Vi-Ko, senior councilor from Triangulum, tell me why you serve on the Council." Again, the statement was made with compulsion to tell the truth.

"At first it was to protect the people of Triangulum from persecution from the Inspector's office. That is still true, but it came at a high cost in terms of the favors and gifts I was forced to give to the Inspector."

"But you did not vote in favor of dissolving the Department of Military Intelligence, rather you voted in favor of installing Ha-Ke."

The councilor bowed his head in shame. "True, I did not vote to dissolve Military Intelligence. I had my chance, but I didn't believe the department would actually be shut down, and feared retribution. I no longer wish to serve on the Council."

The councilor had been compelled to tell the truth and did. David knew this. What surprised him was the sincerity of the regret.

"Thank you. I judge your intentions as worthy, despite your lack of courage to enact them. You may resign if you want, but I ask you to serve out your term."

...

David proceeded to question all the Councilors, including Michael. Only one other was found unworthy, Councilor Ku-Ka, the junior Councilor from Andromeda.

The two Councilors being removed from the Council were escorted out of the room and taken into custody.

"Only four remain. For now, I will hold the Speaker's position. We will eventually want to appoint a new Speaker, but that can wait. The short-term priority will be adding four more councilors. Two must come from Andromeda. I want one more each from Triangulum and the Milky Way. Given that we are years from elections, a special election will be called. But that will take a year and we cannot wait that long. So, I will appoint temporary Councilors. Do I hear nominations?"

Michael was quick to speak up.

"From the Milky Way, I nominate Ambassador Fe-Va, currently serving on Fatafatu. He is the one spearheading our 'Spread the Prosperity' program."

"Good call, Mi-Ku." Councilor Ke-Ve added. "In 3A, our ambassadors are younger, less experienced. I think all the real candidates are in sector 3F. I also back Fe-Va, but in the spirit of honoring another one of our ambassadors, I nominate Ambassador Va-Mu, currently serving on Edukatar. He is older and more experienced. And he has done a tremendous job of integrating his people into the Confederation."

Mo-Mo raised his hand.

"Please." David nodded back.

"I'd like to nominate Ambassador Ja-Fa, currently serving on Dalfanito. He is on the younger side, but his people have suffered at the Inspector's hands more than almost any other. He will be a strong voice against the corruption that has reigned for so long."

There was silence for a moment.

"What about Andromeda? Any nominations?"

Again, Michael spoke up. "Admiral Jo-Na, head of the High Command. He knows where much of the corruption is."

Again there was a moment of silence, then Councilor Vi-Ko raised his hand. "If I may."

David nodded his consent.

"Governor Na-To, of Do-To-Jo-Ka, one of the core worlds. He is an Ascendant, a governor, not an Ambassador. He has led a major cleanup of the corruption on his planet. His was one of the planets targeted by the Enemy when Inspector Ra-Tu's ship was hijacked. He used the disruption to oust most of the Inspector's agents. He's had a hard time of it since but continues to be an example for all in Andromeda."

David's image waivered a bit, then returned.

"Excellent suggestion. Others?"

Silence.

"I will speak with the nominees. I see that Governor Na-To has already responded. He will appear at one of the witness tables momentarily."

David moved over into the Speaker's chair. Then the Governor appeared at the witness table.

David put on a welcoming smile and flooded the room with good will.

"Governor Na-To. Welcome. I am Da'Vit Wa'Ton, newly assigned Speaker of the Central Council. As you may know, the Confederation's founding documents specify that the Ancient assigned to oversee the Confederation is the designated Speaker, a job that he can assign to another councilor. The corruption within the Confederation has finally reached a level where we needed to reassert ourselves. Four of the previous councilors have been indicted on corruption charges. Those seats are vacant. Councilor Vi-Ko has nominated you for one of those seats. Councilor, will you please tell the Governor why you nominated him."

...

When Vi-Ko finished, the Governor said, "Thank you, my friend. And thank you, Ancient One, for considering me."

"As we are still early in the term for this seat, I will appoint a temporary councilor. A special election will be scheduled to choose a replacement for the remainder of the term. I have two questions for you. Would you like to fill this temporary position? And if so, why?"

"Yes, I would like to fill this temporary position. I want to do this for the very reason Councilor Vi-Ko stated. I want to root out the corruption and restore balance, and I think my work as a governor has prepared me in a unique way."

Michael noticed the way David was looking at the Governor. Apparently, his conversion gave him tremendous power to read other's minds.

David turned to Michael with a hint of a smile. "I would like a few words of advice on this nomination from each of the Councilors. Mi-Ku, please start."

"I am in favor."

The remaining three said the same.

"Councilor Na-To, welcome to the Central Council. You will be assigned to this seat on my right."

The room reconfigured and the new Councilor appeared in the designated seat.

"Admiral Jo-Na is here. Please enter, Admiral."

A door opened and the Admiral walked to the witness table and took a seat. He had come in person.

David quickly repeated the same process and asked the same questions.

"I am a patriot. If this is where I'm needed for service, then this is where I will serve. But I'm not an expert on the law. Is it permissible for the Head of the High Command to have a seat on the Central Council? My understanding has been that it's not."

"The founding documents allow it but restrict it to times of emergency. My presence here is the Ancients' declaration of a state of emergency. This provision has been invoked three times in the past. I invoke it now."

"Then yes. I want to serve and want to do so for a simple reason. The Confederation has been on a path to civil war. I believe your presence will stop it. And I believe I can help you in that quest."

David smiled. His pleasure with the Admiral's response leaked to all present. He indicated a chair on his left. "Welcome to the Central Council. This will be your seat."

The process repeated for Ambassadors Fe-Va and Ja-Fa.

...

"I now open this session for normal business. I have one, maybe two items. Are there other items that need to be discussed?"

Admiral Jo-Na raised his hand.

"Admiral?" David yielded the floor.

"The moon known as the Rock was destroyed in a great calamity last night. We do not understand the cause yet, but the planet simply fell apart into a jumble of debris. It has already started spreading and will soon be an asteroid belt around its parent.

"The Rock was the primary center of operations for the Department of Military Intelligence. And it housed the restoration chambers for the vast majority of Ascendants working as spies for the Inspector. Much of the so-called rot in the Confederation originated on the Rock. I think this one event alone will take us a long way toward your goal."

"Agreed," David replied. "The Rock fell under the judgement of the Ancients. The sentence was carried out last night. Are there other items of business we should tend to today?"

Michael raised his hand.

"Mi-Ku, please."

"We had to suspend the trading activities at the heart of our 'Spread the Prosperity' program after the recent events on Togarotu. We would like to re-engage as quickly as possible. The main source of piracy within the Confederation now seems to come from Fleet ships gone rogue. Is there anything we can do to stop this?"

All eyes turned to Admiral Jo-Na.

"I would like to do two things. The first is reinstate the old transponder system. This is under way. I will send an order to all ships forbidding them from interdicting ships with transponders still in use elsewhere in the Confederation.

"I would also like to begin a purge. Too many of our captains have sworn an oath to the Military Intelligence organization. I do not have the authority to prosecute such individuals. I hereby request it."

"Is there anyone opposed to such a resolution?" David asked.

"Hearing none, I declare unanimous consent. A document appeared in David's hand. "Please pass this to the Admiral. Here are new orders for you in your role as head of the High Command."

"Thank you, Mr. Speaker."

"Are there other issues anyone would like to raise?"

"May I ask what happened to your predecessor?" It was the question all the councilors wanted to know the answer to, but the Admiral was the only one with the courage to ask.

"You called him the Ancient Sentient. We know him as So'Gen La'Hoya. He is truly one of the greats among us. He was the one that championed your cause, the one that convinced us to come to your aid all those years ago. And he has been with you for over 2 million years, which is a long time even by our standards. But he needed rest.

"He knew what needed to be done here, and no longer had the strength to do it. So, I was appointed to take his place for a period of time. He will eventually return. But for now, you have me. And together we will cleanse and restore the Confederation."

"Are you sure it can be done?" The Admiral asked hopefully.

David let the question hang there for a moment.

"Later today, I will be releasing evidence packages on 200 people associated with the Office of Military Intelligence. Admiral, you will be receiving several for officers under your command.

"This will be a test of sorts. If the people in question are prosecuted, then we will be on a good path. If not, I will enquire why. If they are acquitted, I will similarly inquire why.

"You see, there will be a cleansing. Preferably it will be done by you, the peoples of the Confederation. If it is not, then I will do it, as I did on the Rock. But let me warn you. If it takes too long, or I grow tired of it, then another will come. And that one will come with a torch."

...

Despite the worrisome comment at the end, Michael felt good about what they'd accomplished today. Fe-Va agreed to connect with him later in the afternoon to see how they could re-start the 'Spread the Prosperity' program. So, Michael decided to head over to Eugene and Kelly's lab to see what new miracle they'd come up with.

EUGENE AND KELLY'S LAB

"Michael, welcome. I didn't expect to see you so soon." Kelly bubbled with excitement.

"I got a note from Eugene this morning. He said that you were working on a proof of concept that I might find interesting. I had an unexpected break in my schedule this morning, so thought I'd go for a walk."

"Well, we've discovered something truly incredible. I've been beating my head against the wall on this one for a year now. I surrendered and gave it to Eugene a week or so back and bingo, he came up with a solution."

"Don't count yourself short, Kelly. You may have been working on this a while, but with everything else you've produced this year, it's hard to believe there was much time left for this one."

"Point taken, but Eugene really does have more horsepower than I do for problems like this."

Eugene came walking in.

"Michael, welcome. I didn't expect to see you this afternoon."

"So, what's this new proof of concept?"

"Something I'm calling a power tap. Similar in function to a power cube, just a lot more power in a much smaller package that uses a lot less Transluminide."

"And you have a proof of concept?"

"Did."

Kelly snickered.

"What happened?"

"Short answer? It puts out a lot of power. I didn't use heavy enough wire and poof, I melted it. But we have a good video of the whole experiment, even me with a fire extinguisher at the end."

"Before we go there, you said you thought this was big. So far, I'm not hearing that. What am I missing?"

"Ah. Take a look at this." Eugene popped up a picture on the holoprojector. It showed a box made from thousands of layers of laminated metal that was maybe 20 feet on a side. A Lorexian was standing next to it indicating its size.

"This is one of the giant 25-terawatt power cubes that power the Fleet's Capital ships. They use 8 of these to power their way across the intergalactic void. Each of those cubes requires about 2 kg of Transluminide to build."

"I've seen them. They're enormous," Michael confirmed.

"This is what we could replace it with."

Another image popped up, showing a similarly constructed box less than 2 feet on a side.

"This box actually produces more power. It requires less than 10 grams of Transluminide. The big challenge, as I found out today, is getting cables heavy enough to conduct all that power. This is the after image."

An image popped up of Eugene with an old-fashioned CO_2 fire extinguisher, spraying the deformed metal remains of his box.

Michael sat quietly for a moment. The so-called Transluminide Economy really boiled down to unlimited, free electricity. If there was a way to get thousands of times more electricity using less Transluminide, then it would, as Eugene had said in his email, change everything.

"What can you tell me about this technology Eugene?"

"We have been using the Transluminide directly to generate electricity. One atom of Transluminide produces 1 electron per millisecond, or some number like that. That electron is essentially coming from another dimension that is electron rich. The Transluminide is what pulls it across the barrier.

"This device creates a selective field that punches a hole into that dimension allowing a torrent of electrons to pour through. The controls allow us to regulate the size of the hole. We know how to do that in principle. My first trial allowed too much through, causing the field that forms the pipe to collapse.

"But proof of concept for the power tap idea is a success. At this point we can tap into immense amounts of power using only the smallest amount of Transluminide. The next hurdle will be making failsafe controls. But it's a low hurdle. Human technology has been making power controls for decades. It's the Power Tap that's new here."

"How long before you have something we can take to market?"

"Weeks, maybe months. Not years."

"Incredible." A pause. "Changing the subject, how is the project with Lisette going?"

Eugene smiled. "She came up with a halfway decent idea. It didn't take long to turn it into something impenetrable to anyone that doesn't have the technology. Kelly and I have a couple pieces of equipment we need to make for her. We were actually supposed to be working on that this week. But when the solution for the power tap came to me Sunday night, I kind of got distracted."

Michael stood. "Eugene, Kelly. Thanks again for all your work. At the moment, we have an abundance of Transluminide. So, I'd appreciate it if you prioritized your work with Lisette.

"But we won't have that abundance forever. So, the Power Tap will be critical to securing the future for Earth and the Confederation as a whole. Please keep me posted."

...

Once Michael was gone, Kelly asked, "Did Michael's reaction seem a bit odd to you?"

"How so?"

"Most of our stuff, he wants immediately. This, probably the biggest thing we will ever do, ends with a 'Keep me posted?' It's as if he wants to keep this in reserve for now or something."

"Maybe. He said there was an abundance of Transluminide at the moment."

"Well, I think something's up," Kelly announced, bringing the discussion to a close.

EAS MUMBAI

The trip back to Earth had been a bit surreal. Her little ship held a million kilograms of pure Transluminide ingots and over 1,000 kilograms of unprocessed wonder stones. And they were being escorted back by two giant cruisers that dwarfed her ship. They'd just passed the orbit of Mars and were now on final approach.

"We were just hailed by Space Force Command. They are asking to speak with you, ma'am."

"Thanks, Rani. Please put them on."

The image of Admiral Scott appeared on the forward view screen.

"Lt. Cmdr. Parikh, welcome home."

"Thank you, Admiral Scott."

"You've received your unloading instructions?"

"Yes, sir."

"Excellent. Word should have reached you about arrangements for leave."

"It did. Thank you, sir."

"Excellent, we will see you at the debrief meeting at 2:00."

"Thank you, sir."

...

Unloading happened in two steps. The first was for the wonder stones. They were transported down to a secure facility in the Space Force technical complex. There they would be unpacked, cut into gemstones, then placed in a secret storage location. The remaining unrefined Transluminide would be transported to one of the alliance worlds for refining.

The second step was underway. A team from Security had transported aboard. Their process was tedious and Bumati was glad they were doing it, not her crew. Each ingot was tested for purity, weighed, stamped with a unique identifier, then loaded onto special grav carts that the security team had brought. The carts were sturdy. Each could hold 100 of the small 100-kg ingots. Once loaded, each cart would be sealed, then transported to a secret location on Earth using a specialized transporter that the security team had brought with them.

It would take the better part of a week to process all 10,000 ingots. Each ingot took about 5 minutes. Five processing lines had been set up on the mining level. Two security people operated each line. The supervisor inspected each processed ingot, then placed it on the cart.

They'd been at it an hour. Sixty ingots sat on the cart. A rotating team would work round the clock, finishing seven days from now.

"Ms. Parikh. I couldn't help but notice the crystals in the claims room on the command deck."

It concerned Bumati that the head of domestic security, Lisette Lefevre was inspecting her ship. "Yes. We need to pull a crystal to validate the claim type. We can't add them to the crates holding the mined material. So we have been gluing them in place in the claims room."

"A practical solution. Are these being logged somewhere?"

"Yes. They're noted in the ship's log which syncs back to Command. They will eventually be removed and processed into jewels. Command has approved this handling of the material."

"Understood. I'm required to file a report when I finish here. Items like this must be included, so it will be. But I'll explicitly call out that there is no suspicion of wrongdoing."

"Will you be staying on the ship?" Bumati asked.

"I'll be spending most of the day here every day until the job is done, but plan to return to the surface for sleep. Same for the processing teams."

"If you should change your mind, we have several spare cabins. The officer on watch or Rani, the ship's AI, can help assign them for you."

"Thank you."

"Will this be the standard process going forward, inspecting and carting on the ship then transporting down?"

"No. We will be setting up a secure facility on the ground. It's not ready yet but will be before too long."

"Well, I'll leave this in your hands. I have meetings at Space Force Command starting in about an hour."

Bumati would be going down shortly. The crew leave rotation would start soon after. Each crew member would get seven days leave over the next ten. And everyone was anxious to set their feet back on the Earth and breathe fresh air.

PRESENCE PROJECTOR, AMBASSADOR'S OFFICE

Michael stepped into the presence projector expecting to see Ambassador Fe-Va, but several others were waiting for him as well.

"Welcome Mi-Ku. I hope you don't mind that I asked some others to join us." Ambassador Fe-Va started quietly.

Already seated were Councilor Mo-Mo from Togarotu and newly appointed Councilor Ja-Fa from Dalfanito, Councilor Ke-Ve from Ardessa in 3A, and Ambassador Va-Mu from Edukatar.

"Gentlemen, an unexpected pleasure to see you." Michael locked eyes momentarily with each, then turned back to Fe-Va.

"Are we here to discuss restarting the program, or is there another purpose?" Michael asked calmly.

"The purpose is primarily the program, but there is the issue of the Ancients, which seems to overshadow everything else."

Michael nodded acknowledgement of the statement but didn't say any more.

"We all suspect that you know more than you've let on. In fact, several of us believe that the newly chosen is the apprentice that we met at the wedding. The one we thought was human."

"And the issue?" Michael replied cautiously.

"Mi-Ku..." Fe-Va started a little exasperated. "We are about to start something very bold and exciting. And something that may be dangerous to each of us and our people. It requires a great deal of trust. Yet, you seem to be holding back. That won't work.

"If we are to continue this process, one we have a lot of hope in, you need to come clean."

There was silence for a second.

"You're right, of course. We are taking on something bold and dangerous, as we have already found out. We risk ourselves and our people, but do so in expectation of great reward.

"And, as you point out, it'll only work if there's trust between us. I'm happy to tell you what I know, but I know a lot less than you probably expect."

Again, a moment of silence.

"Then, let's start there. What do you know about the Ancients?" Fe-Va asked respectfully.

"I was mentored for years by the one you knew as the Ancient Sentient. Over the last two years, he spent a lot of time on Earth, where he went by the name James. I recently learned for the first time his Ancient name, which is So'Gen La'Hoya."

"He told me that he was the last of his kind. A statement that apparently meant something different than I thought it did. If it helps at all, I was called on privately by the new Ancient. The sentinel that accompanies him referred to James in the same way—the last of his kind.

"The new Ancient is the human apprentice that James took. He has gone through a transformation that I know nothing about other than the result. He has all the capabilities of his predecessor, but considerably more power.

"When he called upon me privately, he told me that the Ancients were very unhappy about the corruption that has flourished in the Confederation, and they've decided to take steps to correct it.

"They chose him, turned him into one of them, then gave him the task of cleaning up the Confederation. Their preferred solution would be to simply destroy Andromeda. He has a timeframe, which I do not know, and flexibility.

"He more or less told us that he was the one who destroyed the Rock and that he's the one who called the Inspector and others to judgement."

Michael paused and looked at each of his colleagues.

"I believe that he respects me, but I have no control over him, no means to influence him except when he comes to me and asks for advice. Something he has done twice.

"I've asked him to give us a chance to work our 'Spread the Prosperity' program. His reply was that we should proceed, but it won't work fast enough to satisfy the Ancients. He has a list of targets to take down, but at this point I think it's mostly individuals, not systems, planets, or moons."

Several seconds of silence.

"One other thing. His sentinel scans everyone that comes into his presence. It frequently names the person and species, then declares them as compatible or incompatible. He further declares whether a compatible species is transformed or not transformed.

"Lorexians are not compatible. Humans and Zorossans are apparently compatible. And from what I've come to understand, the Ancients come in two groups, originals and non-originals. Maybe James was the last of the originals."

Michael put his hands out as if to say that was all he knew. And the room broke into chatter.

...

After several minutes, Fe-Va called the meeting back to order.

"Mi-Ku, thank you. It's my sense that the Ancients will not block or take offense to our program. It also seems that we were given explicit permission to proceed at the Council meeting today. Do you agree?"

"I do."

"Then, one more question for you. We know you have ships that can travel quickly across the void. We know that you've come into possession of wonder stones. We also know that you have access to or knowledge of tremendous Transluminide assets.

370

"Can you come clean on that also? We have faith, but we need to know what we're working with."

A moment of silence, then a chuckle.

"My biggest learning on Earth is that nothing stays still for long. I can tell you what I have today and what I see coming in the next couple months. But much of what we have today, we didn't have three months ago.

"What I have now... Approximately 300 ships with intergalactic jump drives, instantaneous travel between about a thousand pairs of destinations along the galactic rims. More pairs seem to come available every day. More ships come available every week.

"Each ship is equipped to defend itself with shields and weapons beyond anything the Confederation has ever imagined.

"The upshot is that we have secure transportation to make the trade deals work."

"The next item is Transluminide. We have a lot. In the process of discovering it, we found several wonder stone deposits that we mined. So, we have a lot of those as well.

"I do not have approval yet, but in short order, maybe this week, we will be announcing a new hard currency backed by 100 thousand kilograms of Transluminide bullion. You might ask, why a currency?

"The answer is simple, efficiency. It will allow us to create restricted use grant and loan programs that will allow underdeveloped worlds access. Access to buy products sold by the developed worlds. Access to Transluminide bullion for use in building out their own infrastructure.

"I have sample grant and loan contracts for discussion, if anyone would like to look at them."

"That's what I have today relevant to the 'Spread the Prosperity' program."

Again, the room erupted into noise, but Michael put his hands up to quiet the room.

"The rate of change here on Earth is mind bending. Consider this. Three months ago, I did not have an intergalactic jump drive, didn't even know such a thing was possible.

"Last week, I had a couple thousand kilograms of Transluminide bullion, more than enough to satisfy Earth, not enough to swing the dial for the sector or the Confederation. I had lots of claims, but no mining ability. Today, I have well over 100,000 kg of Transluminide bullion and expect to have millions more over the next couple weeks.

"The humans move at a speed never seen before. So if you should find out next week that Earth has some other wonder, it's not because I'm holding out. It's because that's what happens here. The Ancient Sentient told me that this is what our ancestors used to be like, which is why he liked it so much here."

"Thank you, Mi-Ku," Fe-Va said, bowing his head in respect. "I think the loan and grant programs are vital to our project's long- and short-term success. I would like to look at them before we wrap up today.

"But before we go there, I'd like to propose adding those present to the management team for the project. I'm already at my limit as I know you are."

"I'm good with that."

"Then let's move on to discuss next steps."

...

Two hours later, Michael emerged from the presence projector more optimistic about the Confederation's future than he'd been in a long time.

HEADQUARTERS, SPACE FORCE COMMAND

Bumati was once again sitting in Admiral Scott's outer office, getting increasingly nervous as the minutes ticked away. Finally, the door opened. It was the Admiral. She popped up at attention and saluted.

The Admiral acknowledged.

"Lt. Cmdr. Parikh, please come in." He indicated the conference table area at the far end of the office.

As she came in, she saw Michael, the Secretary and President Lee at the table.

She took the open chair opposite them, noticing several documents face down on the opposite side of the table.

"First, congratulations on the success of your mission."

He turned one of the documents over and slid it across the table.

"This commendation will be added to your file. It is rare that we get to issue ones like this."

She took a moment to look at the document, but in truth couldn't process it.

"This commendation allows us to do something that usually is only done during war time, giving you another promotion, skipping a rank after only a month on the job. Congratulations, Captain Parikh."

He pushed a small box containing a pair of gold captain's bars across the table to her.

"The last item is a bit unusual."

He pushed the last document across the table to her.

"This is an amendment to the standing orders that apply to your ship. It basically allows you discretion to maintain a collection of samples on your ship. This is functionally the agreement we've had in place. We are making it formal to avoid misunderstanding."

"Thank you, sir. The leader of the security team that transported aboard the ship, already asked me about the collection of samples glued onto the shelf in the Claims room. This will make discussions like that less awkward."

Michael spoke up.

"Captain Parikh, on behalf of the Earth and 3F Alliances I want to thank you for your work. These finds are ushering in a new age of prosperity for Earth, our sector and the entire Confederation."

VALERIE JENSEN'S APARTMENT

It had been over a week since Valerie had heard from David and she desperately missed him. She had tried calling him, even went looking for him at his apartment, but nothing. It wasn't like him to be distant like this and the anxiety of his absence increasingly wore on her.

Her communicator sounded. Picking it up, she saw no source listed. She started to put the communicator down, then thought better of it.

"Hello."

"Hi Valerie. It's David. I miss you."

"David. Where are you?" It was all she could do to maintain her composure.

"I've been called away. James is ill and I had to help him."

"Where did you go?"

"We're in interdimensional space, near New Lorexi. In a place where we can rest and be restored."

"When will you come home?"

"I don't know, but it will be a while. The Ancients have given me a job to do. I can't really come back before it's done. But I miss you."

TEMPLE OF THE ANCIENTS

"*Da-Vit Wa-Ton, you have returned.*"

David sensed the presence of the non-originals collective.

"Yes. Have you had success assembling the evidence packages?"

Assembling the evidence packages was a tedious job. David had been at it for days when the non-originals collective had offered to help yesterday. His original goal was only 100. Yesterday, they'd promised to assemble another 100 for him by this evening.

"Yes. This turned out to be interesting and stimulating work. Several of the other collectives pitched in as well. We have well over 1,000 packages at this point. We have even prioritized them for you."

David was speechless.

"Would you like to view our biggest offender?"

Before David could reply, the images started flashing by. He was shocked by the depravity of what he saw.

"Terrible, isn't it. Maybe now you understand why several of the original's collectives want to burn it all."

"I want to review these before they're sent out."

"Good idea. We've provided several recipient options for each."

"Ah. I see that. This one is recommended to go to the planetary governor and his chief prosecutor. Are those two clean?"

Again, David heard something he could only describe as a laugh track.

"No one is clean. But all the recommended recipients are clean enough."

"OK. Send the first one."

CHAPTER 29: ANNOUNCEMENTS

Two weeks later...
[Thursday, 08.22.2032] EARTH ALLIANCE BANK

The third delivery of ingots had arrived earlier this morning, carried in on the EAS Petra. The first cart of 100 ingots had just been received into the bank's new secure storage system, bringing its inventory up to 20,100. By the end of the week, that number would grow to 30,000.

Today 1,000 of those ingots would be audited in a very public way. The serial numbers for the ingots had been provided to the auditors and would become available to the public when the audit was complete. The auditors would be confirming the existence, weight and purity of the ingot associated with each serial number. The ingots would back the issuance of the first one-million Trade Alliance (TA) dollars. Over the course of the year, more audits would be done as required to support the growth of the money supply. Today was the first.

Nelly had just received word that the auditors were ready to begin.

...

A small crowd had gathered in the vault room. Three auditors, selected by the Alliance's three largest sponsors, stood in front of the vault. Three news crews from around the world, and two from other worlds, clustered outside the roped off area, waiting for the reveal. Nelly emerged from a side door and walked to a podium 15 feet in front of the vault door. Recording lights came up amidst a flurry of camera flashes.

"Thank you. Today is a momentous day. The Earth Alliance in partnership with the Confederation Trade Alliance is launching a new currency for the purpose of simplifying trade. Although this will help all members of our expanded trade alliance, it will disproportionly help the small, less developed members of our Alliance, those who do not have the trading volume to otherwise participate.

"The new Confederation Trade Alliance dollar, or TA dollar as we refer to it, is a hard currency. Every dollar issued can be exchanged for 100 grams of Transluminide bullion. Today, we will create 1 million TA dollars, backed by 100,000 kilograms of Transluminide bullion. The bullion will be presented as 1,000 ingots of 99.999% pure Transluminide, each 100 kg.

"Our auditors will confirm the number, mass, purity, and markings of each ingot. When they are done and the ingots have been returned to the vault, the TA dollars will be created."

"Ms. Hayley McCrae, chief auditor with the Canadian Central Bank, the Bank of Canada, will lead the team of auditors today. Ms. McCrae has a few words to share with you about the process before they begin.

"Ms. McCrae." Nelly yielded the floor.

...

Some hours later, the process finished, the vault doors closed, the ingots were distributed back to their resting places in another dimension, and a million new TA dollars came into existence.

ABOVE CORE WORLD 1A2-C

David made no attempt to hide his arrival flash. His work here would be short. Over the last two weeks the Confederation had been shaken by the number of arrests made among their senior officials. In every case, the evidence was overwhelming. In a hand full of cases, some of the evidence was leaked, leading to a great outcry of anger from the masses. Many of the core worlds experienced civil unrest for the first time in millennia.

But things on the world below him had gone differently. None of the cases here had been prosecuted. Several people on his top 1,000 list had fled here and found shelter. Today, all those people and the judge that had blocked the prosecution would die of 'natural' causes. And each would have a data chip in their possession containing the evidence.

David had come under pressure from one of the original's collectives to simply burn the world. David argued that the lives of millions should not be extinguished because of the crimes of a few.

SUPREME COURT, CORE WORLD 1A2-C

Senior Justice, Ka-Lo, of the planetary Supreme Court was not a happy person. Despite his earlier refusals to hear any of the phantom cases, one was on the docket today. Prosecutors had independently verified enough of the evidence that had mysteriously appeared, that his refusal of the case had been overruled. Today, the prosecutors would present their case to a panel of judges.

Ka-Lo's argument was simple. The evidence was inadmissible. It had originated off world, and the chain of custody, evidentiary requirements had not been fulfilled.

The case had been called. It was his turn to ask a question. He knew the accused was guilty, but he'd sworn an oath to protect the Inspector's allies from prosecution. The tactic today would be to attack the integrity of evidence being presented.

Senior Justice Ka-Lo opened his mouth to begin but could not draw a breath. After 30 seconds of increasing panic, his racing heart stopped. An hour later, the medical examiner listed the cause of death to be myocardial infarction. Massive blood clots had formed in both the arteries and lungs. Nanobot therapy administered on site was insufficient to clear the circulatory system in time. Tragic, but not exceptional among males his age.

The only curiosity found was the medical alert data chip in his pocket. It was scanned when he was received at the hospital. Chips like these were encoded with data about existing medical conditions. Doctors were required to scan them when a new patient came into emergency. This one contained information about the judge's crimes and was turned over to the police.

ASCENDANT VAULT, CORE WORLD 1A2-C

An alarm went off in the vault's control room.

"We have a restoration chamber malfunction!"

"Problem?"

"Overheating power cell."

"What? I've never heard of such a thing."

The two technicians were in a control room that sat above the main floor of the vault, environmentally separated from it by a thick pane of glass. As the lights in the vault came up, they spotted the malfunctioning unit immediately. Smoke was wafting up from it.

"We need to eject the ascendant and shut the unit down."

"Deactivating. Send a bot."

"Bot on its way."

"Oh no. The unit is not responding."

Smoke started pouring out.

They watched helplessly as the bot approached the unit and started dispensing fire retardant. It pushed the emergency eject button, but the door did not open. Grabbing the lid, the bot forced the door up. Air rushed into the super-heated chamber and a fraction of a second later, a huge billow of flames blew out, knocking the bot over.

...

It took nearly a week for the vault to be restored to operation. Despite all the drama, only one Ascendant was hurt, its remains charred beyond recovery. A data chip was found on its avatar. The chip contained extensive evidence of its Ascendant's crimes.

EUGENE AND KELLY'S LAB

"Activating power tap in 3, 2, 1... Power."

Kelly was at the controls; Eugene was on the instrumentation.

"100-watt load. Holding steady."

Getting control over the power tap had been harder than Eugene expected. Nadia had been the one to solve it.

"Told you it would work," her disembodied voice teased.

Kelly looked at Eugene. "Ready to ramp up to 1,000."

Eugene wanted to wait a bit. The last time they tried this, they lost control. But unlike their first prototype, this one had a failsafe circuit breaker in it, so the experiment would shut down instead of catching on fire.

"Still waiting." Kelly whined.

"Ramp it up."

"Increasing to 1,000 watts in 3, 2, 1... Ramp."

Today's test bench used a heating coil to heat water. The water was in a 10-gallon glass jar with a magnetic stir stick whirling away at the bottom. The coil had heating capacity up to 10,000 watts.

"Power meter reads 1,000 watts. Water temperature is moving up faster. Voltage and current are rock steady."

"Ready to go to 10,000 watts?" Kelly asked excitedly.

Eugene rolled his eyes. He preferred testing that moved a little slower.

"What the heck?"

Nadia chuckled at Eugene's reluctance.

"Increasing to 10,000 watts in 3, 2, 1... Go."

Eugene had pulled the fire extinguisher closer during the count down.

"Power steady at 10,000 watts. But we're getting big thermal gradients forming in the water. We need a better test set up for power levels this high."

The water around the coil was boiling rapidly, even though sensors near the surface showed water temperature at 85°C.

"Power is holding steady." Eugene called out. "But let's shut it down. I don't want to melt the heating coil."

...

"So, where to next with this?" Nadia asked. "I would think the apps for this power density would be in gigawatt range ship propulsion and shielding."

"Agreed," Eugene replied. "But we really need failsafe controls before putting it on a ship. The Confederation has had over a million years to get the controls right on their power cubes. They are amazingly safe devices. These have orders of magnitude higher power density and are intrinsically less stable, which makes them much more dangerous.

PRESENCE PROJECTOR, AMBASSADOR'S OFFICE

Michael entered the presence projector to the familiar comfort of the Admiral's mountain cabin. A call had not been scheduled, rather he'd been messaged asking if he had a minute.

"Mi-Ku. Thank you for connecting with me. Odd happenings on 1A2-C today. Many of the Inspector's people have fled there. A judge was functionally giving them asylum."

"What happened?"

"So far, none of the 26 evidence packages sent to that planet have led to prosecutions. Today, the judge who had been blocking the prosecutions died of a heart attack. All 26 people died as well. Some in accidents, others of seemingly natural causes. And all of them carried a medical alert data chip that held evidence of crimes instead of medical alert data."

"Let me guess, the data chips were scanned in the hospitals and the data has leaked?"

"Exactly. Your human Ancient is very clever."

"That is undoubtedly true, but you might not want him to hear you say, or even think, that."

"Point taken."

A pause.

"He provided me with evidence against 32 of my officers. It all checked out. Most confessed when confronted with it. A couple confessed before being confronted. I'm actually starting to think they're under my command again."

"How have your trade runs been going?"

"The Alliance is expanding. We're up to 21 members. We've made our third run to 3A, and now have a standing schedule for three runs a week to 2B.

"We've been contacted by several worlds in Andromeda that want to join. Even more in the less populated sectors here and in Triangulum."

"Congratulations my friend."

"Sadly, I need to go. I'll see you at the Central Council meeting tomorrow."

TEMPLE OF THE ANCIENTS

David was back in the Temple. He tried not to move, not to think. There wasn't the same grief as when he'd destroyed the Rock. Two weeks of constant purge numbed him. He just felt cold, empty.

He felt a presence approach. It was enormously old.

"We, the original Ancients, are much older than you know. One of the other collectives told you that the Confederation was not the first to come under judgement. It is far from the first. There have been hundreds. Most survived the purge and now thrive.

"The purge usually hurts the judge more than the judged. All of us have been judges. We know your hurt. But take comfort in the knowledge that you are handling this well."

The presence receded and David fell into a dreamlike state.

Chapter 30: DESTINY

Michael entered the presence projector excited for today's Central Council meeting. It was the first one he'd looked forward to in years. After the first meeting two and a half weeks ago, David had put them on a regular schedule until the crisis was resolved. This would be their fourth meeting under David's speakership.

...

David called the session to order. "Quite a few items on the agenda. I'd like to start with an update on the Fleet purge. Admiral?"

"Thank you, Ancient One. The lists you provided included 31 admirals and captains, 19 other senior officers. All but three of the admirals and captains are being court martialed, several on capital charges. The three not being court marshalled have been dishonorably discharged with reduced rank and pension. Twelve of the senior officers are being court martialed, three on capital charges. The other seven have received dishonorable discharges with reduced pension.

"A number of things became clear in this process. The most glaring has been the lax enforcement of orders. Far too many officers do not enact any discipline when their orders are not followed. We are starting a retraining process that all officers will be required to pass. Those that don't will be stripped of rank.

"The second most glaring item is the dilapidated condition of our ships. Lax standards have led to undermaintained ships that are not mission worthy. A review is in process that will likely result in disciplinary action against many more officers."

"Questions or comments?" David asked.

Mo-Mo indicated that he wanted to speak.

"Councilor Mo-Mo."

"I'm thinking that we should reconsider the role of the Fleet. I don't have a specific proposal, just the thought that the Fleet is much less relevant to the Confederation than it's been in the past.

"Its ships are obsolete. Their defensive power is still stronger than ships from most non-aligned worlds. But the operative word there is most. My superficial take is that we would be better off with collaborating Defensive Alliances than one large, centralized fleet. It would take years and enormous resources to restore the Fleet to its former glory.

"Maybe we could use the Fleet differently. It still has much to offer. But the Fleet of old no longer seems relevant."

Michael could see the sadness in his friend's eyes. Jo-Na had inherited a mess and generally agreed with Mo-Mo's assessment of the state of the Fleet.

"Thank you for those thoughts, Councilor. I mostly agree with your assessment." David nodded to Mo-Mo, then turned to the Admiral.

"Admiral Jo-Na, I see that you agree with at least some of the Councilor's points. I don't want to drive this any further today. But could you give some thought to this? Maybe come back to us with some alternatives for us to consider regarding the role and equipping of the Fleet."

Jo-Na bowed his head in respect. "I will do as you ask."

"Thank you." David turned to Councilor Fe-Va. "Fe-Va, please give us an update on the Trade Alliance."

"The Trade Alliance has grown significantly over the last two weeks. We've added 18 new members in the Milky Way, 10 in Triangulum. And our systems are getting good enough to take on members in Andromeda when you're ready to open it to us."

David turned to the Admiral. "Are you confident at this point that the Trade Alliance can operate safely in Andromeda?"

"I am confident that there are no more rogue Fleet ships in the core worlds. The rest of Andromeda may be safe as well, but I cannot say that with the same level of confidence."

David turned to Fe-Va, then Michael. "Would you be willing to start with a policy that explicitly allowed you to defend yourselves?"

Michael took the lead on the question. "I'm sure Space Force would consider doing some initial runs to test the waters."

David turned back to Fe-Va. "Then you have my approval to start trade at your discretion."

David turned to Michael. "Councilor Mi-Ku, could you give us an update on your currency, grant, and loan programs."

Michael smiled broadly. "The TA dollar is already a success. Large trade partners really don't need to use it, but most have. The smaller trading partners really can't participate without it. They don't have the collateral trade or Transluminide bullion reserves.

"We have already expanded the money supply to 10 million TA dollars, backed by a million kilograms of bullion in our vaults. And we have the reserves to expand it further as required.

"We have issued our first four grants, totaling 4,000 TA dollars. And are working approvals on the first loans. This is a game changer for the smaller, less developed worlds."

"Truly!" Fa-Va pitched in.

"Excellent." David nodded, then paused for a moment.

"I have several proposals I'd like to bring to a vote today. The first regards the formal dissolution of the Department of Military Intelligence. We still have over 12 million people and numerous facilities assigned to that department. A committee of Ancients has drafted an asset distribution program for our consideration.

"This distribution program is not something we are imposing on you, simply a suggestion offered for your consideration and amendment.

"My proposed resolution simply requires that we take up this topic, assign committees as necessary, and bring forward a recommendation for distribution of assets within the next month."

A copy of the resolution and plan appeared in front of each Councilor.

Michael quickly read through the resolution. "I move that we adopt the resolution as presented."

"Second," Admiral Jo-Na called out.

"Would anyone like to make a motion against the resolution."

David paused.

"Hearing none, I call the vote."

All hands went up.

"The resolution is approved. Admiral Jo-Na will take the lead on moving this forward."

The Admiral nodded his agreement.

"My next item relates to the earlier discussion of the Fleet. It is a formal request to the Earth and 3F Alliance for a plan to start making your ships available to other worlds.

"The Confederation charter allows us to compel the Earth Alliance to do this, but the list of requirements for such compulsion is long and tedious. Therefore, I'd like to start the discussion by asking the Earth Alliance to come forward with a set of terms under which they would do this without being compelled."

Michael indicated his desire to reply.

"Mi-Ku?"

"This is a big ask of a new member, one that has been relentlessly attacked by its allies for several years."

"A new member that has had the blessing of an Ancient since before the first attack."

The two locked eyes long enough to draw the attention of the other councilors.

"New members, nonetheless. I will raise the issue, but caution that this is a big ask."

David smiled. "Perhaps. But one you will see the wisdom of soon."

David held Michael's gaze for several seconds. "I will not press this issue at this time.

"The next issue I would like to raise is the cleansing. It is far from complete, but the worst is behind us. I will continue to hold my seat on the council until So'Gen La'Hoya returns, but I am no longer compelled to hold the Speaker's chair. I will reclaim it if I must. But I exercise my right to assign it for now.

"Mi-Ku. I choose you as the next Speaker of the Central Council. Do you accept this responsibility? It is the one you've been groomed for."

All eyes shifted to Michael, who was slow to reply. David's announcement took him by surprise.

"I will serve as I have been chosen to serve." Michael bowed his head low in respect.

"Then, so be it. You know the agenda, and you know the Ancients' intentions in this matter."

TEMPLE OF THE ANCIENTS

David returned to the Temple. It was still in Central Council Plaza and throbbed with intensity as he entered. Crowds were still drawn to it but those present stepped back a bit as the steady beat increased.

David retreated into a quiet place within and allowed its energy to fill him. His work here was mostly done. There was only one more thing he needed to do before he could go home, but he needed restoration before he would take it on.

...

"Da'Vit Wa'Ton."

David stirred from his dreamlike state feeling surprisingly refreshed, and immediately recognized the presence of the Judges collective.

"We perceive that your work is done. You have brought what So'Gen La'Hoya started to a successful close. There is little hierarchy here, but you now stand honored among us. When the time comes, you will be welcome to join our collective, as you will certainly be welcome to join any of the others."

"Thank you," David sent back.

As the Judges' presence receded, David roused himself. It was time!

CENTRAL COUNCIL PLAZA

Through the afternoon, the crowd had grown, drawn by the crystal's rhythmic pounding. Suddenly, the Ancient appeared with Ma-Ka the warrior next to him. And the crystal dimmed.

"People of the Confederation. My work here is done. Soon, we will retreat to our place of rest. We wish you peace and prosperity."

Just as David was going to flash into energy, he saw the sentinel scan someone who had stepped close to the outer rope, but he made no announcement.

Looking at the person that had come forward, David saw that it was an odd-looking young boy. Then, understanding dawned. The child was of mixed blood. His mother was Lorexian, his father human.

How?

David stepped toward the child, inextricably drawn by its outstretched hand. He knelt and instinctively took the child's hand, causing the child to flash into a small cloud of energy.

"Come back to me, Jo-Ku," David whispered.

The child returned to his natural form.

"Jo-Ku, you are blessed with a great gift. I must go now but will return to teach you."

David saw Ma-Ka scan someone else and knew immediately that it was the child's mother, rushing forward in a panic to retrieve her son.

"Ma-Na. Lorexian. Incompatible species. You are forbidden to approach the Temple of the Ancients."

David held up his other hand. "Ma-Ka, she may approach."

David looked at the mother. "When I let go of his hand, Jo-Ku will fall into a deep sleep. Converting as he did will have drained a great deal of energy. I will return to train him."

Then looking at Jo-Ku. "Promise me that you will not do that again before I return." David pushed compulsion to obey.

"I will not." Little Jo-Ku promised.

"The same thing happened to me when I was a little older than you. I will return to train you, but I must go now."

Looking to Ma-Na. "Please take him. He will fall asleep immediately. It may be a full day before you can rouse him, but do not fear. He is safe."

David released the child's hand, and Jo-Ku fell into his mother's arms.

There was a flash of light and the Temple was gone.

FORBIDDEN PLANET

The crystal reappeared in the place where it had been when David first saw it. David emerged as a cloud of brilliant light, then coalesced into his human form. The small koala-like creatures came forward to greet him.

The sentinel appeared next to him.

"Sentinel. I release you from my service. Guard the Temple."

"David Washington, you will always be welcome here."

VALERIE JENSENS APARTMENT

Valerie sat at the counter in her kitchen. The sun had just set, the last of its light draining from the sky. David had been gone for nearly three weeks and the despair of her life before they'd met was settling back over her.

There was a flash of light outside, bright enough to be noticeable in the kitchen. She turned to see what happened, then heard a knock on her door.

Slowly, she got up to answer, wondering who would come to her place unannounced. She opened the door and saw David standing there.

Heart pounding, she stepped into his outstretched arms, tears flowing. "I missed you."

"Missed you too, but I'm back now. My work is done."

EPILOGUE

SPACE FORCE MEDICAL FACILITY

Daniel was back in the hospital, his anemia now dangerously severe. The doctors would not answer him directly, but Daniel was so weak, he knew he must be close to death.

There was a flash of light and David appeared.

"Admiral Porter, word just reached me of your condition. I wish I'd known sooner."

David placed his hand on Daniel's healed arm and released some diagnostic nanobots into Daniel's blood. Within moments, David knew the problem. He'd released a huge hoard of reconstructive nanobots into Daniel's system to heal him in the short time they had to evacuate. A surprising number had survived the healing process and had moved on to upgrade many of Daniel's other sub-clinical issues. Their best source of energy was Daniel's red blood cells.

David sent a command, triggering the nanobots to exit Daniel's system. Within minutes, white smoke could be seen rising off Daniel's body.

David heard the door open, but his concentration was on his patient.

"Who are you?" It was Dr. Dylan Shaw, Daniel's attending physician.

"The Admiral needs an immediate transfusion."

"What are you doing?" Dr. Shaw just noticed the white smoke rising up from beneath his still patient's sheets.

Clicking the talk button on his collar, Dr. Shaw called for security.

"Too many reconstructive nanobots were in his system. I'd swarmed them in on Togarotu to save him. Too many were still active. They were consuming his red blood cells. They are exiting now, but he is dangerously anemic and needs a transfusion immediately."

"You are the alien that saved him?"

"Human mostly," David replied.

Seeing that the doctor was not ordering a transfusion, David calmly said, "Order a transfusion." Though calmly said, it was sent with massive compulsion.

"Emergency transfusion." Dr. Shaw sent over the comm.

A minute later, David could hear a nurse coming. He knew she was bringing blood, so flashed away. His work here was done.

EAS MUMBAI

"We will enter the system momentarily, ma'am."

"Thank you, Rani."

This was the eighth and last system on Bumati's list. They'd found Transluminide on all the other systems and she expected to find more here. The finds on the last four were small compared to the first three and her expectations for this one were low. It was at the far limit of the ejecta cone she had forecast from the neutron star merger.

But this system had one interesting characteristic that the others didn't. It was further out in the void between the arms. The Confederation database also speculated that it had originated much further out and was slowly creeping in. So there was a chance it had been in the ejecta cone at one point and had been closer to the neutron star merger than the others. Her calculations suggested a 90% chance that this would be her smallest find, which is why it was the last one on the list. They also gave it a 10% chance of being the largest find, the swing variable being its location at the time of the merger.

"Entering the system ma'am."

"Thank you, Rani."

"Mr. Masami, prepare for a long-distance ghosting scan."

"Yes, ma'am. We'll be in range in 15 minutes."

...

"Scanning now. Putting it on the main view screen."

At max resolution, a small black dot showed against the white backdrop of a Class A, main sequence star.

"No ghosting ma'am."

"What separation did you use?"

"100 kilometers."

"Inch it up to 1,000."

The image slowly changed, but no ghost appeared.

"Sorry, ma'am."

"Let's try one more thing. Open it really wide, a million kilometers."

"Ma'am?"

"Ghosting occurs when you have one scan below the deposit and the other above. So let's open it wide, so there's no doubt we have the planet inside, then narrow it down."

"As you say, ma'am."

It was obvious her science officer wasn't buying her theory, but would do as she requested.

"Scan in place. And there it is. A little bit of ghosting."

"OK, tighten it up. Step the gap down 10,000 km at a time."

"Stepping. This will take a while."

"Can you automate. A step a second?"

"Automating."

The image danced around a bit, then suddenly flashed large, then retreated again.

"Back up!"

After a few moments, the ghosting swelled reaching a peak about three times the size of the planet.

"Looks like we may have another core. Take us in Rani."

AMBASSADORS RESIDENCE

Michael and Sarah sat alone in the kitchen. Julissa was in Timothy's room giving him a bath, the sound of splashing and baby giggles reaching them now and again.

Michael had just told Sarah that he had been appointed Speaker.

"What are the implications of becoming Central Council Speaker?"

"The Speaker's position is like a Prime Minister's position, head of the legislative bodies and executive of the Government."

"You're like the president of the Confederation now?" Sarah asked, clearly not sure she liked the idea.

"That would be the closest analogy in the American system, but the job is different."

"Does that mean you have to move into the Confederation's version of the White House?"

"It's more like 10 Downing, but yes. That's what normally happens."

"Well how's that going to work?"

Michael knew Sarah would be upset when they had this conversation, so had put it off a day in the hope of finding an alternative.

"I don't know. I thought this might happen at some point in the distant future, after the kids were grown and you were an Ascendent. I did not expect it now."

"When are you going to leave?"

"I'm still sorting that out. I'd like to move the Confederation capital here but can't wrap my head around the immensity of it."

"Can James help?"

"James has withdrawn for a while. David has taken his place. He's actually the one that appointed me."

"David?"

"David's transformation is complete. He doesn't have James' personality or experience. But he does have James' knowledge and considerably more power. And he's growing into the role quickly."

"Well. I can't go with you. Timothy is human and decades away from becoming an Ascendant."

"Funny thing," Michael mused. "I assumed that James was grooming me for this job, that Earth would be my last steppingstone, and there would be great celebration when the day finally came.

"I didn't expect it now, and in truth, don't want the job. I'm functionally human at this point and have zero interest in returning to New Lorexi. But it has been thrust upon me and I really cannot turn it down. The Ancients were ready to burn down the Confederation. David brought it back from the brink and handed it to me with the warning that it would be burnt down if I wasn't successful."

"Then move the capital here."

Three months later...
[Thursday, 11.25.2032] CHEF MARCO'S

There were enough Americans living in the Embassy complex that Thanksgiving was a thing. But for the vast majority of its residents, it was just another Thursday. Sarah's parents, Tim and Susan, had come to visit Sarah and the baby for Thanksgiving. Sarah had booked the large upstairs private dining room at Chef Marcos for their Thanksgiving celebration.

Sarah and the baby were running late, so Tim and Susan came over early to greet the other guests. Emmanuel and Bahati arrived shortly after Tim and Susan.

A few minutes later, Ta'Sha and Ka-Tu arrived. Since the wedding, the two of them had been seeing quite a bit of each other.

David and Valerie came in next, escorted up by the Chef himself. "I have pulled a special bottle of champaign for you, one you liked once before."

The chef nodded to one of the waiters who brought two champagne flutes, bubbling with pink effervescence.

Thank you, David sent telepathically. *Do you have the gift I send over earlier?*

"Yes, signal me when you're ready for it." The chef whispered conspiratorially.

"What did he say?" Valerie asked. "I really couldn't hear him."

"That he has something special for us." David smiled.

Michael and Sarah arrived last. Julissa pushed Timothy in his stroller, accompanied by Alexi, who was holding Timothy's favorite toy, the Juufa stuffy.

Once everyone was seated, Michael clinked his glass with his knife then stood. "This has been an amazing year. One that's featured much drama and more than a little change. And from it all, there is much to be thankful for. For me, there is my sweet wife, Sarah; our precious son, Timothy; our adopted family member, Julissa; our friend and protector, Alexi; and of course, all of you. I offer this toast to you with thanks."

A series of other toasts and various expressions of thanks were offered. Only David had yet to say something.

David locked eyes with the Chef. *Please bring the gift.* Then he pushed back his chair to stand.

"I started life well. Had a great family and was mostly surrounded by love. Then the Enemy came, and my life turned into a living hell."

The words hung there for a second.

"Then James found me. Brought me here. Started my training and brought me to the point where I could fulfill my destiny. He also introduced me to Valerie, someone I love with all my heart."

David dropped to a knee. "Valerie, will you marry me?"

"I've been wanting to ask you the same question but know it's not the human tradition. Yes, I'll marry you."

Everyone clapped as David kissed her. A waiter approached with a silver tray. A jeweler's box sat atop. David took the box, presented it to Valerie and opened it. Inside was a gold engagement ring with a 10-carat ruby-red wonder stone.

"Is this what I think it is?" she asked shyly.

"Yes."

"Where did you get it?"

"They're plentiful if you know where to look. This one came from the planet that the Temple of the Ancients calls home."

Another toast was offered to David and Valerie.

"Anyone else?" Michael asked.

"I have something else I'd like to say."

All eyes turned to Sarah. She stood, hand on her belly. "I'm going to have another baby."

After more congratulations and another toast, everyone settled. Then Sarah's father, Tim, stood to offer a blessing on the meal.

As the waiters started filing in with plates of food, there was a flash of brilliant light.

"Is there room for me to join?"

It was James.

THE END

COMING EARLY IN 2021

THE RISE OF DAAN
By
D. Ward Cornell

I was born on a protected world. You'd think that would be a good thing, but in truth, not so much.

The underlying problem is that Protected Worlds are, by definition, marginally habitable ones that can't support a significant population. Worlds on which it's difficult to scrape out a living.

It's not like there aren't any benefits. Protected worlds have the fastest, most reliable network access in the Confederation. All essential services available online are ours for free. I got to attend the best online schools as a kid, and I'm currently studying in the online Electrical Engineering program at the Faraday Institute on New London. It's truly one of the best programs in existence. Few students on the central worlds get to do their studies there. But growing up in a place this isolated, where opportunities are so limited... It's hard to describe how difficult it is.

You might ask why anyone would want to live in such a place. I ask that question all the time. The short answer is that these worlds were given away to anyone that had the means to claim and settle them. A lot of adventurers couldn't resist the opportunity. My grandfather, six generations back, was one of those people.

His name was Jared Daan. He was a rugged individualist who struggled under the boot of government oppression. He leaped at the possibility of escape, of becoming the king of his own world. And, as the idea took hold, he decided he wanted a big one.

He filed a claim for a world that was 1.2 times the diameter of the Earth, the largest one available. When his claim was granted, he named the planet Jaredaan in honor of himself. These days, most people just call it Daan.

Daan is cold and dry. It's located at the far edge of the habitable zone in this system. Its only water comes from the great ice fields at the north and south poles.

Despite the cold, most of us live near the north pole. It's the warmer of the two and has the most easily accessible water.

There's a narrow green zone near the equator that turned green for the first time some years before I was born. My great uncle Herold Daan came up with a scheme to move ice from the poles to the equator. The family granted him a large swath of land along the equator as an incentive to build the system. He spent most of his life doing it. The only green on the planet now belongs to his children.

Most of the rest of the world is desert. It's cold, dry, and barren. Forgive me if I mentioned that already, but for the uninitiated, its more cold, dry, and barren than you can probably imagine.

You might wonder how we survive here. The answer is simple. There are massive deposits of precious metals near the north pole. This was known at the time my ancestor claimed our world. The major mining consortiums also knew of these deposits. They deemed them unprofitable to mine because they were too deep in the ground, and in too deep a gravity well.

They were mostly right. What they failed to understand was the strength of our planet's magnetic field and the magnitude of charged particles in our air. My ancestor was an electrical engineer, apparently an incredibly good one. He came up with a scheme to harness the electricity in the air. It powers our town, the mines, and the rail gun we use to launch our metals into orbit. The metal trade is what powers our economy.

One of the few benefits of being a 'protected world' is that we are guaranteed duty-free trade with every planet in the Confederation. Even though we are far from the nearest populated world, we are one of the lowest cost providers of high-end raw metal for use in space in this sector. We are completely free of taxes and have more or less free access to space because of my ancestor's cleverness.

There are many stories about my ancestral grandfather. He was apparently quite a character, eccentric as well. Many of his sayings are built deeply into our culture, and most involve the number six. Spend a day in town and you're likely to hear them. 'Better to do one thing well than six things poorly.' Or 'better to have six good days than one good week.'

Of his many sayings, there's the one my mother quotes all the time. 'The sixth son of the sixth generation will stand above them all.'

Well, it turns out that I'm the sixth son of the sixth generation. My father, and all his forefathers, were the first son of the great Jared Daan. I was his sixth son. Son of the sixth most direct connection to our founder. My parents gave me the name of my ancestor, Jared Daan. I'm the first to bear that name since the great man passed. My mother says I'm destined for greatness. I think that's crazy talk. But my five brothers hate me for it.

CELEBRATION

I come from a big family. Mother, father and six sons. I've read in history books that colony worlds tend to have large families. Their authors claim that large families were needed to work the land. Children were cheap seasonal laborers, so the more kids, the more economically successful the family would be. It sounds like a reasonable explanation, but it surely doesn't apply here. Our family of eight is one of the largest. Most families only have two kids. Three is considered large.

You might ask why. In some sense the answer's obvious. We live on a marginally habitable world. On worlds like ours, the biggest shortage is food. And unlike the agricultural worlds in the history books, there's little work here that kids can actually do. So generally speaking, large families here are less prosperous. Ours is probably the only large family that's not on assistance.

That's kind of what makes today so crazy. It's my birthday. I've reached my majority, been granted my rights under the colony's charter, and Mom and Dad are throwing me a big party. I'm sixteen years old today.

"Jared? Could you come here for a second, sweetie?"

That's my Mom. Whenever she wants me to do something, she tacks a 'sweetie' on the end. It's always my first clue that she's going to ask me to do something I don't want to do.

"Coming."

I've got to give her credit. She's making more or less all the food for this party. She's rented the community party hall on the second level. My dad and five brothers are up there now getting things set up. My oldest brother, Jonah, is even helping. His wife Esther is here in our apartment, helping Mom get ready.

"Hey, Mom. What do you need?"

"Hi Sweetie. Could you run up to the garden for me? I need a bunch of carrots. I forgot to pick them up yesterday.

"Sure Mom. I'll be back in a few minutes."

ESCALATOR UP TO LEVEL ONE

Our town is named Jaredstown in honor of our founder. There aren't that many places like it. It's located near the north pole and is 3,500 feet underground. The garden is on the top level, level one. Our home is on level three. There are three ways to get up to level one: the elevator, the escalator, and the stairs. I've suffered a little elevator-phobia since the incident last year, so I'm opting for the escalator today. The top 24 levels of our town are connected by escalator. The escalator shaft is isolated from each floor by a pair of double doors. You enter the escalator lobby by coming through the outer doors, then enter the escalator shaft itself by coming through another set of inner doors. This system helps mitigate the flow of heat from floor to floor. The escalators aren't as popular as the elevators, so I make the trip quickly.

THE GARDEN, LEVEL ONE

Level One is where all the surface feeds come down to. The feed of consequence for the garden is the light pipes. The garden uses air, water and electricity of course, but plants and animals both do better when there's natural light available.

Level One is the coolest level in town because of its proximity to the surface. It gets increasingly warmer as you go down. Down at the lowest mining levels, about 6,000 feet down, it's just plain hot. I don't see how people can work down there.

On coming out of the escalator lobby, I turn left toward the garden. It's at the end of a long access way. The power company, where I hope to get my first paying job, is at the other end.

The entrance to the garden is through a pair of glass doors. The doors are closed, as most doors in the colony are, to control air flow. On the other side of the doors is the reception area where customers can pick up orders they've placed.

As I walk in, I see that Nana is on duty.

"Well, if it isn't the birthday boy himself."

"Hey, Nana."

I've been sweet on Nana for years, but she's 18 and I don't have a chance. Still, she's pleasant to think about.

"I have your carrots." She holds up a basket with carrots in it, then sets the basket on the counter. "I'm coming to your party."

That's probably the best news I'll get today.

"Good." I can feel a big goofy smile spreading across my face. "I look forward to seeing you there."

I'm back in the hallway, heading toward the escalator. I have to pass the elevator to get there. It's on the right, so I walk close to the left wall. Elevators creep me out.

As I think I mentioned earlier, I have five brothers that hate me. The two oldest, Jonah and Aaron, have both moved out. Jonah is married and has a couple kids of his own. Aaron works in the mine. He's apparently quite good at it. He has a cheap place on a lower level that's closer to his friends. For the most part these two don't bother me that much anymore. But I still do my best to keep a distance.

The other three, Asher, Seth, and Jude are a different story. They still live at home and take every opportunity to mess with me. Mom clamped down on them after the incident with the elevator that nearly killed me. But they still get in every dig they can.

So, about the elevator incident. Seth, who has a real knack for mechanical things, got the elevator to stop one story below the level our home is on, even though the electronics showed it as arriving on our level. Jude, pretending to be nice to me, offered to take me to the movies, seven levels below. I was standing with my back to the elevator door talking with Jude when the doors slid open. Jude stepped toward the door, saying something like, "We need to hurry. The movie's about to start."

I turned and stepped into oblivion. Thankfully, there was an old fiberboard landing I managed to grab. It was rotten and broke but slowed my fall. I woke up two days later in the hospital.

Seth and Jude were arrested, which they'd apparently expected. Because shortly after arriving at the jail, witness after witness came in to tell the cops that the brothers were not there at the time of the incident. They'd rounded up enough liars to get them off the hook.

As I said before, my brothers hate me.

ESCALATOR TO LEVEL 3

I enter the escalator shaft and start down. I'm maybe a quarter of the way to Level 2 when there is a sudden pressure drop and I hear music. Several people have apparently just come into the shaft. The music sounded like the band warming up for the party. Just as suddenly the music drops, pressure increases, and I hear the voices of the new entrants. By the sound of it, two are going down, one is about to come up. The one coming up steps into view and its Asher. A smile spreads across his face.

"Well, if it isn't the little Runt."

The up and down escalators are about 2 feet apart from each other. He will pass me on the left, so I scooch over to the right as far as I can without scraping against the wall.

As we pass, he leans way over into my side. "Hey, I've got a present for you." I see the fist coming but have no place to go. Red hot pain explodes in my left shoulder. My head hits the wall, seriously scraping my ear. And the carrots go flying.

"Happy Birthday piss ant. Hopefully, this one will be the last."

That's the kind of crap I get all the time.

I scurry to collect the carrots before they get ground up at the bottom of the escalator.

HOME

When I get home, Mom takes one look and knows something happened.

"Why's your ear bleeding? And what happened to these carrots? Did you fall?"

"No. Asher punched me. My head hit the wall of the escalator and I dropped the carrots. He said it was my birthday present."

"Oh, sweetie. I'm so sorry. I'll have your father speak with him."

Can't tell you how many times I've heard that line. I love my Dad. He's a genuinely nice guy, and my mentor. But he's not much of a cop and definitely not a disciplinarian. If he's the one in charge, nothing will happen.

...

There are still a couple hours before the party, so I head back to my room to work on my project.

One of the miracles of the modern Confederation is that the worlds are all connected by what's become known as the exo-net, the internet of interworld communications. It has truly allowed remote places like Daan to have access to first-class education and training. My entire formal education has been done remotely, using online training materials and course work. It allows reasonably smart and motivated people like me to get education that's almost as good as the best universities, and to do it at my own pace.

I have one course left to complete and I need to get it done quickly. My dream job, engineer with the power company, is about to open up. Dad's friend and colleague Levi Grayson is retiring at the end of the month. There are three other candidates for the position, none of which are very good. The company wants to hire me. But I need to have finished my power engineering degree to be eligible.

At the university, where this course is taught live, it takes 12 weeks. When I started the course, I only had 26 days to finish before Mr. Grayson's retirement. I'm done except for the project and I have 5 days left.

My project is kind of cool. It's a bit of an adaptation of my ancestor's technology for energy capture, but for personal use. My ancestor's big idea was to use huge arrays of carbon nanotubes to capture lightning bolts. Configured as a capacitor, nanotube arrays can hold almost as much power as a regular battery of the same size. Well maybe a battery of half the size.

But that's only half of what he did. He added nanotube thyristors to the entry and exit points of the array. Ah, sorry about that. Not that many people know what a thyristor is. They've been around forever, but only people into electrical power have ever heard of them. Thyristors are devices that allow one-way current flow, the direction and duration of which can be controlled electronically. They were discovered in the semiconductor days of prehistory. Now they're made from nanotubes. My ancestor's big idea was to combine types that are useful for short-term energy storage with the types used in control circuits.

Why hadn't anyone else figured this out? Well, I'm sure they did, but to what end? This is one of those things that's only a competitive solution in super-high current flow applications, like capturing lightning strikes.

But back to my school project, my device is a capacitor made from nanotubes, both types. I can store enough energy in a 1-inch cube to power most personal electronics for a couple days. It can be charged from any source. Anything from electrostatic shocks, like you get when shuffling your feed on the carpet, to just plugging it in the wall. But, unlike regular batteries that take hours to charge, these can charge more or less instantly given the right power source, two minutes max with standard Confederation household power distribution. Plug it in, come back two minutes later, and bingo! A full charge.

I plan to finish the design this afternoon, well probably tonight given the party this afternoon. Tomorrow, I'll fabricate one. Dad has access to everything I need. The next day, I'll file my project.

PARTY

Commotion in the kitchen breaks my concentration. Looking at the clock, I see that the party is going to start in a few minutes. The last two hours seemed to have just vanished.

I save my work, jot down a note on where to restart tonight, then get up to go see what's going on.

"Hey, Mom. Need any help?"

She smiles at me. "No, sweetie. We've got it covered. Except for this cart, your dad, Jonah, and Esther just took the last of the food and supplies up. I can push this last cart. Unless you want to go up the elevator with me."

The thought of the elevator makes my blood pressure spike.

Mom shakes her head. "You know you're going to have to come to terms with the accident someday. They won't give you the power job if you won't take the elevator to the surface."

I deflate a bit. "OK. I'll go with you."

She smiles. "Good." I get a hug and kiss on the top of my head.

"Hurry up and change, we need to leave."

...

As the elevator doors open, I can hear the music and a lot of noise. It seems the party is well underway. I push the cart slowly in the direction of the sound, Mom coaxing me to go a little faster. As we round the last corner, I see that the doors to the community party hall have been propped open and there must be a hundred people inside. The band is playing some kind of swing music and people are already up dancing.

"Over here."

I turn and see my dad talking with Mr. Grayson, the older man who's job I am going to be taking. They each have a pint of beer in their hand.

I redirect the cart his way as Dad steps toward me.

"I can take that from here."

Dad hands me his beer, and he takes the cart. I'm waiting for the standard admonishment not to drink any.

"Your 16 today. You can take a sip if you'd like. Just take it easy."

I'm flabbergasted. The legal drinking age is 16, but I didn't expect my father to suggest that I have a drink.

"Jared, congratulations."

It's Mr. Grayson. I shift the beer to my left hand, quickly wiping my right hand off on my dress trousers, then shake his outstretched hand.

"Thank you, sir."

He laughs. "I hear you're going to be working at the company starting a week from Monday."

"That's the plan." I smile at the thought of working for the power company. It really excites me.

I get a massive slap on the back. One so hard, it nearly knocks the wind out of me. Beer sloshes out of the glass, but thankfully I don't drop it. "So, the baby of the family finally comes of age. Congratulations kiddo.

"Hi, Mr. Grayson. Good to see you."

"Hello, Seth."

I can tell Mr. Grayson doesn't approve of Seth's antics. He turns and points to the other end of the party hall.

"The beer is over there."

My eyes follow in the direction he's pointing, where I see my dad talking quietly with the police chief. Although they are calm and quiet, I can tell my dad is a bit upset.

"Don't worry, it's nothing."

I look at Mr. Grayson. "There was a minor incident at the company the other day. It's nothing to worry about."

"Hi, Jared."

I turn to see Nana, who's just come in through the door. She's wearing jeans and a tailored blouse with the top two buttons undone. I feel like I'm going to swoon.

I manage to choke out a "Hi, Nana."

She steps up and gives me a big hug.

I want to hug her back but am afraid of spilling the beer on her.

Releasing me, she says, "I see you already have a beer."

"No, just holding it for my Dad."

"Hi, Nana." The voice is my Dad's. He's apparently come back.

"Hi, Mr. Daan."

He smiles at Nana, then says to me, "I'll take that. Why don't you show Nana where the bar is?"

Nana smiles. "Lead the way."

As we step away, I hear Mr. Grayson speaking in a low voice.

"How did it go?"

"They want to..."

I didn't get the last couple words, but it sounded like he was saying the police wanted to go 'top side' to check something out.

...

Approaching the bar, Nana asks, "Are you going to have something?"

"I suppose I ought to."

Nana laughs. "Jared, you're so innocent."

I wonder how I should take that, then am distracted by a commotion over by the beer. A guy, someone I don't know but has the look of a miner, is having cross words with Aaron. I can see that Aaron is really pissed and wants to clobber the guy, who makes the mistake of pushing him.

"Enough of that!" My mom's voice cuts above the sound of the band and everyone turns to look at the two she's pointing at.

Police Chief Darren Hill walks over toward the two.

"Is there a problem here, gentlemen?"

I can tell that Aaron's fuming but have no idea why. Then I notice the concerned look on Nana's face.

She sees me looking at her and whispers, "That's my brother, Lucas. He told me there was some issue down in the mine. It appears that Aaron is involved somehow."

She points back at the two of them. Apparently, the Chief was persuasive. Aaron and Lucas are shaking hands.

"Come on," The Chief says, then he and Lucas head toward the door.

"Jared, I'm sorry. But I think I need to go. Lucas..." She shakes her head.

I can tell she's upset.

"Happy Birthday." The words spill out just before she kisses me on the cheek.

Then she turns to follow Lucas and the Chief out. I just want to cry but shake the whole thing off. She's out of my league. No sense getting wound up about it. I still have work to do tonight.

THE THIRD AGE OF MAN

I ended up leaving the party early. It lost its sizzle when Nana left. But most of the melancholy wore off as I powered through the rest of my design.

I hit the sack once my work was saved, but here I lay, my mind pondering the fact that I came of age today. I'm sure our founder would find delight in it. The sixth son of the sixth generation turning 16 on the first day of the sixth month of 7260 TA. In case you're wondering, 7260 TA means 7,260th year of the Third Age of Man.

Historians have divided the history of mankind into three ages. The first age was that period of time that humans were on Earth, from the dawn of civilization until the cosmic cataclysm that destroyed the Earth in 3123 AD. That year ultimately became year one of the second age (1 SA). The second age ran until the completion of the Great Alien war in 4451 SA. The war claimed the lives of nearly half of all humanity. The day the last alien was sent to meet its maker, the human world celebrated, and the Third Age began.

It gives me pause to think. What will be the event that marks the dawn of the fourth age? I hope that day comes well after I'm gone. I can't imagine living with the fear of an approaching black hole, the way the people did at the end of the first age. Or living with the terror of sudden death falling from the skies as they did at the end of the second age.

I wonder if everyone has thoughts like this, worries for the future, when they come of age.

AFTERWORD

I hope you enjoyed *Return of the Ancients*, as well as the expanded preview of the new series, *The Rise of Daan*. I started writing The Rise of Daan a month or so after I'd started *Alliance* (Ascendancy Book 4). I'd originally planned to put out the first book in the new series before *Return of the Ancients*. Both books were well underway as Alliance entered the editorial process. But as the publication date for Alliance approached, I realized that the Return of the Ancients' piece of the Ascendancy series really needed to get out while Alliance was fresh in readers' minds.

As I mentioned in Alliance's Afterword, the world of the Ascendancy series is very well developed at this point. I love the characters, love the richness of the situation. And the universe it reveals offers so many places for the story to go. But I think this portion of the series is done. It's gone from First Contact to Earth becoming the capital of an Intergalactic Confederation. From humans struggling to understand alien technology, to mastering it and pressing it forward.

So, be on the lookout for a new derivative series in the same universe in 2021. I left several clues in the main body of this book about where the story might restart. The tentative title of the new series is Transcendence; its first book will be titled Vergence.

I'd love to hear your thoughts on where you'd like to see the story go. You're welcome to contact me at dw.cornell@kahakaicg.com.

...

Each of the books in the Ascendance series has what I like to call a story challenge. For *Revelation*, it was how to make an advanced species millions of years older than humanity approachable to humans. For *The Institute*, it was what could humans do to make themselves relevant to the advanced civilization they were now a part of. In *Return of the Ancients*, the challenge was how to represent the Ancients.

I'm sure you've heard Arthur C. Clarke's Third Law: "Any sufficiently advanced technology is indistinguishable from magic."

I've received both published reviews and private communications from readers citing James and the Ancients as being magic or fantasy.

At one level, these comments affirm the idea that I've envisioned Ancients that satisfy Clarke's 3rd Law. But at the end of the day, my genre is science fiction, not fantasy.

So where is the line? What distinguishes a story as being hard science fiction instead of fantasy. My answer has to do with the presentation. Has the story element been tied back to some application of scientific principles? Or, has the element been tied to properties of an individual wielding some sort of magic?

Beginning in **The Institute** (Ascendancy: Book 2), the characters Eugene Xu and Kelly Williamson go to great lengths to describe how they take Confederation scientific findings and turn them into an engineered technology. The underlying Confederation science is loosely described in **Revelation** (Ascendancy: Book 1). It's elaborated more in the Afterword of The Institute. Both tie key aspects of Confederation science to current human theories of the multiverse.

For more perspective on that, see MIT Professor Max Tegmark's four levels of the multiverse classification system. Confederation zero-point energy devices are consistent with a Level 3 or higher multiverse. All the other dimensional mechanisms are consistent with a Level Four multiverse. Although, I've admittedly taken some artistic liberty with the language and scientific terms.
(https://en.wikipedia.org/wiki/Multiverse)

But, back to the point at hand. One of the major plot lines in the book is the return of the Ancients. For that to work with any credibility, everything about the Ancients needs to be consistent with Clarke's 3rd Law. I chose to walk that line by having Eugene and Kelly develop technologies that drive the story from the human perspective.

Then when the Ancients return, in the form of David Washington, they fix the mess that's overtaken the Confederation using technologies that have already been described.

Anyway, that's the challenge I laid out for myself. I'm reasonably happy with the way it played out. But what I think really doesn't matter. It's whether it worked for you. Let me know what you think.

...

Thank you for having read **Return of the Ancients**. There is great joy in writing a book like this, even more in knowing that someone read and enjoyed it. Please put some stars on a review and stay tuned for more to come.

If you have comments, suggestions, or just want to say 'Hi,' drop me a note. I do my best to answer every email. If you'd be interested in joining my pre-reader program, please contact me.

You can reach me at dw.cornell@kahakaicg.com.

ABOUT THE AUTHOR

D. Ward Cornell lives on the Kohala Coast of the Big Island of Hawaii. His work as an engineer, consultant and entrepreneur has taken him all over the world. Many of those places are featured in his writings. Although still dabbling in those fields, his passions are now writing and entertaining.

Made in the USA
Las Vegas, NV
08 April 2021